THE SAINTLY BUCCANEER

BOOKS BY GILBERT MORRIS

THE HOUSE OF WINSLOW SERIES

1. *The Honorable Imposter*
2. *The Captive Bride*
3. *The Indentured Heart*
4. *The Gentle Rebel*
5. *The Saintly Buccaneer*
6. *The Holy Warrior*
7. *The Reluctant Bridegroom*
8. *The Last Confederate*
9. *The Dixie Widow*
10. *The Wounded Yankee*
11. *The Union Belle*
12. *The Final Adversary*
13. *The Crossed Sabres*
14. *The Valiant Gunman*
15. *The Gallant Outlaw*
16. *The Jeweled Spur*
17. *The Yukon Queen*
18. *The Rough Rider*
19. *The Iron Lady*
20. *The Silver Star*
21. *The Shadow Portrait*
22. *The White Hunter*
23. *The Flying Cavalier*
24. *The Glorious Prodigal*
25. *The Amazon Quest*
26. *The Golden Angel*
27. *The Heavenly Fugitive*
28. *The Fiery Ring*
29. *The Pilgrim Song*
30. *The Beloved Enemy*
31. *The Shining Badge*
32. *The Royal Handmaid*
33. *The Silent Harp*

CHENEY DUVALL, M.D.[1]

1. *The Stars for a Light*
2. *Shadow of the Mountains*
3. *A City Not Forsaken*
4. *Toward the Sunrising*
5. *Secret Place of Thunder*
6. *In the Twilight, in the Evening*
7. *Island of the Innocent*
8. *Driven With the Wind*

CHENEY AND SHILOH: THE INHERITANCE[1]

1. *Where Two Seas Met*
2. *The Moon by Night*

THE SPIRIT OF APPALACHIA[2]

1. *Over the Misty Mountains*
2. *Beyond the Quiet Hills*
3. *Among the King's Soldiers*
4. *Beneath the Mockingbird's Wings*
5. *Around the River's Bend*

LIONS OF JUDAH

1. *Heart of a Lion*
2. *No Woman So Fair*
3. *The Gate of Heaven*

[1]with Lynn Morris   [2]with Aaron McCarver

GILBERT MORRIS

the SAINTLY BUCCANEER

BETHANYHOUSE
Minneapolis, Minnesota

Published by Bethany House Publishers
11400 Hampshire Avenue South
Bloomington, Minnesota 55438
www.bethanyhouse.com

Bethany House Publishers is a division of
Baker Publishing Group, Grand Rapids, Michigan.

Printed in the United States of America

Library of Congress Cataloging-in-Publication Data

Morris, Gilbert.
    The saintly buccaneer / by Gilbert Morris.
        p.   cm. — (The House of Winslow ; 1777)
    ISBN 0-7642-2948-6 (pbk.)
    1. United States—History—Revolution, 1775-1783—Fiction. 2. Winslow family (Fictitious characters)—Fiction. 3. American loyalists—Fiction.
4. Impressment—Fiction. 5. Frigates—Fiction. 6. Amnesia—Fiction. I. Title
II. Series: Morris, Gilbert. House of Winslow.

    PS3563.O8742S25   2004
    813'.54—dc22   2004012900

To my special granddaughter—Laura Michelle Smith

All children are "special," of course, and all grandchildren are *extra* special—because all of them come from God; they are the fruit of the womb—the reward of the Lord. No two have the same laugh, the same fingerprints, and each of them forges a special golden chain to bind himself to the heart of a parent or a grandparent.

You are "special," Laura, because you have "special" parents. If it were not for their faith, you would not be alive on this earth! Stacy—my "special" daughter, the handmaiden of the Lord—and the light of her father's eyes! Ronnie, my "special" son-in-law who walked by faith!

You are "special," my Laura, because God has used you to increase the faith of others.

You are "special" because although God has not yet made you complete, He has given His promise that what He has begun he will complete.

And you are "special" because you exactly fill that space in my heart that no other child or grandchild could fill. Without you, I would be incomplete.

GILBERT MORRIS spent ten years as a pastor before becoming Professor of English at Ouachita Baptist University in Arkansas and earning a Ph.D. at the University of Arkansas. A prolific writer, he has had over 25 scholarly articles and 200 poems published in various periodicals, and over the past years has had more than 180 novels published. His family includes three grown children. He and his wife live in Gulf Shores, Alabama.

CONTENTS

THE
🍃 HOUSE OF WINSLOW 🍃

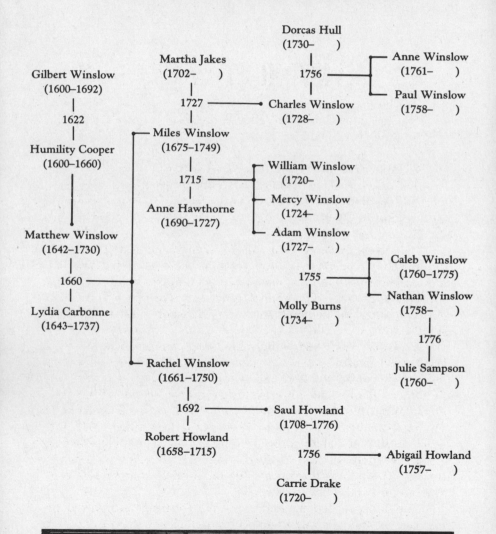

Dorcas Hull
(1730–   )

Martha Jakes
(1702–   )

Gilbert Winslow
(1600–1692)

1622

Humility Cooper
(1600–1660)

1727 ——— Charles Winslow
(1728–   )

1756 ——— Anne Winslow
(1761–   )

Paul Winslow
(1758–   )

Miles Winslow
(1675–1749)

1715 ——— William Winslow
(1720–   )

Mercy Winslow
(1724–   )

Adam Winslow
(1727–   )

Anne Hawthorne
(1690–1727)

Matthew Winslow
(1642–1730)

1660

Lydia Carbonne
(1643–1737)

1755 ——— Caleb Winslow
(1760–1775)

Nathan Winslow
(1758–   )

Molly Burns
(1734–   )

1776

Julie Sampson
(1760–   )

Rachel Winslow
(1661–1750)

1692 ——— Saul Howland
(1708–1776)

Robert Howland
(1658–1715)

1756 ——— Abigail Howland
(1757–   )

Carrie Drake
(1720–   )

CHAPTER ONE

VISITOR AT CAMP

★　★　★　★

The bitter cold probed with icy fingers beneath Charity's thick fur coat, and it took an effort of will for her to ignore its grip. Her face had been stiffened by the bite of the frigid December wind, and despite the thick woolen gloves, she could not feel the reins that guided her rangy bay.

"Come on, Pompey!" she called out as the horse stopped suddenly. She was surprised at how weak her voice sounded, and her lips were stiff as wood as she spoke. Pulling the whip from the socket, she gave the tired animal a cut; and as he broke into a trot, she muttered, "Better find that camp pretty soon—else I'll be froze solid!"

The small black buggy careened along the frozen ruts, but in less than twenty minutes it crested a long hill, and there between a sweep of frozen meadowland on one side and a thick forest on the other, Charity saw with relief the campfires blossoming in the quick-falling darkness. An elderly woman with a wrinkled face but the body of a young girl had told her four hours earlier: "Ye'll find them soldiers at Valley Forge." Pointing toward the hills she had added, "Over there's the Schuylkill—ain't but a leetle ways to whur they is—was a forge thar once—but ain't nothin' there now—'cept Washington and them soldier fellers."

The horse sensed the end of the long journey and picked up his pace, so that she had to hold him back as she drew even with the first fires. Her first clear look at the men who stood around the feeble blaze brought a shock. She had pictured in her mind rows of sturdy tents with men dressed in neat uniforms; what she saw was a group of scarecrows! Their faces were blue with the cold, and their eyes looked enormous as they stared at her. And the clothing! Not a good coat or a pair of boots among the lot. Parts of the body showed through huge rents—one man even exposed a portion of bare, blue buttocks where the pants had worn away! Most of them looked deformed, elephantine, with their feet wrapped in blankets.

She saw them stare at her. Then several of them started toward her, their voices thin on the cold air. "Hup! Pompey!" she commanded quickly, and as she sped down between the ragged tents and flimsy huts, she heard their raucous, obscene cries fade behind her. She was not a girl given to idle fears, but there was a wolfish hunger in their faces.

Now the dusk was closing in and she grew a little desperate, searching for an officer. The huts grew closer together, and somewhere somebody was singing:

"Yankee Doodle went to London,
Riding on a pony—"

The space narrowed, forcing her to guide the horse between two rows of shacks that seemed to rise out of the ground, specter-like. Suddenly there was a shrill cry, and she caught a startled glimpse of a figure that darted from the shadows, rising up to grab Pompey's harness and pull him to an abrupt halt.

"Get out of my way!" she cried out, but even as she snatched the whip from its socket to slash at the man, she felt a pair of hands grab her and drag her off the buggy seat.

"Well, now! Whut we got here?"

Charity found herself in the grip of a huge man with yellowish teeth. He was grinning down at her, and his rank odor almost paralyzed her. He kept an iron grip on one arm and ran his free hand over her body, laughing in a shrill manner. "Looky here whut we done got us for a Chrismus gif', Sam!"

"Ain't that a fact, now?" Another man thrust his face close to hers, a thick-bodied man with a huge bulbous nose and small gleaming eyes.

"Let me go!" Charity tried to pull herself free, but the first man merely laughed at her struggles.

"You can take the wench first, Charlie," the one called Sam grinned. He nodded at Pompey, saying, "I'll cut us some steaks out of that there horse. Blast my eyes, but we'll have us steaks and a woman tonight—but keep her still so's them other fellers won't know 'bout it!"

Terror ran like fire through Charity, and she opened her mouth to scream, but the tall man named Charlie promptly clapped his dirty paw over her face and said, while dragging her to the shack to his left, "You take that beast and dress him out, Sam. Time you get back, you'll 'preciate a pretty leetle thing like this!"

Charity kicked and tried to claw at his face, but he laughed in evil delight. "Thet's right, honey, you keep it up! I likes a gal with some fight in 'er!"

Desperately she fought, and just as he was dragging her through the low door, she wrenched her head and his little finger slipped into her mouth. Instantly she bit down with all her might and tasted blood!

"Owww . . . !" The soldier instinctively shoved her away, yanking his hand free and sending her sprawling on the ground. But she was up like a flash and let out a piercing cry, "Help! Help me, somebody!"

She darted toward the buggy, but Sam grabbed her, and with a curse Charlie came racing after Charity, shaking the blood from his wounded finger. There was an ugly expression on his dirty face, and he snarled, "Bite me, will you? Well, maybe you need a lesson 'fore—!"

"Get away from that woman, both of you!"

Charity looked wildly toward her left, her eyes lighting on a very tall man dressed in a loose-fitting, shapeless gray smock. He had reddish hair curling out from beneath his fur cap, and the bluest eyes Charity had ever seen. A long rifle rested loosely in one hand. "I said let that woman alone," he commanded as the men around Charity began moving in.

Sam Macklin gave a quick look around and was reassured as he saw the ranks closing in, much like wolves circling a wounded deer. "Why, you fool!" he snarled and took one step forward, pulling a knife from his belt. "You git back there with the rest of your kind!" He gestured with the knife, the cold steel glittering in the fading light. "I'll cut your gizzard out, Winslow!"

"Do it, Sam!" Charlie urged wickedly. "Like to see one of them Virginia men cut right down the middle like a hawg!"

A chorus went up from the men and they closed around Charity, but the man named Winslow said evenly, as though he were making a remark about the weather, "I'd rather shoot a lobsterback than one of you; but I'm telling you now, one of you is going to die if you don't let that woman go."

"Aw, he's only got one shot!" Macklin shouted. "Git him!"

"Only one—want it, Sam?" Quick as a flash, Winslow brought the rifle up, and Macklin found himself staring down the cold steel muzzle. The blue eyes above it did not waver, but the voice matched the steel in his hands. "You think this is a good day to die? No? I didn't think you would. Miss, you come over here."

Charity jerked free of the hands holding her and ran to the tall man who seemed to hold the others with his eyes.

"You ain't gonna do it, Winslow!" Macklin breathed heavily, his face pale. He moved forward and said, "If he gets me, you boys cut him to pieces!"

With terror Charity saw he was not going to stop, that he was willing to take the bullet, and she knew the tall Virginian would not be able to resist the rest—but suddenly, there was the sound of a horse approaching, and a sharp voice cut through the air: "What the devil? What's that woman doing here?"

A man in a blue uniform pulled up, looking down at Charity. He had cold blue eyes, and she sensed the hurried withdrawal of the ragged men.

"I—I've come to see my brother," she answered quickly. "My name is Charity Alden."

He stared at her, a frown on his face. Then Winslow spoke. "I know him, General Wayne. He's in the hospital."

"All right. Take her there, Winslow." The steely eyes moved to Sam Macklin, and he said evenly, "I'll cut the heart out of any man who touches a decent woman. You understand that?" Without waiting for an answer, he turned to Winslow. "See to Miss Alden." He wheeled his mount and rode off swiftly into the maze of huts.

"I'll kill you for this, Winslow!" Macklin threatened.

"Sam, you can't even kill the lice that're crawlin' all over you," the tall Virginian grinned. Then ignoring the angry stares, he said, "I'll take you to your brother, Miss."

A lump seemed to have lodged in Charity's throat, and her legs wanted to give way. She had never known such terror, and without Winslow's help, she would have been lost. "I—I can't thank you enough, Mr. Winslow! But, won't those men try to get at you?"

He looked down at her from his great height and smiled. "Oh, they'll cuss and rare, but they're too beat to fool with revenge." He took Pompey's bit and laughed, "I think you'd better watch this horse day and night, though. We've eaten most of ours—and this one would be prime cut!"

"You know my brother—Curtis?" she asked, trying to keep up with his long paces.

"Sure. He's right down the line from one of my friends." He glanced at her curiously. "How'd you hear about him being hurt?"

"He sent word by a friend of his—Malcolm Ruggle." She bit her lip and asked the question that had been gnawing at her ever since the raw-boned Scot had come to Boston with his message. "Is he hurt bad?"

Winslow nodded slowly. "Bad enough." He hesitated, then added, "You see, it has to be *very* bad before we go to the hospital. Most things we take care of ourselves."

"He's . . . he's not going to die?"

Winslow put a hand on her shoulder, his eyes filled with compassion. "He's bad, miss—but God is able!"

God had played little part in Charity's life, and what she heard the Virginian saying was, *Only God can save your brother.* Fear shot through her at the thought. Winslow soon turned down an alley of sorts, a winding path between two rows of huts, and stopped before one of them. "I'll tell my wife about you—and we can leave the horse with a friend of mine."

He tied the horse to a slender stump, led her to the door, and called out, "Julie—we've got company!"

The room Charity entered was very dark, for there were no windows and only one small candle flickered, casting deep shadows over the interior. She had time to see a crude table, a small bed, and various objects hanging from pegs along the rough boards that made up the walls. There was an odor of bodies, cooking, and raw earth; it was much like a cave, she thought.

"This is Charity Alden, Julie—you've met her brother at the hospital. And this is my wife—and my son."

Charity's eyes rested on a young woman with black hair and eyes dark as pools. She was moving carefully, for she was very close to the time of giving birth. When she spoke her voice was very husky, and there was a gentle smile on her broad lips. "Welcome to Valley Forge, Miss Alden," she said. "Your brother is such a fine young man. I only wish we could have done more for him— but it's so crowded—and there's so little to do *with*."

"I'm going to take her there now," Winslow told her. "Tell Jed to watch the horse, will you?"

"Yes, Nathan." There was a calmness in the young woman that Charity envied, a stillness and a patience some women seemed to have. "Do you have any place to stay? No? Then you'd better come back here."

"Oh, I don't want to be a bother!"

Julie did not do more than smile, but turned and got a covered pot and handed it to her. "See if you can get your brother to eat something. I'll be praying for you."

The kindness of Julie Winslow caught at Charity, and she could only nod. Following Nathan outside, she commented as they walked along, "Your wife—she's so kind!"

"She's that."

Curiosity nibbled at Charity, and she asked tentatively, "Isn't she . . . nervous? About having a baby under such . . . conditions?"

"I tried to get her to go home, but she wants me to be with her when the boy comes."

"You seem sure about it—that it'll be a boy."

"Well, Julie says that's what God's told her—and I don't recall that she's ever missed when she says something like that."

Charity was flustered, for when people said "God told me to do this," it always made her slightly angry somehow. She didn't understand such things and felt they were attempting to be *spiritual* in some unfair way. But she could not feel resentment toward the kind young woman who had taken care of her brother.

"There's the hospital."

A long, low building was perched on top of a knoll, the wind tearing the spark-studded smoke that rose from the chimney, dissipating it into the darkness. She followed Winslow to the door, and a sentry in rags blocked their way. "No more room," he mumbled through blue lips.

"Want to visit, Soldier," Winslow answered shortly, his breath labored from the steep climb.

The sentry shrugged and stepped aside just as the door opened. A short man with a long gray apron splattered with blood came to stand inside the frame. He peered at the two of them through small spectacles. He had a long face, a thin nose and very red lips. "What's this?"

"This is Miss Alden, Doctor," Winslow said quickly. "She's come to see her brother."

The doctor peered at her and asked incredulously, "How in

the holy hades did you *get* here?" Then he caught himself, saying abruptly, "Oh, never mind."

"How is he, Doctor?"

"Your brother?" The question seemed to disturb him, and finally after a short pause, he shrugged. "Not well." Then an angry light leaped into his eyes, and he snapped bitterly, "How could he be doing *well* in a hellish place like this? No medicine—no bandages—nothing!"

"Maybe it'll help to have his sister here," Nathan offered hopefully.

The doctor stared at him, and finally said, "I trust it will help." The futility in his tone sent fear through Charity, and she stared at him as he stalked away to a path that led down the hill.

"Come along, Miss Alden."

Nathan stepped aside to let her enter. It was a simple log cabin thirty feet long at most, but there must have been more than a hundred men inside. They lay close together on beds built the length of the hut. Some of them were asleep, but most of them moved restlessly in the bitter cold. There was a continual groaning, and the stench was overwhelming.

She followed the tall Virginian to a tiny corner partitioned off in the back, and gave a gasp when she looked down at her brother's pale face, the hollows of his cheeks made deeper by the yellow glare of the lantern hanging from the ceiling.

"Curtis!" she cried, tears filling her eyes as she fell beside him. His thin hand was like ice, and for one brief instant terror filled her as she thought, *He's dead!* But then he stirred, and as she dashed the tears out of her eyes she saw that he had moved his head to face her. He was her baby brother, only sixteen, but he had been wild to become a soldier. Nothing she nor their father could say would keep him back—and now he lay dying in a miserable hut!

"Charity?" he asked in a thin, reedy voice—and when she leaned over and kissed him, he stared at her, his eyes enormous in his thin face. "How—did you get here?"

"Oh, Curtis!" She forced herself to smile. "Why, I heard you'd been wounded, so I just up and came to nurse you. I'll have you out of this place in no time!"

His eyes seemed to be all there was to him—all eyes and skin and bones. But then he smiled, and it broke her heart to see, for it made him look younger, childlike—and she could not speak for the tightness that gripped her throat.

"Sister—I'm—glad you came." His voice fell, and his eyelids dropped. "I—didn't want to—go out—by myself . . ."

He closed his eyes and his head lolled. Charity shot a look of fear at Nathan, but he shook his head. "Just fell asleep. He does that a lot. Maybe he'll eat a few bites when he wakes up again." He added, "I'll go give some of this to my friend over there while you sit with him."

Charity sat in the dim hut beside her brother for a long time. Nathan came back after a time, looked down, then left, leaving the soup with her. "Stay as long as you like; I'll take you home whenever you want."

As she continued the vigil, holding the thin hand, memories swept through her—mostly about the days when Curtis was a small boy. They had been very close, and now she was afraid. If she had been a woman of prayer, she would have prayed, but that part of her life had been perfunctory—a few memorized forms that meant nothing in this place of pain and darkness and death. Fear was not something lurking outside—it was a sharp blade slicing away at her deep down inside.

Her thoughts flew back and forth as she tried to think—but the fear that had paralyzed her since she had walked into the hospital seemed to have destroyed her power to think. She longed for her father or for her grandmother to be there. Always she had depended on them, and now they were far away. She was the only one who could help Curtis.

Finally she felt a hand on her shoulder and looked up with a start to see Winslow standing over her. He spoke quietly. "Charity—would you like to get Curtis out of this place?"

A sudden hope seized her, and she exclaimed with a wild urgency, "Oh, yes!"

"I've been praying on it," he replied slowly, his face still in the flickering lamplight. "And I think the Lord has told me that we better take Curtis home. I'll go get your buggy and tell Julie to fix up a place for him."

"Thank you!" was all she could say, and when he left, she let her hot tears fall on Curtis's thin hand. She moved her lips in a whisper. "Oh, God! Don't let him die!"

CHAPTER TWO

DEATH AT VALLEY FORGE

★　★　★　★

Snowflakes large as shillings fell out of the sky—not drifting down gently but plummeting to the frozen earth. Charity had to stop frequently and clear her lashes, because the heavy flakes froze instantly as they touched her face. For the last week, since she had arrived at Valley Forge, she had made a daily journey from the Winslow hut to the hospital, taking food to several of Nathan's friends. He had been sent on some sort of military mission, and when Julie had started to put on her thin coat to make the trip, Charity had quickly insisted on taking her place.

"I hate to have you out in this weather, Charity," Julie had protested.

"Me? Why, I'm used to it, Julie," Charity had laughed as she slipped into her fur coat. "The last trip we made on *The Gallant Lady*, a snowstorm caught us. Father stayed at the wheel so long he froze his feet, and I almost did the same. I'm an old salt—and tough as boot leather!"

"But it's—"

"Julie, I want you to lie down and rest until I get back. Come on, now—let me cover you up." She practically forced her onto the low bed strung with rawhide, pulled a heap of ragged quilts over her, then impulsively leaned over and kissed her. "You've done so much for Curtis—and for me. Don't refuse me this one little thing!" Then she had darted over to pull the covers up on Curtis before leaving the hut.

The visits to the hospital had been difficult, for she hated the stench and squalor of the place. She had to carry the food past those who were starving, and the hollow eyes that followed her made her ache. They were dying, most of them, she realized, and they cried out silently for her to stop and talk. Some were young, not over fourteen, and they cried out for their mothers in their delirium. Charity forced herself to smile, spending most of the time that Curtis lay unconscious trying to bring some hope to the sick and wounded.

She made her way through the curtain of falling snow, muttering through stiff lips, "Worse than a fog off the Banks!" Finally she stumbled up to the hospital and entered. Dr. Williams looked up from where he was bending over one of the men, and rose instantly to come to her. "Glad you came, Charity," he nodded, his face grim. "Billy's bad—maybe you can stay with him a little."

"Is he . . . going to die, Dr. Williams?"

She had not liked the physician at first, thinking him surly and uncaring, but she had soon discovered that his gruff manner was a facade, that he hurt for the men under his care. She had discovered this on her third visit when he had drawn her to one side, saying harshly, "Wish you'd say a word to Sills—boy needs a little comfort."

"Which one is he?"

"Over there by the window. He's only fifteen—" She saw the look of pain surface in his face involuntarily. "Just the age of my own boy." Then the curtain dropped, and he went on, his lips tight. "Lost a leg last month, and it's gone to gangrene. Won't last long— but I expect he'd like a little word from a woman."

Billy Sills was a towheaded boy from Virginia, emaciated and bright-eyed with fever. He had been pathetically grateful when Charity had stopped and offered him a little of the thin stew, but it had been her presence rather than the food that had cheered him. She led him to talk, and soon she knew his family by name. His favorite sister was Melissa, "Missy"—and he used that name for Charity, saying, "You look a heap like her, you do."

Dr. Williams went on quietly. "We made a little place for him over by the corner," motioning to where a tattered blanket was tacked up. He hesitated, shook his head, then added, "Don't expect he'll know you. Been in a coma since this morning."

"I—I'll sit with him for a while." Charity worked her way around the room, making the food go as far as possible, speaking with a tight smile to the patients, then went to Billy with a mug of tepid water. Lifting the blanket, she sat down on the floor using her coat for a pad, and leaned closer to see the boy's face. The feeble yellow rays of a lantern barely enabled her to make out his features. His lips were drawn back and his eyes were fluttering, revealing a glimpse of the whites as they rolled up in his skull. His chest was rising and falling erratically, and the rasping sound of his breathing struck against her nerves. Desperately she wanted to run away, but she forced herself to mop his clammy brow with a bit of cloth from her pocket.

Her touch seemed to arouse him, for he rolled his head weakly from side to side. Then his eyes slowly opened and focused on her as she bent over him. He licked his dry lips, and his voice was a croak as he whispered, "Missy—that you?"

"Yes, Billy. It's Missy."

"Aw—I'm glad—you got here . . ."

She reached down, lifted his head, and put the water to his lips. He took a few quick swallows, then pulled his head back and looked up into Charity's eyes. "Missy—I ain't—gonna—make it."

"Billy . . . !"

"Good you came—though. Hate to die—Missy!"

Tears scalded her eyes and she set the cup down and reached out to embrace his emaciated form, holding him to her breast. "Billy—Billy!" she moaned, but could say no more, for her body was shaken by uncontrollable sobs. She held him like a baby, rocking back and forth and calling his name for a long time; then he pulled back and a spasm racked his body—a violent shudder that shook him until his teeth rattled.

"Missy!" he cried out, pulling at her weakly. "Don't let me die, sister! I—I'm afraid!" He gave a great wrenching cough, and when it passed, he asked, "Missy—you reckon—you could say—a prayer?" His eyes were enormous in the golden light of the lantern, and his lips trembled as he whispered, "I—I never got—religion, did I? Mother—she tried to—to talk about God—but I never did—"

Then his whole body arched and he began to kick the floor, his bare heel drumming in a horrible pattern. The blanket flew back, and Dr. Williams entered hastily, but even as he reached out, Billy took a deep breath, held it for a brief moment, and then his body went limp, the rattling cough raking against Charity's nerves.

"He's gone," the doctor said. He took the thin hands, folded them over the boy's chest, and dropped the blanket over the worn face. He pulled Charity to her feet and led her out of the space. She almost stumbled over a sleeping man, but Dr. Williams caught her with a surprising strength and helped her to the only open space in the room—a small cubicle where he kept his meager supplies and slept when he could on a cot made of saplings and rawhide. She was so blinded by tears she could see nothing, but suddenly felt Dr. Williams jerk to an abrupt halt. "Why, General Washington—I didn't know you were here."

Charity brushed the tears from her eyes and looked up to see two men standing in the open space. One was a thin man wearing a blue uniform greatcoat with black facing and silk scarf; the other, a very large man, over six feet. Charity looked at him with startled interest.

The general had a large nose, gray eyes, and deep pockmarks on his long face. He had very large hands, she saw, giving an impression of tremendous strength, though his eyes and voice betrayed a great weariness.

"How many, Doctor?"

"Well, not as bad as it might be—but we just this moment lost Billy."

"Billy Sills?" The gray eyes fell, and the big man stood there silently. Finally he raised his head, and Charity saw the pain etched across his face. "He was from my state. I know his parents, Colonel Hamilton. They are fine people."

This, she gathered, was Alexander Hamilton, the general's most trusted aide. "It's hard, Your Excellency." His voice was sharp and clipped, but he seemed almost boyish with violet eyes and lashes long and thick like a girl's. "It never gets easy, does it?"

Dr. Williams interjected, "This is Miss Charity Alden, Your Excellency. She came to see her brother—but she's been a great source of encouragement to all the men."

"We are in your debt, Miss Alden," the general returned, his gray eyes weighing her. As he took her hand in his, hers seemed lost in the massive grip. For a moment she felt the power of the man; then he released her hand, saying, "I hope your brother is doing well?"

"Not very well, sir." She bit her lip and added, "One of your Virginia men has taken us in—Nathan Winslow."

"That's Adam's son, isn't it?" Hamilton asked.

"Yes. I had to send Adam on a mission." Turning to Charity, Washington nodded, "Miss Alden, I pray that our merciful God will spare your brother. And we are grateful for your kindness to our poor men. Let me help you."

She put her arms into the coat he held for her, then said as she turned to go, "I'm—sorry about Billy."

"I'm sorry, too—for all of them."

She left the hospital quickly, and as she made her way back to the cabin, she wondered why the boy's death had affected her so deeply. The presence of Washington had taken the pain away momentarily, but now it swept back as the whining wind that purled around the evergreens and sent scuds of new snow everywhere reminded her of his cries.

What if Curtis should die like Billy?

The question came again and again, and by the time she got to the hut, she was so filled with fear for him that she did not even feel the cold.

Julie was sitting beside Curtis as she entered, and looking up she said, "He's been asking for you, Charity. See if you can get him to take a little broth."

"Why, sure I can, can't I, Curtis?" she asked with a forced heartiness. Taking the cup from Julie, she sat down and began to cajole him into swallowing a little of the broth. "I could always make you eat, couldn't I? Remember when you had measles, and I took care of you?"

A faint smile touched his pale lips. "I remember. Gave you the measles, didn't I?" he answered weakly.

"You sure did! Take another swallow—that's good! Now another. . . ."

He ate a little of the broth, then lay back wearily while she fussed over him. He had developed an alarming cough which would, on occasion, seize him in a frightful manner. It was as if a giant hand suddenly closed on him, shaking him from side to side and racking him until his breath was spent. It was getting worse, more frequent, and after a bout that made Charity want to cry out at his agony, he fell into a drugged and unhealthy sleep.

The two women did what they could, then sat down and talked as the stub of a candle sputtered in its own tallow. Charity was too exhausted by the death of Billy Sills and the tension over Curtis to say much, but Julie's voice had a soothing effect. Charity put her head back, closed her eyes, and listened as the young woman spoke of things other than disease and death.

Often the two had sat into the night, and Charity had listened as Julie told her of her meeting and marriage with Nathan. The story was so incredible that at first she had suspected the young woman was one of the most creative liars she'd ever met, but others in the camp had confirmed the story.

Julie had fled her home after her father's death to escape the rapacious attentions of her uncle. In desperation, she had disguised herself as a man, and Nathan had saved her from freezing to death on a wharf in Boston. Through a strange set of circumstances, she had joined the Continental Army as an aide to Colonel Henry Knox. Nathan, his attention occupied by a young woman he was courting, had never suspected her secret. He and his cousin, Paul Winslow, were engaged in such fierce competition for Abigail Howland that Nathan was blind to all else. Soon after Julie's secret finally got out, Nathan was made painfully aware of Abigail's deceit.

"I caught him as he was dropped, Charity," Julie had laughed as she recounted the story. "He was easy pickings."

But this, Charity discovered, was not true. The love of Nathan for Julie—and hers for him—was of a storybook quality, and the warmth in Julie's eyes when she spoke of her young husband spoke volumes.

Now as they sat there in the cold room, the hoarse breathing of Curtis was very loud in the quietness. Julie finally stopped speaking, and for a long time there was no other sound. In the dim light Charity saw that Julie's lips were moving, and she knew the girl was praying; it was something Charity had noted and been troubled about. Now the death of the boy was a fresh wound in her spirit, and she finally began to speak, telling her friend how it had been. She ended by saying, "It was so—hard! So awful, Julie!" Then she plunged in and added, "Julie—he said he didn't know God. Do you think he's in . . . ?"

Julie sat there for what seemed a long time; then she began to speak. At first it seemed to Charity the young woman had not heard what Charity had asked, for she said nothing about Billy or his death. She talked about God, about His love for man—and most of all she spoke of Jesus Christ and how He died on a cross to save all men. Her voice went on and Charity sat there listening. Finally Julie picked up her worn black Bible from the table by her side and, leaning over close to catch the feeble rays of the candle, read slowly: "This is a faithful saying, and worthy of all acceptation, that Christ Jesus died to save sinners, of whom I am chief."

Then she looked up, the tears shining in her eyes in the yellow light. "Charity, never question the love of God! No matter what you see in this world, remember that God sent His only Son, and Jesus died a terrible death on a cross. He died because He loves us all—you—and me—and Billy—and Curtis."

Charity swallowed, fighting back the sobs that rose to her throat. "But what about Billy?"

"I don't know, Charity," she answered quietly. "I *do* know that he will meet a loving God—and I never lose hope."

"I wanted to help Billy—but I couldn't!"

"I know, Charity." Julie put her hand on Charity's. "I think if you want to be able to help others—like Curtis and Billy—you've got to find your own peace with the Lord. Would you like that?"

Somehow the thought frightened Charity, and she said quickly, "Oh, I couldn't!" And she begged in a faltering voice, "Won't *you* help him, Julie? Please!"

The silence ran on and Charity saw that the other girl was praying. Finally Julie looked up and smiled. "Of course I will, Charity."

★ ★ ★ ★

Three days later Curtis died. During those three days Charity was helpless. She took care of her brother's physical needs, but the presence of death was over the hut. Nathan came back, and he would sit for long hours beside Curtis, often with Julie by his side.

Julie would read the Bible aloud as she sat beside the dying boy, and once she said, "Maybe he doesn't understand it, Charity, but the scripture says, 'The entrance of thy word giveth light.' "

From time to time Curtis would rouse, always a little weaker, but he seemed to live on the prayers of the couple who was always there. He would hold on to Charity's hand, speaking of their early days, but he grew restless, his eyes searching for something, and only when Julie or Nathan would come and sit beside him would he relax.

On the day before he died, Julie was reading from the Gospel of John, late in the afternoon. Charity sat on the floor, her head leaning against the cot, and she heard the words:

> And as Moses lifted up the serpent in the wilderness, even so must the Son of man be lifted up: that whosoever believeth in him should not perish, but have eternal life. For God so loved the world, that he gave his only begotten son, that whosoever believeth in him should not perish, but have everlasting life. For God sent not his Son into the world to condemn the world, but

that the world through him might be saved.

"Does that mean me?" Curtis's voice interrupted the reading, and when Charity lifted her head, she saw that he had pulled himself up and was staring at Julie with a strange hope in his eyes. "Can I be saved, Julie?"

Julie said quietly, "Why, Curtis, Jesus *died* to save you. There's nothing God longs for more than to see us trust Him for salvation."

He lay back down and the silence ran on. There was an ache in Charity's throat, and she clenched her fists together until they hurt. Then she heard him say, "Would you help me, Julie?"

Julie sat there reading scripture after scripture, pausing to answer his questions, and finally she said, "I think you're ready to put your faith in Jesus, Curtis." She put the Bible down and got awkwardly to her knees, saying, "I'm in poor shape for this, but God is waiting. Let's pray—and you simply tell the Lord you have sinned, and that you want Jesus in your heart—"

She began to pray, and Charity went to kneel beside her, both of them bending over the thin form of Curtis. Charity never knew what happened. She found herself weeping uncontrollably, and with that, a sudden desire to pray. She tried, but there was something within her resisting.

Finally she looked up to see Julie struggling to get up. "Give me a hand, Charity," she gasped. As she was pulled to her feet, she laughed freely, tears running down her cheeks—but there was a light of joy in her eyes. "Your brother is in the family of God, Charity! Look at him!"

Curtis had tears in his eyes, but there was a smile on his lips as he exclaimed "Bless the Lord! Bless the Lord!" over and over again.

Julie put her arms around Charity. "It'll be your time one day. God has promised me that!"

Charity could not speak, but the peace that had come to the thin face of Curtis brought joy to her own heart.

Curtis died in his sleep the next day. He had awakened at dawn, and his eyes were clear as he held up his arms to kiss his sister for the last time. He gave a few messages for family and friends, said his farewell to Nathan and Julie, then looked at Charity, a quiet smile on his lips. "I'll be waiting for you." As he closed his eyes, Charity knew with a startling clarity and an aching heart that her brother would never open them again—not on this earth.

CHAPTER THREE

BACK TO BOSTON

★ ★ ★ ★

"Charity, I wish you'd change your mind." Nathan had come inside, slamming the door against the blast of freezing air that rattled the entire shack. His eyebrows were crusted white with ice, and there was a worried look in his eyes as he moved to where Charity sat beside Julie. "If this snow keeps up, you'll never make it through."

"I'll be all right, Nathan."

"Just wait until tomorrow, please, Charity," Julie whispered. Her voice was weak, and pain was dulling her eyes. Ever since Curtis's death, she had seemed to weaken, taking to her bed with a fever. Charity had grown to love the Winslows, but a plan had formed in her mind, and she smiled and leaned over to kiss Julie, saying, "Don't fret yourself about me, Julie Winslow." She felt the girl's arms close round her neck, and allowed herself to be held, then drew back and forced a smile, saying with artificial conviviality, "Now, you just take care of yourself and that big boy—if you're good, maybe I'll have a surprise for you!"

She pulled away, snatched up the small bundle containing her clothes, and dashed outside. The freezing cold bit at her lungs, causing her to catch her breath as the wind whipped tiny crystals of snow into her eyes.

"Everything's ready, Charity," Nathan informed her, motioning to the waiting buggy. "We had to do a little carpentry work to make the coffin fit, but it's all secure."

"Thank you, Nathan." Charity forced herself to walk toward the buggy, which had been stripped to accommodate the pine coffin that bore Curtis's body. When she had announced her intention of taking her brother back to be buried in the family plot, there had been incredulous looks on every face. But no persuasion could change her mind, so Nathan had made provisions for her trip. The back seat of the buggy had been ripped out, and an extension built on the floor, so that the coffin protruded past the rear wheels, and was tied down with ropes. The canvas top had been roughly sewn together to make a shelter over the front seat, providing at least some protection from the stormy weather. Most important, the wheels had been removed and a pair of runners thrust under a crudely built undercarriage, transforming the buggy into a sleigh. "If the snow gets deep," Nathan had told her, "you'll have a better chance with a sled than a buggy."

"Looks shipshape, Nathan," Charity stated, tilting her head back to smile up into his face. "Now, you listen to me! I'm going to make a record trip to Boston, and I'll be back here with a good doctor and supplies quicker than you can think!"

His mouth dropped open and he exclaimed, "Why, you can't do that, Charity!"

She slapped him on the chest and laughed shortly. "I never let any man tell me what I can or can't do! Now, you take care of your wife until I get back!"

Nathan stared at her; then a smile broke across his broad mouth. "Well, devil fly off! I reckon you'll do just that, Charity Alden! However," he added, his eyes twinkling, "you can argue all you like—but I'm sending a man with you."

"I don't need—!"

"This is Daniel Greene," he went on, ignoring her protests. "He's a preacher, but don't put too much stock in that. He appreciates a pretty woman well enough."

"Pay no attention to him, Miss Alden," the man who had stepped up interjected quickly. He was, Charity saw, a well-built individual, just under six feet. He had wide shoulders and warm brown eyes, and his voice was deep as the bass on an organ. "I need to get to Boston, and if thee would permit me to join thee, it would be most helpful."

"See? He can charm the birds out of the trees," Nathan grinned. Sobering, he added, "But most important, he's a chaplain in the Continental Army and a nephew of General Greene's. You get that pass from the general, Dan?"

"Yes, right here, Nathan."

"All right." Nathan hesitated, then reached out and hugged Charity. "Bless you, girl! God keep you."

Charity returned his hug and climbed into the buggy, noting that the chaplain did not attempt to help her but settled himself beside her as she took the reins. "Watch for me, Nathan," she called out. Turning her head back, she raised her voice, "Hup! Pompey!" and the sleigh lurched ahead so fast that Greene, giving her a startled look, had to grab at a brace.

Except for sentries and one squad bringing in firewood, there was no one stirring; all were buried inside the huts seeking relief from the biting cold. The sky was a clear gray, scored on the horizon by the naked black branches of trees, and the tiny crystals of snow bit like fire on Charity's face as the two made their way out of the camp. The smooth ride and the hissing sound of the runners over the frozen snow was so different from the lurching of a buggy over rutted roads that she delighted in the experience.

Looking at her from under the rim of a black-brimmed hat, Dan Greene noted her confident handling of the horse and the eager thrust of her firm chin. *Likes to have her own way*, he thought. There was an independence about her that was in abrupt contrast to the feminine grace of her face and figure. *Might give a husband a hard time!* was his first judgment, but as the miles spun on and the bleak sun rose feebly and she said nothing, he began to be interested, for not many women could hold their tongues like this one.

They were stopped twice by armed patrols—ragged Continentals who gave them a queer look, but let them through at once when they saw the pass signed by General Greene. "Better watch yourself, Chaplain," one of them warned. "Looks like a blizzard brewin' for sure."

As they drove on, Charity turned to look at him, and there was a directness in her glance that searched him thoroughly. "You're a Quaker, I take it?"

"That's right."

"I thought Quakers didn't believe in fighting."

"Well, that's what *I* thought, Miss Alden," Dan said wryly. "But my uncle somehow found his way into this war—and now I'm in it, too—though I can't say just how I reconcile my views as a man of peace with being in a shooting war."

She smiled at him quizzically, and then laughed out loud.

"Maybe you'll have to find some way to kill the Redcoats in a good Christian way!"

He shook his head sorrowfully as he murmured quietly, "Don't know about that."

She gave him a quick glance, feeling embarrassed at her satiric remark. "I didn't mean to make light of your beliefs, sir."

"No offense." He pointed at a deadfall down the road and asked, "How does some hot soup and tea sound?"

"Wonderful!"

She pulled the sleigh up to a line of trees and got down, stamping her feet to restore circulation.

"I'll build a fire if thee will get the food out of that box," Dan offered, and began at once breaking off small branches. He made the fire swiftly and efficiently, using a wad of punk lit by a spark from some flint and steel he carried in a small leather pouch, and soon the crackling fire had put some color and warmth into the bleak day. The singing of the small kettle sounded like a tiny trumpet on the cold air, and they sat down on a log to sip the scalding soup and coffee.

The intimacy of the meal and the warmth of the steaming food made them both more talkative, and as they ate, Charity learned more about the Winslows. The muscular chaplain, she discovered, knew their history well, and as he ate he spoke warmly of the couple. The solidness in his speech matched that of his body, but despite the slight strangeness of his Quaker speech, he had a way with words—managing somehow to convey a great deal with simple, direct language.

Finally they finished the meal, and she accepted his offer to drive. As they made their way down the desolate road, she asked abruptly, "What about Charles Winslow? Didn't I hear Julie say that he lives in Boston? I've heard of him, I think. A rich man?"

She did not miss the hesitation in Greene's manner nor the dubious quality in his deep voice as he replied slowly, "Well, yes— that's Nathan's uncle, his father's brother—or half brother."

"They don't get along?"

"Oh, yes, I suppose they do, but . . ." Dan searched for a phrase, then shrugged. "I really don't know much about it, Miss Alden. They had trouble at one time—but I heard that it's gotten better now. Why does thee ask?"

"I'm wondering why these Boston Winslows don't send some help to Nathan and Julie."

"Oh, Nathan would never ask! In the first place, I reckon Charles is a Loyalist." He guided Pompey skillfully around a fallen tree before continuing. "Well, there was some trouble between Paul and Nathan."

"Paul?"

"Paul Winslow—that's Charles's son."

"What kind of trouble?"

"Woman trouble!" The brown eyes of Dan Greene met the green eyes of Charity, and he grinned sourly, adding, "Both of them were in love with the same woman."

"This was before Nathan married Julie?"

"Yes." He sat silently. The restraint in his manner made her wonder. Finally he spoke. "Guess thee heard about the way Julie dressed up like a man and joined the Army?"

"I heard. Hard to think a woman could get by with that in the Army."

"Well, she did—mostly because she was General Knox's aide and didn't have to be around the troops. But the thing was, Nathan was in love with this rich girl named Abigail Howland—and so was Paul."

"Did she marry Paul?"

"No. She turned out to be a wench—and Paul Winslow was no better. The way it was, Nathan and Paul were both after her; but when it turned out she was a deceitful baggage, why, neither of them would have her."

"What about Julie? How did Nathan come to marry her?"

"She loved him." As the bleak words rolled from his lips, Charity shot a glance at Greene and read something in his square face that gave him away. *Why—he had been in love with Julie!* she thought.

She said only, "But, that's no reason for the Winslows to refuse to help their kin."

"Can't say. Nathan told me once that his uncle was pretty sick, so he may not even know about it. But they won't talk much about the rest of the family."

He changed the subject briefly, and then they settled down in silence for the long drive. As darkness fell, they found shelter at the home of a farmer. Charity fell asleep as soon as she hit the bed in the small room at the back of the house, but Greene sat up late talking about the war. They left at dawn after a good breakfast.

"I'm right sorry about your brother, Miss Alden," the farmer's wife said gently as she bade Charity goodbye.

"Thank you," she nodded.

The next two days were like the first, but the snow held off and they managed to find a place to sleep both nights. Late Wednesday afternoon, each lost in his own thoughts, Greene broke the long silence by saying, "I will leave thee here, Miss Alden."

Charity looked around in surprise, seeing only a small cluster of houses off the road ahead. "Aren't you going into Boston?"

"No. I have to find a man—and I can get a coach out of here."

She stopped the horse, and he reached back and pulled his small valise from where it was lodged. He got out and stood there looking up at her. "The rest of the journey will be safe now. I hope to see thee again."

She smiled warmly and thrust her hand out like a man, and he took it. "You've been a comfort, Chaplain Greene. Will I see you back at Valley Forge?"

He stared at her. "Thee is really going back with that doctor?"

"Didn't you hear me say it to Nathan?"

"Yes." Then he squeezed her hand, saying loudly, "Thee is a fine girl, Charity Alden! God bless thee!"

He stepped back, and she left him standing beside the road staring at her. As she closed the distance to Boston, she thought long about what he had said—and about what he had not said. "He was in love with Julie," she murmured as Pompey pulled the sleigh into the outskirts of the city. "But he loves Nathan—and Paul Winslow, why, he hates Nathan." She shook her head, remarking aloud, "Love sure is a messy thing!"

People turned to stare at the sleigh with the coffin protruding out of the rear, but she paid no heed. Charity dreaded her arrival, and as she drove along the waterfront, she sought for a way to make the news easier for her father. The harbor was a forest of icy masts, the pale sun reflecting in glittering flecks, dying them a deep reddish hue. She rode past the shops lining the shore, expertly guiding Pompey through the traffic. A mile farther she glanced out and saw *The Gallant Lady*. Seeing the ship should have lifted her spirits, for she had spent most of her life on board the three-masted schooner, the happiest part of her existence. But it brought no joy to her now as she caught sight of the weathered salt-box house perching on a high dune-like hill back off the rocky shore.

Her heart almost failed her then, but the lights gleamed in the low windows, and she straightened her back and set her jaw as she approached the house. The night was quiet except for the clopping of Pompey's hooves and the hissing of the runners along the icy road. She pulled the horse up at the picket fence, tied the reins, and stepped stiffly down. As she turned she saw the door open and her father framed in the lamplight. She could not see his face, and she could not move. There was no way to help, no way to shield him from the truth, so she stood there watching helplessly as he came slowly down the steps and walked down the path to the gate in his peculiar rolling gait, as if he were walking across the deck of a ship.

William Alden opened the gate and came to stand beside her. He was short and stocky, but not fat. His weathered red face, she saw, was pale in the fading light, and she leaned against him, suddenly weak, and whispered, "Father—I've—I've brought Curtis home!"

He did not answer, and she could feel his powerful heart beating. He stood there looking over her shoulder at the coffin, and when she pulled back, she saw that his eyes were filled with tears—the first she'd ever seen there in all her life.

In his erect frame, the heritage of the sea was noticeably strong in him. He came from a race that was all too familiar with the loss of sons, for the sea takes its toll of those who live on it. He had lost two brothers, and his own father had gone down in the South Seas when William was but a boy.

Now he slowly nodded and stated stoically, "We'll lay him beside the others tomorrow."

"Yes, Father."

As his eyes returned to her, he asked, "Did he die well, Charity?"

She nodded, her eyes filling with tears; but not wishing to seem weak, she dashed them away and spoke in a strong voice. "Yes. Yes, he died well." Taking his arm she said, "I'll tell you all about it." Then she hesitated, holding his arm firmly. "And I'll tell you why I have to go back to Valley Forge."

He stared at her in surprise and nodded, with just the touch of a smile on his lips. "All right—you'll do as you please, Charity. It's a way you have." Then they put the horse and the sleigh in the barn and went into the house.

CHAPTER FOUR

THE BAD SEED

★ ★ ★ ★

Charity pulled Pompey to a stop in front of the large white house with the eight pillars. She had passed by it often, for it was only two miles out of Boston, perched on a ridge of high ground, but as she got down from the buggy she considered it thoughtfully. *Not a poor man's house*, she thought as she wrapped the reins around an iron ring set in a huge oak. The freezing rain had put a bluish glaze of ice on the house, and she almost slipped once on the glassy surface of the tiled walk leading up to the front porch. A heavy brass knocker, sheathed in ice, was set in the center of the massive oak door. Breaking the ice, Charity lifted the knocker and gave a series of heavy blows on the door.

As she stood there waiting, she glanced back toward town, as if she could see the small cemetery where they had buried Curtis earlier in the day. It had been necessary to break up the frozen ground with steel crowbars to get below the frost line, and the memory of it now sent a quiver across her face as she seemed to see again the small group of mourners as they circled the stark hole in the frozen ground. The words of the minister had sounded thin on the cold air, and only the thought of how Curtis had called on God in the Winslows' rough cabin at Valley Forge kept her from giving way to the grief that had shaken her terribly.

The preacher had read from the Bible the words, *I am the resurrection and the life*, and then had made a few simple remarks about loss being made right when all God's people would be raised from the dust. *But that doesn't mean me!* The thought had raked across Charity's mind. Though not unfamiliar with death, this encounter with its presence had shaken her as never before.

The door swung open and a thin black woman peered at her. "Yas'um? Somethin' fo' you?"

"I'd like to see Mr. Winslow."

The slave looked at her, shook her head doubtfully, but opened the door wider, saying, "Mistuh Charles Winslow—he sick—but Miz Winslow will mebby see you."

The interior of the foyer was dark, but Charity's eyes adjusted as she followed the woman down a broad hallway. "Miz Winslow? Kin I come in?" the servant asked. A voice answered faintly, and she opened the door. Stepping back to let Charity in, she said, "Lady wants to see Mistuh Charles."

Charity entered, and as the door closed behind her, she walked toward the far side of the room where two women were sitting in chairs beside a large bay window. The younger of them was fashionably dressed, and she rose slowly, saying, "Yes? What is it?"

"My name is Charity Alden. I came to see Mr. Winslow, but I understand he's ill."

"What is your business with my husband?" There was a hardness in the woman's voice, as there was in her face. She spoke sharply as she would have to a servant. "I'm Mrs. Winslow."

Charity hesitated, not certain how best to speak of her errand. There was nothing in the face of the woman who stood opposite her that gave encouragement, but she was a direct girl accustomed to dealing with business.

"I've just come back from Valley Forge, Mrs. Winslow." She saw a flicker of interest in Mrs. Winslow's dark eyes and added quickly, "I was there to visit my brother, and I met Nathan Winslow and his wife."

"I suppose they sent you to beg for help?" The other woman was almost hidden by the large overstuffed chair she sat in, but the flickering light of the fire suddenly threw its beams across her face. She was, Charity saw, shrunken with age, and had the same hardness in her old eyes as in the countenance of the younger woman. "We've nothing for them," she rasped. "Let them get help from their precious 'Patriots'!"

"Don't upset yourself, Martha," Mrs. Winslow said; the words were a command, void of compassion. She gave Charity a direct look, saying, "This is Mrs. Martha Winslow—my husband's mother." Then she asked, "Do you have a message from my husband's people?"

"No—but I think you ought to know that Julie is quite ill, Mrs. Winslow," Charity told her. "The Army is starving—and if she doesn't get some decent food soon, I don't think she'll live. At best, she could lose the baby."

A strange angular light seemed to flicker in Dorcas Winslow's eyes, and as soon as she began to speak, Charity realized there was no hope of help from this person. She was an attractive woman, but it was not a gentle beauty; there was an adamant quality to her features, and even her figure was somehow rigid as she spoke in clipped tones: "I'm sorry you've made the trip for nothing, Miss Alden, but my husband is quite unable to have visitors. Even if he were, there's nothing he can do. We have nothing to do with this insane rebellion—and on the day when the King's power is once again in place, what you're asking us to do could be called treason!"

When Charity saw that neither of these two women would give any help, she prepared to leave. As she turned, a thought struck her and she faced them again. "If I can't speak with your husband, could I speak with your son?"

"Paul?" The request caught Mrs. Winslow off guard, and she lifted her head with a haughty anger. "I don't think you know very much about my son, Miss Alden. He has no reason to love Nathan Winslow!"

"I see." Charity considered the faces of the two women, then said, "Thank you for your time; I'll not intrude on you any longer."

She turned and left the room, almost running over the slave who had apparently been listening outside the door. She hurried down the hall, the black woman racing to open the door. There was a peculiar look on the servant's face as she said softly, "You kin fin' Mistuh Paul at the Black Horse Tavern."

Taken by surprise, Charity paused, searched the black face of the woman, and asked, "Why do you tell me that?"

A secretive air shrouded the woman's face, but there was a bright look of intelligence in her eyes. "Mistuh Adam—thet's Mistuh Nathan's pa—he wuz good to my pa. They is bof' good men, missy. I don' know if he'll help you. Mistuh Paul—he ain't good like Mistuh Charles and Mistuh Adam—but if he takes a notion to help you, he do it!"

Charity tried to remember what the burly chaplain, Dan Greene, had told her about Paul Winslow. "I heard he had trouble with Nathan. It doesn't seem likely he'll want to help him."

"Mistuh Paul—he do whut he want, missy! Him and Mistuh Nathan, they fight over that Abigail wench—but if Mistuh Paul ain't drunk, he mebby will remember dat it wuz Mistuh Adam who kept Mistuh Charles and all de rest of dis fambly from bein' put in jail when dem Redcoats got run outta Boston!"

"The Black Horse Tavern? That's down near the wharf." She smiled warmly and reached into her pocket to get a coin.

"No, missy!" the woman objected, drawing herself up. "I don' wants nuthin' fo' helpin' none of Mistuh Adam's folks! He was real good to me and my pa!" Her eyes opened in surprise as the young girl held out her hand, but she took it timidly. Then as she heard a call from inside, she lowered her voice. "You go see Mistuh Paul!"

★　★　★　★

The Black Horse Tavern was nearly full, even though it was only late afternoon. Jacob Spelling, the owner, looked with satisfaction across the low-ceilinged room that took up the entire first floor of the half-timbered building. Ordinarily he could have counted the customers on the fingers of one hand at such a time, but the cold weather had stopped all outdoor work, and most of the shops were closed for lack of business. The warmth of the tavern drew men, and Spelling smiled, calculating his profits; liquor and talk flowed freely as the men downed the potent ale and brandy.

Spelling moved with alacrity toward a table set in front of the wide window that provided a view of the harbor crowded with ships. He deftly removed an empty brown bottle, wiped the table, then poured a fresh drink into the pewter mug of the young man who sprawled carelessly in his chair. "Another bit, is it, Mr. Winslow? Just to keep this cold off your bones."

"Leave the bottle, Spelling." The speech of Paul Winslow was only slightly slurred, although he had been drinking for several hours. He picked up the tankard, motioned to the three men seated at the table, and offered languidly, "Drink up."

"What'll we drink to, Paul?" The speaker was a heavy young man with piercing eyes and a mouth like a catfish—wide and ugly.

"Didn't know you had to have something to drink to, Ralph."

"That's right, I don't!" Ralph Courtney grinned and downed his drink, then filled it again.

The other two men were obviously brothers, for they bore a strong family resemblance. They were both tall and rawboned, and both had the same shock of sandy hair and hooked nose. Mason Bright was twenty-eight; his brother Moses, two years younger. Like the other two men, they were well dressed and had a general air of prosperity that set them off from the rest of the men in the room.

"Let's drink to a timely demise of General George Washington," Paul suggested with a wicked grin, and leaned back waiting for the warnings he knew would follow his words. There was a raking look in his face, a dissatisfaction on his lips and in his eyes that dared trouble to come.

"Not so loud, you fool!" Mason Bright hissed, giving a nervous look around the room. "You want to get us all thrown in the hulks?"

"That's right," Moses spoke up. "I'd hate to spend Christmas in one of those things." He spoke of the rotting ships used as prisons for captives taken in battle.

Paul looked around the room and spat out contemptuously, "I don't see anybody here who could put any good Englishman in jail, do you, Ralph?"

Ralph Courtney had a boldness of his own, but it was mixed with a wily sense of self-preservation. He did not miss the sullen looks on the faces of the men sitting close enough to hear Winslow, and he put a restraining hand on Paul's arm. His wide mouth scarcely moved as he spoke quietly. "I reckon Mason's right this time. Our turn will come soon enough, Paul!"

There was a reckless light in Winslow's eyes, but he shrugged and growled, "Bunch of old women!" then took a long pull at his ale. He slumped back in his chair and stared out the window at the forest of masts that scored the harbor. "I'd like to get on board one of those and take a voyage to the South Seas."

"You better watch out, Paul," Ralph grinned, "or the press gang will get you!"

"They're not taking anybody now," Moses said. He shook his head and added in a low tone, "The rebels don't have enough ships to need more men."

"Different with the English," Mason went on. He glanced out at the ships and shook his head. "Got a letter last week from my cousin who's a second lieutenant on a King's ship. He said they're so short of men they're having to take the dregs out of the prisons to keep full crews."

"Well, I don't think we have to worry about getting pressed into His Majesty's Royal Navy here in Boston," Paul shrugged.

"No, but when you get to New York, you'd better watch your-self," Ralph insisted. "You done a lot of sailing, Paul, but from what I hear the lot of a sailor in the Royal Navy is pretty grim!"

"So I hear, but—" Paul Winslow stopped abruptly as a young woman in a heavy fur coat walked in through the front door and after taking a quick look around the room, went up to speak with Spelling.

"Well, what have we here, gentlemen?" he grinned. "Haven't seen a morsel that juicy in some time."

"She don't look like a tavern wench, for sure," Ralph leered. "Look at that!"

The girl had spoken with the burly Spelling who had motioned toward the table where the four young men were sitting. She had followed his gesture, then made her way toward them.

"Mr. Winslow?"

The four men all rose, and Paul stated, "I'm Paul Winslow."

There was a direct look in the young woman's eyes, but she hesitated slightly. "Could I—speak with you a moment, sir?"

"Of course," Paul agreed quickly, and giving a wink that she could not see, he said, "Would you gentlemen mind giving this lady a little privacy?"

She waited until the others left. "My name is Charity Alden, Mr. Winslow. I've just come from your home."

"Oh?" Winslow was not drunk, but his wits were moving rather slower than usual. He could not imagine why this beautiful creature had been to see his family, but he was bored, and any attractive woman he looked upon was a challenge to his skill. "Will you sit down, Miss Alden?"

"Thank you." She sat down and gave her attention to him, trying to think of the best way to gain his help. He was one of those men who have a neatness about them both in feature and in figure. He was of average height but there was a natural grace in his body, and as he took his seat, she knew he would do most things well. He was not massively built, but there was a depth to his chest that hinted of strength. He had a handsome face, his dark hair smoothly in place like a cap. His eyes were large and dark brown, the planes of his face smoothly joined to form a pleasing picture.

He came very close to having a feminine beauty—but there was nothing feminine about Paul Winslow, Charity saw at once. On the contrary! There was something of the predator in his smile, and she stirred uncomfortably as she forced herself to explain her mission. Quickly she told him of her trip to Valley Forge, and when she mentioned Nathan and Julie, his head shot up and he stared at her, an unreadable thought in his eyes. When she finished by telling of her visit with his mother and grandmother, he leaned back in his chair, a sardonic smile on his face.

"I don't imagine you got much encouragement from either of them, Miss Alden?"

"Well . . ."

He laughed and leaned across the table to put his hand on her arm, saying, "We have our family problems—Father would help you like a shot. But neither my mother nor my grandmother have any time for Nathan or his father."

The pressure of his hand made Charity uncomfortable. Not only was his touch too intimate, but she was aware that they were the target of all eyes in the crowded room. She pulled her arm free, her eyes flashing. "I'm going back with a doctor to help Julie, Mr. Winslow—with or without help!"

He looked at her with interest, then suddenly laughed. It was an easy laughter, the laughter of a man who finds amusement in many things. "Well, that's speaking right out," he remarked. "What do you want me to do?"

"I—I thought you might help get some supplies for me to take back."

"What kind of supplies?"

"Food, blankets, shoes—anything! They have nothing!"

Paul Winslow was a creature of impulse, and he blurted out without thinking, "I'll do that."

Her face lit up, showing an openness in her expression—a sudden trust. Winslow added, "When will you need the food?"

"I'm leaving tomorrow morning. I have to find a doctor who'll go with me, though."

"I'll get on it, Miss Alden," Winslow promised at once. "Maybe you could stop by here in a couple of hours to check over the supplies?"

"Oh, yes, I can do that," Charity said. She rose quickly and after an instant's hesitation put her hand out and gave him a firm grip. "I—I know you and Nathan have had . . . problems in the past. It's good of you, sir, to put it aside."

"Nothing at all, Miss Alden," he protested.

She gave him another smile. "I'll be back by six, Mr. Winslow."

As soon as she left the room, Winslow's friends came rushing back to pump him for details. When he told them what she wanted, Ralph's catfish mouth drew tight, and he gave a sharp look at this friend. "You're going to help him, Paul?"

"Why not?"

"He gave you a hard time with that Howland girl, didn't he?"

"Well—that's over."

Courtney said no more, but his question had changed Winslow's mood. He had offered his help on impulse, but the mention of Abigail Howland brought a scowl to his face. He threw himself into his chair, picked up his mug and drained it. "Spelling!" He raised his voice over the rabble of voices. "Blast you! Why can't you keep this cup filled?"

Ralph Courtney knew Paul Winslow well, and he saw immediately that the volatile element in the man had surfaced. *Winslow's a good chap*, he had confided to Mason earlier, *but he's as changeable as the wind!*

Courtney sat down and said nothing more about the girl. He was aware of Paul's sensitive nature, as sensitive as a man without a skin; and the loss of Abigail Howland to Nathan was something he had not forgotten. The afternoon wore on and they all drank steadily, especially Paul. There was a scowl on his face as he put down tankard after tankard of liquor, and Courtney knew that the man was building up to one of the fits of anger that came on him like a sudden squall.

The Bright brothers left, and the two men were left alone. Paul finally broke the silence, his voice husky with drink. "He cut me out, Ralph, didn't he? Took Abigail away from me!"

"Ancient history, Paul. Forget it."

"Never going to—forget it!"

"You're drunk, Paul."

"That is correct, my friend—but I'm sober enough to handle Miss Charity Alden."

Ralph peered at him sharply, then shook his head. "Better be careful, Paul. Girls like her have fathers and brothers who have the bad habit of calling fellows like us to account."

"Like to see 'em try it!" Winslow lifted his head and there was a gleam in his eyes. He got up and went over to the bar, and Ralph watched as some sort of argument went on. The husky tavern keeper shook his head, but finally seemed to agree to something reluctantly, and Paul came back to the table with a smile of satisfaction on his face.

"I don't like it, Paul."

"You don't have to like it. Go on home to your mother."

It was part of Winslow's manner to become insulting when he drank too much, and Ralph got up angrily. "All right, I will!"

He left, his back stiff with outrage, but Paul only laughed at him. He leaned back and there was a look of pleased anticipation on his face. The time ran by, and he drank little more.

Finally he looked up to see Charity enter, and he got up and went straight to her. "Well, you're back," he said warmly. "Did you get a doctor?"

"Yes!" There was an excitement in her green eyes, and he admired her flawless complexion as she continued. "He's really too old to make the trip, but he's a real Patriot! I was ready to pay him anything he asked, but when he found out it was for the son of one of General Washington's officers, why, he jumped at the chance!"

"Splendid!" Paul said. "Now, I've been working on the supplies, but there are still a few problems."

"Problems?"

"Oh, you know how difficult it is to get some things with the war and all." He snapped his fingers and said ruefully, "I say, Miss Alden, I'm just about starved, and I'll wager you haven't taken time to eat a bite, have you now?"

"Well, there's hasn't been much time—"

"Of course not," Paul agreed, adding quickly, "I've arranged to have the innkeeper bring a supper to one of the rooms upstairs. Why don't you join me?"

Charity looked startled, and he hurried on. "There are really a couple of items about the supplies that we ought to discuss."

"Well—I suppose it will be all right."

"Fine! Fine! Let me show you the way." He led her across the room, saying to Spelling as they passed by, "Oh, Innkeeper, you can bring that food along—and Miss Alden will be having a bite with me!"

As Charity walked up the stairs she felt the eyes of the men in the room follow her—and she had an impulse to turn and leave. The tavern was respectable enough, but it was the first time she had ever been in one alone. And while the supper upstairs had sounded harmless enough, as she entered the room and he closed the door, a shock of fear ran along her nerves. It was a bedroom, and though there was a table and two straight-backed chairs, there was something about the whole thing that seemed improper.

He talked easily about food supplies and drew her out on the hard conditions of the Army in camp, and soon a knock at the door came, and Spelling brought in a large tray and left it on the table.

"Well, this looks good—try some of this ale, won't you?" he offered with a smile and picked up one of the tankards while handing her the other one.

"Oh no, really, Mr. Winslow. I don't care for anything to drink."

He sipped his own drink, and then said, "Well, perhaps later."

She sat down at his urging and ate a little, but the uneasiness she felt increased. He began to drink steadily, talking all the while and refilling his tankard from a large jug.

At first the talk was about supplies, but soon the tenor of the conversation changed, and he began paying her personal compliments. He was, she realized, not entirely sober, and she got up at once, saying, "I must go."

He looked at her, then put his tankard down and got to his feet. "But, Charity, we've not had time to get to know one another." There was a light in his eyes that shot fear into her heart, and she turned to leave, only to find herself whirled around to face him.

"Let me go!" she cried out, struggling wildly, but his strength was tremendous. He held her as easily as if she were a child.

"Now, sweet, be still!" he admonished, and suddenly he pulled her close and kissed her full on the lips.

Charity's heart raced wildly, and she struggled in vain to free herself. He was, she saw, enjoying her struggles, and she stopped at once.

"Now, *that's* more like it!" he grinned, and his grip relaxed a fraction. It was not much, but it was, Charity thought swiftly, the best opportunity she was likely to have. If she tried to scream, he would clamp his hand over her mouth, and there was no way she could overcome his superior strength. She made herself smile and said, "Well, sir, you *are* a forceful man!"

"Ah," he smiled, "but I am hoping force will not be necessary, Charity."

"You startled me, Mr. Winslow!"

"Call me Paul," he said. His eyes fell to the food and he asked, "Shall we continue our meal, Charity?"

"Well, I could eat a little, Paul."

They sat down, and she began to eat—not much but enough

to keep him from questioning her. He ate nothing, but drank steadily, going to the door once and calling down to Spelling for more ale. He began to tell her about Nathan and soon his face grew angry. The more he drank the more she encouraged him, and soon he was so intoxicated that his speech was slurred and his movements clumsy.

All at once he looked across the table at her accusingly. "You're trying to get me drunk, aren't you?"

"No, Paul," she returned quickly. All the while she had been talking she had thought wildly, trying to find some way to escape, but there was no way. Then her eyes fell on a long whip-like rod nearly two feet long with a cup on one end—a candle snuffer. It was leaning against the wall next to the door, and she measured the distance to it carefully.

He rose unexpectedly and started around the table, saying, "Come here, Charity!"

She had only a brief second, but she leaned over and in one motion grabbed the rod and with all the strength in her arm slashed him across the face.

The force of the blow sent him reeling to the side, and the sharp, thin rod split his cheek from his ear to his lower jaw. The pain of it sliced through him, and he threw up his hands as she slashed at him again, taking the blow on his forearm. He stumbled backward, falling to the floor over a stool, and as he fell, she cried out, "You dog! I ought to cut you to ribbons!"

But he was struggling to his feet, and though the blood was running through the fingers he had clapped to his cheek, he was strong and dangerous. She struck at him once more. Then as he reeled backward, she threw the snuffer at him and with one sure motion, opened the door and fled so quickly down the stairs and across the broad taproom that Spelling's jaw dropped with amazement as she disappeared through the door.

He mounted the stairs swiftly and found Winslow cursing and raving. When Spelling looked at the cut, he said quietly, "You'll have to have a doctor stitch that up, Winslow—and even then, you're going to have a nasty scar." He stared at the young man, distaste in his eyes, and added, "I hope it heals badly! Maybe you'll learn to leave decent girls alone!"

CHAPTER FIVE

CHRISTMAS COMES TO VALLEY FORGE

★ ★ ★ ★

Giant flakes of snow swirled earthward as the heavily loaded sled drawn by a matched set of roan geldings pulled over the rise. Dr. Aaron Bergen's head jolted as Charity yanked the team to an abrupt halt, and his nearsighted eyes peered around the frozen wasteland in confusion. "What's this?"

"Valley Forge," Charity said stiffly through frozen lips. "We made it." The strain of the hard journey was revealed by the lines around her eyes and mouth, and she had to force herself to keep her shoulders square. They had pulled out of Boston with the threat of a howling blizzard lurking in the lowering clouds, but by hard driving they had made the journey in record time.

As they continued down the slope, Dr. Bergen peered through the whirling flakes at the scarecrow-like men who were making some effort at marching their posts, staggering stiffly through the deep drifts. He shook his head, saying sadly, "Guess I've had the wrong idea about the Army, Charity."

"I know." She did not try to tell him that her own impressions had been the same, for the bitter cold made it necessary to limit words. Nothing had changed, she saw, as they passed along the rows of tents and shacks—except that the steadily falling snow had sculptured the rough, ill-built shacks into beautifully shaped, smooth structures. The leaning fieldstone chimneys breathed reluctant blue-white vapors that tried to rise but were immediately swept away by the moaning wind.

"This is it." Charity pulled the tired team to a stop in front of the Winslow hut, climbed down and stamped her feet to restore circulation. Dr. Bergen groaned slightly and staggered stiffly toward the cabin.

The door had opened as soon as the horses stopped and two men rushed out. "What'd I tell you, Father?" Nathan's face was split in a wide grin as he came forward to steady Charity, who was stumbling in the drifts lying in high ridges around the cabin. "This is Charity Alden—and I'd lay a wager this is some doctor she forced to come at gunpoint!"

The older Winslow stepped forward, and although he was shorter and darker, Charity saw at once that this man had the same strong face and calm assurance as his son. Charity was struck by the long scar that ran along one side of his face—it reminded her, with an agonizing stab, of her experience with Paul Winslow.

But Adam Winslow's manner soon put Charity at ease and helped her forget that frightening encounter. "My son puts a high value on you, Miss Alden," he said with a smile. "I tried to tell him it wouldn't be possible to get back in this weather, but he never doubted."

"Good heavens, Charity!" Nathan had lifted the tarpaulin, and his face was filled with astonishment as he stared at her. "Looks like you brought the whole store!"

"All we could pile on," Charity grinned. "Most of it is food, with as much warm clothing as we could carry—and Dr. Bergen brought all the medicine he could lay his hands on." She smiled and stepped toward the doctor to lay her hand on his shoulder. "I didn't have to threaten him at all, Nathan. He's a true Patriot—and when he found out that one of General Washington's officers had a need—why, he tore around like a crazy man getting supplies!"

"Never mind all that!" The doctor snorted and waved aside the thanks that the men tried to voice. "Where's my patient? I didn't freeze my tail off to stand here gossiping!"

"This way, Doctor," Nathan directed, a relieved look on his face and a grateful expression in his blue eyes that made all the effort worthwhile to Charity. "Father, you look after Charity, will you?"

"Of course." As the two disappeared through the low doorway, Major Winslow took the harness in his hand, then turned to

Charity. "Would you like to ride over to the quartermaster's shed? We have to get these supplies under armed guard at once, you know."

"No, thank you—I need some exercise, Major." She fell into step with him as they moved down the winding trail and asked, "How is Julie? I've been uneasy."

"Not good—but I feel much better now that you and the doctor are here. Our own doctor is pretty rough, and he's got enough patients to keep ten doctors busy." He paused and after a few steps he dropped his right hand on her shoulder and said, "We're in your debt—all of us."

"Oh, no!" Charity shook her head quickly, her cheeks rosy. "Your daughter-in-law was so good to my brother Curtis. If she hadn't talked to him about God, Major, I . . . don't think I could've had a peaceful day the rest of my life."

"I heard about it. We're all sorry about Curtis—but if he had to go, I'm glad he was under the blood."

Under the blood. The phrase would have sounded pious, almost sanctimonious, in the mouths of most men—but there was the same easy acceptance of God in Major Winslow that Charity had marveled at in his son and in Julie. It made her nervous—but at the same time she was drawn to that quality in the Winslows which made God as acceptable a topic of conversation as water or earth.

She listened as Major Winslow spoke of Julie's certain conviction that she would have a boy, and smiled with him as he shrugged and added quietly, "I'll not argue with her, Charity. When that girl says God has spoken, you can be absolutely sure she is right!"

"I think that's true, Major. She is as fixed as the pole star!" She halted abruptly and gave him a guarded look, saying, "I'd better tell you, sir, I went to see your family in Boston."

"My brother?"

"Well, no—that is, I went to see him, but he was ill. I spoke to his wife, but—"

She could not finish, and he smiled gently at her discomfort. "I would imagine you didn't get much encouragement from Dorcas—but I thank you for trying."

Charity bit her lip, and he saw that she was bothered, but he let the silence run on. Finally she continued. "There was a slave there at the house, named Cory. She told me to go see your nephew."

He saw instantly that she was uneasy, and shrugged. "She's a good girl, that Cory. Did you see Paul?"

By the time they pulled up to the quartermaster's building, he had the whole sordid story out of her, including how she had wounded Paul, and how shocked she was to see a similar scar on Adam Winslow's face. But there was a kindness in his dark eyes as he looked at her. "Don't blame yourself, Charity. It wasn't your fault." He sighed and shook his head sadly. "Paul's got the makings of a good man—but he's been spoiled beyond belief. He's spent his inheritance—and more beside. His father could never say no to him, and Dorcas is even worse. Why, he's spent enough on *boats* to start a business!"

"Boats?" Charity questioned. "What kind of boats?"

"Ah, yes," Adam smiled. "Nathan said you were a seafaring lass. Well, Paul started out with a small boat, got a bigger one, then bigger—and he's made quite a sailor of himself. I've often thought that it would have been a good thing if he'd gone to sea—but he doesn't have the discipline for that, I'm afraid."

Charity wanted to know more, but the sentries approached, and Major Winslow gave orders for unloading the sleigh. "There's plenty of room, I'm afraid," he remarked ruefully as the supplies were placed almost reverently in the large building by a brace of privates. "But it's a gift from God, all this; and in the name of His Excellency, I thank you, Charity."

"It's so *little*," she lamented sadly. She had noted that the hands of the soldiers unloading the food had trembled as they touched it, and that they had to put it down with force of will. The hunger of Valley Forge marked their eyes, and she whispered, "How can it happen, Major Winslow? How can our people let our men *starve*?"

"Some don't know," he answered. "But," he continued, anger raking his dark face and his mouth drawn to a thin line, "some don't care. Lots of people think we're fools out here, led by a madman who wants to make himself a king."

Charity looked at the pitiful heap of supplies, then at the wolf-lean faces of the soldiers, and she murmured, "It seems . . . impossible!"

"With God all things are possible, Charity!" There was such strength in Major Winslow's voice and such determination in his lean face that he frightened her. She had never seen such dedication as she found in these people, and knew instinctively that for this man the war was to the death. When he smiled, she was amazed at how these Winslow men, with all their strength, could have such gentleness! Then she thought of the drunken lust etched on the face of Paul Winslow, and she mused: *They're not all like Nathan and his father*.

⋆　⋆　⋆　⋆

For the next four days Charity and Dr. Bergen worked from dawn until dusk, and even later. There were four long huts packed wall-to-wall with the sick and dying, and the pair of them were found long after sundown moving down the narrow aisles between bodies illuminated by the feeble yellow lantern light.

Dr. Bergen and Dr. Williams appreciated each other, but would not admit it. They had stared at each other suspiciously at first; then slowly, as each man discovered the quality of the other, they began to spend their spare time together arguing endlessly—and loudly!—over treatment of the sick men. Once Nathan and Charity had listened to them reach the yelling stage over a fine point of medicine, and Charity had whispered in wonder, "The way they scream at each other, you'd think they were the worst of enemies, wouldn't you?"

"Good men—both of them," Nathan had said, and it was true that Williams' load was lightened by the arrival of his colleague. As for Bergen, any sacrifice he might have made in coming became as nothing, for General Washington himself had made a visit, and his warm thanks to the little doctor had brought tears to Bergen's eyes. "Such a man!" Bergen had murmured huskily as he told Charity about it. "Such a man our general is! And did I tell you, Charity, he talked with me for half an hour—to me, Aaron Bergen!"

"What did he say, Dr. Bergen?"

"Oh, all about the men, of course." He shook his head and there was wonder in his bearded face as he said in such a low tone she had to lean forward to hear it: "He loves them—these men of his! How he loves them!"

When not at the hospital, Charity was with Julie, and it was a joy to her to see the improvement from the food and medicine. A rich glow had come to the pregnant woman's face, and the feebleness that had struck her down was replaced by a vigor that delighted not only Nathan but all of them.

Dr. Bergen argued loudly with Dr. Williams that it was the presence of a *real* doctor which made the difference, but privately he admitted to Charity that it was as much Julie's faith as his doctoring that had brought improvement, and Charity agreed.

Christmas Eve, Charity and Dr. Bergen made their rounds, taking such small fragments of food and drink as could be spared to the men. Julie was awake when they returned, and seeing the look on her face made Bergen question, "Is it something, Mrs. Winslow?"

"Maybe." There was no fear in Julie's face, but she moved carefully as she walked across the room to sit in the one chair. "I think it will be tomorrow."

"A Christmas child!" Bergen chuckled. "Well, send for me when it's time!" Then he wheeled and left the hut.

Charity went to sit on the floor beside Julie. The two of them had spent many hours in that position, with Julie listening as Charity spoke of her life. At other times Julie had read from her Bible, always amazing Charity at how the words of the old book—words she'd heard a hundred times—came to life as the young woman read them and commented on their meaning. Charity had never thought of the Bible as a book for life, but more as an ancient tome of philosophy that one could study or read for an hour. As for making it a principle or guide to *practical* matters—why, that had never entered her head, nor had she ever known another human being who thought of it like that.

The night wore on, and finally Julie went to bed, saying to her husband with a calm smile on her lips, "He'll be here tomorrow, Nathan. Our son."

Charity looked at the faces of the couple and wondered, *How many people are in warm, safe places, but don't have the peace and joy of these two in these miserable conditions!*

She slept fitfully in a corner of the hut, wrapped in a blanket and expecting at any moment to hear Julie call for help. But dawn came, and with it a knock on the door. She got to her feet to open it and was surprised to find the Quaker chaplain outside. "Why, it's you, Friend Daniel!" she said with a smile.

He beamed at her use of the title so beloved by the Quakers. "I'm glad to see thee, Miss Alden," he nodded, then added, "I thought thee might like to go to service with me."

"Service?"

"Christmas service," he said simply.

Hearing his voice Julie called, "Friend Dan, come in."

The burly Quaker entered, and as he bent over Julie, there was a light in his eyes that Charity did not miss. She had known from the way he had spoken of this woman that there was a special feeling for her—and now she saw the mixture of pain and admiration in his eyes.

"Is it well with thee, Julie?"

"Yes, very well. Now, you take this young woman along. I'll be all right," she added quickly, seeing Charity hesitate. "Nathan will be here in a few minutes."

"He's on his way," Greene informed her. "I thought Miss Alden might like to go to our service. His Excellency will be there—in fact, the whole Army will be attending."

"Preach the word, Friend Dan," Julie smiled. "Go along, both of you."

They moved outside and headed for the drill ground just as Nathan came hurrying along with Dr. Bergen. The snow had stopped and now reflected a ruby glow as the sun cast its first rays over the mountains. The shadows lay like long fingers over the camp, dark and sinister at first, but as they moved out of the heavy timber onto the flat plain used as a drill field by the troops, the light swelled into a brilliant display of color—blue-white ice, dark green firs, the crimson reflections of the sun on the snow, and overhead a sky that was for the first time in days a delicate pale blue instead of iron gray.

The Army had already arrived, closely packed in a fan-shaped formation. "There it is," Greene commented quietly. "The Continental Army of the United States."

"It's not very big, is it, Friend Dan?"

"No. Not big." He led her to where the officers were mounted in a cluster, then added clearly, "Not many, Miss Alden. But it's all pure grain—the chaff has been blown away. These are the men—these pitiful few—who will make this nation free, or it will become a slavish colony forever."

He said no more but led her to a small platform in the center of the semicircle made by the troops. She could see Washington clearly, and once again she was struck by the massive presence of the man. His eyes, she saw, were fixed on the ranks, and she knew, as did the men, that he was weighing the possibilities. Would they be enough? Would they stand fast? Would they stay when the skies were falling?

The other officers, including von Steuben, Mad Anthony Wayne, and Hamilton, never took their eyes off their commander. They waited, and finally Washington began to speak. His voice, rising and falling in even cadences, carried clearly across the open space to the rear ranks. When he spoke of "our country," there was something in the way he said it that made every man on that frozen field believe it was true.

They were starving, freezing, dead with fatigue. They had been deserted by their supporters, cornered and beaten by the British, scorned by the powerful nations of the world—but when Washington said *our country*, they believed it. There was a meaning to their suffering, and as Washington spoke simply of their sacrifice and of the suffering yet to come, they accepted it because he said so.

It was simple, Charity saw at once. Washington was the keystone to the arch; he held the Army together, and without him the whole experiment in democracy would fall to ruins.

Then he said, "And now, our chaplain will speak to us, to all of us. May Almighty God, who rules over this new nation as He rules over the stars in their courses, bless his words to our hearing."

Dan Greene stepped forward, opened his Bible, and read the words:

> Behold, a king shall reign in righteousness, and princes shall rule in judgment. And a man shall be as an hiding place from the wind, and a covert from the tempest; as rivers of water in a dry place, as the shadow of a great rock in a weary land.

Raising his head, he lifted up his voice and began to preach. "This scripture refers to the Lord Jesus Christ. One day He will come. Kingdoms may rise and fall, but He will come. That is the one certain thing in this earth—that one day the earth will be under the authority of Him who can do no wrong." Then he stopped, and when he paused, the silence was almost palpable in its intensity.

"But *until* He comes, the Lord of Glory," he cried out suddenly in a tone that rang like a great bell over the frozen ground, "we are men who must occupy this earth—and we believe that He, this almighty God who will come, wants us to live as free men and not as serfs!"

Charity stood there transfixed. This was no sermon delivered as a religious duty by a hired parson! It was a prophetic cry from the heart of one man, but it caught the hungers of all who listened; and as Dan Greene spoke of God's love and purpose, he forged it to the cause for liberty for which these men were asked to lay down their lives.

She couldn't remember much of the sermon, but she would

never forgot that scene—never! Washington, his face set like a flint, staring out at the troops. The ragged, bearded men with hollow eyes grown suddenly bright with hope. The hush that was broken by Greene's voice—and the ragged but powerful *Amen* that went up as he closed with prayer. She was certain that when she became an old woman, she would see this scene as sharply and clearly in her mind's eye as she had seen it with her physical eyes just now.

Commands were given, the troops were dismissed, and Dan came to stand beside her. "I expect thee is cold."

"No, I don't think so." She hesitated, then said, "I—I thought your sermon was moving."

He didn't answer, but took her arm and they made their way back to the hut. He seemed to be constrained, so she remained silent, but as they came in sight of the hut, he lifted his head quickly. "Look! There's Nathan—something's happened!"

He broke into a run, and Nathan shouted as he saw them, "He's here! By the good Lord—he's here!"

He was laughing, tears running down his face as Greene caught him in a bear hug, and the two of them danced around in the snow.

Dr. Bergen came outside, considered the two big men waltzing in the snow, and remarked with a grin, "Pair of blasted fools!" But there was light in his small eyes, and he nodded to Charity, "Go on in and greet the newest member of the House of Winslow."

Julie was sitting up, holding a white bundle. "Come and see him, Charity," she called, her eyes bright with joy.

Hesitantly, Charity approached the bed. As she knelt and Julie pulled the blanket back, she exclaimed, "Oh, he's got red hair!"

"Yes," Nathan voiced from behind her. "And he's got a name, too."

"A name?" Charity asked. "What is it?"

Julie had a playful look in her eyes, and she reached out to take Nathan's hand as she announced, "His name is Christmas. Christmas Winslow."

"Christmas?" Charity smiled. "What a wonderful name! I never heard of a man named Christmas."

"He came on Christmas—and the Lord has promised me that he'll be a blessing to his people—just as the Lord Jesus came to be."

Charity's eyes filled with tears and she put out a timid hand and stroked the fine red hair. "Christmas Winslow—may you be as good a man as your father and your grandfather!"

"Amen!" Dan Greene affirmed fervently, which was echoed by the rest as they sat gazing at the newest arrival at Valley Forge— and wondering what his life would be like.

CHAPTER SIX

Ring Out the Old

★ ★ ★ ★

"He'll make a fine American—and from the sound of that crying, he's got the lungs to be a preacher as well!"

Charity pressed herself against the rough log wall and stared at General Washington. If the room had seemed small before, now the general's bulk seemed to take all the available space. He was standing in the center of the floor, his head almost brushing the shakes of the ceiling, smiling down at Julie, who was holding the baby up for him to admire.

Christmas Winslow was the only person in the room not impressed with the imposing stature of General George Washington. He had just had his meal cut short, and his face was red with rage as he protested vigorously. Washington put out a finger gingerly, and the flailing hand of the baby encountered it, grasped it, and to everyone's surprise, Christmas stopped crying.

"You have a way with babies, Your Excellency," the tall, bald man standing to one side commented. This was Daniel's uncle, General Nathaniel Greene, one of Washington's most trusted officers.

Washington raised his head at Greene's statement, then looked back at the baby, saying with a wistful look in his gray eyes, "I love children." He said no more, but Charity knew, as did the others, that the great sorrow of his life was his lack of sons.

It had been a shock to Charity when she had opened the door to find the general standing there that morning. He had greeted her warmly by name and thanked her again for the supplies. She was not accustomed to the attention of famous men, and none was more famous than Washington. He was, she was amazed to find, a simple man. Though the richest man in America, yet he had laid his position and his fortune on the line for the cause of liberty. As he spoke with Nathan and Julie, Charity watched him intently and was taken off guard when he turned and faced her, saying, "I understand you're a ship owner, Miss Alden."

"Why—yes, sir. My people have always been sailors."

He began asking her about the ship, about cargoes and speed, and she answered his steady flow of questions a little bewildered. Once she glanced at Daniel and saw a faint smile on his face, but she had no time to think of that.

Finally Washington paused and looked at her silently, with some of the same calculation in his eyes that she'd noted when he'd looked at the troops during the Christmas service. The room was silent save for the small whistle of a teakettle on the small hearth. Finally he spoke. "I am become a beggar, Miss Alden."

"A beggar, Your Excellency?"

"Yes, a beggar." A bitterness ran along the edge of the general's thin lips, and he added curtly, "I must go with my hat in my hand to our Congress for the bare necessities of life for my poor men—"

"And often as not, they keep you waiting like some peasant!" Greene exploded. "It's an outrage, sir, an outrage!"

"I am the servant of the Congress, General Greene," Washington rebuked the older man gently, then fixed his eyes on Charity. "A ship is on its way from France with a hold full of supplies— cannon, powder, muskets, food—everything an army needs!"

"That's Franklin's work, I'd warrant!" Daniel exclaimed.

"Yes. He worked like a slave to get these supplies—and now it may all be wasted." He stopped and looked straight into Charity's eyes, adding slowly, "Unless we can find a Patriot who will help us. A Patriot with a fast ship."

It was all clear to Charity then, for she knew that the British fleet had sewn a tight web around the coast of America with the intent of strangling the flickering revolution by a blockade. It had been, she knew as well, a successful move, for the British Navy was paramount among the navies of the world. There had been no losses on the British side in single ship actions, so it was taken for granted that England's fleet was invincible.

There was only one thing the general could mean, and Charity voiced it. "You want me to bring the supplies to our shores at Boston?"

"Yes. The French ship cannot be caught even *close* to our shores," Washington nodded, pleased with her alertness. "The best we could do is arrange to send a ship to Port-au-Prince and transfer the supplies."

"Why, we make that run several times a year, Your Excellency," Charity replied, quickly analyzing the best routes and anticipating the dangers. "It would be no trick at all for *The Gallant Lady*."

"If the British stop you," Washington insisted with a warning shake of his heavy head, "your ship will be seized. You'll lose her."

Charity laughed at the idea. "Those wallowing hulks catch *my* ship? Not in a million years."

Washington was still apprehensive. "The Army must have food, clothing, and weapons. I've made General Greene quartermaster. If you feel you can do this, work it out with him. We have little to offer you in the way of reward, but if the gratitude of one old soldier is of any value to you, Miss Alden, you will have my heartfelt thanks—and that of my men."

For some reason, the simple words brought tears to Charity's eyes, for she knew this man would die before asking anything for himself. She blinked the tears back and stated, "Sir, if my father will agree, we will get your supplies." Then she added as an afterthought, "And Father usually lets me have my own way."

A laugh went up and Charity blushed, but the general nodded with a soft smile, saying just as he turned to go, "I believe, Miss Alden, that most of us men would let you have your own way. God bless you."

Washington turned and left, followed closely by the two Greenes, and as soon as the door slammed shut, the baby set up a howl that stopped the moment Julie began to feed him. Nathan smiled at the pair. Turning to Charity, he asked, "Do you really think you might be able to get those supplies?"

"Don't see why not. Like I told the general, no Britisher can catch the *Lady*. Besides, they'll never suspect our cargo, because they're used to seeing us make voyages in that area."

Nathan grinned at her. "You sure are a better looking sailor than any I've ever laid eyes on, Charity."

★ ★ ★ ★

For three days Charity did little but ponder Washington's

words. She helped Julie with the baby, but that young woman made such an astonishing recovery that by the last day of the year, she was able to carry on without help.

All morning on the thirty-first, Charity walked around the camp, being greeted constantly by the soldiers who had come to recognize her. The sight of a woman was a rare thing, and more than once she had seen the ugly face of lust, but every soldier in the Continental Army knew with an iron certainty that the man who touched Charity Alden would hang in the cold wind the next day.

She stood and watched as Baron von Steuben, that strange import from Europe, drilled a picked squad on a hard-packed field of snow. He howled and wept and cursed in German, and the men laughed at him, and then he would laugh at himself. But Charity had heard Major Winslow say, "That fat Prussian has made soldiers out of them! They'll never break and run again!"

During the afternoon, Charity walked along the perimeters of the camp, staring at the miserable huts and tattered tents, gazing from time to time into the hungry eyes of a sentry or some of the men on wood detail, wondering why they stayed.

The sun paled and seemed to cast no heat on the frozen ground as she finally returned late in the afternoon, weary from the over-whelming situation. A resolve had come to her, and the import of her decision brought no comfort, for she had seen neighbors and relatives who had paid a heavy price for throwing their strength into the battle for freedom.

Deep in thought as she walked, she was unaware of anyone until a shadow came across her path. Looking up, she saw that Dan Greene was standing patiently with his hands in his pockets. Something about his attitude told her he had been waiting for her.

"Getting dark, Miss Alden."

She fell in beside him, and he spoke of casual things, but finally he stopped and she halted as well, looking up at him.

"Has thee made up thy mind?"

"Yes—but how'd you know?" she asked.

"Ah, now, that's not been too hard." He kicked the snow off one of his boots, lifted his eyes, and gave her that gentle smile so often seen in his strong features. "Thee has been walking around for three days now practically talking to thyself. But I know what thee is going to do, Charity."

His use of her given name surprised and pleased her somehow, and she smiled up at him. "Oh, do you now, Dan? And what *am* I going to do?"

"Why, thee is going to get the supplies for the general," he answered and laughed at her expression, adding, "And I am going with thee!"

"What!"

"Surely thee didn't think the general would let thee go alone?"

"I don't need any help!"

He stared at her, shaking his head. "Oh, there's no doubt thee would do it, but my uncle is the quartermaster of the Continental Army, and he's assigned me to be liaison officer in this matter."

It irked Charity to see the assurance in Greene's face. She had made up her mind to go, but there had been nothing said about taking anyone along. She had spent years proving that she was as good a sailor as any man, and now it seemed that she had to prove it to the Continental Army. "Take you along? Are you a sailor? Can you skip up a foremast and set a top gallant? Can you navigate?"

He shrugged, ignoring her flash of anger, and admitted, "I'm no sailor, Charity. Matter of fact, the only time I ever got in a boat bigger than our little fishing skiff, I got so sick I couldn't hold my head up. So thee will have to help me along—if I'm allowed to go, that is. And the general would really prefer to have a member of his staff along to negotiate with the captain of the French ship."

His words soothed her ruffled emotions, and she laughed lightly and put her hand on his arm, hard as iron beneath her touch. "Well, maybe we'll make a sailor out of you, Dan. Don't know of any Quaker sailors, though."

He put his hard, square hand over hers and there was a queer feeling in her as he murmured softly, "It's a good thing thee is doing, Charity Alden—and God will bless thee for it."

Her face flushed as he pressed her hand. He was a powerful man, his thick chest and broad shoulders making her feel almost unsubstantial. He had, she realized, a physical strength that was prodigious—but it was the spirit which flared out of his warm brown eyes that she had learned to admire.

Finally he released her hand and looked off into the distance. "Listen!" Far off some bells were ringing. Church bells, probably, but far away, heard only as a silver tinkling that floated across the white frozen world.

"Ringing out the old year," he told her. Then he smiled. "And for thee, Charity Alden, the bells are ringing out a great deal. Thee is leaving the old world—coming into something new."

There was something almost prophetic in his deep voice, and a quick stab of fear ran through her. Her life had been fixed, and now she was moving out of it, into an unknown and uncertain time. She took a deep breath, and looking across Valley Forge, she whispered, "I think you're right, Dan—but it'll be all right."

"So help us God!" he murmured as if in a benediction.

★ ★ ★ ★

"What's the date?"

Dan looked up at Charity, who had come below to the small cabin used by the first mate, and answered, "The fifteenth, isn't it?" He rose and the top of his head almost brushed the low ceiling. He had almost beaten his brains out at first aboard the *Lady*, for the doors were just low enough to catch him right in the center of the forehead. "Look, I can't make head nor tails of this awful stuff! Now what in the world does *this* mean?"

Charity looked down at the problem in navigation that he was wrestling with, and then shook her head. Taking the book from him, she tossed it on the small desk, saying, "You've not got the head to make a navigator—but you make a fine foretopman, Dan!"

"Never mind that!" He grimaced, then forced a grin, thinking of the only time he'd climbed to the top pinnacle of the mainmast. A wind had been rocking the ship at anchor, and he'd made it to the top, but when he looked down, he immediately got sick and froze to the spar. His grip was so powerful that none of the sailors had been able to break his grasp, so Charity had gone aloft and, after a time of soft talking, had persuaded him to turn loose. He'd followed her down and fallen to the deck instantly.

The crew had laughed, of course, but when the mild-mannered Quaker had refused to be offended, they had been forced to like the man. He had, after all, proven himself to be the strongest man on board. Years of work on the farm had given his fingers a steel-trap grip; after he had put Stevens, the biggest man among the crew, on his back as if he had been a child, he had gotten along famously.

Greene had been accepted by William Alden almost at once. Charity's father was not an educated man, but he had a wisdom that lies deep in seafaring men, and he saw the quality of the husky Quaker almost at once. This had surprised Charity considerably, for she knew her father made up his mind slowly. She was, however, not at all unaware of Daniel Greene's ability to move among men—an ability she had observed as he gained the respect from the soldiers at Valley Forge.

Persuading her father to make the voyage had been simple. He had a slow-moving mind, but like a glacier, once in motion, he was difficult to stop. He blamed the British for his son's death, and had cast about in his mind for some way to repay them. So when he heard it was Washington's personal request, and was made to understand that the cargo would give the Continental Army what it needed to stand up to the hated English, he agreed at once.

The Gallant Lady carried a crew of fourteen as a rule, but none of them were told of the mission—with the exception of Alden's nephew, Thaddeus. Thad Alden was a young man of seventeen, the best sailor for his age out of Boston, many believed, and he was also part owner of the ship. His father had been Alden's only brother, and it had been a blow when he had been lost off the coast of Africa on another ship.

Thaddeus had been stand-offish with Greene, which puzzled the officer, for the boy was characteristically friendly with all others. Greene had finally asked Charity, "Why doesn't Thad like me?"

"Oh . . ." Charity had become flustered, and her face turned pink. "He's—he's jealous of you, Dan."

"Of me?"

"Well, not just *you*. He thinks—"

She could not finish and Greene smiled. "I see. The lad's in love with thee. Well, it'd be surprising if he weren't, Charity."

The compliment disturbed her, and she'd flounced off, muttering about how silly men were, but Greene had looked at her with a new light of interest in his eyes.

Since that time there had been an air of constraint between them, but now as she peered out the only small window in the cabin, she seemed herself again. "Father wants us to go pick up the papers from the harbor master before setting sail, and there are a few more things to bring from the chandler's shop. Want to come along?"

"Maybe we can get some more of that chowder at the inn," he said hopefully. "Still planning on leaving day after tomorrow?"

"We'll go out after dark. I don't think the British would stop us, but no sense taking chances."

One of the sailors, a squatty man with a bristling beard, followed them to the chandler's shop, shouldered the supplies, and headed back to the ship. They made their way to the harbor master's office, got the papers Captain Alden needed, then came outside onto the street. "Now, how about that chowder?" Greene suggested.

"All right," Charity smiled up at him. "But you better enjoy it, because I have the feeling that day after tomorrow you're going to hate the sight of food!"

"Give no thought for the morrow—or the day after, either, as the scripture says!" He walked with her along the cobblestone street, enjoying the warm air that had driven the chilling winds away from the city. She knew the city well, and pointed out several interesting spots to him. Finally they turned into The Eagle's Nest, a small tavern where she often came with her father. The food was good and reasonably priced, and the tavern was frequented by a more respectable spectrum of seafaring men than many of the others.

They sat down at a table against the back wall, and the innkeeper, a small man with a patch over one eye and several fingers missing, took their order. "One wouldn't think being an innkeeper would maim a fellow like that," Dan remarked.

"He's a real sailor of the old school," Charity answered.

Greene shifted and lowered his voice. "Isn't it a little dangerous for us to be in here?"

Charity laughed at him, saying, "If you try to stay away from every man in Boston who fought on a King's ship, you'll be pretty lonely." She traced with her finger a design cut deep into the blackened oak table, and her face grew serious. "Don't worry about Tompkins. Most of the men who served in the British navy got their belly full. You don't know much about life on board a ship of the line—a fighting ship, do you, Dan?"

"Nothing at all."

"It's about as close to hell on earth as you want to come," she replied. There was a frankness in this girl that intrigued Dan. She was blunt, plain-spoken to the point of abruptness. It was her life on board ship since she was a child that had molded her, and her manner of thinking was almost masculine, in a way that contrasted sharply with the trim feminine lines of her figure and the grace of her features.

She spoke of the floggings that cut the flesh to the bone, the biscuits filled with weevils, the rotten salt pork that made up the boring and unhealthy diet. She was eloquent in her own way as she painted a stark and ugly picture of the brutal life that the common sailor endured for a pittance, which was often withheld from him for little or no cause—or which he lost in the brothels and gambling houses that lined the harbors of every deep-water port in the world.

The food came—steaming clam chowder with fragrant fresh-baked bread and a jug of clear cider to wash it down. They ate with enjoyment, and Charity more than once realized that this man—so foreign in so many ways, with his strange religion and ignorance of the sea—had some quality that was potent enough to bring a fellowship to her that she had known only with one other man.

They talked long, and were so engrossed in conversation that it came as a rude shock when a shadow fell across Charity's face and a venomous voice declared, "Here's the filthy vixen, Courtney!"

Both Charity and Greene were startled, and when she looked up, she saw Paul Winslow standing over them, a ragged bandage covering his left cheek. The man he'd called Courtney stood behind him, and he reached out and pulled at Winslow, saying in an urgent whisper, "Now, Paul, you don't want to get yourself involved with this woman!"

"Who says I don't? Blast you, Courtney. If you can't be a man, go home to Mama as you always do!" He grinned wickedly as the heavyset Courtney shrugged and stepped back. Then he turned and put his left hand on the bandage and stared angrily down at Charity. He was weaving slightly, his eyes glazed as he stood there. Then he reached out and grabbed Charity by the hair and gave a yank.

Greene was up in a flash, and his fist moved so fast that it was only a blur. Charity heard a solid *thunk*! and then her hair was free. She saw Winslow driven backward into Courtney by the powerful blow, and both of them careened into a table, falling to the floor with a crash of dishes.

"I think we can leave now," Greene said quietly. He took Charity's arm and they walked past the two men—Courtney struggling to his feet and Winslow lying as still as a corpse, with his mouth open and a livid bruise on his forehead where Greene's blow had landed.

They walked out of the tavern, which had fallen silent, and as soon as they were outside the impact of what had happened hit Charity. She began to tremble, and Greene held her arm firmly as they made their way back to the ship. "Let's not go on board, Dan," she said quietly. "Can't we just sit here a while?"

"Surely." He sat beside her, and soon she began to tell him the story. He listened silently, and finally, moved by the ugly account, he put his arm around her and she leaned against him. She was a proud girl, but the scene had frightened her, and she let him hold her until the trembling passed.

After a while she took a deep breath, pulled away from him, and looked up with some embarrassment in her face. "Sorry, Dan. Guess I'm not as tough as I thought. But it's all over now."

"Not quite over, I think." He stood up and she saw the man called Courtney coming down the street, his eyes fixed on them. "Maybe you better go aboard."

"No, I'll stay with you."

Courtney came straight up to them, and there was a reluctance in him. "A word, sir?"

"I'm standing here, friend," Dan said quietly. The odd greeting took the man off-guard, and Dan added, "How's Winslow?"

Courtney shifted, his catfish mouth drawn tight. He scuffed his feet, then said, "This is none of my doing, sir, but my friend demands satisfaction."

"A duel?"

"Certainly!"

"I let my dog take care of fighting of that sort."

Courtney shrugged. "I must tell you, sir, that if you refuse, my friend will take a horsewhip to you on the public street."

"Don't do it, Dan!" Charity whispered.

"I would pay attention to the lady, sir," Courtney suggested. "You would have no chance at all in such an affair with Paul Winslow. Much better that you leave town and never return."

Although Dan Greene's training in nonviolence was strong, it had been considerably weakened since he had left his home to join his uncle and Washington's troops. He was a chaplain, and a noncombatant, but because he had lived in the atmosphere of war too long, he responded instantly. "Name the time and the place, sir!"

"Tomorrow morning at dawn—there's a beach down there a quarter of a mile." He pointed with his left hand and added, "It'll be most private. We'll see to a physician, and you have your second there with you. The choice of weapons belongs to my friend, of course?"

"Anything!"

"The rapier, then—foils will be provided if you have none."

"At seven."

Courtney nodded and moved away. After walking a few paces, he quickly turned and came back, a queer light in his piercing black eyes. "I've done as Winslow asked—now I want to say one word on my own." He hesitated, then blurted out, "Man, don't do it! He's a devil! There's no man in this country—perhaps nowhere—that can touch him!"

"At seven," Greene repeated stubbornly.

Courtney stared at him, shaking his head. "Very well—at seven. But make your peace with God!"

No sooner had Courtney moved away than Charity was at Greene like a terrier. "You can't do it! He'll kill you!"

She argued and reasoned until he finally stated, "A man can't get off the earth because another man says so. That's one thing this war is about!"

"It's not the same thing! And besides, he's Nathan's cousin—doesn't that mean something to you?"

"I can't help that."

Charity argued until she was hoarse, but finally gave in. Looking up at Dan's stubborn face, she murmured resignedly, "All right, Dan—let's go on board."

He was surprised at her subdued manner, but agreed. They went down to the cabin, both lost in their own thoughts. After she left, he sat on the bunk staring at the wall for what seemed like hours.

She came in later with some soup. "I'm not hungry," he told her.

"Eat it and don't argue!" she snapped.

After they had eaten, he said simply, "Charity, I'd like to be alone if thee doesn't mind."

"All right, Dan."

She left without another word, and he lay down on his bunk, his mind in an agony of indecision. He hated the idea of violence, but he had already settled in his mind that he would fight for the honor of his country. Could he do less for his own honor—or for Charity's? *Is it pride?* he asked himself. *Will I be a coward? Can I face up to cold steel?*

Time passed, and his mind grew fuzzy. Once he started to get up to open the window, but to his astonishment he was drowsy. *How can I be sleepy facing death in a few hours?* he thought. As his eyelids grew heavy again, the outlines of the cabin lost their sharpness, and the sounds of the ship grew faint.

He awoke with a start, sitting up so abruptly that his head swam. There was an awful, bitter taste in his mouth, and as he stood up he was so weak he had to grab at the bulkhead to keep from pitching onto the floor. Then, suddenly, the floor tilted and he fell headlong to the deck. As the floor began to move in the other direction, he became sick—sicker than he had ever been in his life—a sickness that made him fearful—not that he would die but that he would live!

He crawled out of the cabin, up steep steps to the deck, where he pulled himself up to the rail and vomited violently.

"Are you all right, Dan?"

He turned and with an effort focused his eyes on Charity, who had come up behind him and was watching with compassion.

"We're—at sea!" he muttered. "How'd I sleep so long?"

"I dosed your soup with laudanum," she answered. "You were bound and determined to be a fool—and there's only one way to treat a fool!"

He grew indignant and started to argue, but the ship nosed down into the green waters, and he groaned and grew sick again.

She watched him carefully, then nodded. "We'll have lots of time to talk about it on the way to Port-au-Prince and before we get back to Boston, Dan."

★   ★   ★   ★

Six weeks later, in the mild March winds, Charity and Dan pulled up in front of Charles Winslow's house. "Are you sure you want to do this, Dan?" Charity asked.

"It's a thing that can't be avoided, Charity," he answered, his voice subdued. As he got out of the buggy and came to help her down, the memories of the voyage they'd just completed flashed across her mind. It had been entirely successful from a military point of view. They had met the French ship, transferred the cargo, and not a single English ship had challenged them on the return voyage. They'd dropped anchor at the rendezvous point—a natural harbor ten miles north of Boston—and wagons had been waiting. Henry Knox had gotten his cannon, and Washington's hungry men would eat well for the first time in many months.

Taking Dan's arm, Charity thought of the long days under the southern sun and the long warm nights on deck. The two of them had spoken little at first, but gradually the barriers had come down, and finally they had fallen under the spell of sail and surf and warm sunny skies.

One night off the coast of Port-au-Prince when the cargo was safely aboard, she had stood looking up into a sky alive with stars, and he had come to stand by her. Both of them were elated that their mission was accomplished—part of it, at least. They had talked excitedly long after the crew was asleep.

And then, they had grown quiet. The sea was laid out like green glass with flashes like gold flakes breaking up the reflection of the yellow moon. The waves were slapping the sides of the ship, and she became acutely aware of him as a man. He turned to her, his face still, but his eyes searching hers.

He had never touched her, and even now he seemed to be unaware that he had put his hands on her shoulders. She looked up, unable to move, and as he slowly let his arms go around her, she had unconsciously lifted her arms and put them around his neck. He pulled her close and kissed her slowly, and she returned his kiss.

Which of them pulled back first neither knew, but he held her just one moment, saying, "Charity Alden—thee is a woman to unsettle a man's mind!"

As they moved up the steps now and he knocked on the Winslows' front door, she still remembered the touch of his lips—and she wondered then, as she had since that night, what he thought of her. Neither of them had spoken of the kiss, but he had not forgotten, she knew.

"Yas'um?"

"We'd like to see Mr. Charles Winslow," Greene said to the slave, whom Charity recognized as Cory.

"Come in, please." The black woman did not speak further, but there was a bitterness in her eyes as she cast a look at Charity. "I'll see if Mistuh Winslow kin see you."

They waited in the spacious foyer, and the black woman came back, saying, "Come wif' me, please."

Charity was reluctant, but there was no way out, so she accompanied Dan to the same room where she had visited with Mrs. Winslow.

Charles Winslow was standing beside one of the tall windows, and he turned slightly to face the pair as they entered. "I'm Charles

Winslow," he said in a voice that barely carried across the room. His illness had marked him radically, making his cheeks hollow and giving his blue eyes an unhealthy bleak look—nonetheless, both Charity and Greene saw the resemblance to Nathan.

"I'm sorry to trouble thee, sir," Dan apologized, at the same time casting a look at the woman who sat glaring at them from a chair by the wall. He went on hurriedly, making no attempt to defend himself, but giving a straightforward version of the quarrel.

"Why have you come here, Mr. Greene?" Winslow inquired.

"I would like to settle the matter in a civilized way, sir." Greene stood straight, his face revealing no weakness as he put the matter into words. "I do not believe in duels, and if an apology will satisfy thy son, I will make it."

"Charles!" Dorcas Winslow started to her feet, her face distorted with rage, and rushed to stand before Dan and Charity, lifting her hand in a gesture of accusation. "How can you let that person into our home?"

She would have said more, her voice on the verge of a scream, but Winslow commanded sharply, "Dorcas, please leave the room!"

With a baleful glance at her husband, she ran out of the room weeping.

"I apologize for my wife, but there is some cause."

"Certainly, Mr. Winslow. These things are always unpleasant," Dan replied quickly. "I might add that thy nephew, Nathan, is my good friend, and thy brother, Major Winslow, is a man of whom I cannot speak too highly. That is why I am willing to apologize— even though there was provocation."

Winslow stared at the honest face of Dan Greene and then he walked to the window and stared out at the trees without a word. Dan and Charity exchanged glances, mystified. After a lengthy silence, Winslow spoke without turning. "I appreciate your generosity, sir—but it is no longer a matter of importance."

"But—Mr. Winslow, we must settle this matter!"

"There is nothing to settle, Mr. Greene." Winslow turned, and grief lined his face. "My son is dead."

The stark words hit like a blow, and when neither visitor spoke, Winslow added, "Three days after your quarrel, Paul went to New York. He disappeared, and no trace of him can be found."

"Mr. Winslow," Charity offered hopefully, "could he have been taken in the press—for the British Navy? I've heard they're impressing whomever they can get."

"That was my first thought," Winslow nodded. "But it was not the press. I have strong connections in England—particularly with the Navy. A post rank investigation was made, and my son was not taken in the press. The only other explanation is that he was murdered for his money and his jewelry."

"I hope not, Mr. Winslow," Greene expressed compassionately.

"There is no other answer." Charles Winslow stared woodenly at the floor and said quietly, "My son was last seen in a notorious brothel on the waterfront—in the worst district. He was drunk—as usual—and the authorities tell me that more than one man has been murdered, stripped, and thrown into the sea there."

"Sir, may I—?"

"I bid you good day." Winslow's face broke and he left the room abruptly, leaving them standing alone.

"We'd better go," Dan suggested. They made their way to the front door and left without another word. Standing beside the buggy, Charity exclaimed, "Such a waste! Such a waste!"

Dan nodded slowly, and said painfully, "He was a Winslow, Charity. I wonder how men of the same blood can be so different?"

There was no answer, and after helping her into the buggy and taking the reins, he drove slowly away from the magnificent home of the Winslows of Boston.

CHAPTER SEVEN

THE *NEPTUNE*

★ ★ ★ ★

His Majesty's ship *Neptune*, with thirty-two guns, slipped bow-first into the green trough between two steep waves, seeming to burrow into the cold brine like a huge mole tunneling into loam. Clarence Langley, first lieutenant, had not regained his sea legs. He was thrown forward and would have sprawled on the deck if Angus Burns, the second lieutenant, had not grabbed his arm and hauled him upright.

Langley cursed under his breath, and was rebuked instantly by the other. "Better give thanks to God ye didn't fall, Langley. If He hadna put me here, ye'd have made a pretty sight fallin' like a landlubber in full view o' the crew." Burns was a small man, slight in build and not over five six. He spoke with the thick burr of Scotland, and he would have been attractive except that a bout of scurvy off the African coast had cost him many of his teeth. He was religious to the bone, holding to the iron-forged, hyper-Calvinistic creed of his fathers, convinced that God's hand was in everything, that all of them were playing out roles that Jehovah had long ago written out in fine detail.

Langley opened his mouth to argue angrily, but casting a quick look at Burns's dour face, laughed and gave it up. "I'd as soon argue with the sun, as you, Angus." He clapped a hand on the smaller man's shoulder, and there was affection in his eyes as he added, "Well, I'm glad that God put you here to keep me from making a clumsy oaf of myself before the crew. This is the only decent uniform I've got—nothing fit to wear to the captain's table. I look like a scarecrow!"

Burns grunted, taking in the tall form of the first lieutenant, noting the neat brown hair and regular features. The Scotsman placed no value on outer appearance, and it was Langley's seamanship and honesty that drew him rather than his dashing appearance. He shrugged, glanced down at his own worn dress uniform, not caring one pin if the captain would be impressed with it or not, but he realized that Langley's mind was on the ladies who would dine with them. He said, "I see nae sense in hauling females on this ship. It's nae guid practice."

"Haven't you heard why they're on board, Angus? Scuttlebutt is that the daughter got into a torrid romance in New York with some rotter, and Captain Rommey hauled her aboard to break the thing off."

"It'll come to nae guid," Burns warned.

Langley stopped and spoke to a thick-chested sailor who was passing. "You've got all the new men out, Whitefield?"

"Yes, sir—'cept him I told you 'bout." Enoch Whitefield was a slight man of thirty. He was the best gunner in the fleet, some said, and was so effective with new hands that Langley often ordered him to take charge of them until they got their heads straight.

"What's wrong with him? Can't be drunk this long!"

"No, sir. He mighta been drunk, but he got some kind of bad bust in the head. Left side's all swelled up. My guess is he tried to fight it out with the press gang and they laid into 'im with a club. Thing is, he got hit right on top of a right fresh cut—a bad one all stitched up."

"One of the pressed men?" Burns asked.

Whitefield nodded his head.

Burns grunted dourly, "I've nae confidence in any o' that breed!"

Langley hesitated, then stated, "I'll have the doctor take a look at him, Whitefield."

"Yes, sir," Whitefield returned, saying no more, but both officers caught the sudden flash of mistrust that flickered in the gunner's eyes. None of the crew wanted anything to do with the ship's surgeon; for that matter, neither did either of the officers, but it would not do to let a seaman hear them say so.

"We'd best hurry, Lieutenant Langley," Burns urged. "Captain Rommey's nae a man to keep waitin'."

"Certainly!" As the two men hurried along toward the stern, both of them were searching the ship surreptitiously. The *Neptune* had been refitted in Southampton, brought to America by a skeleton crew—only the officers and a few experienced hands on board. The blockade that stretched along the eastern coast was thin—not nearly tight enough to pin the rebellious Colonists inside, and King George chose to ignore the fact that England had other commitments for the Royal Navy. The Naval Office was sending out anything that would float, and the abysmal conditions which the average seaman lived under in the fighting ships of England enticed few men to join the navy. The long, drawn-out wars had bled the service white, and both officers knew, as they carefully noted the hands, that it would not be an easy task to whip the crew into fighting trim.

The ship itself, the *Neptune*, was much more impressive than her crew. One hundred and thirty feet long on her gun deck, and built of good English oak, she was the picture of a shipbuilder's art. She had cost nearly fourteen thousand pounds, and being a frigate, was well worth it. Frigates were meant for speed and hit-and-run fighting. They were fast enough to catch any fighting ship, and the *Neptune's* thirty-two guns gave her power enough to take on any vessel except a ship of the line.

The two lieutenants moved swiftly toward the poop deck, descending the steep steps quickly to the great cabin. Langley knocked firmly on the oak door. "Come in!" the captain's voice sounded. Langley opened the door and stepped inside, closely followed by Burns.

Captain William Rommey was standing by the stern windows, his feet firmly planted against the ship's motion. He was a bulky man in his early fifties, square of face and blunt of feature. His mouth was very wide, but thin and pressed together in a habitual expression of suppressed anger. There was a pugnacious air about him, his heavy chin thrusting forward, his body constantly shifting as if seeking to move against a foe, the restless pale blue eyes now falling on the two officers, searching them as for some unconfessed fault.

"Sit down, gentlemen," he rasped, motioning with his hand. "I was about to send a search party for you." He ignored their apology and moved to the table. "The food is probably cold," he complained.

The great cabin was the most ornate area of the *Neptune*. The large stern windows rose almost to the ceiling, allowing the reddish gleams of the sinking sun to filter through, tinting everything with a warm rosy glow. The bench seat around the stern was covered with rich green leather; Rommey's desk, made out of finely carved mahogany, stood against the starboard bulkhead; and a French-made post bed occupied the space on the port side. Beside the bed was a large walnut bookcase filled to overflowing with expensive leather-bound books; the captain was a great reader. The large table had been extended in order to accommodate the party, and except for the two sixteen-pound guns extending from their ports into the cabin, it looked very much like a fine room in a mansion on shore.

It was typical of the two men as they seated themselves at the table that Langley began to talk while Burns sat silently, examining the faces of the others. He gave only a glance to Dr. Erich Mann, a burly German of fifty with a bald head, a round face, and small piggish eyes; there was nothing there to interest Burns. He noted, not for the first time, the butcher's hands that were unsteady now—the result of too much wine. Sooner or later, Burns knew, Mann would inform them all that it was his last voyage, that he would leave the ship and take up a private practice so that he could live like a gentleman. But the private practice, they all realized, would never be, for he was an incompetent, drunken boor, and only men who were helpless—such as seamen in the navy—would let him treat them.

Robert Baxter, the debonair captain of marines, was a different story. He was highly intelligent, shoulders always squared, and his uniforms molded around his limbs like wax. He spoke in short, clipped sentences. His marines were his whole life, although he hardly ever seemed to utter much in the way of orders. His massive sergeant, Potter, took care of the close contact with the men.

Burns had little respect for Captain Baxter, for the marine was an atheist, and the Scot thought that any man who held such a view was mentally defective. He gave a quick glance at the three midshipmen, a hulking, bully-faced seventeen-year-old named Rackam, a sharp-featured individual named Symmes, and one small, undersized lad named Arthur Pink. Pink was going to be a problem, Burns realized, for he was not only sickly but totally unfit for life at sea. His relatives no doubt had shuffled him off to the navy to get rid of him.

That left the two women—and the captain's wife, though highly decorative, was not a matter for much speculation. She was an attractive woman of about fifty, with a gorgeous head of auburn hair, a pair of beautiful eyes—bright but unintelligent—and a languid manner that never seemed to change. She had the incredible ability to sew for eight hours at a stretch (Angus had discovered on the voyage from England), and he wondered at the vacuity of mind that could concentrate on the trivial for such periods. She had long ago lost any force of influence (if she ever had any) with her husband and her daughter. To Burns, she seemed like an attractive life-sized doll.

If Captain Rommey's wife was insipid, his daughter lived as a sharp contrast—for Blanche Rommey was a heady article, indeed! Even the dour Burns could not keep from being somewhat overwhelmed by the girl, and he let his eyes rest on her as she carried on a spirited conversation with Langley over a play they had seen in London.

Tall, with a beautiful figure, Blanche Rommey was one of the most *alive* human beings Burns had ever seen. Her face was not pretty, but it was highly mobile, and her eyes moved constantly— huge eyes, almond-shaped, and blue as the sea off the coast appears at times. Her mouth was well shaped, but too wide and full for real beauty, and her high cheekbones were just a shade too high for the perfect proportion. She was, Burns realized, *overdone* somehow, in a way that was compelling and made mere beauty of no moment.

Even though the slight second lieutenant had very limited experiences with women, he discerned immediately something predatory about the girl. She was conscious of men, interested in them, and had no doubt for a long time drawn many with her almost overwhelming feminine presence. Langley was flattered by her attention, but Burns knew instinctively that Blanche Rommey was not really interested in the lieutenant. It was simply impossible for her to do other than to fix her attention on the most available man in her sphere, as she was doing now—but if a more interesting or challenging one walked through the door, poor Langley would be dropped at once like a toy no longer desirable.

"Better enjoy this fresh meat," Rommey offered as the steward placed platters of fresh beef and a saddle of ham on the table. "After it's gone we may be eating salt pork until we get sick of it."

Baxter looked up and asked languidly, "We'll not be in touch with the mainland, then?" He cut a geometrically perfect square of beef, examined it, then greedily stuck it into his mouth. "I rather expected we'd be a part of the American blockade."

"We'll be doing a little more than that," Rommey grunted, then looked up with a smile on his thin lips, adding, "Better get your gun crews trained as quickly as possible."

"I thought we were at peace with the world—except for these rebels," Blanche commented. "Whom do you intend to fight?"

Rommey grinned at her and then shot a quick look at his officers. There was a rebuke in his manner as he growled, "I rather expected my first officer would ask that question."

"I didn't want to be impertinent, sir," Langley said quickly, his face reddening at the reprimand.

"I don't expect my officers to stand on ceremony when there's a matter of tactics involved, Mr. Langley." This remark made the face of the first lieutenant grow even more rosy, for he knew—as did Burns—that Captain Rommey was not at all satisfied that his second in command had the aggressive character required of the first lieutenant of a fighting ship. Burns had some of the same apprehension, for he had noted, even in the short time they had served together, that Langley tended to lean more on the judgment of others and was reluctant to drive the crew. It was only a sign, but in the midst of battle when the heavens were falling, one wanted to know that the first lieutenant was capable of instant and sometimes even reckless decisions.

Burns spoke up hurriedly in an attempt to give Langley time to regain his composure. "If it's action right away, sir, we'd be hard put to hold our own. The gun crews are raw, as ye weel know."

"Of course, Lieutenant Burns. We have some time to shake them down, make seamen out of them. I doubt if we'll go into action tomorrow, but sooner or later we'll have to whip the Frenchies again."

"I thought that was taken care of in the war, Father," Blanche queried. She referred to the Seven Years War, which had ended in 1763. "I thought Admiral Hawke sank the entire French fleet."

"Would God he had!" Rommey said. He took a huge bite of beef, chewed it thoughtfully, and then began to give a lecture— which was his way. "Hawke did defeat the French. I commanded the *Dominant* in that action, you remember? By Harry, we put them to rout!" He slammed the table and his eyes glowed with the memory, but then he grimaced and added, "We had our chance, and we made the Frenchies renounce to England all Canada and the Ohio Valley, and we routed the Dons out of business in the War of Spanish Succession."

"Well, who's left to fight, then?" Blanche asked impudently. She smiled across the table, her blue eyes catching the lights of the candles, giving her a feline look. "You can't mean to fight the red Indians, can you?"

Langley spoke up, attempting to regain some ground with his captain. "I suppose you think we'll have to fight the French again, sir?"

"Blast it! Of *course* we'll have to put them down again!" Rommey's craggy face grew grim, and he almost tipped the wine glasses as he threw his hands up in disgust. "Our intelligence tells us that the French have eighty first-class ships of the line, and Spain has sixty more. England has only a hundred fifty, and they're scattered all over the world from Calcutta to Jamaica, not to mention our fleet in the blockade."

Burns added quietly, "And the Frenchies have been longin' fer revenge after the trouncin' they got in '63."

"Right you are, sir—and this insurrection is just the opportunity they've been looking for." Rommey gritted his teeth. "It may not come for a time—but sooner or later we'll be forced to take the French on again. When that time comes, I want the *Neptune* to be the best fighting ship carrying the British flag—the *best!*"

"Ach! It will not be easy, my Captain." Dr. Mann belched and took a tremendous draught of wine, then wiped his mouth with his napkin and nodded. "Make a silk purse out of a sow's ear, you cannot—and these pressed men will not make a crew. The press gang must have scraped bottom—the scourings of the earth! Half of them have the pox, all of them are drunks, and there's not a drop of honorable blood in the lot!"

Baxter nodded slightly. "Not far wrong. Can't expect to make a well-trained fighting crew out of that material." Baxter could afford to be critical, for his marines were all volunteers, but the remark displeased Rommey.

"Captain Baxter, the Royal Navy has utilized the press for more years than you have lived—and we shall continue in the tradition!" He shot a command at the surgeon, "Dr. Mann, it is your responsibility to get these men fit for duty!"

"But, sir—!"

Ignoring him, Rommey directed his remarks to his officers, smoldering impatience in his snapping eyes. "You are officers in His Majesty's Royal Navy, and you will take these men—no matter what methods you must use—and make fighting men out of them.

I will accept no excuses from them—or from you!"

The lieutenants knew enough not to argue, but Dr. Mann had taken on too much port, and was rash enough to say, "But, my Captain, I cannot work miracles! There is one of the pressed men who was hauled aboard unconscious—is still not awake. His face is scarred from a drunken brawl, I'd guess, and he's got a concussion. What can I do with him?"

Rommey paused, letting a silence build up. Finally he stood to his feet, his bulk blotting out the light from the stern windows, and addressed the men in a cold, hard voice. "I will make myself plain this one time. We have on this ship a certain number of shot for our guns. We have so many pounds of powder. We have water and food in casks. And we have a certain number of seamen. All of these are expendable." His eyes were fixed on Langley, and he added, "Use up the powder, the shot, the food, the water—and use up the men, Lieutenant Langley. Do you understand?"

Langley swallowed, his face losing its color, then nodded slightly and answered in a low voice, "Yes, sir, I understand."

The deadly seriousness of Rommey fell heavily on the guests, and the meal was finished with little talk. Excusing themselves as soon as it was polite, the two lieutenants left, both drawing sighs of relief as they came up on deck.

Burns took a deep breath of cold air. "Weel, Clarence, I feel like a schoolboy who's had his bottom whacked by a stern schoolmaster."

"Too right, Angus!" Langley swore and slapped the rail, shaking his head apprehensively. "It's not going to be a tea party."

"Captain Rommey's a hard man, but he's fair enough—which is more than ye can say aboot others I could name."

"We'll lose some of the men if we drive them too hard."

"It's God's will." Angus put his hand on the taller man's arm, something he'd never done before, and smiled. "We're all in God's hands, Langley—the crew, me, you. Even Captain William Rommey is just as much under God's rod as that poor lad below who may never wake up. Think o' it like that."

Langley felt a lift of his spirit. "I'm glad you're aboard, Angus. Can't say I agree with your gloomy theology—but you're a comfort." Then the two went below and dreamed their private dreams as the ship was driven by a sharp wind toward a warmer world.

★　★　★　★

The clear morning brought a promise of the warmth that lay to the south, and the wind held firm. Captain Rommey stood motionless on the forecastle watching his officers and men work the ship.

Each mast had its own division of seamen, from the swift-footed topmen to the older, less agile hands that worked the braces and halyards from the deck. As the calls shrilled and the men poured up on deck through every hatch and companion, it seemed incredible that *Neptune*'s hull could contain so many. The deck swarmed with figures of seamen and marines formed into compact groups, each being checked by leather-lunged petty officers against their various lists and watch-bills.

Like the mass of seamen and marines, the officers, too, were at their stations. Langley stood beside the captain on the forecastle, the foremast his responsibility. Burns commanded the upper gun deck and the ship's mainmast, which was her real strength, with all the spars, cordage, canvas and miles of rigging that gave life to the hull beneath. Lattrimer, the third lieutenant, kept close watch on the crew managing the mizzenmast.

"Hands aloft! Loose tops'ls!" Langley cried with all his might through a trumpet. "Loose the heads'ls!"

Released to the wind, the canvas erupted and flapped in wild confusion; while spread along the swaying yards like monkeys, the topmen fought for the right moment to bring it under control.

Burns called, "Man your braces. Bosun, take that man's name!"

"Aye, sir!"

Take that man's name. It was a cry often repeated, for the old hands were few and the new men were many. The bosun ran around the deck like a madman constantly, using his starter, a thick rope with a knot on one end. It fell on the backs of the pressed men most often—for they were totally confused by the mass of ropes and the billowing sails above.

Burns felt a pity for them that the captain did not, for the lieutenant's sensitive spirit could empathize with the utter bewilderment they had been thrown into.

"Will they ever learn, Lieutenant?"

Burns turned to find Blanche Rommey standing behind him. She was dressed in a fine dress of blue satin that brought out the color of her eyes and clearly outlined her figure as the whipping wind pressed the thin cloth against her body. She was watching with interest as the bosun drew a cry from a thin lad on whom he was slashing viciously with his starter. There was, Burns saw, no real compassion in the girl's face. She was no doubt accustomed to the hard life of seamen, but it was the first actual sight she'd had of it.

"Aye, in time, most o' them will, Miss Rommey."

She came to stand beside him, and at her request, he explained the basic structure of the sails and spars. She was listening intently when a movement to her left caused her to turn. "What's the matter with that man?" she asked.

Burns followed her gaze and saw Enoch Whitefield and another seaman placing the limp form of a man on an unoccupied section of the deck. "That's one of the pressed men—the one Dr. Mann spoke of last night." He checked the progress of the men, then added, "I believe I'll see how he is, if you'll excuse me."

She ignored his implied order to remain at the rail and followed him as he went to where Whitefield was bracing the man against the rail in a sitting position.

"Has he come around yet, Whitefield?"

"No, sir."

"What a frightful scar!" The captain's daughter had moved to stand over the unconscious man, and was staring down at him with interest. "Except for that, he'd be very nice looking."

Burns glanced at the man and saw that she spoke the truth. The man was naked from the waist up, wearing only a pair of patched canvas breeches. He was not over five ten, but the muscles of his arms and chest were hard and well defined. His dark hair, dirty and uncombed, would lie neatly, Burns could tell, if it were clean. Clean-cut features were marred by a livid, half-healed scar that ran from his lower jaw to disappear into his hair. The wound had been stitched and was puckered, drawing the left side of his mouth up slightly and pulling his left eye into a squint.

"He ain't no weaklin', sir," Whitefield voiced thoughtfully, looking at the dark face. "Look at them forearms! I ain't never seen such. He's got smallish hands, but mighty strong, I'd venture!"

"Will he die?" the girl asked, staring down at the man.

"Mebby so, miss." Whitefield was a simple man, and added only, "It's in the great God's hands now."

"Blanche—" She turned to see her father who had approached and was staring at her, displeasure in his eyes. "It would be best if you did not come in contact with the deckhands."

A stubborn light leaped into the girl's eyes, and she retorted instantly, "Father, you have put me on this ship against my will. Now you are telling me that I must not speak with those in the world you've consigned me to."

"These men are not your sort. They're dangerous."

She laughed and glanced down at the unconscious man. "I very much doubt if he's any great danger to me."

His daughter was, Captain Rommey saw clearly, ready to make a scene right there on the deck. He'd had several with her in the process of separating her from a dissolute French nobleman, and desired no more—especially not in front of his crew. Rommey was not a man to deceive himself, and he realized that while he could command a ship of the line with eight hundred souls aboard, he was totally unequipped to handle this fiery daughter of his.

"Lieutenant Burns, my daughter is your responsibility. See that she is watched at all times." He felt like a coward as he whirled and left the deck.

"Miss Rommey, your father's point is weel taken." Burns bit his lip and gestured at the man at his feet. "This one seems harmless enough right now—but if he was to come to himself, I wouldna trust ye alone with him for one second."

Blanche Rommey was a strong-willed young woman, and the rebellious fury that had burned in her since her father had snatched her almost bodily from her affair with Jean D'amont still rankled. She looked down at the still figure at her feet, then deliberately took her delicate silk handkerchief and wiped the grime from his face.

"I wouldna do that if I were ye, miss," Burns warned nervously.

She looked up at him with a challenging smile in her eyes, saying sharply, "But you're not me, Lieutenant Burns!" She brushed the dark hair back from the unconscious man's wide forehead and then murmured so quietly that Burns barely heard her words: "And nobody else is me!"

She'll nurse the fellow to spite her father, Burns thought, and he caught a brief smile on Whitefield's lips, and quickly turned away, happy to deal with spars and sails instead of a beautiful, rebellious captain's daughter who had no place on board the *Neptune* in the first place.

CHAPTER EIGHT

ABLE SEAMAN HAWKE

★ ★ ★ ★

"You don't give a hang about the man!"

Captain Rommey had attempted for two days to ignore what every man on the *Neptune* was fully aware of—that his daughter had disrupted the entire ship. There are no secrets on a frigate. A ship of war manned for active service is the most crowded place in the world—more crowded than the most run-down tenement in London's Cheapside. Every square foot of the vessel was spoken for, planned for, and even now as Rommey stood on the deck, he had to lower his voice to keep from being overheard as he spoke to Blanche, who sat beside the still figure of the injured man.

Forward there were groups of men yarning, men skylarking; there were solitary men who had each preempted a square yard of deck for himself and sat, cross-legged, with tools and materials, doing embroidery or whittling at models, oblivious to the tumult about them. Similarly aft on the crowded quarterdeck the groups of officers strolled and chatted, avoiding the other groups without conscious effort.

Blanche had had the injured seaman brought up out of the stuffy crew's quarters below, as she had done on the previous two days. The wind had grown balmier, and Whitefield had rigged a hammock on the port deck aft of the mizzenmast; there he had gotten well acquainted with his captain's willful daughter as they had sat beside the man. He admired her spirit, but realized clearly that the same impetuous impulse that had been the means of caring for the helpless man would be just as likely to lead her into less noble causes.

The two of them had been idly talking when Captain Rommey appeared unexpectedly, and Whitefield, wily enough to see a storm cloud in the face of Blanche's father, hastily slipped away. Rommey, towering over the girl, said with obvious displeasure, "You don't give a hang about this man!"

"Neither do you, Father," Blanche retorted sharply. She threw her head back, her eyes flashing. His daughter took a perverse delight, he saw, in taking him on in the matter, and added defiantly, "Perhaps you're right. He's just a common sailor. But you pulled me out of the only life I cared for—now I have to do something to entertain myself."

He bit his lip, pondering how to answer her. Finally giving up, his mouth drawn in displeasure, he said sternly, "The whole ship is rumbling about this thing. It's not good for discipline!" He waited for her to answer, but saw that she intended no such thing. Her rebellious disrespect flooded him with anger, for he was a man who could brook no opposition. Now he could only add, "You're doing this to spite me, Blanche. Or maybe you're playing dolls again."

His words stung her, and she stood up to face him, her features hard and her voice brittle. "What does *that* mean?"

"It means that you've always liked to play god with people. Even when you were a child, you had to rule the other children you played with. And as an older child, you learned you were smarter than most girls, and better looking, so you did as you pleased. Later when you became a woman, you played with men— just as you'd played with your dolls—pulling them to pieces when you got bored with them."

"Oh, Father, that's *wonderful* coming from *you!*" He knew her, and his words had cut deep—so deep that her face for all its rich color was a trifle pale. "You've done nothing all your life but rule people—and now you're saying that I'm the one who's spoiled!"

He looked around uneasily, for her voice had risen, and he realized that she did not care a pin if every seaman on deck heard her—but *he* cared, for he was jealous of his dignity and knew well that a captain must be aloof from his men. He shook his head and turned, saying only, "I'll be glad to get you to the Indies!"

She glared at his broad back as he wheeled and marched away toward the forecastle deck; then as quickly as it had arisen, her anger faded and she laughed aloud at herself. It was typical of the girl to shrug off anger so easily, for her emotions were quick rather than deep. Her father, she realized wryly, was right, and it was part of her charm that she was able to see a weakness in herself as readily as she could in another.

Curiously, she moved beside the gently swaying hammock, and with a gesture made easy by the practice of the last two days, lifted the battered head of the sailor and spooned some thin soup between his lips. She held his head, not missing the finely structured bones, the broad forehead, the high-bridged English nose, the small, neat ears, and the wide mouth, firmly molded and somehow a little stubborn even when relaxed. She paused before giving him more soup, and thought, *I wonder if I'd be doing this if he weren't so good-looking?* She smiled disdainfully and admitted, *Of course not! If he were homely, I'd never come near him.*

Blanche Rommey was a fickle, changeable, spoiled girl—but she had the rare gift of being honest with herself, and she knew that her father had been entirely correct in his evaluation of her motives—that she was doing it just to spite him and to play god.

She was furious with him for interfering with her life and bored to tears with the ship. She was not a girl given to books; her very being was the essence of action, and tending the sick man was just one handy way of burning up the energy that seethed inside her—and had the additional benefit of irritating her father!

Forward on the deck, as he emerged from the hold, Whitefield had been stopped by Oscar Grimes, the cooper. Grimes was shaped like a spider with a huge torso supported on thin legs, and his abnormally long arms, thin and sinewy, completed the illusion. His head was small, covered with a thatch of stiff black hair, and he had a pair of small, beady eyes, black as tar. Most of the crew were rough in their ways, but Grimes had the kind of evil in him that fascinated normal men. Repulsive as he was, in person as well as in mind, he drew a segment of the crew by the very power of his warped spirit.

"Wait up there, Whitefield," he called in an oily voice, and with a simian gesture reached out and caught the gunner by the arm. "Wot's this agoin' on?" he queried, nodding his head toward the spot where Blanche was tending her patient. Leering slyly, he added, "If that gel is that hot to 'ave a man—why, I reckon I can accommodate 'er!"

Whitefield was a small man and seemed dwarfed by Grimes's

powerful bulk, but there was something in his light blue eyes that made the cooper hurriedly remove his hand. "You just fly right at it, Grimes," he said menacingly. "Touch one hair on that woman's head, and you'll be hangin' from the yard arm by sundown—and feedin' the fish by dark."

His words angered Grimes, and the cooper's neck swelled; however, he well knew that Whitefield spoke no more than simple truth. In spite of that, he raised his voice as the gunner walked away, "All right, holy man—but I've got me ways! Oh, I've got me ways!"

Whitefield walked up to the hammock, looked down at the still face, and asked, "Any change, miss?"

"No, Whitefield."

"Aye—well, if you'd like to rest a bit, I'm off for four hours."

"Nothing to do on this awful ship!"

"Not much, miss—not for a lady like yourself." As he spoke his eyes caught sight of a large bird gracefully flying back toward the coast on powerful wings.

"What sort of bird is that?" she asked, following his gaze.

"Frigate bird, miss."

"Looks like an eagle. What do they eat?"

"Oh, pretty much what all sea birds eat—but they *are* different. They don't bother with doing much fishin' themselves, you see."

She looked at him with a puzzled light in her eyes before turning back to the bird. "How do they get their food?"

"Take it away from them what does work for it," Whitefield answered. "Like—a pelican will dive and get himself a nice fish; afterward he'll likely rise up and head off with it. But Mr. Frigate Bird, why, he's been asailin' round up there just waitin' like—and finally he says, 'Why, there's my supper, right in Mr. Pelican's beak!' So down he dives—and it's a fair sight, Miss Rommey, to see a frigate in a dive! So he hits Mr. Pelican and knocks 'im loose from the fish—and there's his supper!"

Blanche stared intently at the disappearing bird. "That," she said with a quick grin at Whitefield, "is the kind of bird I'd want to be if I had to be a bird."

He chuckled and nodded, pulling at a lock of his hair. "I thought you was a bit in that way—if you'll pardon me for sayin' so, miss." He waved his arm around and added, "That's why they call this kind of ship a *frigate*, you see? Light, fast, strong, and got enough guns to throw plenty of iron. She sees a ship filled up with good things, hits like a lightning bolt, and *bam*! She's got the goods and the poor old merchant ship ain't got no more than the pelican!"

She laughed, and although Whitefield would never have felt comfortable speaking freely with the captain, this girl had a natural quality that won his confidence. She was curious about everything, and for over an hour he kept her entertained with yarns of the sea. Her eyes glowed as he related some of the stories of sea fights between the great ships of the line, her desire for action and activity drawn to the excitement of that part of life.

Eventually she grew sleepy, and put her head back against the wooden bulkhead. He sat there quietly, finally pulled a small book out of his pocket and began reading. He looked up with a start when she said, "You read the Bible a lot, don't you, Whitefield?"

"Why, yes, miss. It's 'bout all the books I do read, you might say."

"Are you any relation to the Methodist preacher—what's his name?"

"That'd be my cousin George, miss."

"Of course." Blanche acknowledged, looking curiously at the sailor before responding. "Your kinsman, he's set the whole world buzzing! He's the talk of the court, you know. I was at a ball given by the Countess of Huntington, and *everyone* was there. The actor, David Garrick? Well, he said that he'd give anything to have a voice like Rev. Whitefield." She laughed and added, "I remember he said that Whitefield could make a congregation weep by pronouncing the word *Mesopotamia*!"

"I reckon the gentleman ain't far wrong, miss. George is a powerful man of the Word."

"Tell me about him."

Whitefield was reluctant, thinking that this wealthy girl would scoff at his simple beliefs, but she did not. She was, on the contrary, as fascinated by the phenomena of the enormous successes of the outdoor preaching of Whitefield and the Wesleys as she had been with the habits of the frigate bird.

Finally, she remarked, "Some people really dislike him, White-field—especially the clergy, I understand. Why is that?"

"Well, that's because he insists that people have to be born again."

"Born again?"

"Yes, miss." He opened his Bible and read her the opening lines of the third chapter of John, concluding with the words, 'Ye must be born again.' " He looked at her earnestly, saying, "You see, Miss Rommey, most people in the Established church of England thinks that if a man behaves himself, don't do no big sin, is good to his family and attends services—why, he's all right in the sight of the Lord."

"Well—isn't he?" Blanche asked instantly.

"Not according to what the Lord Jesus said," Whitefield shrugged. He explained in his rough way what it meant to have a change on the *inside*, but he saw at once that the girl had no concept of the matter.

She was just beginning to argue when a slight noise caused her to look at the man in the hammock, and she leaped to her feet, crying out, "Whitefield! Look, he's waking up!"

"Glory to God!" Whitefield exclaimed, breaking into a broad smile. "So he is!"

They stood there staring down, watching in anticipation as the eyelids seemed to flutter, then slowly opened, revealing a pair of murky eyes. They closed almost at once, but Whitefield moved to shade them. "Come, lad—open your eyes now." And once again the eyes opened. At first there was no expression in them, but as the two waited with bated breath, the gaze shifted, focusing on something to the left, later coming back to stare up at the face of Whitefield, who was leaning over the side of the hammock.

They were strange eyes, Whitefield decided. There was a bright intelligence behind them, giving them life, but there was something else—something the gunner could not identify. *Poor lad is terrible confused*, he thought, and he said in a mild, soothing voice, "Don't be too quick now, lad. Just lie easy till you gets your bearings."

Blanche moved closer, and immediately the eyes turned, taking her in. But there was no response on seeing her. He lay there considering her face, then looked back to Whitefield. They both waited for him to speak, but he seemed either unable or unwilling to open his lips.

"Are you all right?" Blanche asked. Once again his eyes shifted to look up at her, but as before there was no sign of recognition and no attempt to speak.

The wind was whistling through the shrouds, and the noise of the men's voices was like a hum of distant bees. Both Whitefield and Blanche unconsciously leaned forward to hear what the man would say—but he remained mute. Finally Blanche gave the sailor a puzzled look, somewhat fearful, and whispered, "Whitefield—something's *wrong!*"

He did not answer at once, but considered the eyes focusing on him. "Well, Miss Rommey, he's come a long way. You have to remember, this is all new to the lad. He was on shore, maybe in a cold, dark place, and now he wakes up in this warm sun on a ship. Let's not rush the poor chap."

"Water . . . !" They both jumped at the sound of the man's hoarse voice, rusty with disuse, but Blanche whirled and poured a cup of fresh water from the jug beside the hammock. She lifted his head and held it while he drank thirstily. When he stopped, she let his head fall back, holding it gently. "Do you feel better?" she asked.

He looked at her, slowly nodded, closed his eyes again and relaxed so completely that it frightened her. "Whitefield—he's dead!"

"Not a bit of it, miss," the sailor assured her. "Just went to sleep right sudden-like. Ain't uncommon in such cases. Men that's been wounded bad, they fall off like that—especially at first. But he'll wake up soon, and it's hungry he'll be."

"He looked at us so strangely," she murmured, looking down at the still face. "Do you think he'll be all right?"

"Oh, I should think so," Whitefield responded. "I been afraid he'd go out without waking up at all."

"You mean—die?"

"Yes, miss."

The thought troubled her, and she shivered slightly. "I've never seen anyone die. It would frighten me, I think."

"Takes most of us that way," he shrugged. "I'll be glad to talk to the lad—see if he's ready to meet the good Lord."

She stared at him, offering hurriedly, "We'll take turns watching him, Whitefield. I'll nap a little so when you go on duty I can sit with him."

"Yes, miss."

For the next forty-eight hours neither Blanche nor Whitefield slept a great deal. There was something a little frightening about the way the sick man would wake up, stare at them with a directness that was disconcerting, and after a time fall back into sleep as fast as a rock falling to the ground. It was as if he came from death, stared at them briefly, then descended back into a nameless cavern of unknowing. Always they tried to talk to him, but never did either one break through; the eyes would watch for a span, and, as though pulled by an invisible force, soon return to that dark place.

It was on the twenty-fourth, a Sunday morning, when he spoke for the second time. Most of the men slept late or came up on deck for their usual recreation or personal work, but Whitefield and half a dozen other hands held a service on the afterdeck. The sick man had been brought up and placed in the hammock. During the singing, which lasted for about ten minutes, Blanche had listened and watched everything with great interest, for she had never met anyone like the gunner. He was a simple man, truly religious—with the variety of religion called *enthusiastic*—that is, emotional to an abnormal degree. To be labeled an "enthusiast" was pretty much the same as being called a madman or a fanatic. With the exception of a handful of nobility, such as the Countess of Huntington, most Methodists and other varieties of "enthusiasts" came from the poorer class.

There was, however, something genuine about Whitefield, and as little inclined as Blanche herself was to becoming religious, she had a sharp ear for the counterfeit. She was convinced that if Whitefield was a fanatic, he was as gentle and honest a man as she had rarely met. So it was that she listened carefully as he spoke after the song service was finished.

But before the simple "sermon" had gotten well under way, she was startled when the words "Where is this?" came to her. She whirled around and saw immediately that this time something was different. The somber eyes were fixed on her, but now they held an awareness that was unmistakable. As if to prove that he was himself, he said slowly, "I don't—know this place."

She responded quickly, placing a hand on his head in an act of reassurance. "Don't be frightened—you're going to be all right."

The commotion had halted the service as everyone watched intently.

For a moment the man looked out at the fleecy clouds drifting across the azure sky, then brought his gaze back to her and asked again in a voice that was clear and distinct, "Where is this—place?"

"You're on the King's ship—*Neptune*. My father is the captain—Captain William Rommey."

He stared at her perplexed, trying to comprehend. As if thinking action would help, he tried to get up. She helped him into a sitting position, and as she did so, the swinging of the hammock confused him. He grabbed wildly at her, flinging his arms around her neck, and only by grabbing him around his waist did she manage to keep the man from crashing to the deck. "Be careful!" she panted, struggling with his weight. "You've been hurt. Here, lean against this wall."

He clung to her as she swung him around, setting him carefully against the bulkhead. Leaning back he took a deep breath, looked around, and murmured, "I—feel very queer."

"You've been very ill—don't try to do too much."

She was holding on to his hands, noting his strength even in his weakened condition. The white shirt that Whitefield had loaned him was thin as silk as a result of many washings, and she was very much aware that his torso was taut, swelling with a set of rippling muscles—not massive, but like a cat, lithe and elastic.

By now the man leaning against the outer bulkhead was surrounded by the other men. Whitefield asked Blanche, "Is he well?"

"I think so."

Whitefield stepped in front of the man, peered sharply into his eyes, and said exuberantly, "Well, bless God, you're out of it, are you? I'm glad to see you up and well."

The man stared at him, saying simply, "Thank you—but I'm not very clear on—"

"Don't be havin' to know everything," the gunner responded. "First thing is to get some real food down your gullet!" He helped the man down the stairs, and closely followed by Blanche, led the way to the kitchen where the cook, a fat Dutchman named Hans Boerner, used two of the few eggs left, and some of the bacon and fresh bread to make a meal. The man devoured it wolfishly, washing the food down with a cup of coffee.

"That was . . . good." There was a very slight hesitation in his speech, noticeable to both his listeners, as if he were learning a new language. He reached up and touched the side of his head, now only slightly swollen. "That hurts," he remarked quietly, a puzzled look on his face.

"It was a pretty hard lick you got, I'd venture," Whitefield replied. "Now, I expect you maybe have some questions—but first, what's your name, lad?"

"My name?"

"Sure. We have to know how to call you," Whitefield smiled. "My name is Whitefield—and this is Miss Blanche Rommey—our captain's daughter. Now, what's your name, lad?"

He stared at them, and his brow wrinkled with a sudden strain.

He bit his full lower lip, confused. Finally he shook his head slowly, saying in a voice that was thready with panic, "I—I can't seem to remember."

Blanche and Whitefield looked at each other questioningly. "Well," she assured him, "you've been badly hurt. Don't be afraid. It'll come in a little while. But maybe you remember where you came from. Where in America?"

"I don't—seem to know that, either," he answered, the hesitation in his voice now much more noticeable. He rose suddenly, grabbed at his temples, and tried to take a couple steps, but Whitefield caught him.

"Now, don't fret! It'll all come back."

"I don't . . . know much . . . about anything," he whispered. There was fear and confusion in his eyes, and he implored them, "Tell me . . . how did I . . . get here?"

The next half hour was unpleasant for all of them. The man was on the verge of panic, and Blanche and Whitefield had all they could do to keep him calm. It was fortunate that he tired quickly, going to sleep almost at once as Whitefield put him in a hammock next to his own.

Blanche had gone back on deck where Whitefield now found her standing at the rail, waiting for him. "He's asleep," he said, "but I fear the lad is not right."

"He seems not to be. What if he—what if he doesn't ever remember, Whitefield?"

"That would be bad indeed, miss." He shook his head. "Don't know as I ever heard of a man who didn't know who he was. Be a little like bein' a livin' dead man, wouldn't it now?"

The thought frightened her. "Keep me informed as to how he is, will you?"

"Yes, miss."

★ ★ ★ ★

Three days later the captain questioned Burns about the injured man.

"Lieutenant Burns, about this man who doesn't know who he is—give me some facts."

Burns shrugged. "Weel, sir, I canna tell ye much." He had been expecting the captain's question, for as second lieutenant, he was responsible for the muster book, and therefore was expected to know the condition of the crew. But he spoke with even more caution than his Scottish reticence provided.

"Speak up, man!"

"Weel, sir, physically, the man is in guid condition. It's only been three days since he came out of the coma—and he's fit so far as his body goes—but his mind—?"

"Claims he doesn't know his name, is that it?"

"Yes, sir, and I think he's tellin' the truth. I've had a talk with him, Captain, and it's no act. Matter of fact, sir, the thing frightens him—as it would any man."

Captain Rommey stared at his feet as the silence ran on. Finally he looked up, perplexity marking his square face. "Well, we'll have to use the fellow, Lieutenant. Put him to work."

"Aye, sir. I've put him in Whitefield's care. He's a steady man, and he tells me the man's quite able—a quick learner."

"All right. Use him."

"Aye, sir, but what shall I put down in the muster book?"

"Put down—oh, you mean a name."

"We must have that, Captain."

"Of course." There was little humor in Rommey, but something caught at his mind and brought a light into his frosty eyes. "Little like naming a baby, isn't it, Burns? Well, I've named a few ships, but never a baby. Let me see . . ." he pondered. Shortly he exclaimed, "I've got it! You know the Hebrews had a genius for naming their babies, Burns. Like Jacob. Name means *deceiver*—and he didn't miss it far, did he now?"

"No, sir."

"Well, I need seamen—so I'm going to name this infant of ours after the best seaman I ever knew."

Burns grinned, knowing the captain's idol. "Admiral Hawke, that'd be, sir?"

"Of course! Name the fellow that—*Hawke!*"

"Aye, sir—and the first name?"

"Blast the first name! *Hawke*—that's good enough for the fellow—probably too good!"

"Aye, sir. I'll put it in the book. Hawke, able seaman."

CHAPTER NINE

I'D LET THE DEVIL HIMSELF MAN THE GUNS!

★ ★ ★ ★

Neptune's bell struck two double strokes. It was six o'clock in the evening, and the first dogwatch had come to an end in the gathering darkness.

"Sunset, sir," reported Burns.

"I see that," Captain Rommey answered, biting off his words.

"Six o'clock exactly. The equinox, sir. Now we'll have a westerly gale, or I'll miss my guess."

"I would not be opposed to a breeze, Mr. Burns. And I do believe the wind's freshening and the sea's getting up a bit, sir."

Burns shifted his feet and said uncomfortably, "We're vurry short o' water, Captain."

"Put the men on a pint a day."

"Yes, sir."

Rommey glanced at the small officer, noting the unhappy light in his eyes. "It won't kill them," he barked. The captain was not a man to explain his actions. And it wasn't as if he didn't know that the entire crew was rebellious and unhappy with the water shortage. Every man on board was aware that the *Neptune* could make port in five days, and they resented the captain's stubborn refusal to do what seemed reasonable.

Rommey thought back over the past five weeks, musing as to how he might have done differently, but nothing came to him. He thought of the first day the pressed men had been forced out on deck, naked and shivering, to rid themselves of vermin.

Their heads were shaved to the bare skin, accentuating the prison pallor many of them still wore. They had been driven by Thompson, the captain of the forecastle, to the wash-deck pump, fright making them shiver as much as cold. Most of them had never had a bath before, and Thompson's blood-curdling remarks terrified them: "Perhaps we'll make sailors of you, but if we don't, overside with a shot at your feet! Come on with the pump there! Let's see the color of your hides, jailbirds! When the cat gets at you, we see the color o' your backbones, too!"

Rommey had watched, and contrary to the opinion of most on the ship, he took no pleasure in seeing the pain or discomfort of these men. The shearing and the bath were necessary if the ship was to be kept clear of fleas and bugs and lice which would make life miserable.

The next day had brought one of those sudden, violent storms that seem to rise out of nowhere, ripping the seas to tatters, seemingly possessed with a demonic desire to destroy ships. It had been, in Rommey's judgment, a miracle that the *Neptune* had not gone to the bottom, for the new hands had been worthless. Only extraordinary courage on the part of the few old hands had saved them.

It had not saved their water or their food, however. The planking had been sprung, flooding the compartment containing fresh food and water, spoiling everything. There was one other compartment, very small, which held a few casks of fresh water and some staples, and it was on this that the crew had lived for three weeks.

Both his lieutenants had been surprised when he had not made straight for the Indies, but there had been a method to his seeming madness. *The men have got to be made into good seamen*, he'd thought stubbornly. *If they get thirsty enough—that may do it.* Such was his plan, and he was assisted by a lull following the storm that had becalmed the ship, preventing them from making any headway no matter what the captain decided.

The days had grown to weeks, and the water and food dwindled down so that rations were cut three times. But there had been no letup of drill! From dawn to dark the men ran up the lines and worked the sails at the commands of the officers. Below decks the gun crews labored harder than miners, running the heavy guns out, firing them, then doing it again. Every day, hour after hour, the drills were repeated as the *Neptune* drifted with slack sails across a windless glassy sea, which grew hotter and hotter as the days wore on.

Uncomfortable with the situation, Rommey was now anxious for someone to approve his action. "We've had a hard cruise, Mr. Burns," he acknowledged, "and I know the men are unhappy."

"Aye, sir."

Rommey looked up, smote his meaty hands together, saying brusquely, "It's hard to make first-rate seamen out of pressed men. Easy ways won't do."

Burns turned to stare at the captain, for he realized it was a plea for some sort of understanding. *Weel, now,* he thought in surprise, *the man is actually human!* Aloud he said only, "That's the sea, sir. You had to give them a little pride."

Now it was Rommey's turn to be surprised, for he had not thought the second lieutenant had that sort of discernment. Realizing that he had mistaken the Scot's reticence for a lack of intelligence, he smiled briefly. "I'm glad you see that, Mr. Burns."

"They got a bit o' it, sir—but if I may make a suggestion?"

"Of course."

"Weel, I don't think we'll get much more out o' them just now. They're landsmen, sir, an' not toughened up. But if we could make for port, get some fresh food an' water, why, I think we might see a better spirit."

"I agree. We'll set all sail and make for port. You may give the orders as soon as the wind picks up. I'll have Lieutenant Langley plot the course."

"Aye, sir." Burns was somewhat embarrassed, for he was a poor navigator, though excellent in every other aspect of seamanship. He spoke up hurriedly to cover his shame. "The men will have a heart for it."

"How's that man doing—Hawke?"

"Not bad, Captain. He's vurry strong an' healthy. Whitefield say's he's a first-class hand with the gun."

"Keep an eye on him," Rommey suggested, then left the deck to Burns. He thought sourly as he went wearily to his cabin: *And if you don't have time to keep an eye on him, Burns, my daughter will take care of the duty!*

The captain was not wrong, for at the same time that he was speaking with Burns on the forecastle deck, Blanche and Hawke were sitting at the small table in the galley. The men were in their hammocks, exhausted from the day's taxing drill, and Hans, the cook, had watched the pair furtively as he made dough for bread. He was a gossip, as most ship's cooks were, but the couple spoke so quietly that he was unable to hear. As he finally left the galley and went to bed, he was thinking up ways to improve on the telling of the thing—the captain's daughter and the strange man called Hawke who didn't even have his own name. He licked his lips and thought of how he could report their being alone in the galley, sitting *very* close indeed . . . and so his fertile imagination built on the incident until he dropped off to sleep.

Blanche looked up as the cook left. "I think he suspects us."

"Suspects us of what?"

The question took the girl off guard—as Hawke's remarks often did, and she colored slightly, an unusual thing for Blanche Rommey!

"Why, he suspects us of—of being—" She broke off, unable to meet his steady, inquiring gaze. "You know, Hawke."

"No."

The stark simplicity of his remark and the clear, dark eyes looking directly into hers made her give an uncertain laugh. "You are a difficult man to talk to!"

"I am?"

"Yes. Any other man in the world would have known *exactly* what the cook suspects. But you really don't know, do you?"

"No."

"No!" she mocked him, then leaned forward and tapped her finger against her chin, studying him as if he were some exotic specimen. She had done that a great deal for the past three weeks, and there was still an excitement in it that she could not explain. He was an enigma to her, of course, as he was to all, even to himself, and she was fascinated by what she was constantly finding out about him.

Things he didn't know himself came to light as they sat for hours in the dimly lit galley. She'd discovered that he knew the names of the newest fashions, exotic foods, a little about French dances and manners, though he spoke no French. He was not a common man, she had discovered quickly.

He had grown well and strong, she saw, staring at him directly. His face was reddish with a slight sunburn, which was evening out to a golden tan. The work he'd done with the ropes and the tackle of the ship had roughened his hands, but they were well-shaped, not the hands of a laboring man.

"What would Hans be suspicious of, Miss Rommey?" he asked when she did not respond.

"Oh, Hawke, he's thinking it's not right for a man and a woman to be alone like this."

"Why not?"

"Because they might—do things they shouldn't," she answered with some discomfort in her face.

"What things?"

Impulsively she shook her heavy hair in an extremely feminine gesture, and quickly put her hand on his arm and squeezed it, feeling the steely muscle beneath the thin cotton shirt. "Why, most men would try to kiss me if they were here alone with me."

He thought about that, and she watched his face carefully, wondering at the openness in his eyes. That, she knew, was what fascinated her. She had tried to explain the man's innocent behavior to her mother in answer to the charge that she was spending too much time with a deckhand. "Oh, Mother, he's not a deckhand— he's not anything. At least, no one *knows* what he is. He doesn't know himself. He's like a baby, really. Most people put on a mask, try to be somebody else. But Hawke doesn't even know enough to do that. He's the only person I'm aware of who doesn't have anything to cover up—or who doesn't *know* anything he has to hide."

Her mother had been totally bewildered, but now as Blanche sat there with her hand on his arm, she knew that part of the thrill of being with Hawke was his extreme attractiveness, and part of it was the excitement of discovery—finding out who he was. But, at the same time, she knew that once she had found out his identity, he would not be nearly so interesting.

She looked at him, a glint in her eyes. "We've talked about so many things, but we've never talked about women."

He flashed her a smile and said with the trace of humor that sometimes burst from him, "I don't know anything about women— just about you. You're the only woman I know, Miss Rommey."

"Now that's fascinating! All men say the same thing!"

"What do they say?"

"Oh, they all say 'I love only you!' "

"And they don't mean it?"

"No. Certainly not."

"Why do they say it then?"

"Why—!"

She halted, and he said frankly, "You're the only woman I love."

She gasped and then shook her head. "You are a danger, Hawke. It would be unsafe to let you go into society."

"A danger?"

"Yes. Either you'd charm the ladies out of their virtue with your point-blank simplicity—or you'd get snared by some hussy—or you'd marry a widow with six children because you felt sorry for her!" The last amused her and she laughed until the tears ran down her face.

Hawke rarely laughed, but he smiled as he watched her. His body had healed, but he felt incomplete, and for this reason said practically nothing to anyone but Blanche and Whitefield. Those two he felt safe with, for they never probed at him unkindly as a few of the crew had tried to do.

He sat there relaxed, trusting the woman, and submitting to her questions, for they were kind. Finally she rose and he got up with her. "I hate to go to bed. I always hate to go to bed."

"Why is that?"

"Oh, I don't know," she shrugged. "Afraid I'll miss something."

"But nothing happens at night. Everybody's asleep."

She could never get used to the absolute simplicity of his mind, and she smiled, coming closer to him. "I know," she stated, hating to leave. The ship swayed slightly, bringing her mind back to why she was on board. "Wind is picking up. Father told me we'll be in the Indies in a few days with a good breeze."

"Will you be glad?"

"No. It'll be boring." She stirred restlessly, and added, "I won't be able to see you. The ship will sail in a few days." She waited for him to ask where, and when he didn't, she questioned, "Don't you want to know where you're going?"

"No. Places are all alike to me," he answered quietly.

"One of them isn't! Your home."

"I—can't remember it."

A thought struck her and she voiced it, looking carefully at him. "You may be married."

He shrugged his shoulders, and then replied with one of his small smiles, "I don't *feel* married."

The statement pleased her, but there was a light of speculation in her eyes. The ship was still except for the creaking of timbers, and impulsively she turned fully to him and asked a little breathlessly, "Do you know what a kiss is?"

"Yes."

She looked at him, then put her hands up and drew his head down, kissing him full on the mouth. She held him there, and was not displeased to feel his arms go around her waist. But as he pulled her closer she drew away. Looking at him with a smile, she remarked, "You are very proficient in that area, Hawke. I think you must have had practice."

He stood there, a look of sadness in his eyes. "I can't say, Miss Rommey."

The hurt she saw pulled at her and she was sorry she had teased him. "Forgive me, Hawke. My father says I like to play with people as if they were toys. I hope you don't think I've done that with you."

"No. If you hadn't helped me, I couldn't have borne it."

"What's it *like*? Can you tell me?" All of a sudden she found herself filled with compassion, a rare emotion for Blanche, and she waited expectantly.

"It's—like being in a large room with all sorts of objects. I see them and I know what they're for—but I don't know how I know. And when I'm alone, in my hammock, I have bad dreams—or not dreams, really, but thoughts that come as I lie there in the darkness."

He paused and she whispered, "What do you dream?"

"Faces—all sorts of faces. People I don't know—but who seem to know me. And sometimes it's—scenes, like in a play. I seem to be in the play and I'm doing things—sometimes just simple things like eating a meal with someone. Sometimes doing something I don't even understand—that seems to make no sense."

He had grown pale, and she realized that beneath the even demeanor of Hawke, there was a frightening void, and she longed to comfort him. "It'll come to you, Hawke," she murmured, putting her arms around him. This time she did not kiss him, but held him as he stood there with an emptiness in his eyes. Then she drew back and said, "Good night. I'll see you in the morning."

"Good night, Miss Rommey."

After she had left, he went to the crew's quarters. A single candle threw a feeble yellow beam over the swaying hammocks, and he slipped quietly into his, not knowing that more than one set of eyes marked his progress. He lay there quietly, and for once slipped into a deep sleep, not awakening until the sun piped all hands up.

Whitefield had already risen and was gone, but a few of the hands still there spoke to Hawke as they began to pull their clothes on and stow their hammocks. As he left the cabin, he was abruptly caught by a strong hand and whirled about to look into the face of a tall, strongly built man with jet black hair and eyes to match— Dion Sullivan, an Irishman. He was the carpenter and also part of a gun crew. Hawke had been aware that the man was considered a bully. Sullivan had whipped one man badly, one of the new pressed men; and most of the crew suffered his bluster, fearing his powerful fists. He was a crony of the cooper, Grimes, and Hawke saw that the spider-like man was standing beside Sullivan, an ugly gleam in his beady eyes.

"Well, looky wot we got, Mates," Sullivan yelled. "A real ladies' man, that's what we got!" He did not notice that Pickens, a foretopman, had slipped out of the door. The Irishman continued holding Hawke in an iron grip, an unpleasant smile on his lips. "Now, wot I says is, when a fellow has himself a woman friend as purty as that there captain's daughter, why he owes it to his mates to give some details! Now that ain't askin' too much, is it?"

"Too right, Sullivan!" Grimes moved to block the way when Hawke would have pushed by the Irishman. "You've been cuddlin' up to that gel fer weeks now. Come on, wot's it like, eh?"

Hawke stared at the pair, confused, and several servile followers of Grimes began to join in, yelping like dogs.

Hawke pulled free from Sullivan's grip—and the ease with which he did it both surprised and angered the carpenter. "I have to be at my station," he said quietly, and would have gone through the door but Sullivan caught a wink from Grimes. He made a leap and threw a blow that caught the smaller man between the shoulder blades with such force that Hawke was driven against the bulkhead with a crash. Sullivan cried, "You ain't learned 'ow to act to yer betters, lubber!"

He threw a punch that caught Hawke high on the forehead and knocked him to the floor. A small protest went up from one or two of the hands, but Grimes cried, "Shut yer face!" and Sullivan pulled the smaller man to his feet and began to strike him in the face and body with hard, driving blows. Hawke held his hands up to protect his face, but made no attempt to strike back, which pleased and infuriated Sullivan.

"Look at the rat!" he cried with a twisted grin. "Won't even put his hands up!"

He began to strike again, but at that moment Whitefield came flying through the door with a marlin spike in his hand. He took a swing and knocked Sullivan to the floor with one fierce blow, dropping the spike in the process. Quick as a flash Grimes reached out one arm, plucked the spike, and proceeded to beat Whitefield to the deck with it. Grimes would have killed him, but Lieutenant Langley shot in, shouting, "Blast you, Grimes! Drop that spike!"

That was the end of the fight, but it was not the end of the matter itself. Langley was in a fit of rage, and he reported to the captain instantly. Rommey stared at him and said, "I'll have the lot flogged!"

Immediately Langley lost his anger, saying, "Oh no, sir, that would be too severe!"

Burns had come along with the first lieutenant, and he agreed. "It would nae be a guid thing to blow this up, Captain. The men will fight, an' that's all there is to it."

Rommey was angry, but allowed himself to be pacified. He said impatiently, "Well, take care of it. If it happens again, we'll see what a taste of the cat will do." Then he had a thought. "One of them was Hawke?"

"Yes, sir."

"I'll see the man in my cabin."

As the two officers walked away, Langley told Burns, "I'll work the tallow off Grimes and Sullivan. You send Hawke to the captain."

Ten minutes later Rommey opened the door at the sound of a knock, and found the seaman there. "Seaman Hawke reporting, sir," he stated, well schooled by Whitefield.

"Yes." Rommey beckoned impatiently and went back to sit at his desk. He stared at the sailor with a hard glance, noting the livid bruises on his face. When there was no response, he continued. "I understand there was a fight and you were involved, Hawke."

"Yes, sir."

Captain Rommey waited for an excuse, but none came, so he probed further. "I'm aware of your misfortune, Hawke, and am inclined to believe that you are innocent." He waited to be thanked, but Hawke simply stood there, his eyes alert but revealing nothing.

"I want to ask you—"

The door suddenly opened and Rommey turned angrily to find

Blanche coming in with an innocent look on her face. "I'm sorry to interrupt, Father, but Mother wants me to get a book for her."

He knew instantly that was a lie, for his wife read practically nothing. She had come, he knew, because she was fascinated by the man Hawke. Going to the bookcase, she looked over the books, took one, then stood there. "Good morning, Hawke," she nodded.

"I would appreciate it if you would take the book to your mother, Blanche. I need to talk to this man."

"Perhaps I can help." She sat down, settled herself firmly and added with a disarming smile, "Hawke and I have spent some time together, and I believe I understand more of his problem than anyone else."

She would not be budged by anything less than a charge of gun powder, Rommey saw. And not willing to give her the satisfaction of an argument, he gave in. "Very well. Stay if you must, but remain silent!"

"Certainly, Father. Anything you say."

He gritted his teeth at the over-sweet reply and turned to ask, "You remember nothing, Hawke—not even your name?"

"No, sir."

Puzzled, Rommey began to inquire further, asking technical questions about ships and the sea. Hawke answered them slowly and with great care, and finally Rommey stated, "You can answer all my questions about the tackle of ships—except for arms, and you even know a smattering of that."

"I've learned all that from Whitefield, sir," Hawke responded. "He's taught me that since I . . . came on the ship."

"I see," Rommey nodded slowly. "That means, of course, that you've done considerable sailing—but not on a warship."

"Yes, sir. That's what Whitefield decided."

Captain Rommey caught a smile on Blanche's face and flushed, for he knew what she was thinking: *A lowly seaman—but he found out as much as the captain!* It flustered him, and he continued his inquiry but could find no pattern.

Finally he remarked, "Well, Hawke, I don't know what you *were*—but I know what you are now. You're a seaman aboard the frigate *Neptune*, and I will expect you to do your duty."

"Yes, sir. I'll do my best."

Rommey was caught off guard by the quick, respectful answer, and he turned and walked to the window. He stood there silently staring out. After a few minutes he spoke as he continued to gaze at the waves and the sky. "England is on the brink of a war, and it is ships like this one that will save her. It always comes to that— the navy is England's strength."

He began to pace the floor, forgetting momentarily the pair who were watching. His next words were intense. "The politicians and the merchants and the public—they all want peace. Good for business!" he snorted. "But they'll not get peace. Never! Then when war comes, they start to cry for the soldier and the sailor!" He shrugged and went on, "We'd all like peace, but when war comes, what good is a man of peace? That's when we need men of war. Let me see, there's a blasted good line about that . . ." He paused and tugged at his ear, staring at his books. "What is it? Something about a tiger! Imitate a tiger? No, that's not right. What is it?"

Suddenly Hawke quoted:

> In peace there's nothing so becomes a man
> As modest stillness and humility.
> But when the blast of war blows in our ears,
> Then imitate the action of the tiger.

Captain Rommey stared dumbfounded at Hawke, shot a startled glance at Blanche, then back to Hawke. "Do you know that line? Who said it?"

Hawke closed his eyes, thought for a moment, his brow wrinkled. "I believe," he replied, "it was Henry V, wasn't it, Captain?"

"By Harry, that's the piece!" Amazed, he burst into laughter, saying, "A scholar in our midst! And I need gunners!"

Immediately a thought struck him, and his eyes gleamed. He wheeled, walked to the large table that was covered with a nautical map, and picked up a scrap of paper and a quill. After scribbling something on it, Rommey extended the paper to Hawke, who took it and read it.

"Do you recognize what that is?"

"I suppose, sir, they are two positions."

"Exactly! The first is our present position. The other is our destination." He hesitated, looking at him intently. "Do you think you can take those two figures and plot a course on that map?"

Hawke bit his lip, stared at the paper, shrugged slightly and answered, "I can try, sir."

"Do it then!"

Hawke walked to the table and surveyed the project. He seemed to forget the captain and Blanche as he pored over the figures and the map. Finally he picked up the dividers, moved them across the map, then looked at the paper again. He checked his figures carefully, using some of the tools on the table. After several movements and rechecking, he put a mark on the map, traced a line, and stepped back. "I believe that's right, sir."

Rommey came over, stared at the map for a long time, and without looking up, said, "You may go, Hawke."

Blanche, fascinated by this unusual man, watched him leave. As soon as the door closed, she rushed over to stand beside her father. "Is it correct?"

"Yes," he said in a strange tone.

"What's the matter, Father?" She saw he was troubled, the cloud of anguish evident in his eyes, and for the first time in weeks Blanche felt a compassion toward him.

"What's the matter? I'll tell you what's wrong," he said quietly. "There are only two men who can navigate this ship—myself and Langley. And three times in my life I've known of ships that lost their captain and first mates in action. A ship without a navigator is a piece of wreckage, Blanche."

"But—!"

"And now I have a man who can navigate this vessel—and he doesn't even know his name! Can you imagine what they'd say at home if I put a man like that in any sort of position of responsibility?"

She stood there appraising him. "You would never let a common seaman chart a course."

He stared at her, then declared slowly, "Daughter, this is a fighting ship and I am a fighting man. That's all either of us is good for. And if fighting comes, and if it means victory—I'd let the devil himself man the guns of the *Neptune!*"

CHAPTER TEN

THE BLADE

★ ★ ★ ★

The frigid cold of the North Atlantic and the American shore was only a faint memory now to the crew of the *Neptune* as they sailed toward the Indies. The blazing June sun beat down like a fist on the crew as they sought the small islands of shade on the deck, and the southern breeze baked the lips dry and turned the pallid hides of the pressed men to a rich copper.

Whitefield glanced to where Hawke was sitting with his back against the bulkhead, his eyes half shut as he stared across the rolling troughs of green topped with sparkling white caps of spray. The young man was a source of never-ending wonder to the gunner, who had kept close watch on him since the trouble with Sullivan and Grimes—and the thought of that time prompted him to speak.

"Hawke?"

"Yes?"

"You ain't never said a word about that pair—" He waved a hand toward the stern where the two sat in the middle of a small group laughing loudly. "I been waitin' for you to complain about the way they beat you up—but you ain't said not one word."

"Nothing to say about it, Enoch." Hawke did not even shift his gaze, but suddenly his eyes opened and he said in excitement, "Look—what's that?"

"What? Oh, them's flyin' fish." Enoch watched carefully, and as usual tried to make some sort of connection with the remark. "You never seen flyin' fish?"

"No—at least, I don't think so."

"You ain't never been in these waters, then." He pondered that, chewing on his lower lip. But he was a stubborn man, and he went on doggedly, "Now, it ain't in a natural man to take a beatin' like you took from that pair an' not get mad."

Hawke took his eyes off the fish and considered the older man with a glint of amusement. "Why do you think that is, Enoch?"

"Well, I've been ponderin' on it—and it come to me that you might be a Christian man. The Bible teaches us to turn the other cheek, and that's just what you done, Hawke. And besides, you know more 'bout the Scripture than a sinner would know."

Whitefield was a single-minded man, eager to see all men embrace Jesus Christ; in that he was much like his cousin, George Whitefield. Hawke had been aware of the gunner's fervent desire, and had listened carefully to Enoch's preaching as well as to their conversations.

But he now shook his head, saying quietly, "I don't know what I am, Enoch. From what you've told me, a Christian has some feelings—but I'm just a blank. Maybe I had parents who read the Bible—or perhaps I attended a school where it was read aloud. And as for not wanting to get revenge on Sullivan and Grimes, it could be that I'm a coward."

The answer did not satisfy Whitefield, but he said no more. For the next hour they sat there quietly, Enoch from time to time relating some of his life to the young man. They were disturbed by the crowd on the stern who came milling to the mizzenmast with loud cries.

"They're tormentin' young Jones again," Whitefield said in disgust. He got to his feet, spat over the rail, and then shook his head, saying, "Why can't they leave the poor boy alone? He's sick. A fool could see that!"

Will Jones was one of the pressed men and, unfortunately, one of those human beings who is constitutionally unfit for life at sea. He had been seasick since the day he was brought aboard, unable to keep down any food, much less the unpalatable, rough fare served on a warship. He was nothing but skin and bones, his clothes flapping about him in the breeze as he was pulled roughly along by Sullivan toward the mast.

"Bully boy!" Whitefield said. "Ain't happy unless he's makin' some poor devil weaker than himself miserable! He'd 'ave been after you, Hawke, if Lieutenant Burns hadn't put the fear of the cat in him."

That, Hawke realized, was true. Burns had stood looking up into the face of the hulking Sullivan and in his quiet Scottish burr, had informed the sailor that if he laid one hand on Hawke, he would kiss the Gunner's Daughter—an expression that meant he would be tied over a cannon and flogged.

Since that hour Sullivan had not touched Hawke, but there was a burning hatred in his eyes, and now, as he held fast to the unfortunate Jones, his eyes were fixed on Whitefield and Hawke, addressing his words more to them than to the trembling sailor in his grasp.

"See here, Jones," he snarled loudly, "I've had enough of your play actin'! You ain't done nothin' but lay around and let these good men do your work. Now you climb them shrouds or I'll make you wish you had!"

Hawke saw that young Jones's thin face trembled as he looked up to the top of the towering mizzenmast; and bloodless as he was, his pallor seemed to wash to an even paler hue. "I—I can't do it!" he whispered. "Never could bear high places."

"Never could bear high places!" Sullivan mocked the boy with a grin, then gave him a shake that made the thin frame tremble violently. He held up his large fist in front of Jones's eyes. "I'm tellin' you, boy," he warned; "you climb that mast, or I'll bust you up!"

Pickens, one of the foretopmen, protested, "Sullivan, he's not lying. He tried once, and we had to pry his fingers loose. Some men is like that—can't stand no height."

"Shut your mouth, Pickens! I say he's a whining quitter and I aim to cure him right now."

"Let the boy alone." Whitefield left his place and came to stand beside Jones. "I don't remember nobody makin' you an officer on this ship."

"The officers expect us to make sailors out of these lubbers, Whitefield, and you can't deny it!"

There was some truth in that, and Enoch could only say, "They do expect that—but this boy is sick."

Hawke did not miss the look that passed between Sullivan and Grimes, and he realized instantly that this scene was directed at him. Then, when Sullivan spoke again, he was certain of it.

"Every man on this ship knows you're a great one for taking care of strays, Whitefield—like that one there." Sullivan gave a nod at Hawke, adding with a sneer, "You sold Burns a bill of goods on that dummy, didn't you?"

"He does his work!"

"He's a bleedin' coward, that's wot he is!" Sullivan said. "Won't fight like a man! Well, I can't touch your stray cat—not till I catch him ashore—but I can build a fire under this one!"

Hawke had been standing with his back to a bulkhead, watching as he always did. He was not touched by the plight of Jones, for he had seen much suffering on the part of the landsmen who'd been roughly handled on the *Neptune*. But he was disturbed by the troubled face of Whitefield. The gunner had become his touchstone with the world, and it was only through Enoch's constant attention that Hawke had been able to keep his mind off the sinister darkness—the frightening void that lay behind him. He saw Enoch's helplessness, and suddenly without knowing why, he stated quietly, "The boy's pretty small game for you, Sullivan."

Instantly the big Irishman swung his head, his eyes fixed on Hawke. "Well, well—another country heard from!" His eyes gleamed and he jabbed a thumb toward Hawke, saying, "And it's yourself who's takin' this lubber's part, *Mister* Hawke—who can't even do his own fightin'?"

"Let him alone. I'll fight you if that'll make you happy."

The challenge came so quickly that Sullivan's jaw dropped, and he retorted, "Well, that's what I'd like—"

"Don't do it, Mate!" Grimes, his ungainly body a blot on the bright sunlight, moved forward and put a restraining hand on Sullivan's arm. "Burns would 'ave you cut to rags." Then he smiled craftily and suggested with a sly look toward Hawke, "But just make a friendly wager with the man."

"What sort o' bet?" Whitefield broke in.

"Oh, a fair show, Enoch!" Grimes offered, lifting his hand in a mock oath. "Like, mebby, if Hawke can beat Sullivan to the crow's nest, why, Jones will 'ave no more trouble."

"And if I lose?" Hawke asked.

"I'd say six months' wages to my friend here would be fair."

"What?" Whitefield was enraged. "Why, Sullivan's a first-rate foretopman, and—"

"I'll take the bet." Hawke spoke almost with indifference, and moved toward the shrouds, the network of rope that formed a weblike ladder to the tops of the masts.

A shout went up from the men who loved any sort of contest, and Whitefield asked nervously, "Hawke, have you ever climbed a mizzenmast?"

"Why, I have no idea, Enoch." A trace of amusement was on the lean face of the younger man, and he added, "I suppose we'll find out in a few minutes."

Enoch could do nothing, but stood there helplessly as the two men took station on opposite sides of the ship, Hawke on the starboard and Sullivan to port. "You give the signal, Whitefield," Grimes grinned. "Just so all is fair and square. And we'll all be the judge of who's the winner!"

Enoch was sick at heart, for he knew that Sullivan, for all his bulk, was agile as a monkey. He was by far the best and fastest in climbing up the shrouds; and there was no hope, he felt, for Hawke. Just the way the two men stood revealed the difference, for Sullivan was crouched, his hands clutching the shrouds, while Hawke had one hand lightly, as if for balance, on one of the horizontal strands, and was looking bored with the whole affair.

"Go!" Whitefield shouted, and a cry went up from the deck, mostly cheers for Sullivan. The big man moved with practiced speed, not one wasted motion as he sped upward. *No man can beat him—he's too good!* Enoch thought. But he kept his eyes fixed on the smaller man—and what he saw made him shout with glee!

Hawke did not move as quickly at first as Sullivan. He seemed to fumble slightly as he climbed hand over hand, and his feet had to search for the horizontals. But then he seemed to take wing, and he flew up the web of ropes with a rapidity that not a one of them had ever seen. The cheering stopped abruptly, and Grimes alone raised his voice to yell, "Sullivan! Don't let the blackguard do you in!"

Sullivan paused long enough to look across at his counterpart and nearly fell off the shrouds as he saw the flying figure of Hawke come even with him, then leave him behind even as he watched. He cursed and drove himself upward with all his might, but a cry from the deck caught him; and ten feet from the top he looked up to see Hawke standing there looking down at him with a slight smile.

"Looks like you're getting old, Sullivan," he remarked, then grabbed a loose rope and slid down, almost falling to the deck before catching himself in time to step lightly onto the oak planks.

Whitefield pounded him on the back, exclaiming, "You did it! By the grace of the good Lord, you did it!" Looking up he yelled to the stunned foretopman, who was staring in rage at Hawke, "Mind you, keep your end, Sullivan. I can't abide a gambler—but a welcher is something the ship won't stand!"

Jones moved over to Whitefield and Hawke as the crowd broke up. Tears filled his eyes. "I—I can't say how . . ."

He paused, and Hawke put a brown hand on his shoulder, reassuring him. "Why, it was nothing, Will."

Jones looked at him, but could only say to Enoch as the other walked away, "He's a Christian man—ain't he, Enoch?"

"Will," Whitefield agreed slowly, "it's looking more like that all the time."

A fighting ship is a small cosmos, a microcosm of the world. And as in the world, news can travel with incredible speed. By nightfall every man on the ship knew the story. The crew was bored, for life at sea is monotonous, and any juicy tidbit was chewed over and over until every morsel was extracted.

The officers had heard a little, but at the captain's table that night, they got the full story from Burns, who'd gotten it out of Whitefield. When Burns finished, they all looked at Rommey expectantly, but he said only, "We'll need all the foretopmen we can muster—especially in light of our new orders."

A hum of excitement went around the room. That morning they had sighted a sail which proved to be HMS *Centaur*, a sixteen-gun sloop fresh out of England. Rommey had gone on board and returned later with a waterproof pouch which everyone had identified as a container from Flag Command in London.

Now there was satisfaction in the craggy face of the captain, and he nodded with a smile. "We have been given some time to get the crew toughened up and the ship smoothed out. Now we can do the job *Neptune* was built for."

"Action, sir?" Langley asked.

"Yes, Langley. Action!" He rose and pointed to a map tacked to the bulkhead. "We now know that the rebels are sending their ships along these lanes—both privateers and merchant ships."

"But the winds aren't favorable in those latitudes, Captain!" Burns protested. Then the truth dawned and he smiled. "Weel, of course! That's the reason they're there!"

"Exactly! Now that we know where the scoundrels are, we'll bag them," Rommey said fiercely. Then he added, "We'll head for home at once. On our return voyage and while we're provisioning the ship, Captain Baxter, I want you to train the seamen in small arms."

"Small arms, Captain?" Baxter gave a languid look around the room and asked, "May I ask for what purpose, sir?"

"I think it not unlikely that we'll have to board an enemy ship, and it's not impossible that we might make a raid on a port city. Your marines are well trained—but we may need to fill out our numbers with men who can handle a musket and a blade."

"If you wish, sir—but they're a scrub lot."

"Do the best you can, Captain."

During this exchange Burns had been watching Langley, and saw what he expected—disappointment. The tall lieutenant had fallen hopelessly in love with Blanche Rommey, and the thought of not seeing her turned him to putty! Burns shook his head in despair, for he had watched the one-sided courtship closely. The captain had installed his wife and daughter in a fine mansion twenty miles in the interior of Jamaica. After each short venture to sea in the *Neptune*, Rommey had gone there, usually accompanied by Langley and Burns.

Mrs. Rommey was satisfied—as she would have been in any place. She did her embroidery, went for rides through the countryside, and made infrequent trips to the port city. She seemed not to grieve when her husband left, not happy when he returned. She was, Burns had thought, the closest thing to a vegetable he'd ever seen.

But Blanche Rommey was a different story. She was almost out of her mind with boredom. Her quick spirit and impulsive nature were the worst possible combination to fit her for living in a secluded rural paradise, and she had been so hungry for company and excitement that she had practically forced Burns to take her to a party at a plantation over fifteen miles away.

He thought of it as he sat at the table looking at Clarence Langley, and felt very sorry for the man. Blanche had flirted with every man she saw at the party, even with Burns himself on the way home. When the Scot had cut that short by mentioning Langley, she had laughed and said lightly, "Clarence? He's a dear—but such a *stick!*"

Burns had tried to warn his friend, but given up in despair, for the tall lieutenant was deaf to his words. The meeting broke up, and Langley went to set the new course. "Lieutenant Burns, a word," Captain Rommey requested, catching him as the other left.

"I have a rather *unusual* order; that's the best word I can apply to it," he hesitated.

"Yes, sir?"

"We will be taking prizes, almost certainly, when we get into the lanes."

"I've nae doot we will." All the crew would share in the prize money, and Burns was as thrifty as his ancestors in far-off Scotland.

"There is a problem," Rommey frowned. "The prizemaster I put on board to take the captured ship to port must be able to navigate."

Burns flushed and shook his head. "Sir, I'm embarrassed to say I canna!"

"No time for that now, Burns. It's a weakness, but there are worse things in a King's officer. I have a plan I believe will work— but it's so unusual, I'm not going to order you to do it. You'll have to volunteer."

Burns was mystified, for this captain was not the sort to avoid giving orders. "I'll do anything to help, sir."

"I thought you would. Now, I trust that soon we'll be getting some new midshipmen who *can* navigate, but until we do, you'll have to learn. When we make port, I'm leaving Langley in charge of provisioning the ship. It will take about a week. I want you to learn to navigate during that time. You'll have no other duties— and I have a teacher in mind."

"Yes, sir?"

"This man Hawke, he's an excellent navigator." Rommey shrugged and gave a slight grimace, but went on. "I know he's only a seaman, and you're an officer. But he's all we've got. Will you let him teach you?"

"Why, I'll nae make any promises, but I'll do my best, Captain Rommey."

Rommey smiled and put his large hand on Burns's thin shoulder. "I knew you'd take it like that," he beamed. "Some officers have too confounded much pride, but I'd take instruction from Lucifer if it would make a better seaman of me!"

The next morning every hand knew that he would have shore leave, and the officers were careful to mention the rich possibility of prize money. "Just one fat merchant ship, men," they promised, "and you can retire for life."

After that Captain Baxter had no problem getting the men to

drill. Sergeant Potter drilled the hands in the use of the musket, and reported to Baxter, "Captain, they'd do more damage if they throwed rocks at the enemy! Never seen such rotten shots."

"Well, we thought it would be that way, didn't we, Sergeant?" Baxter smiled. "In the morning I'll find out if there's a good blade in the lot of them. Which I most sincerely doubt."

The exercise the next day was no better than Baxter had anticipated. Most of the ship's crew had never had a sword in their hands, and only three showed any skill. Most of them hacked away as if they were threshing wheat, but Baxter said to Potter after about half of the crew had been tested, "Sir, I reckon we may have six men who are fair. Sullivan is the best, in my judgment."

"Quite so, Sergeant. He's had some training. I'll try a bout with him."

Captain Baxter loved the sword. It was the only thing that ever caused him to drop his languid air and come alive. He had been a student of the foil, the saber, the cutlass, and every other form of blade for years, and his reputation was formidable among those who knew the art.

It had been boring to watch the heavy-handed crew hacking away, but when he squared away with Sullivan and saw that the big man was no amateur, he allowed a smile of excitement to crease his thin lips. "Have at me, Sullivan!" he cried out.

"Sir! These blades ain't got no buttons!"

It was the custom to blunt the tips of the foils for use in practice, but Baxter waved his free hand, saying, "Oh, I think it'll be safe enough."

Sullivan grinned and began advancing, his left foot extended in a long stretch behind him, his right knee bent at a sharp angle, his left hand well back. He came in quickly, so quickly and so skillfully that Baxter was taken aback, in fact, and was hard put to keep himself from getting embarrassed. But he was very good, and soon he controlled the bout. He did not have to exert all his skill, and he did not want to discourage the best prospect among the crew, so finally he called a halt. "Very good, Sullivan! Very good, indeed! If we had twenty like you, I'd not hesitate to tackle a ship of the line."

The drill continued until the last day; and Baxter had Potter pair the men off for practice. "Don't let them cut each other to bits, Sergeant," he warned. "And you might use Sullivan to help with the more clumsy fellows."

The last drill was at sunset, and most of the crew gathered either to participate or to watch. Baxter and Potter had grown tired of the routine, but were forced to stay and watch. They were paying little attention, so when Sullivan called Hawke out of the crowd they paid no heed.

"You there, Hawke," Sullivan called out. "I ain't seen you in the drill. Give him that blade, Atkins, and let's see what he's got."

Immediately the entire crew sensed that a drama was about to unfold. The officers were not paying attention and everyone knew that Sullivan was smarting under his defeat at the hands of Hawke. Several men had received minor wounds at the sword drill, and it would be easy for Sullivan to stab Hawke—and then protest that it was an accident. Who would there be to say differently? Surely not the officers.

Sullivan had waited for the right time, but had despaired. Always either Burns or Langley was in charge of the deck, or else Whitefield was present. But now Burns was far aft drilling some boat crews, and neither Whitefield nor the first lieutenant were in sight, so he had grabbed at the chance.

Hawke came forward slowly, taking the foil from Atkins, and he saw the cruel gleam in Sullivan's eye; this was not to be a drill! He slowly lifted the blade as Sullivan came forward with a grunt of pleasure, and the blades rang with a silver sound on the salt air.

Sullivan came in dancing, his blade flashing like liquid lightning, and there was no pretense of a "drill." He lunged with all his force, directing his blade straight at the heart of his opponent—but he did not succeed.

Hawke had known the moment the hilt of the sword nestled in his hand earlier that day that this was not a new thing. Now, after some fresh practice he felt like a *natural* as he picked the tip of Sullivan's blade out of the air with the tip of his own foil, directing it to one side with an ease he knew was born of a thousand hours of practice.

I've done this before, he thought as Sullivan recovered, his face red with murderous desire. *I've stood and faced men and I've felt my blood run down—and I've seen them fall to the ground pierced to the heart.*

And he could have killed Sullivan, he knew. For the man, for all his skill, seemed slow and clumsy. Hawke moved little, standing in one spot for the most part, parrying the thrusts of the other with ease, refusing to drive his own blade home.

Captain Baxter heard the rapid clashing blades and saw in one experienced glance that Sullivan was in the hands of a master. *Why, that fellow could have killed him half a dozen times!* he thought. Then he hurried forward, calling out, "Good enough for now!"

Sullivan was gasping for breath and his eyes were filled with astonishment and rage. "Sir, just let me have—!"

"Oh, you've done too much, Sullivan." Baxter reached out and took the blade from the Irishman, and moved to stand before the man with the scar. "I see you've done a little along this line before, Seaman Hawke."

"I couldn't say, Captain."

The even tenor of Hawke's voice and the bland look in his eyes stirred the captain's temper. He was not at all certain that the fellow was really all he claimed, and in any case he was anxious for a good bout.

"Well, let's see how good you are," he said, and raising his blade he began to advance toward Hawke. They circled one another, for Baxter had seen enough of the man to be cautious. He tried a feint, and to his chagrin, it was parried; for one instant he saw the tip of Hawke's blade poised and knew that he was helpless to prevent the thrust. But the thrust did not come, and a smile on Hawke's face caused Baxter's face to redden. *This one is no beginner*, he thought, and tightened his guard, taking no chances.

The crew saw two men, both light as a breeze on their feet, both quick as a striking snake with their hands. They circled slowly, but their blades rang and clashed so rapidly that it was impossible to follow the motion. Captain Rommey had come up out of his cabin and stood on the forecastle watching the contest with an inscrutable expression on his craggy face.

On and on it went, and suddenly Baxter realized that his opponent was *playing* with him! The dark face of the man was not triumphant—if anything, he looked slightly *bored*!

Desperately the marine tried to break Hawke's composure, driving at him like a madman, but always the flashing tip of the sword caught his own and parried it with ease.

Finally, Baxter stepped back, lowered his foil and stared at the man in front of him. It was almost dark, and the deep-set eyes of Hawke were hidden by the shadows of his brow and high cheekbones. He was not smiling now, and for one instant a sadness pulled his lips into a hard line—and at that moment Captain Baxter knew that Hawke was indeed a man without a past.

"You are a fine swordsman, Seaman Hawke," Baxter told the

man quietly. "I never saw one finer."

The compliment slid off the other man, and he said only, "Yes, sir. May I go now?"

"Certainly." Baxter watched him go to stand alone peering out over the rail into the gathering darkness, then said, "Drill is over, Sergeant. Dismiss the men." Looking up, the captain saw Rommey staring down from the forecastle, and he went to stand beside him. "Well, sir, what did you make of that?"

Rommey shook his head. "Another surprise from the man from nowhere, eh, Baxter?" He shook his head slowly. "He's educated, knows the world, handles a sword like a demon out of the pit—I don't know *what* the fellow is! A broken-down gentleman, perhaps?"

"I didn't get the 'broken down' part," Baxter replied with a rueful expression. "What are you going to do with him?"

Rommey looked at Hawke, who was still standing alone at the rail. "Do with him, Baxter? Why, I'll *use* him—just as I use you and myself and every other soul on this vessel. He may not have a past," he added grimly, "but I'll see to it he has a future!"

CHAPTER ELEVEN

BEAT TO QUARTERS!

★ ★ ★ ★

"I canna learn this blasted book!" Lieutenant Burns was a mild man, but his struggles with math had almost destroyed his patience. He stood up abruptly and threw the thick book he had been poring over against the wall. "Blast!" he cried in despair, pulling his sandy hair as if to remove it from his head. "I can do anything on the *Neptune* as weel as any man—but this—this accursed navigation—"

Hawke rose from his chair and walked over to pick up the book. Bringing it back to the small desk where the two of them had been seated, he said evenly, "Let's just go over it one more time, sir." He began to go over the problem, pointing from time to time at a large map stretched out on a table, and was pleased to see the officer stop glaring at him and come back to resume his seat.

Hawke could sympathize with Burns, for he realized that there was some part of the canny Scot's brain that was almost impervious to anything mathematical. For nearly a week the two had met to study at Captain Rommey's house, and the seaman had patiently gone over the fundamentals of the science of navigation, wondering at how difficult it was for Burns. Time after time the lieutenant had given up, but Hawke had sat there calmly, then continued his instruction as if nothing had happened.

Burns had become so distracted with his slow progress that he had allowed his temper to boil over, at time fastening fury on Hawke, but the seaman had never shown the least reaction. And now a light of respect came to the eyes of the Scot, and he laughed aloud. "Hawke—I dinna see how ye've put up with me! I know how tedious it is to drill a banana-fingered deckhand—but it's worse to work with a slow-witted lieutenant." He nodded, and added sincerely, "I thank ye for your patience, Seaman Hawke."

"Why, you're not slow-witted, sir." Hawke gave the other a rare smile. He had learned to respect the tenacity of the man who sat there; for many, he knew, would have given up. "It's just not your strong point. You're a fine sailor."

Burns's face flushed at the compliment, and he wondered at it, for he had never cared particularly what the crew thought of him. But his feeling for Hawke was different, and he was kept from forming a more personal tie only by the vast gulf that had to exist between officer and common seaman.

"Weel, that's guid of ye to say so, Hawke." He looked up as a clock chimed somewhere in the distance, and closed the book, saying, "It's time for dinner."

"Yes, sir. Tomorrow at the same time?"

"I don't rightly know. We may sail tomorrow—Langley tells me the *Neptune*'s fully provisioned." He walked to the wall, plucked up his coat, and slipping it on, remarked thoughtfully, "This partying every night is a bit much for a simple lad like myself. I'll be glad to put to sea."

He referred to the nightly festivities that went on at the house, for Blanche Rommey had made it a point to have a formal dinner each night, with dancing and cards after the meal. Since Burns neither danced nor played cards, he had gone to fill out the number, but had returned to his room as soon as possible.

Burns left, saying, "Better be ready, Hawke, in case we pull out early."

"Yes, sir." He picked up the books and shoved them into a small leather case; next, he took down the map and folded it carefully, placing it with the books. Closing the case, he put it on a mahogany table beside the bed and left the room.

Passing down the wide hall, he heard the sound of music—the small orchestra of native musicians. He smiled slightly, then turned left and passed out of the house into the warm night air. The mosquitoes made a whining harmony, and he brushed them away automatically with each step. He followed a stone path beside the house, down a line of *flagrante* plants rich with perfumed blossoms to a long, low stone building in a grove of mango trees.

Most of the building was taken up with a blacksmith shop, and he found Whitefield at the forge. He had been working for most of the week making spare parts for the ship, and when not instructing Burns, Hawke had watched and even helped a little.

"What's that you're making, Enoch?"

"Vent fittings."

Hawke came over to look more closely at a row of tapered cast-iron plugs laid out neatly beside the forge. Picking one up, he turned it over. "These go in the vent hole?"

"Right." Enoch gave him an approving glance and nodded, "You've picked up a heap 'bout gunnery in a short time, Hawke."

Hawke shrugged and asked, "How many of these do you need?"

"Well—a gun ain't worth spit without one, is it, now? So I thinks we better have fifty at least."

"Show me how."

"Right, lad."

Enoch had found Hawke to be a quick learner, and in less than an hour he had gone through the process. "If you think you can carry on, I'd like to get some sleep."

"Seems simple enough—and I'm not sleepy. Lieutenant says we may sail tomorrow."

"Figured we might. Don't worry if you don't do all them vent fittings, Hawke. We probably got enough."

After he left, Hawke worked steadily at the forge. It was not a demanding task, but he was getting little exercise and as a result could not sleep well. As he methodically filed the fittings, time slipped away. It was quiet in the forge, the silence broken only by the sounds of horses stomping the ground outside and the faint sound of music drifting across on the night air from the big house.

He realized after some time that his fingers were aching, and also that he was thirsty. There was an *olla* of water hanging on the wall, but he thought of the cold spring that fed the house, and left the smithy to get a drink.

The water was cold, and he sipped it slowly, thinking of what Whitefield had told him about water on ship. *In a few weeks, the water will be getting thick. Bless me! I've seen it so thick and green with stuff it wouldn't hardly pour!* The thought ran through his mind, and he lowered his head to drink, savoring the coldness and flavor of it.

He made his way back to the shop, and was startled when a

voice caught at him as he reached the door.

"Well, Hawke . . . ?"

He turned quickly, peering into the darkness, and relaxed when Blanche Rommey moved toward him. She was wearing a white dress, cut low in the neck, which set off her dark hair. "Hello, Miss Rommey," he said.

She stepped up beside him, saying, "I'm tired of that hot stuffy room." There was a husky quality in her voice, and she laughed as she took his arm, saying, "Let's walk a little."

He knew instinctively that it was not the right thing to do, but she gave him little choice. He found himself walking along the paved walk, listening as she spoke of trivial things. The sweet odor of frangipani was strong, but some scent that she was wearing mixed with it, stirring his senses.

They came to a low wall with a gate, and he stopped. "I don't think we should go outside the compound, Miss Rommey."

"What are you afraid of, Hawke?" she smiled. "Me?"

"No—snakes," he said evenly. "There's one kind here they call a Five-stepper."

"A Five-stepper?"

"Yes, because if one of them bites you, you have five steps to get help before the venom kills you."

She took a quick look at the ground, stepping closer to him involuntarily. "I don't like snakes." She took his arm, pressing against him as they walked back toward the shop. The sky was velvet black with icy points of stars, and she looked up and wondered aloud, "Look how bright that star is! I wonder what name it has?"

He looked up casually and said without thinking, "That's Sirius—the Dog Star."

She paused, stared at him, then shook her head. There was a smile on her rich, full lips. "I wonder how you know that, Hawke?"

"Common star—Sirius."

"Perhaps." She suddenly drew him to a halt, and all of the thoughts she had had of him the past days flashed across her mind. She had enjoyed the nightly parties, but the men had been insipid: a seventeen-year-old son of a planter on the neighboring property (with bad teeth and little charm); two cousins in the military, one aggressive, the other timid (both equally boorish); several cousins of the owner of the plantation (who thought of little but planting sugar cane); and one aging diplomat who fancied himself a ladies' man. Lieutenant Langley had come twice, and had done everything but throw himself at her feet. She had allowed him to follow her, but his fumbling attempts to pay compliments were so awkward that it was tedious to her.

She had thought often of Hawke, and now as he stood there, she saw he was better looking than she remembered. He had filled out, and there was a regularity in his features that was entirely masculine, but the long lashes and contoured features would have been effeminate in a man with less vigor. He was saved from this, Blanche saw, by the strength of his neck and the direct look in his large eyes, and by the scar on his cheek.

Suddenly she reached up and touched the scar on the side of his face. "I wonder where you got that?"

The touch of her hand on his cheek ran along his nerves, and he was intensely aware of her womanly figure revealed in the dress. "Probably my just deserts," he said.

"Do you remember any more?"

"Nothing." The pressure of her hand remained, but he did not know how to react, so he stood motionless.

The silence ran on. Finally Blanche spoke in an enticing voice. "You are a very attractive man, Hawke." Turning to him she whispered, "Have you thought about the time you kissed me?"

"Yes."

"So have I!" And then she lifted her face and came into his arms. There was a heavy silence over the earth, broken by the cry of a night bird, and as he lowered his head and met her full lips, softer than down, he did not *think* at all. Her body came against him, and there was only that moment, only a time of coming together, and he pulled her roughly into his arms with a hunger that suddenly came from a depth that he did not know.

She did not draw back, but gave him her kiss freely. She had been kissed many times, but always before, she had been in command of the moment; now she found that she was helpless in his arms, like a swimmer caught by a rip tide, and the thought flashed through her: *He can do anything with me!*

This shocked her, for she was a proud woman, and the sense that he was the stronger made her draw back abruptly.

He released her at once, saying shortly, "You'd better go back to the party, Miss Rommey."

She was breathing raggedly, and bit her lower lip. "Yes . . . I suppose so." Pausing for a moment, she continued. "You'll be leaving tomorrow. My father told us so at dinner." She waited for him to speak, and when he did not, she asked coyly, "Will you think of me?"

Anger suddenly rose up in Hawke's chest, and he took her by the arms and held her pinioned. His hands were frighteningly strong, but his eyes and voice had a paralyzing effect on her. "You like to play with men. I have no family, no wife, no country—and no God, as far as I can tell." His voice grew rough, and he released her so quickly that she staggered. "Don't play with me, Blanche!"

He turned to go, but she caught his arm, pulling him around. The moonlight changed the tears in her eyes to silver as she whispered brokenly, "I—don't want to do that, Hawke! Forgive me!"

Knowing instinctively that her pride had been hurt as perhaps never before, his anger receded. He shook his head, and a smile came to his lips touched by the depth of sadness in his eyes.

"It was my fault. But it won't happen again. I'm a common sailor, Blanche, and for you to think of me any differently would be wrong. So—I thank you for taking care of me—but this can't happen again."

He turned and walked away, and she slowly moved along the line of flowers toward the house. The scene had left her trembling and empty, but there was a stubborn and rebellious streak that ran deep in Blanche Rommey, and she thought, *No, he's not a common seaman. I don't know what he is—but he's not a common man—in any way!*

★　★　★　★

The sultry heat of summer gave way to the cool breezes of winter, bringing refreshment to the crew of the *Neptune*—at least to those not stricken by the virulent attack of fever that had fallen on the ship.

It was mid-January, and for six months Captain Rommey had been highly satisfied with the crew and the ship. They had taken three heavily laden American merchant ships, and even had a slight taste of combat with a fast frigate that had refused to be fully engaged. "Fine training exercise for the men!" Rommey had smiled grimly. "Not enough to bloody them, but a taste of powder and the sound of the guns. Now—we're ready for *real* action!"

But then on the second of February, Jenson, one of the lower deckhands, had fallen to a bone-cracking fever, and in five days, a quarter of the crew was down. Dr. Mann's treatment was the same as for every other illness—purging and bleeding. His brutal methods almost destroyed those he treated, and many of the crew dragged around sick to keep out of his hands.

Langley nervously approached Captain Rommey on the poop deck, saying, "Captain, wouldn't it be wise to put about? I mean, we don't have enough men to fight an engagement."

Rommey's frosty eyes considered the young lieutenant briefly; then he shook his head. "We're able to handle any rebels that come our way."

There was no room for argument, so Langley moved aft and said moodily to Burns, who was staring off in the hazy distance, "Captain won't hear of going back to port—so I pray God we don't run into an enemy frigate!"

"That's as God wills, Clarence." The dour Calvinism of the reply angered Langley, and he turned and left the deck. Two hours later when the lookout cried, "Deck! Sail off port bow!" Langley had a premonition, and he yelled, "What ship?"

"Sloop, sir! Twenty-four guns!"

Ordinarily the *Neptune* would be able to take care of such an adversary with ease, but with so many men ill, there would be little difference in the firepower of the two ships, and the sloop had the advantage of being faster and far more maneuverable.

"Beat to quarter!" Captain Rommey called the order loudly, and two small marine drummers ran to the larboard gangway, pulling on their black shakos and fumbling with their sticks. They beat a tattoo, their faces tight with concentration, and men poured up from below. The marines hurried aft and aloft to the tops, their uniforms shining like blood in the sunlight, with Captain Baxter in the lead.

Below deck Burns had the guns run out, and then walked along the larboard guns, his heart filled with doubt as he saw the pickup crews. At one gun a man stared without comprehension as a captain put a rope into his hand. Burns tried to instill some courage in the crew, calling out, "Men, we are going to engage that ship. Do nae hurry—just take your time and obey orders, and all will be well."

Hawke crouched beside his gun, sweating freely in spite of the breeze blowing through the open port. He saw the sloop, rebel flag flying, making a turn and his heart pumped against his ribs like the beating of a drum. It was like one of his nightmares with every detail clear and stark, but he was not afraid.

The men he had been given were pallid with fear, so he said easily, "Well, lads, we'll give the rebels a lesson, eh? Come, Harry, see to the slow match—quickly now!" He gave them something to do, keeping their minds off the ship that drew ever closer; and his eyes met those of Whitefield, who gave him a nod and a wink.

Topside Rommey was waiting until the last moment to set his sail, for if he timed it right, the smaller ship would come under his guns for one brief moment sooner than the sloop could bring her own guns to bear. "It has to be just right, Langley," he insisted, then watched the closing ship carefully. Finally he shouted, "Stand by to go about!"

The mizzen yard was squeaking and the helmsman, Spence, cried out, "Ready, sir!"

"Put the helm down!"

The order came from Rommey. Up forward the headsail sheets had already been released, and as the wheel went over and the great hull began to swing very slowly into the wind, Langley urged the men at the braces to even greater efforts as they strained back, their eyes on the yards above them.

Sails boomed and swelled, and as the ship continued to swing, Rommey commanded, "Off tacks and sheets!"

This was the moment, they all knew, and there was a tangle of flapping sails and jerking shrouds—and then they saw it! "Captain! There's not enough men to handle the sail!" Langley called out in horror. The ship fell back, helpless in the water as the fore-topmen struggled like madmen to set the sail.

"She'll blow us out of the water!" Langley moaned.

"Order the marines to open fire!" the captain ordered, disgusted with Langley's fright. "Get more men on those sails!"

Below deck, Burns felt the ship fall back and knew what to expect. He stood near Whitefield and their eyes met. "For what we are about to receive," Burns said so quietly that only the gunner could hear him, "may we be duly grateful!"

Looking out the port, Hawke realized that in the next few moments he might be dead. He took a deep breath, studied the sloop, then said, "Lads, we'll have to let them have first shot—but our turn will come!"

Suddenly the hull shuddered beneath his feet and splintering woodwork flew in every direction. The air quivered and shook with the crash of guns and the nerve-jarring scream of cannon balls as they whipped through the smoke like beings from hell.

The scream of passing shot mingled with closer, more unearthly sounds as flying splinters ripped into the packed gunners and bathed the smooth deck with scarlet. In the midst of this, men ran blindly, hopelessly trying to escape. Midshipman Symmes, who was in charge of gun number seven, fell to the floor clawing at it as if he could burrow into it and hide. Burns hurried to him immediately and kicked him hard, screaming, "Get up, you coward!" and lashed at him with a cane until he resumed his position with wild, mad eyes.

Hawke saw splashes of blood and gristle on the bulkhead, and as he turned he realized that one of the guns had been upended and its crew annihilated. One man lay legless, a handspike still gripped and ready.

Panic ran through the gun deck, and only the will of Lieutenant Burns and a few old hands like Whitefield kept the men at their stations.

Another broadside like that, Burns thought, *and we're done!* He waited, knowing that only if the ship regained the wind could they avoid the hail of metal that would sweep them to bloody death. Slowly he felt the ship tilt and he shouted, "She's comin' about; get ready to fire!"

But just at that moment, a ball came screaming across the water and flew right through a gunport. The shot struck a deck support, which broke its powerful flight—but a splinter went whirring through the air, striking Lieutenant Burns in the back.

He fell to the floor with a cry—panic, until now held in check, spilling over. Helplessly, he writhed on the deck, pain driving him half mad. Still he struggled to regain his feet, for he saw the crews leaving their guns, running mindlessly toward the hatch.

If we don't return their fire, they'll blow us out of the water! he thought—and he called on his God to help.

Hawke knew nothing about tactics—but even in the midst of the screaming shot and the terror-stricken men, he saw clearly through the port that the sloop was coming back to finish them off. He felt also the ship lift beneath his feet, and quick as flash, he knew that if the *Neptune* could get off a broadside, they would not be lost.

But how? He leaped to his feet, and was almost knocked down by the blind, stampeding crew. Then he saw Enoch and three other gun captains fighting to keep the men away from the hatch—but it was a losing battle, he realized instantly. The crew was clawing blindly, deaf to any orders; only a miracle would turn them.

Suddenly Hawke caught sight of Burns writhing on the floor, bathed in his own blood, but struggling to get to his feet. Without a logical process of thought, Hawke sprang to his side, and Burns looked up with a plea in his eyes. With a sudden gesture, Hawke ripped the man's sword from his side, and with a piercing cry threw himself into the fray.

He was a madman among madmen—but there was more fury in his madness than they could face. Like a screaming banshee, he ran along the line of men who were forcing Whitefield and the other gunners to the wall, and he slashed them with a blade that was a mere flash of silver in the smoke-filled air. "Back to those guns!" he screamed. There was no man able to face that blade—so they fell back, one, then another; and finally, as Whitefield and the others grabbed their weapons, the tide turned.

From where he lay, Burns watched in awe, and as the men were driven back to the guns, he looked up and breathed a faint prayer, "Thank ye, God!"

Back and forth down the line, Hawke shouted, pushing men into position, cursing and slashing with his sword. "Load!" he screamed. "Look, the captain's got us moving! All we have to do is let her have a belly full, lads! Fire! Fire! Bring your guns to bear!"

Topside, Captain Rommey was staring at the sloop as she took the full brunt of the heavy guns. He had been expecting nothing but death and disaster. After the terrible pounding the ship had taken, he had scarcely dared hope that his men could return the fire—but now he saw the sloop riddled by the heavy shot, and the crew gave a shout as she suddenly turned and fled.

"Not a victory, perhaps," he said quietly to himself. "But we'll fight another day."

"I'm going below," he announced to Langley. "Handle the ship."

He hurried to the gun deck, swept the scene quickly, then went to where the hands were pulling Lieutenant Burns to a sitting position.

"How bad is it, Burns?"

"Painful, sir—but it'll nae be the death o' me."

"You did well, sir!" the captain expressed with thankfulness, kneeling beside the wounded man. "You saved the ship."

"No, sir," Burns objected through white lips. "I was doon on the deck. It was Seaman Hawke who rallied the men. We'd ha' been gone if he hadna taken over when I went doon."

"I see." Slowly Captain Rommey rose, his eyes fixed on Hawke, who was trying to stop the flow of blood from a wounded man. "He did that, did he?"

"Aye, sir, he did." Burns was gritting his teeth against the pain, but he nodded across the gun deck, adding, "Midshipman Symmes is dead, sir."

"Let's get you to the surgeon, Burns," Rommey said. "And I'll see to it that he does a good job—or I'll keelhaul the butcher!" He did exactly that, standing right behind Mann, who was so nervous he did the best job of his life, extracting the splinter from Burns's back.

Then Rommey left, and when the battle damage was being repaired, he sent for Hawke. He was seated at his desk staring out the stern windows when the man came in.

"Yes, sir?"

Rommey stood up and came to stand before Hawke, saying, "Burns told me how you rose higher than your duty during the action. I commend you."

"Why—"

"And I have a daring scheme to propose to you. I intend to make you midshipman, effective at once. You are old for that rank, but I'll give you a brevet commission as an ensign, or even as a junior lieutenant, depending on how rapidly you advance. I *must* have a navigator, and now that Lieutenant Burns is out of action for an indeterminate period, I need a man who can stand watch." He paused and studied Hawke's face. "Well, what do you think?"

Hawke's face did not change, though a light leaped into his eyes. He considered the face of the captain, then slowly smiled. "Sir, I think you'll be letting yourself in for a great deal of trouble. I'm not an officer."

"How do you know?"

"Why . . . !"

"You're a man who isn't anything—which means really, you can *be* anything." The stern features of Rommey softened, and he said warmly, "I'm aware that this is an unusual action—but we are in an unusual situation, Hawke. I *must* have help to sail this ship, and there's precious little help coming from the Admiralty! So—I'll use what I can lay my hands on, and let the Lords of the Admiralty whistle up a dead tree! Now, will you be my officer?"

Hawke stared at the tall captain, doubt in his even features.

Finally he nodded. "I'll do my best, Captain."

"Fine! Fine!" Rommey beamed. "It'll be a shock to the crew—but you'll just have to make them like it! Now, we have to get you a uniform, Midshipman Hawke—and then we have to let my officers know they have help."

The new midshipman smiled, and reminded his superior, "I'm an American, Captain. Have you thought of that? What if my memory comes back? You'll have a rebel for an officer."

"Blast it, no!" Captain Rommey growled. "You're too good a chap to be one of those wild-eyed fanatics! I'll wager when you recall who you are, you'll be delighted to find yourself a good, safe servant of King George!"

"Well, sir, I'm your man for now. God knows what I'll be in the future."

"We all must say that, sir," Rommey stated soberly, then turned to his work as the newest ensign in the Royal Navy left the cabin.

CHAPTER TWELVE

THE LIEUTENANT

★ ★ ★ ★

Accustomed as he was to being in command, it was a rare thing for Captain William Rommey to feel intimidated—but as he passed under the massive arch of the Admiralty House and asked a rigid guard in full dress for directions to Admiral Hood's office, he had to clear his throat to make the request.

"Down the hall, sir," the guard replied sternly. "The big double doors to your left."

Rommey almost thanked the man, but bit off the words. Wheeling quickly, he made his way down the marbled floors and found another secretary, a lieutenant with a pinched face and skin that had not seen the open sea for some time. "Can I help you, Captain?" he asked languidly.

"Captain William Rommey to see Admiral Hood!"

"Oh, yes, Captain. The admiral is expecting you."

The quick change in the fop's manner made Rommey feel better. He followed him inside and found the grizzled Hood turning from his huge window, and the admiral's warm handshake made him feel even more relieved.

"Well, now, Rommey, it's been a long time!" He motioned at a chair, and the two seated themselves in the glare of the May sunlight that flooded through the high-arched windows. "Let's see—I believe it was on the old *Dominant*, was it not—back in '64?"

"Yes, sir." Rommey gave the older man an admiring glance. Hood might be aging, but there was still that quick intelligence in his smallish brown eyes. "I was a midshipman under you in that fight with the *Fleur de Rose*."

"Ah, by gad—that *was* a hot one!" Hood laughed with delight and slapped his thigh. "You made a name for yourself that day, Rommey! Gad, sir, you did!"

The captain shifted uneasily, but as the admiral went on reminiscing about the old days, he felt a twinge of relief. He hated to ask favors, but that was exactly what he had come for.

His opportunity came quickly, for Hood soon asked, "Well, Captain, what is it? I know you've been in for refitting. Let's see, didn't I sign an order for you to put back to sea duty this week? I know you must want something—everybody does who comes through that door."

"Well—yes, sir."

Hood laughed again, and waved a hand in the air. "Gad, sir! You're a breath of fresh air! Most fellows come in here wanting something and they're too sly to come out with it! I like a man like you, Rommey! Now, what is it?"

Rommey cleared his throat and then pulled a paper from his pocket and handed it to the admiral. "This is what I want in writing, Admiral Hood, but I can put it very plainly in just a few words if you'll permit me."

"What is it? A bigger ship?"

"No, sir, I'm happy with my command."

"I've read your reports. Good work you've done with the *Neptune* in the Indies. How long have you been there?"

"Almost two years, sir. I set up my family in a house in Jamaica but have brought my wife and daughter back to England for a visit."

"Yes, I'd heard you had been forced to get your daughter out of the hands of some Frenchman. The Lords of Admiralty have been most pleased with your work—especially with the prizes you've taken. Every American ship you take puts that much of a crimp in this rebellion!"

"How does the matter look to you, Admiral?"

"Why, very well. That bumpkin Washington lost at Brandywine and Germantown—and I heard that their best general, Benedict Arnold, came to his senses and joined our side." The admiral took a pinch of snuff from a silver case on his desk, sniffed it, then sneezed. "As long as we control the sea—there's no way those clods can win, Rommey. And since they have no navy, they have no hope of winning at sea."

"But everyone knows the French are getting a fleet ready to send to that area."

"Well, let them! I hope they do, sir! Then we can wipe out the Frogs and the blasted rebels at one blow!"

"I must say, though, that some of the rebels have done very well—fitting out ships with guns—privateers."

"Oh, some of them are good seamen, of course—come from good English stock." Then the admiral laughed and tapped the captain on the knee, adding, "But that's what we have you and a few others down there for—to keep the blasted privateers from getting at our merchant ships. A few more like that fellow John Paul Jones, and we'd be in trouble!" Glancing quickly at the clock on the wall, he returned to the business at hand, asking, "Well, Rommey, what is it? You've done a magnificent job, and—within reason—I think I can meet with you on any reasonable request."

Rommey took a deep breath and began. "Well, sir, two years ago last December, we took some pressed men onto the *Neptune*, and one of them was injured. He recovered, but the injury had done something to his mind."

"Crazy?"

"No, sir, but he can't remember anything of his past—not even his name. . . ."

Rommey had thought his speech out, and he saw that the admiral was caught by it. He related how rapidly Hawke had been able to learn, and after being appointed midshipman, had made amazing progress.

"I've made a report, Admiral, of his progress, and I can only say that in all my years at sea, I've never known a man so fitted for command as Midshipman Hawke."

"You gave him a good name, Captain," Hood mused. He looked up with a sharp glance. "I suppose you want him promoted—is that it?"

"Yes, sir." Now that it was out, Rommey expelled his breath and hurried on. "It's a little—personal, sir." He tried to find some way to put the matter, then shrugged, saying bluntly, "My daughter fancies herself in love with the man—that's why I'm here."

"I can't promote a man to please your daughter!" Hood exploded.

"Of course not!" The tone of his commanding officer ruffled Rommey's nerves, and he shot back, "I would not have him on my ship on that basis, sir; but he has mastered the ship—and in action he's proven himself a cool man under fire." He stopped abruptly, rising to his feet, his face tinged with pink. "I'll not bother you about this matter any longer, sir."

"Now, Rommey!" The admiral got up at once and there was a smile of reconciliation on his broad face as he took the arm of the younger man. "You always did go off half-cocked! Not too good for an officer—but on the other hand, most of the good ones do have some temper. Now, sit down, and let me read this report."

As the admiral read through the report, Rommey stared at the fresh blooms on the plum tree outside the window, wondering if he was doing the right thing. *If it is, it'll be the first time I ever did the right thing where Blanche is concerned,* he thought grimly. He'd hinted to the girl about seeking a commission for Hawke, and she'd given him no peace. He thought she'd grow tired of Hawke as she had of others, but during the two years that had passed, she and Hawke had spent practically all the time together that shore leave permitted.

Finally Admiral Hood looked up and gave a shrug. "I have no problem with giving the man a commission, Rommey. From your report, he's a far sight better than most!" Then he tilted his head and looked at him searchingly. "Would you have the man for a son-in-law?"

Captain Rommey made a helpless gesture with his hands, got to his feet, and walked to the window. "With a daughter like mine, sir," he remarked, "I'll pretty well have to have what she gives me. But this man—he's better by far than any she's ever been interested in before."

"I dare say—but there's the matter of your family. You know nothing of the fellow. What sort of blood will he put in your family line? That's not a trifle, is it now?"

Rommey had thought of that many times, so he said evenly, "I think the man is of good stock, sir. Beyond that I can't say. But I *will* say that's he's fine officer material—and we need all we can get."

"Very well, I'll have his commission drawn up."

"Thank you, sir. I am in your debt."

Hood called the vapid lieutenant in and in a few minutes, he was handing the document to the captain, saying, "I don't know if I'm doing you a favor or not, Rommey—but I trust so. Keep me posted, will you?"

"Yes, sir—and thank you."

"You can thank me best by capturing those rebel privateers—" He had a sudden thought and snapped his fingers. "What's the name of the one that did the *Safire* in six months ago?"

"*The Gallant Lady*," Rommey said, a grim line settling along his jaw.

"That's the one. I wouldn't have thought a sloop could take a man like Crafton." The admiral shook his head. "That ship—she's made quite a name for herself."

"She's taken more prizes than the rest of the rebels put together, sir."

"Well, I trust you'll put a stop to that, Rommey!"

Captain Rommey slapped his thigh suddenly, and there was a cold, frosty light in his eyes as he answered, "I think I can promise you *that*, sir! It'll be my first order of business. That ship has got to be stopped—and the *Neptune* is just the ship that can do it!"

He left the Admiralty and walked along the busy street, paying little heed to the mass of people streaming along the way. He was a seaman, and the land for him was a place to stay until he could get back on the ocean—a man's proper place.

The sight of the *Neptune* brought a lift to his spirits, and he stood long enough to admire the clean lines, the new canvas, and the glitter of new brass. Even more than that which he could see, he was pleased with the bottom of the ship, for she had been coated with sheets of thin copper held in place by copper nails. This kept out the teredo, or shipworm, and the gribble, creatures that bored into the oak of the hull—and it had the added advantage of preventing barnacle growth, thereby increasing the speed of the ship. "Ought to get eleven knots out of her!" he gloated as he moved to the dock where his gig was waiting.

He spent the afternoon going over the ship, driving his officers with determination. The purser, the quartermaster, the master gunner, the carpenter, the sailmaker, the boatswain were all summoned to his cabin. Mercilessly he picked their reports apart, until one by one they left with pale faces. Rommey knew he was too hard, but he knew also that battles often were won or lost before a ship weighed anchor, and he was determined that a matter of too-little powder would not be the element that spelled defeat for the *Neptune*!

Finally he rose from his desk, saying, "Mr. Langley, I'm going ashore. We'll weigh anchor at dawn."

"Aye, aye, Captain."

There was a miserable look on Langley's face, and it irritated Rommey. *Won't he ever get over his blasted puppy love for Blanche?* he asked himself, then said harshly, "I'll spend the night on shore."

"What about Midshipman Hawke, sir?"

Rommey shook his head, knowing that his first lieutenant was jealous of Hawke and the relationship he had with Blanche.

"You get the ship ready, Mr. Langley—I'll see to *Lieutenant* Hawke!"

"Lieutenant—!"

"You heard correctly, Mr. Langley. You may pass the word that Mr. Hawke is now third lieutenant on this ship."

"Aye, aye, sir."

He won't like it, Rommey thought as he climbed into the gig. *But Burns will—and so will the men.* That was one thing that had encouraged him to seek a commission for Hawke. The men trusted him—and not because he was soft, either. Some men had that quality, Rommey well knew. He himself ruled by stern force, but he knew a few choice officers whom men would follow blindly with a loyalty that was not easily put into words. *Hawke—he's got it, whatever it is,* he mused. *And I intend to use it!*

By the time he reached the large mansion, the home of a friend who had prevailed upon him to stay during his time in England, where Blanche was enjoying a final party, it was dark. The house was lit up with hundreds of lanterns, and when he entered the large ballroom, he had to adjust his eyes to the brilliance of the huge chandeliers that threw golden gleams over the room. The ballroom was crowded with the cream of London society, but he had no eye for the vivid greens, reds, and blues of the ladies' gowns, nor for the bare shoulders and creamy arms that rose out of them.

Finally he found Blanche standing at a long table covered with crystal goblets and golden plates piled high with morsels of exotic food. He paused suddenly, taken aback by her appearance. She was wearing a low-cut crimson dress; around her neck a single flashing diamond was suspended by a golden chain. Her hair was down, cascading over her smooth shoulders, and the yellow beams of the candles made her blue eyes glow. He wondered, not for the first time, where she got her good looks, then tossed the thought away and moved toward the table.

Hawke, he saw, was there too, a slight smile on his face. *His white and blue uniform sets him off well,* Rommey thought. Usually

Hawke was alert, but the party had dulled his senses, or so it seemed. He looked up and saw Rommey, leaned over and spoke quietly to Blanche.

"Father, you're late! Let me get you some wine."

"Well, just one." His daughter's attitude, he realized, had mellowed toward him, and he wondered how much that was due to her desire to get a commission for Hawke. She was, he knew, determined to get her own way—and since he was that way himself, he could not exactly fault her.

"Come out of this blasted noise," he said, and a look of anticipation leaped into Blanche's eyes. He turned and led the two through a pair of French doors into a garden, and when he closed the doors, the sound of the party was muted.

When he turned to look at them, he stared at Hawke and wondered again if he was being a fool—but it was too late to alter his course. "I've been to the Admiralty, Hawke."

He waited for the other to reply, but Hawke merely waited. It was one of the things the captain liked about the man: he could keep his tongue still.

Blanche, however, could not, and she asked nervously, "Yes, Father?"

Reaching inside his coat, Rommey pulled the commission free and extended it to Hawke who took it, asking quietly, "What is this, Captain?"

"Your commission." Rommey experienced a thrill of pleasure, and grinned as shock leaped into Hawke's face. "Well! For *once*, by heaven, you're taken off guard!"

"Yes, sir—I am!"

"Oh, Hawke!" Blanche cried, taking his arm and staring at the document. "I can't believe it!"

"You ought to," Rommey grinned. "You moved heaven and earth to get me to go after it!"

She laughed in delight, and there was no shame in her. "You wanted to do it—but were just too stubborn."

"As to that, you're probably right," he said ruefully. "But how do you feel about it, *Lieutenant* Hawke?"

There was one sign that gave Hawke away, Blanche had learned: when he was troubled—or pleased—he would touch the scar that ran down his cheek. He did so now, but there was a pleased light in his eyes as he looked at the captain. "I'm very glad, of course." Then a shadow fell on his face as he spoke. "I have no other life other than the one you've made for me, Captain Rommey. I'll serve you the best I can."

"I know you'll do that, Lieutenant Hawke. Now I must go. I'm spending the night at the inn. Take my gig. We'll weigh anchor at dawn, so get a good night's sleep."

"Aye, sir—and thank you."

After her father left the terrace, Blanche took Hawke's arm and shook it fiercely. "Is *that* all you can say? You're an old stick, that's what you are!"

"I'm very happy, Blanche."

"Ah, you're afraid to show how you feel—that's your trouble! You've got a career, Hawke! If you can't shout, why, dance with me!"

She fell into his arms, and they began to dance across the paved surface, and soon he was grinning at her. "You just want me to be a lieutenant because you're ashamed to be seen at your parties with a midshipman."

"That's it," she laughed. "And I won't be happy long with a mere lieutenant. A post captain—that's what you've got to be, Hawke!"

"Why not an admiral?"

"Why not? Shoot for the stars!"

He laughed, and she joined him, saying, "It's taken a long time to make you laugh, Hawke. I've invested two years of my life in you."

He paused, shook his head, and asked, "Why did you bother, Blanche? You could have anybody."

"Oh, I want—"

"You want something *different*," he finished more soberly. "I'm just a freak, you know, Blanche."

"Don't say that!"

His face looked thin in the faint light of the lanterns, and he said quietly, "You think it's romantic having a man who doesn't have a past. But it's not a game, Blanche."

She bit her lip, sobered for once, and then she put her arms around his neck and looked up into his face. "I'm not playing games, Hawke," she whispered. "I want you!"

The air was quiet, and he could hear the sound of cowbells far off on the night air. Holding her, he thought of the past two years, and realized that she had come to be the center of his world. His life with men on the *Neptune* was half of his world—and she was the rest of it.

"When I try to think of life without you," he murmured, looking into her eyes, "I can never do it. If it weren't for you, Blanche, I'd not have made it."

She pulled his head down and kissed him, and was shocked at the emotion running through herself. But she had long known that he was one of the most physically desirable men she had ever known.

"You don't need a past, sweet!" she whispered. "We've got a future—and that's all that counts!"

The rest of the night was like a dream to Hawke. They went back into the ballroom and continued drinking wine, Hawke trying to keep pace with Blanche. When they left the ballroom, it was very late, and he was so dizzy from the wine, he could scarcely give directions to Blanche's home to the cab driver.

He fumbled his way up the stairs, and then she said, "Come inside—just for a moment! You'll be gone for so long!"

It was much later when he left her room and walked all the way to the wharf where the captain's gig was still waiting. The crew of the small boat had been drinking, but he paid no heed. He got out of the boat and made his report to the officer on watch.

"Midshipman Hawke returning to duty, sir."

Burns grinned at him, returned his salute. "Not *Midshipman*, I think!" Then he turned and when they were below deck, he added, "Congratulations, man! Ye'll be a bonny officer."

"Thanks, Angus," he said faintly.

Burns looked at him more closely, and sniffed his breath. "Ah! A bit of the grape, eh? Weel, ye do deserve it."

"I—I think I'll get a bit of air before I turn in," Hawke replied. He left and made his way to the stern, and for a long time stood there staring at the myriad lights of London as they winked across the velvet blackness of the night.

Finally he shook his head, turned, and went below, thinking of the future. That night he dreamed of Blanche and her long black hair spread out like a fan on a linen pillow—and the dream frightened him, bringing him upright in his hammock. He could not remember being afraid, but now he was—and he did not know why.

He had not felt his alien past so keenly before. For long hours, until the first rays of dawn thrust red and gold fingerlike beams across his face, he lay there, and then the boatswain's whistle shrilled, and he got up to face his new world.

CHAPTER THIRTEEN

A New Lady

★ ★ ★ ★

"Why is it every time you two get together you fight like wildcats?"

William Alden looked over his foaming glass of ale toward Charity and Daniel Greene with a mixture of humor and irritation in his sharp blue eyes. Taking a pull at the brew, he added mischievously, his voice rusty, "And I allus thought that you Quaker fellers was set against fightin'. Sure don't seem like it, Friend Daniel. Here you jump into this fight against King George with both feet. Then like that ain't enough action, you get engaged to this girl of mine—and you fight with her worse than with the Redcoats."

"She'd drive an angel to pick a fight, Mr. Alden, and *you* know it better than anyone else!" Dan retorted sharply, dropping the characteristic "thee," as he often did since his association with the Aldens. Greene's square face was ruddy with irritation, and there was a trace of real anger in him when he nodded at Charity and added, "If thee had been brought up with the Friends, thee would have a better idea of how to act like a lady."

"If I don't suit you, Dan, you'd better take your ring back."

"No! Don't say that!" She was, he saw, pulling at the thick band of gold that had been his mother's, and he went to her quickly. Holding her hands tightly he prevented her from pulling the ring from her finger, and shook his head sadly. "Why am I always the one to have to beg? And this time I'm *right*, Charity—even thy father says so."

"Oh, Dan, we've been over it a hundred times!" Charity pulled away from his grip and walked to the window. She stared out at the delicate cherry blossoms beginning to fall from the tree outside, and said nothing, but there was a stubbornness in the straight set of her back. Finally she sighed and turned to face them. As she began to speak, Dan was caught again by the beauty of her face, and thought back to the last two years and his struggle to keep from falling in love with her. He had not wanted it, for there was a reserve in Charity that he could not break down. He knew she did not love him as he did her, but he had gone after her with the same dogged persistence that marked everything he did. But even though she had finally (after six months hard pursuit on his part) agreed to be engaged, Charity seemed to be more distant than ever. Not that she didn't show flashes of affection, but more often she seemed to hold him off at arms' length.

He listened to her words, but he was asking himself silently, *Does she really love me?* And he was so afraid of the answer that he buried the thought and paid closer heed to her words.

". . . so we've done well because we've been able to outsail any ship the British have. But we've missed a dozen rich prizes because the *Lady* doesn't have the guns to take any ship except merchantmen. But if we sell the *Lady* and get a ship with bigger guns, don't you see? Why, we could hit the convoys and take what we pleased!"

Her father stared at her doubtfully. "Sell the *Lady*?" he murmured, then shook his head. "You're talking about a whole new thing, daughter. We can sail a ship—but engage an enemy warship? Why, we'd be lost!"

"Not if we got a good crew—and there are plenty of sailors just begging for a berth. A lot of them served on a ship of the line or one of the king's frigates."

"Thee would have us buy a frigate?" Dan asked sharply, unbelief in his face. "It takes *hundreds* of men for a ship like that. Why, even a brig would be—"

"Oh, Dan, a brig would be no good for a privateer!" Charity's green eyes lit up as she began to speak rapidly. It was an idea which had come to her months earlier, and now that she had shared it with her father and Dan, she was eloquent in her plea. "Look, if you use a schooner, she'll crush like an eggshell if you try to lay her alongside a heavy ship in any kind of sea. They're too delicate!

And if a British sloop of war ever takes out after the *Lady* and the topmast carries away, you know we'd be lost."

"Why can't we put heavier cannon on the *Lady*?" Dan asked.

"She's not made for fighting, but for freighting," Charity returned. "Look, what we need is a smaller craft, a sloop. Then we can use fewer men. You can come down on some lordly merchantman and blow him out of the water. You can tack three times to anybody else's once—and the heavier British ships won't waste time chasing you because they know they'd never catch you."

William Alden rubbed his chin and studied the face of his daughter. He had become a rabid Patriot in the years since his son's death at Valley Forge. Every prize they took from the hated British and consigned to the struggling forces of Washington seemed to be a taste of revenge, and for the first time he began to think that Charity's scheme was not as wild as it had seemed at first.

"Well, I'd do 'bout anything to put a crimp in the Britishers. What sort of ship are you thinking of?" he asked cautiously.

Charity hesitated slightly, and there was just a touch of a blush on her tanned cheeks. "Well, Father, actually, I've already found the ship."

"What!" Dan looked at her in consternation, and then shook his head in despair, but said no more.

"Last month she came through and took on supply. A good fast sloop, bigger than most—about ninety tons. Thirty or forty can fight her as well as a hundred and twenty could fight a brig. But she's already armed with enough guns—and there's plenty of room for a fair load of prisoners and for the prize cargo. And there's not a British-built vessel of any size whatever that can catch her."

"Where's she located?"

"Twenty miles south, Father, in Portleigh Harbor—and I know we can get her cheap. The captain's name is Benteen, and he's afraid he'll lose the ship in this war."

"Tomlison offered me six thousand for the *Lady* last week. He'd go to seven, I reckon."

Charity laughed out loud, pleasure spreading over her face. "Let's go take a look, Father. You'll not be able to say *no* to this one."

Then she went to Dan and put her arm through his, and looking up with a glint of affection in her eyes, urged engagingly, "Come on, Friend Daniel, wipe that frown off your face. You may like my plan better when you hear what I've got planned for you."

"I can't wait," he said grumpily, and stalked off, his pride injured. But later that day when they were on their way to see the ship, he brought the matter up. They were alone in the buggy, Charity's father having gone off on other business. The air was sweet with blossoms and the smell of new grass. Taking off his coat and putting it behind the seat, he looked at the warm blue sky and the rich greenery of the landscape.

"Not much like our buggy ride from Valley Forge, is it, Charity?"

"No." She bit her lip and shook her head, sending her auburn hair cascading like waves in the sun. "I don't like to think about that winter. I thought they'd all die in that place."

"They didn't, though." He smiled at her and added, "Christmas Winslow came through it."

The thought of the fat baby drove the gloom away, and she replied happily, "He's the prettiest thing I ever saw!"

"I've seen one thing prettier," Dan said quickly. He slipped his arm around her and drew her close. She did not resist, but when he kissed her, though her lips were warm and soft, there was something in her that held back. He quickly released her and said hurriedly to cover up his disappointment, "I guess Christmas is about the only high point right now."

"Things aren't going well for Washington, are they?"

That was putting it mildly, for though Washington and his ragtag continentals had lived through the winter of 1778 at Valley Forge, they had been on the run ever since. Clinton, the British general, had attempted to move his army from Philadelphia to New York, and in the battle of Monmouth, the Revolution had nearly gone to pieces. Washington's most trusted general, Charles Lee, had broken and commanded a retreat, and only the dramatic appearance of Washington had saved the day. He had dismissed Lee (which was, in Dan's mind, a move long overdue), and all that year the British had chased the Americans around like foxhounds on the scent.

Late that year a French fleet had come to help, but through a series of misfortunes had given up and left for the West Indies. Washington had almost wept, Dan had told Charity, for the general was convinced that only when they could cut the British off from their navy was there any hope of winning the war.

"It hurt the general when Arnold turned traitor, didn't it, Dan?" Charity remarked.

"Like to have killed him! He was the best we had, Charity."
He studied the landscape, then shook his head. "Never know what
went on in that man's mind. I reckon it was pride. He was sharp,
intelligent, but they never gave him any good posts."

"Are we going to make it?"

He looked at her in surprise. "God knows, Charity. I sure
don't."

They said no more, for the cause they loved was at the lowest
ebb. Finally they pulled into the small harbor and Charity cried,
"There she is!"

He looked up to see a tall-masted ship standing off shore, and
drove down to the landing. He gave a one-eyed fisherman a coin
to take them out, and soon Charity was talking animately with
Captain Thomas Benteen, a tall man with a thick mop of black hair.

Dan ran his eye over the ship while Charity went right at the
bargaining. "Don't think you'll be able to get much of a price for
your vessel, Captain," she expressed with a shrug. "She's too slow
for a privateer."

Benteen snorted and slapped the rail with his hand. "Not fast
enough! Why, she'll do thirteen knots!"

"Not likely!"

The casual treatment of his boast angered the tall man, and he
exploded, "Listen to me! This ship is staunch and she's gentle, but
she's fast. She can do better than ten knots for twenty-four hours
on end, and she ain't never been pushed. This ship is sweet as a
nut and sound as a bell . . . !"

Dan left and wandered around the ship. He had made three
short cruises on the *Lady* and liked the sea. There had been little to
do with the army, and Washington had suggested, "Chaplain, the
best favor you can do for me right now—besides your prayers, of
course—is to do anything you can to get guns, food, and supplies.
That young woman is doing more with the *Lady* than the whole
Congress of the United States." He had clamped his lips shut suddenly, for as everyone knew, he considered himself a servant of
Congress and would permit no one to criticize it. And this despite
the fact that in actuality Congress did practically nothing to help
the starving troops.

He returned from his walk around the deck in time to see
Charity and Benteen shaking hands. "You got yourself a sweet
ship, missy," Benteen was saying, and he looked sadly around the
deck. "I'll never get a better!"

"My father will have to agree, Captain," Charity stated. "But he will!"

For over two hours Dan followed Charity around the ship, taking pleasure in her delight. She poked into every cranny and climbed the spars. Finally he said, "Thee is like a child with a new toy." Then he added ruefully, "Wish thee were as proud of me as of this ship!"

She laughed and took his hand. "You'll love her just as much, Dan."

"Not me. I'm a landsman."

She looked at him soberly, saying, "I want you to do something. I'm not sure if you'll like it."

"What?"

"I want you to join Father and me permanently on the *Lady*." She cut off his startled protest by putting her hands across his lips. "Just listen for one minute. You're not a sailor, Dan, but we need someone we can trust. We're going to be taking thousands of dollars of prize cargo aboard, and it'll be a temptation to some of the crew. You're a strong man, Dan, and I'd feel safer if you'd come with me."

A warmth spread through Dan, and he was pleased with her request. It was the only time she'd ever asked for help, and he replied joyously, "Why, I'd be happy to come, Charity, but I'd feel out of place. I hardly know the mizzenmast from the jib."

"But you know guns," she said quickly. "We're going to arm this vessel until we can take on anything smaller than a frigate, and a good master gunner is hard to find."

He was attracted at once, for he had spent months with Henry Knox's command, the artillery. Much of that time he had helped them train, learning much about ordnance. He was tired of inactivity, so all day long as they drove back to town, he allowed her to persuade him. Finally that night after supper, he told her, "All right, I'll go see if my uncle will let me transfer. And if he will, I'll get the best gunners in Knox's artillery to teach me all they know about cannon."

"Oh, Dan, won't it be wonderful!" Her green eyes glowed, catching the lantern light, and she for the first time threw herself in his arms. "We'll get fitted out as soon as we can, and then look out, King George!"

He was suddenly speechless, for the rich curves of her body pressed against him was unnerving. He smiled warmly, saying hopefully, "Maybe we'll make the first voyage a honeymoon trip?"

She looked up, returning his smile. "Maybe so. You get the new *Lady* ready to fight, and I might just think about it!"

★   ★   ★   ★

"I still don't see why we have to have them here for dinner, Charles!"

Dorcas Winslow had made the same complaint steadily for a week, ever since her husband had told her that he had invited his brother Adam and the rest of the family for a meal. Now as she looked over the glittering white cloth covered with silver plates and polished crystal glasses, she made one final protest.

"What possessed you to do this?" she demanded, staring at him with displeasure. She was an attractive woman, a little overweight, but with fine features and beautiful hair. There was, to be sure, a selfish cast to her face, and it was accented now. It had been a long time since Charles had deliberately ignored her wishes, and she was angry.

Charles glanced at her, weighing his words. "I think it's wise, Dorcas."

"But *why*?"

"Because we're Loyalists. You seem to have forgotten that." He lifted his gaze and considered the room. "If it weren't for Adam, we'd be in a shack or a prison somewhere—like most of our friends. I don't think you'd like that, Dorcas."

Charles had become a silent man since the loss of his son. His sickness had ended, or at least he had overcome it. As the months passed, Dorcas kept waiting for him to become more lively, but even as his health improved, there was a sadness in his countenance, and she could not remember too well the smiling, carefree man she had married. He had gone back to his business, leaving early and coming in rather late, so the house was not a happy place.

"Is—is there something you haven't told me, Charles?" Dorcas lifted a hand to her throat as a sudden spasm of dread gripped her. When the rebels had taken the city, she had nearly gone mad with fear, seeing her best friends torn from their homes and either shipped to England or cast out of their homes to make their way as best they could. She now was caught by that anxiety and came to grasp her husband's arm. "Are we in danger?"

"Why, certainly, we are!" Charles stated with a mild surprise. His broad lips turned upward in a smile, and he added, "We are enemies of this government, Dorcas, in name at least. We've been living on the razor's edge. Only Adam has kept us safe."

There was a sudden sound that made Dorcas give a nervous twitch, and he said, "They're here—and I think you'd be wise to make yourself pleasant to my family."

"Yes, Charles, of course," she assured him, and she was able to compose herself as they made their way to the spacious foyer. Charles was at her side, and she smiled graciously at the guests.

"Adam, you're looking well—and you are looking beautiful, Molly."

Dorcas thought how unlike they were, these two half brothers. Adam was thickset and dark, while Charles had the tall figure and blonde good looks of the Winslow clan. But Molly fit perfectly with her husband, and Dorcas spoke quickly to her, "How nice of you to come."

Molly Winslow was English by birth, with fine facial features. Her ash-blonde hair and gray eyes gave her a youthful look, and she said, "Thank you, Dorcas. We really came just to force you to see our grandson."

Dorcas looked up at the tall figure of Nathan and his wife Julie, and a pang went through her as a thought of Paul forced itself into her mind. Nathan and Paul were almost exactly the same age, and though they did not favor each other physically, there was something about Winslow men that could not be hidden.

To conceal the bitter thought that her own son was gone and this one lived, she looked at the baby Julie held and exclaimed, "What a beautiful child! What's his name?"

Julie held the baby to the light. "His name is Christmas. He was born on Christmas night at Valley Forge, Mrs. Winslow."

"Well, that's a fine name—and a fine boy." Charles Winslow moved to see the child clearly, and Adam, standing to one side, saw what the others missed. He loved his brother, despite the differences they had had in the past, and he knew him well. As Charles looked down on the fat baby and put out a finger for the child to seize, a sudden twitch ran across his lips, and Adam understood that the grief over Paul, his only son, was burning in him like a live coal.

Charles turned away blindly, saying in a husky voice, "Come, let's go eat, Adam—and all of you."

"Well, there's more of us than you invited, Charles," Adam began, then hesitated. Charles paused and turned to see a young couple who had been standing at the door.

Daniel Greene stepped forward and said, "I tried to talk Major Winslow out of bringing us, but—"

"I know about that, Reverend," Charles said with a sudden smile at his brother. "He's a hard man to say no to."

Charity was feeling terribly uncomfortable. Daniel had taken her to see the baby, and Adam had simply swept them along. "We've not had an invitation from my brother for a long time, and I want you to go with us."

"But, Major," Daniel had protested, "thee knows about the trouble I had with their son. It would be very uncomfortable."

Adam had simply overruled. "I want you to come." Molly had remained quiet, but Adam had told her when they were alone, "I'm afraid for Charles and Dorcas. Paul is dead, and they're not accepting it. I hope there's no bitterness in them against Daniel, but if there is, I want them both to face up to it—because a bitterness that isn't voiced eats at a man like a cancer."

But now Charity's eyes met those of Dorcas Winslow, and both of them were speechless. Each was thinking of their last meeting. Besides this, Charity's thoughts went back to the traumatic scene she'd had with their son, and the memory of it was suddenly raw and fresh.

Dorcas, however, merely said, "We're happy to have you all. I'm sorry our daughter Anne is away. Come in, please."

The moment of discomfort was broken as they made their way down the hall, and Dorcas busied herself seating the guests. She paused only when Charles's mother, Martha, a small, arthritic figure, came into the dining room, walking carefully, as if she were terribly afraid that her fragile bones would break.

"Why, Martha, how are you?" Adam went to her at once, and Charity gazed with interest at the sight. She had learned enough of the Winslow family history to know that the relationship between the two had not always been so pleasant. Martha Jakes had married Miles Winslow, and Adam, Miles's son by another woman, had not been a favorite. She had managed to sway her husband's favor from Adam to the son born to her and Miles, so that Charles had been the favorite.

But there was no trace of rancor in Adam Winslow, though the woman who had mistreated him so shamefully was now sickly and at his mercy. He must have sensed that it was gall to her to know that she was safe only because he made it possible. He took her thin hand carefully, and put the other on her frail shoulder, saying,

"It's good to see you again, Martha."

How different these Winslows are! Charity thought as she watched. *I've heard that Charles was a bounder in his youth, and his son was a rotter—but there is such gentleness in Adam and Nathan. There must be a streak of wildness in the Winslow breed!*

The old woman ducked her head, thinking perhaps of the hard treatment she'd inflicted on Adam when she was younger and he was helpless; and when she raised her face, a trace of tears glinted in her faded eyes. "Thank you, Adam. That's—that's like you."

Charles did not miss this, and laid his hand on Adam's burly shoulder. "It is like you, Adam." Then a flash of rare humor struck him and he laughed. "You and Mother weren't quite so friendly when you and I blew father's black Winslow chickens to bits—along with her prize rug! Remember that awful cannon you made?"

The memory brought a smile to Adam's broad face, and he replied ruefully, "I've never forgotten it. Father was so proud of those chickens."

"Well, never mind," Charles laughed. "They survived—or some of them did—we're having their offspring for supper! Come along now."

The meal went well after that, and Charity sat quietly beside Daniel, eating the delicious food, but not missing a word. Adam did most of the talking, mostly about the boyhood he had shared with Charles.

There was something in Charles's face that puzzled Charity. He was a handsome man, thin from sickness, and his face hollowed from the illness that had almost destroyed him. He was, she saw, toying with his food, thinking of other things. Finally he said, "I remember when you and Molly came back from Whitefield's meeting, Adam. You'd been converted." He paused and asked quietly, "Have you changed your mind?"

"In what way, Charles?"

"Well, so many are carried away with these 'revivals,' but after it's over the people don't seem to have been changed."

Adam reached over and took Molly's hand as he asked, "How about you, Molly? Are you still a servant of the Lord?"

Molly answered simply, "Ever since that moment when we took Christ as Savior and Lord, we've wanted nothing else, Charles."

The simplicity of the answer and the light in the eyes of the couple seemed to fascinate Charles, and he stared long at them, saying at last, "I see that you are happy."

Adam longed to speak a word to his brother about his soul, but it didn't seem the right time, so he refrained from saying anything. But he felt Molly squeeze his hand and knew that she would be praying for Charles. She was an intercessor of power, awesome in her efforts when she called on God for someone.

The rest of the meal was pleasant, and the visit in the long drawing room was equally so. But just before they left, a casual remark brought a sense of discomfort to the group.

They had carefully avoided any talk of politics, for the Tory in Charles and the Patriot in Adam would never mix. But a chance remark by Daniel in response to something Charles said brought the comfortable atmosphere to an end.

"How are things with you—in the chaplain business, I mean?" Charles asked Daniel. "Are the soldiers very religious?"

"Well, sir, I'm not with the army any longer. My uncle, General Greene, has assigned me to a new duty."

"What is that?" Charles asked.

"Why, my fiancee and her father are owners of a privateer— *The Gallant Lady.* I'm first mate and master gunner." Ordinarily Daniel Greene was a perceptive man, but he was so full of the past few months on the *Lady* that he did not see the flicker of warning in Adam Winslow's eyes. He said with some excitement, "We've made six voyages in as many months, and we've taken more prizes than we thought possible, Mr. Winslow!"

As he spoke of the sea with all the enthusiasm of a newcomer to an art, he did not see that Charles Winslow's lips were trembling, nor catch the warning shake of his head. Dorcas, too, was visibly shaken. Finally he paused, and realized from the awkward silence in the room that something was wrong.

Charles spoke slowly. "Paul was very fond of the sea. If he'd not died, I think he would have made a most able sailor." Then he turned and said in a whisper, "I'm not feeling well—pray excuse me, Adam—all of you—good of you to come . . ."

As he left the room, the guests felt a sudden urge to take their leave. They made their exits as quickly as possible, and as soon as they were clear of the house, Daniel said to Adam, "I'm awfully sorry, Major! I never once thought—"

"It's not your fault, Dan." He put his hand in a kindly fashion on the young man's arm, adding, "Don't fret."

Later on, Nathan brought up the subject, saying, "I know Uncle Charles wouldn't think so—but it's best that Paul died. He was marked for a bad end."

Charity had been strongly affected by the evening. She wrote in her diary that night:

> I feel so strange tonight. I wish we hadn't gone to Paul Winslow's house. It's like a ghost come back. I remember all the nightmares I had after I struck him and cut his cheek—and then when he disappeared, it was as though I was somehow responsible! But I'm not! I'm not!
>
> How sad they were, Charles and his wife. To lose an only son when you're too old to have another! He was bad, but if he'd lived, maybe he could have become better. Nathan says not, but you never know.
>
> Oh, God, don't let me dream of that time anymore! Let him stay in his grave—Paul Winslow!

But that night, she dreamed again of Paul Winslow seizing her. In the dream she moved in slow motion, cutting his cheek open so that the blood ran in crimson rivulets down his maimed cheek. Suddenly her eyes flew open, and she found herself screaming, "Don't! Don't come back!" as she woke up, drenched with sweat and so terrified that she could hardly breathe. Filled with fright, fists clenched, she sat straight up in bed waiting for dawn.

CHAPTER FOURTEEN

THE PRIVATEER

★ ★ ★ ★

A sea gull, wheeling motionless upwind, suddenly flapped its wings until it hovered stationary, and screamed raucously as it made a swooping dive at the wake of the ship below. Daniel followed it with his eyes from his perch high on the mizzenmast, smiling as he thought how he'd overcome his fear of heights. *Only six months ago,* he thought as he swept the horizon automatically, *I was hanging on to these shrouds until my knuckles were white!*

A fragment of something arrested his gaze, and he instantly whipped the heavy brass telescope up and peered intently across the glittering green waters. He adjusted instinctively to the roll of the *Lady,* and after one quick look called out, "Deck! Sail off port bow!"

He slipped the telescope under his belt and slid down the ratlines as easily as a squirrel. When his feet touched the deck, he handed the telescope to a young sailor, "Thad, get aloft and keep an eye on that ship."

Thad Alden nodded curtly, and his "aye, sir" was barely audible. Dan twisted his head and framed a sharp rebuke, but changed his mind as he watched the slender youth climb upward. He shrugged and tried to forget, but he knew that sooner or later he would have to rebuke the boy. Ever since Dan had come aboard as First Mate, young Alden had been sullen. He was totally in love with Charity, had been since he was thirteen years old, and his bitter hostility was obvious to the crew. Charity had tried to soften his attitude, but he had stubbornly refused to change.

"Maynard, I'll have the guns manned."

"Aye, sir!" Giles Maynard, a husky Frenchman, began to call out orders, and soon the deck was a beehive of activity. The powder monkeys scurried below deck to bring the linen bags of powder topside, while the gun crews freed the guns from the tackle that held them firmly in place.

Dan looked fondly at the twin rows of guns and remembered the long arguments he had had with some of the crew who served as gunners on the King's warships. He'd spent as much time as possible with General Knox's men, especially a tall gunner named Ericson, captain of a gun crew on the *Victory*. Ericson had listened carefully as Dan explained the plan to arm a new privateer, and had given him some revolutionary advice.

"It ain't never been tried that I knows of," Ericson had said. "But was I in your place, I'd use long guns."

"Long guns?" Dan had questioned in a puzzled voice. "I'm afraid of long guns. Their pivots are too high and they weigh too much. They'd make us too slow and heavy."

"Not if you mount 'em on carriages."

"What about carronades?"

"'Course you got to have 'em—but they're for close work. They're fat guns and can sweep a deck, right enough—but you got to remember that other ship's goin' to have carronades as well. What they won't likely have is long guns. You can stand off and take shots at them till you break them up, then get close and finish what's left with the carronades."

Ericson had convinced Dan, and he had spent weeks searching for long eighteens, traversing pieces, and ten eighteen-pound carronades. He moved across the deck now, pleased with the result of his labors, for port and starboard bristled with ominous cannon, and the crews that manned them were sharp and quick in their movements.

"What's away, Dan?" Captain Alden had popped out off the quarter deck and was staring eagerly around the horizon.

"Sail in sight, Captain. Too far to make her out."

Charity cleared the ladder, and as she hurried across the deck to stand beside them, Dan thought once again how impossible it had seemed for a woman to live on a fighting ship—but she had made it possible.

"We're about out of room, Dan." She raised up on her toes to see more clearly through the lines, the brisk wind molding her clothing to the slim lines of her body as she stretched. There had been one scene six months earlier, when Dan had tried to convince her to wear a dress. She had stared at him in surprise, then laughed. "I can't go up the mast in a party dress, can I now?"

She wore a pair of dark blue linen trousers, a red and white cotton shirt, and her hair tied in place with a bright red kerchief. The men, of course, had been slow to adjust to having a pretty, young woman on board, and several of them had taken liberties with their language in speaking to her—but that didn't last long. Dan had simply waited for an example—a hulking brute named Olsen. When the Swede had made a crude remark to Charity in Dan's hearing, he reprimanded, "Olsen, I could have you under the cat for that—but maybe you'd like to face me man-to-man."

Olsen had grinned in anticipation. "Why, I'll take you up on that, mate."

It had been a simple matter; the Swede, for all his strength, was awkward. Dan had let the man wear himself out swinging, then stepped in and with a crashing blow to the sailor's blunt jaw had driven him across the deck. It had taken six more knockdowns, for the man had the stamina of an ox, but finally his face was a bloody mask and he lay there an inert mass. There had been no more incidents, and if the men chose to sneak a look, they did it secretively.

"Looks like a brig," Captain Alden decided after the three had watched carefully. "Lying low in the water—like she's loaded."

"We'll have to go back if she is," Charity advised. "Three fat prizes! Not bad for a month's cruise!"

When they were close enough to make out details, Dan reported, "She's got twelve guns—five on a side and two in the stern."

"Probably carronade as well," Charity added.

The men, eager for prize money, were shouting, "Take her! Take her!"

Captain Alden asked, "You think like I do, Charity?"

"Take her!" Charity responded, and Dan turned and called out, "Double-shot the long guns!"

As they drew nearer, they could clearly see that the ports were open and the guns manned. She was flying a British flag and ran on silently, a beautiful, high-sided ship, her mass of sails ruddy in the sun. A cloud of smoke puffed from her stern and a spout of water shot into the air two hundred yards ahead of the *Lady* well off line.

"That's a twenty-four-pounder!" Dan said quickly. "We can outrange her and take her from here." It was exactly the sort of action he had fitted the *Lady* for, and they had taken nine rich prizes in the same fashion over the past months. "Open fire!"

Lige Smith sighted his long eighteen. The deck jerked, the gun roared, and white smoke covered the deck briefly. There was a distant crackle, like a dog crunching a stick between his jaws. A small cabin on the British ship seemed to fly apart into a million splinters. Almost before the smoke was cleared, the gun was ready. The gun crew moved with what seemed to be leisurely movements, but actually with precision beyond the ability of most gun crews.

"Caught her that time!" Captain Alden yelled. A star-shaped patch of white splinters appeared at the ship's waterline.

It was suicide to resist, and the ship dipped its flag in a surrender sign. It was a matter of minutes until Captain Alden and Dan were aboard. She was the ship *Blue Cloud*, James Tennant, master, from St. Thomas to the Indies, 518 tons and laden with a wealth of cargo.

"I should have stayed with the convoy another day," Tennant mourned. His remark caused Alden and Greene to exchange a quick glance. *Good luck for us and bad for the British*, Dan thought with a surge of pleasure.

"Well," Dan responded carelessly, "we'd have got you in the end. It's probably a small convoy and weakly guarded—like most we find in these waters."

"Not so little—and not so weakly guarded!" Tennant shot back. "Twenty-two sail and guarded by a frigate!"

Dan stared at him, then shrugged. There was no way for the *Lady* to take on a ship of that size, so he gave the orders, and the hard work of shifting the cargo to the smaller ship began. By late afternoon Charity informed him, "No room for any more, Dan. We're stuffed with cargo."

"Hate to sink that ship," Dan commented. "She'd bring forty thousand back home."

"Maybe next time we can bring prize crews," she mused.

"Maybe." Dan gave the order, and Lige blew a hole in the bottom of the ship. She sank quickly, and Dan looked away soberly. "Could be us, Charity."

"No. God's with us, Dan. We'll be all right."

There was a feast for everyone that night, even the prisoners who were stacked together into two small cabins. The enemy ship had been filled with galley stores, and the crew ate as few of them ever had.

In the great cabin, Malloy, the steward, served the captain's table with a liberal hand. The table was small, just large enough for Captain Alden, Charity, Dan, Middles, Conrad, and Lester. Rufus Middles was a fat man who served as sailmaker, but had considerable medical experience—having been apprenticed to a physician at one time. Laurence Conrad, the coxswain, was a tall, thin man, almost cadaverous. He was an incurable pessimist outwardly. Miles Lester was an older man, pushing sixty. But he had the bright eyes and indefatigable stamina of a much younger man.

All of them waded through a dozen courses—a huge joint of beef, chicken, kidney pie, steaming hot vegetables, plum duff and fruit washed down with rough, dry Cape Town wine and topped up with port. The captain did not drink, nor did Dan or Charity, but the others imbibed freely.

Finally they all leaned back, and Lester stated contentedly, "Well, man and boy, I've been aboard ships—but never a meal like that!" He took out a battered briar pipe, and soon the cabin was fragrant with the blue smoke rising from the bowl. "I suppose it's back home, eh, Captain?"

"Well, I suppose . . ."

"I think we might have a nibble at the convoy the captain of that Britisher told us about," Dan suggested.

Conrad stared at him in surprise, his thick eyebrows rising. "Whatever for, Greene? We're loaded to the waterline now!"

"That's right," Middles agreed. His fat face was sweaty in the lamplight, and he was so full of food he groaned as he leaned forward. "We get this ship back and we're all rich. I say set sail right now."

"A few days won't make any difference," Dan argued. "We might be able to pick off a stray."

"And do *what* with her?" Conrad's frown grew stronger and he demanded suddenly, "Didn't that captain say there was a frigate guarding the convoy?"

"Well, he did say that—"

"Then we don't need to be hanging around these waters!"

"I agree with Conrad, Dan. That frigate can throw enough iron to blow the *Lady* out of the water." Lester's wise old eyes were blue as a summer sky, and his wealth of experience commanded everyone's respect.

Charity looked at Dan. "What's your thinking?"

There was a pause as the big Quaker thought about his words. He was quick in action, but there was a characteristic way that came from his Quaker background—a slowness, perhaps the result of many hours sitting in "Meeting" waiting until the Inner Light fell on one of the Friends. Charity had heard him say that it was not unusual for a group to sit stock-still for two hours in absolute silence until one of the number heard from God.

The cabin was quiet as he paused, the silence broken only by the creaking of the timbers and the faint cry of a seaman calling out the watch change topside. Finally he spoke. "Maybe it's a great thing to be rich—though it's not something I've given much thought to. I guess the winter I spent at Valley Forge changed me."

Charity added, "I can understand that, Dan. I'll never forget the sight of bloodstains in the snow from the bleeding feet of those men."

He glanced at her and smiled, then said, "I didn't join this rebellion to get rich."

Middles shot back aggressively, "You're not the only Patriot on this ship, Dan. All of us believe in the cause—but look at it this way, the sooner we get home and unload, the sooner we can go back to sea and strip the bones of King George!"

"I'll drink to that!" Conrad cried, and downed another tankard of pale wine. "We've got nothing to gain nosing around that convoy."

"Every time a British ship is lost," Dan alleged stubbornly, "it's good for us and bad for them. If we do it enough, the British will have to quit. Their ships are scattered all over the world—and if we can make this fight cost them too much, why, they'll leave us alone."

"Not likely, Mr. Greene," Conrad commented gloomily. "Washington is hanging on by a thread—why, I've heard he doesn't have twenty thousand men in the whole Army! And the British blockade has us strangled!"

"God will not desert us, Laurence," Dan encouraged gently.

Laurence Conrad had no more religion than a cat—or so he made his claim. Throwing up his hands he said in exasperation, "Oh, it always comes to that, doesn't it, Friend Dan? No matter how big a mess we make of things, God will see us through!"

"Not a bad way of thinking, Laurence," Miles Lester said quietly, and he gave Dan a smile. "I don't see as how it can hurt to look around a bit. If we run into that frigate, the *Lady* can sail out of range while the British are tryin' to trim their jib!"

Some would have argued, but Captain Alden made the decision. "Just a day or two—then back to Boston." He arose and this was the signal for the party to disperse. Conrad glared at Dan as he left, muttering something about presumption, but the others accepted the captain's decision without comment.

"Come on deck with me, Charity," Dan requested. He left the hot cabin and led her up the ladder to the deck. They made their way to the sharp bow and stood there in the moonlight enjoying the breeze.

The sky was so blue that it seemed purple, and the stars glittered like burning ice—a million points of light scattered like jewels across the curving horizon.

"Makes me feel pretty small, that sky," he remarked. "Reminds me of what God promised Abraham—that his seed would be as the stars of the sky." He looked upward, awestruck. "God is a great maker, isn't He, Charity?"

"Yes. He is," she whispered.

He smiled at her, saying, "Remember what God asked Job when He spoke to him out of the whirlwind? 'Canst thou bind the sweet influences of Pleiades, or loose the bands of Orion? Canst thou bring forth Massaroth in his season? Or canst thou guide Arcturus with his sons?' "

His deep voice stirred something within her, but it was not a comfortable feeling. His walk with God disturbed her, somehow. She stared at him and suddenly asked, "Dan, you love God, don't you? I mean, more than anything else, you love God!"

"Why, certainly!" The question took him off guard, and he looked at her, leaning forward to see her face. She was, he saw, disturbed, and he asked, "Why does thee ask that, Charity?"

She stirred unhappily and did not answer immediately. A star fell off the starboard bow, and she watched as it traced a line of light down the sides of the north. "It's not like that with me, Dan. You don't seem to need anything but God—and that's not the way I am. I know it's what I *ought* to feel—but I just *don't*."

He stood there, making a large shape in the darkness, his face lit by the silver light that flooded the deck. Her words disturbed him, but he had known that she felt something like this. For months they had been together on the small ship, and they had stood many times at the same rail, talking of everything under the sun. She was a creature of moods, he had long known. But he also had discerned that the mood covered a dark side of her character, a part of herself that she kept carefully hidden. It was as if she would let him into her lighter moods, but put a large *KEEP OUT* sign over that part of her life that lay deepest in her soul.

He put his hand on hers as it lay on the rail, saying, "Why, thee does love God, Charity."

"Not like you do, Dan. You've got to realize that. There's something in you, and in Julie and Nathan—and his parents, too—that's different." She struggled to find words for her thoughts, and turned quickly to face him, her face tense and strained. "I don't think any of you know what it's like for the rest of us."

"The rest of you?"

"Yes—those who just have *some* religion—enough to get by, I suppose." She laughed shortly and said, "That sounds terrible! But it's the truth—and it's why I'd make a rotten wife for you, Dan."

"No such thing—!"

She cut him off with a wave of her hand. "You know it's the truth, but you're *stubborn*. You need a girl who's as much in love with God as you are—and I'm not that girl, Dan."

He shook his head, saying, "Thee is not talking sense, Charity!"

"*Thee* is a stubborn fool, Daniel Greene!" She struck him angrily on the chest, and there were tears in her eyes. "If it were any other man, you'd tell him quick enough, 'Get rid of that flighty girl and find yourself a woman who loves God like you do!' That's what you'd tell him, isn't it? *Isn't it?*"

A rare streak of anger ran through him, and he grabbed her suddenly and held her tightly, ignoring her protest and struggle. He lowered his head and kissed her, and though at first she struggled to free herself, gradually she ceased and they stood there under the stars, in each other's arms. For months he had been capping his desire with a steely brand of discipline. Day after day he had watched her; many times he had taken her arm or she had brushed against him, and often the physical desire raged in his flesh. He was not a man to take advantage of a woman, and he had bent over backward to avoid any hint of pressure, despite their engagement.

Now he forgot that, and he held her pinioned in his arms, savoring the softness of her lips and the intense femininity of her body. The slow roll of the ship matched the waves of longing that seemed to rise from deep inside his heart, and he realized that she was not struggling any longer.

Charity was taken off guard; she was so accustomed to the iron control of Daniel the Quaker that she had not sensed the fierce strength of Daniel the man. As he held her in his arms, she found herself responding to his kiss, pulling him closer and surrendering to the magnetic power of his nearness. There was a drumming in her ears, and she was trembling.

Abruptly she pulled away and looked up at him. "What does that prove, Dan?"

"It proves I love thee."

"No! It proves you're a man and I'm a woman. You find me attractive and want to make love to me. And I know you can tell from the way I kissed you that I also find you attractive. But that's nothing."

"Nothing, Charity?" He shook his head and steadied himself. The kiss had shaken him, and he waited as the ship rolled before he went on. "Thee is making too much of this. It was just a kiss. That's part of marriage—a good part, I think. God made them male and female. It's got to be that way."

"Yes—but it's *more* than that, isn't it? We can't spend the next fifty years kissing, can we?" She laughed as he blinked at her outspokenness. "Didn't think I could shock you, Dan! But it's true. Marriage is more than bodies coming together. It's minds and souls and spirits!"

"Thee is right, Charity."

"And we're right back to it. The most important thing in you, Daniel Greene, is God. And you need a woman who's the same way."

He was a stubborn man, awesomely so, she realized. His wide face seemed to settle in determination. "Thee will change, Charity. Thee is young."

She saw that everything she had said made no difference to him, so she reminded him, with a little streak of cruelty, "You were in love with Julie, weren't you, Dan?"

He reddened, for it was the truth. Nathan's wife had been his first love. He had told Charity of it, feeling that it was her right to know, and now he could only say, "I—I thought I was."

"And now you think you're in love with me," she stated quietly. Shaking her hair free, Charity turned to face the horizon, her voice weary as she added, "I don't think we can make it, Dan. I'm afraid it's not going to work. It's not your fault—it's mine."

He did not touch her, but replied calmly, "We'll see, Charity. There's no hurry."

They stood there looking at the stars, the silence of the skies a contrast to the turbulent scene below. The conversation had disturbed them both, and when they parted, there was only a brief word. For a long time Dan lay in his bunk trying to pray, but the heavens seemed like brass. Finally he said huskily, "Lord, I want that girl, but it's as Thee thinks best." He rolled over, feeling miserable and unable to sleep until the motion of the ship finally lulled him into a dream-filled slumber.

Charity fared no better, perhaps worse. She went to sleep but was gripped by an evil and frightening dream. She woke up with a cry caught in her throat, and the terror of it was so great that she rose from her bed and sat in a chair until the first streaks of dawn began to lighten the sky.

The Gallant Lady probed the green billows silently all night. Underneath her hull, millions of sea creatures stirred, while overhead a myriad of stars glittered. The crew slept, except for the watch, and the elderly helmsman, a worn sailor named Hobbes, who thought not of the stars in their courses, but of the leftover plum duff he would have for breakfast. He kept the ship on course and thought of food; such was the simplicity of his soul, and there were those on board the ship who would have traded much to have had his serenity!

CHAPTER FIFTEEN

HAWKE'S BAG

★ ★ ★ ★

Twenty-seven days out of London, the *Neptune* had been making painfully slow progress under light winds, breezes often falling to the merest zephyr, a whisper in the slack, sullen sails. Langley had done all he could, which was little enough: he had set every stitch of canvas available—skysails, studding sails below and aloft, and the seldom-used light moonrakers. He ordered the pumps to be played on the lower sails as far as they could reach and water manhandled aloft to wet the canvas above, and he edged the frigate a few miles north in the hope of finding new winds. In the ship's quieter moments, he had thought of asking Angus to pray for wind, but that would have been *too* much, he decided.

The crew watched him carefully, for they well knew that if the breeze failed entirely, they would have to man the small boats and tow the ship by brute force—a man-killing chore they all dreaded.

The frigate had been in the vanguard of the convoy, and had sighted no other vessels since leaving England. All the officers hated the convoy duty, for it was a slow monotonous task, as they were tied to the speed of the slowest vessel. Not that it mattered much, since the winds were almost nothing, in any case!

The days had merged into one another with little to note their passing in the unvarying routine of a warship at sea, except for the occasional small landmark, a bloody accident during gun practice, or a rare meal of fresh beef—fresh from the barrel, of course. Watch followed watch, four hours on and four hours off, the hands varying their night watches with a two-hour spell in the dog-watches in order for one watch not to suffer continually the detested middle watch. The routine of the day never changed: holystoning, breakfast, dinner, grog, quarters, grog, supper, sleep. In between came gun practice, painting, shot cleaning, punishment, boat drill, clothing inspections—and on fine evenings, singing, dancing and skylarking on the forecastle.

On one of these nights as the *Neptune* inched her way through a sea as smooth and unbroken as glass, Blanche Rommey joined the three lieutenants as they stood on the poop deck and watched the antics of the crew below. All three of them turned, but Angus alone saw the pain that leaped into the eyes of Langley as she appeared, clad in an emerald green dress, her hair falling over her bare shoulders. *Still sick with love of her, poor lad!* he thought. *Better if Mann could cut out that hopeless love like he lops off a leg or an arm!*

He shot a quick glance at Hawke, not surprised to see that the trim officer only smiled at his bride-to-be. *I'd be pleased to know what goes on in that brain of his—he doesn't act much like a man in love, that's certain! It's her that has to do all the lovemaking! A whole month together on this ship, and he acts like he's on parade before the Queen!*

The wily Scotsman had watched the third lieutenant and the captain's daughter no less than did the others on the ship. Hawke had been a target for every eye ever since he had been commissioned an officer; this was not strange, for an officer of any rank in the King's Navy was a demigod to those who lived below the salt. Every man in one way or another would be at his mercy, and all of them had suffered enough under cruel officers to be avidly interested in how this new lieutenant would behave.

But Hawke had not been an easy man for the crew to figure out; he was unlike any other officer they had ever seen. He was, they soon discovered, not unfair, and they all gave a collective sigh of relief when, after finding Will Jones asleep on the late watch, Hawke punished him by cutting off his grog for a week.

"He could've had you torn to bits with the cat, Jones," Spinner had told him. Then he grinned broadly. "We ain't got no worries over this 'un, mates! He's too bleedin' easy!"

But the next week when Spinner himself carelessly brought a bag of black powder into the vicinity of a lighted quick match, he had suddenly found himself grasped and thrown backward into the bulkhead with such force that he could not breathe for a few moments. He got to his feet, his beady eyes blazing with rebellion, an evidence to the crew that he was not cowed by Hawke. But then the husky sailor looked into the raging eyes of Hawke, and something he saw there made him shut his mouth at once.

"I've heard you think I'm an easy man, Spinner. We'll see if you think so tomorrow."

At punishment the next day, all hands were fully expecting that Spinner would get a taste of the cat, and the officers expected no less than three dozen lashes. But Captain Rommey put the option into the hands of Hawke himself: "Punishment will be assigned by Lieutenant Hawke."

Spinner watched fearfully as Hawke motioned to Lattimore, the husky sailmaker, who handed him a small object. It was, Angus saw, a canvas bag with straps. "Put those two shot into the bag, Spinner." Every eye was on the gunner as he picked up the two thirty-two-pound round shot that Lattimore had placed by the rail and put them into the bag. "Now, put that bag on your back," Hawke commanded.

"On—on me *back*, sir?" Spinner stared into the ebony eyes of the officer, swallowed at what he saw, then obeyed. There were two straps for the arms; he struggled into the knapsack-like bag, and the dead weight of sixty-four pounds pulled him backward, so that he could keep himself upright only with an effort.

He stood there with fear in his face, thinking perhaps that he was going to be thrown overboard—a thought which flashed through the mind of Angus Burns as well!

"Now, climb the mizzenmast," Hawke commanded in a hard voice, "all the way to the crow's nest—then back to the deck at once!"

Spinner licked his lips and cast a fearful glance up at the towering mast. He was a gunner, not a foretopman, and had seldom been aloft since his youth. Even then he had been uncomfortable, and his years spent in the small, confined world of the lower gun deck had made any work higher than the deck unwelcome. The empty spaces of sky and the thin lines that he slowly began to climb were alien to him, and the crew saw his fear as they watched him grasp a line and pull himself slowly upward. He was a strong man, but the dead weight of the shot pulled at his shoulders, throwing him off balance, dragging him away from the safety of the lines, and only by grasping the ropes with all his strength was there any hope. There was no relief, Angus saw, from the intense pressure of the weight that threatened at each laborious step to pluck him off the shrouds and send him plunging to the deck below.

By the time he was halfway up the mast, the sound of his ragged breathing was audible to the crew. Every man saw him look down once, saw his face turn pale at the sight of the deck below. They heard the gurgling cry of fear that rose to his lips and for one moment it seemed he would faint and fall, but he recovered and began his creeping progress until he reached the platform. He gave a glad cry of relief and fell into the safety of the small structure. His joy was cut short by a loud command from Hawke below.

"Now—down with you!"

Spinner had no choice but to begin the painful descent to the deck. It was no better going down, for there was still the weight jerking him back.

Something about the punishment frightened the crew. They were accustomed to a world of order, for there is no more rigid order than on a ship of war. All is by count and by routine, and seldom is that order broken. The seamen may have suffered under the rigid discipline of the navy, but even if they did not realize it themselves, they were "comfortable" under its rule.

Now the order was broken, and the crew to a man was touched with something akin to fear. If Spinner had been raked with three dozen lashes of the cat, it would have been hard—however, they were accustomed to that. But there was something frightening in Spinner's white face, his eyes bulging with fear—and his terror communicated itself to the sailors who stared at him as his feet touched the deck.

"Now, back to the top," Hawke barked, adding, "Mr. Rackam, you will see to it that this man carries those shot to the lookout and back."

Rackam looked at the stern face of Hawke, swallowed and asked in a strained voice, "How long, sir?"

"Until I give the command—or until he falls and kills himself."

The words struck against the minds of the crew, and one look at the dark face of Lieutenant Hawke gave them no assurance. Later Pickins, the foretopman, said in awe to Sullivan, "Did you see his face, Sullivan? Like stone it is, and he wouldn't have no more cared if Spinner was mashed to jam on the deck than if he'd squashed a fly!"

"All hands dismissed from punishment." Hawke nodded and turned to his duties, his face a mask of stony indifference for the rest of the morning. He was the only man on the ship who seemed to be unaware of the drama of Spinner's punishment. All morning long the gunner toiled to the top of the mizzenmast, then back to the deck. As time dragged on, the sun rose in a fierce blast of heat, and the weights seemed to grow heavier. By eleven o'clock Spinner had lost count of the journeys he had made, but he was paralyzed with a fear that was worse than anything he had ever known. In battle there was the sound and fury to take a man's mind off the idea of death, but the silence as he went up and down like a crippled beetle made every second a painful reminder that if he relaxed his grip one time, he was a dead man.

His hands, tough as they were, soon were bleeding, rubbed raw by the ropes, and the sun burned his lips and the sweat blinded him so that he had to grope for the lines overhead. Once he asked in a croaking voice for water, but when Rackam relayed his request, Hawke replied indifferently, "He can have water when he's learned to be a seaman."

Captain Rommey and Blanche had been watching the drama, and when Hawke came into the great cabin to report that one of the convoy had gotten out of position, Blanche was there. Rommey heard the report, nodded, then as Hawke turned to leave, cleared his throat and said with a touch of hesitation, "Lieutenant—I must say that your method of punishment is—well, *unorthodox!*"

A flash of humor appeared in Hawke's eyes, and he commented, "I suppose so—but they get so accustomed to the cat that it's lost some of its usefulness. They'll remember this for a little while, I believe."

"But—what if he falls?" Blanche asked uneasily. She was staring at his face intently; this was a side of his nature she had not seen, and she was baffled.

"He'll die."

"That's a little stringent for a small offense, surely!" Rommey protested.

Hawke's lips were wide and mobile, and now the corners of them turned up as he answered, "Well, sir, I remember what Queen Elizabeth once said in such a case as this."

"Queen Elizabeth?"

"Yes, sir. One of her admirals had been accused of treason and was scheduled to be executed the next day. One of the Queen's counselors tried to get her to pardon the man—it seems the evidence against him was very weak. But she refused. She said, 'It's good to have an admiral executed from time to time as an example to the rest of them.' "

The humor left his eyes and there was a steely quality in his voice as he continued. "I may never have the love of these men, but I'll have obedience—or I'll tear the hearts out of them!"

Rommey stared at him, wonder in his eyes. "Obedience is required, of course. You are dismissed, Hawke."

When the door closed behind him, Rommey turned to his daughter. "What do you make of that, Blanche? The man's got ice water in his veins!"

Blanche shook her head, biting her lip nervously. "He's—he's like two men, Father. One man is quiet and gentle. That's the man we've seen. Now we see that it's not that simple. He's got a cruel streak as well—but which of us doesn't have some of that?"

"Yes—but what *other* side will we see of him?" Rommey asked. Then he did something most unusual. He went to her, put his hands on her shoulders and when she looked up at him in surprise, there was a gentleness in his eyes that she had not seen in a long time—not since she had been a child and he would take her onto his lap on rare occasions.

"I know we've been hard on each other—my fault, I think. I've not been gentle. But I care for you—and that's why I ask, Are you *certain* this is the man you want? You can never really know him, can you?"

She shook her head, a far-off look in her eyes. Reaching up, she touched his cheek, saying softly, "No—but I have to have him." She slipped away, and for a long time Rommey stared out of the window, seeing nothing, but filled with the most profound sense of futility he had ever known. He was a hard, demanding man, and fully aware that he had taken his naval habits into his family life. Now he was grieved that he had not spent more time with his daughter—but it was too late. He struck the bulkhead a terrific blow with his fist and slumped down at his desk, defeat graphically written across his face, cursing the moment the battered form of the pressed man without a memory had been brought on board!

By noon there were bets being made in the crew's quarters as to how long it would be until Spinner fell to his death. "That Hawke, why, he's goin' to let the poor blighter die just to show us wot the rest of us can expect from 'im!" Grimes scowled.

"I didn't think he was so bad—up till now," Sullivan responded moodily.

"Bad—you'll think *bad* by the time this voyage is over!" Grimes screwed up his face, spat on the floor, bitterness spilling over.

"Don't make no mistake 'bout this one, lad. He's a bad 'un! Oh, he's been nice as a kidney pie up to now—but nobody crossed him. And now he's an officer—that's the point! Oh, he's a killer, no doubt of it! Ain't I seed enough of that breed!"

"Right you are, Grimes!" Teller, an undersized dwarf of a man, nodded sagely. "Did yer see his face? 'Let him go till he dies!' That's wot he said! Oh, he'll be the death of poor Spinner—just to teach the rest of us a lesson!"

"Spinner won't last till one, is wot I says, and I'll bet on it," Grimes predicted—and soon there were bets made all over the ship on the hour of Spinner's death.

Looking down from the quarterdeck, Langley remarked to Burns, "Like a flock of buzzards! Look at them!" He waved his hand toward the crew, who were all staring skyward as Spinner groped his way up the mast, leaving red bloodstains as he moved. He was moving so slowly now that each step seemed to take forever. When he almost fell off the ropes at the deckward part of his journey, Hawke suddenly appeared and said, "That will do, Spinner. I believe it's your watch."

Spinner fell to the deck limply, the shot in the knapsack making a *clunk* as they struck the oak boards. Rackam took one look at Hawke's face, reached down, and began hauling the exhausted gunner to his feet.

"I trust you'll keep yourself out of trouble from now on, Spinner," Hawke told him in a voice that was a quiet threat. "If I have any problem with you at all, I will have two shot added to your load and you'll carry them for twenty-four hours up the mast."

"No—no, sir! Mr. Hawke!" Spinner gasped and trembled in every joint. Fear sprang his mouth open, terror coursing through him as though the devil himself had appeared. "No trouble, sir—I swear it!"

That had been the end of it, but from that day, Angus reflected as he looked at Hawke's pleasant face, there had been no trouble at all from the crew. The term *Hawke's Bag* had become a symbol of dread, for all the third lieutenant had to say was, "Perhaps you'd like to carry my bag for a time?" and the hardest man on the crew was instantly turned to jelly! There was not a man among them who wouldn't rather fall into the hands of any officer on board than into disfavor with the slender black-eyed Hawke.

★　★　★　★

Now, however, there was a mildness in Hawke's eyes as he spoke. "They're having a good time, aren't they?"

Angus glanced down at the figures of the crew below, detecting at the same time a trace of envy in Hawke's face. "Weel, more power to 'em," Angus growled. "This convoy duty is drivin' me mad! If I could get doon on the lower deck there, and dance a hornpipe like Jenkins there, it might cheer me up a bit."

"It is boring, this duty," Blanche agreed. She smiled brightly and suggested, "When we get to New York, let's have the biggest ball that place has ever seen! I know enough pretty girls to satisfy you two." Taking the arms of Burns and Langley, she teased, "You two can't wind up crusty old bachelors smelling like dirty socks!"

"Weel, now," Angus nodded, "I'll take the party, but like the man once said about marriage, 'Many that set sail on the sea o' matrimony wish they'd missed the boat!' "

"You're just too *stingy*, you old Scot!" Blanche taunted. "And you've got too much religion, too. Why, you wouldn't know what to *do* with a pretty girl!"

"Probably read psalms to her," Hawke agreed with a grin.

"I'd not be so sure o' that—but in any case, it would do neither o' ye harm to read a bit of a psalm now and then."

Blanche was still holding Burns's arm, so Hawke pulled her away, saying lightly, "If you can't appreciate the merchandise, don't handle the goods, Angus!" Then he did something that surprised the three of them. He had never shown any affection for Blanche publicly, but now he put his arm around her and drew her close. Looking into her face with a smile that made him look much younger, he scolded, "You've got *me* going to the altar, woman— now don't torment the rest of the crew!"

She responded at once to his caress, leaning against him. "I'm not sure of you yet! I've seen too many hunters counting the fox as caught only to see him go to cover."

"No—I'm a lost man," he sighed, his lean, tanned face relaxed, almost playful. It was a side of him that Burns and Langley had never seen, and Blanche but rarely. She knew, as they did not, that beneath his stern face lay a lively spirit, playful almost, when he would permit it to be seen.

"I'll go check the course," Langley blurted out, leaving them abruptly, a bitter expression in his blue eyes. Angus and Blanche exchanged a quick glance, for they had spoken of Langley's jealousy—not being able to adjust to her engagement.

"Not much need for that—not with this calm," Hawke remarked, staring at Langley's retreating form. "We couldn't drift off course even if we tried."

"Not quite right, I'm afraid," Angus shook his head glumly. "The *Blue Cloud* managed to get herself lost. I'm a bit worried aboot that one."

"You think a privateer got her?" Hawke asked quickly. His whole manner changed, for in their cruise before going back to England for refitting, he had savored the action they had found. Rommey had been delighted to find that if his first lieutenant was somewhat slow, this third was a fire-eater. He had said as much to the other officers and to Blanche.

"That young fellow is *exactly* like his namesake, Admiral Hawke! He rocks along with that bored manner of his. But let a cannon fire and he's a savage out for blood—loves action like most men love women!"

Now that love of action leaped into Hawke's eyes, and Angus laughed, "Oh, don't get your hopes up! I doubt there's a Yankee within a hundred miles. The *Cloud* just fell behind. Helmsman probably went to sleep from boredom, I expect."

"She should have caught up by now," Hawke argued, his mind probing the possibilities. He had, they both had noted, a determination that would put a bulldog to shame.

"I expect Angus is right," Blanche smiled. "Come—let's join the fun. You're not on duty." Raising her voice she yelled down, "Morgan! Let's have some fiddle music!"

The tiny Welshman, one of the ship's most agile foretopmen as well as an excellent fiddler, caught the words and waved his fiddle at her with a broad grin. "Right you are, miss!" Soon the sprightly music of Ireland floated over the still air.

"Dance with me," she commanded, and with a laugh Hawke took her in his arms, and in the tiny space on the poop deck they moved gracefully in the steps of a dance.

"A praying knee and a dancing foot don't grow on the same leg," Angus lectured sternly, but there was a smile on his face, and he said, "I'm on late watch, so I'll leave ye two to your courtin'."

After he had gone, they seemed to be alone—a rare thing on a crowded ship of war. The crew below could not see them, and it was too dark for the lone lookout to view much of the deck. Blanche moved closer to Hawke, pressing her body close. "You're the best dancer I've ever seen. I wonder where you learned so well?"

She often voiced questions like this, but he never referred to his loss of memory. He only replied lightly, "Probably at the French palace."

"I'd hate to see you exposed to those French girls—they're such predatory evils!" Laughing happily, she looked up into his face. "That's the pot calling the kettle black!" Raising her hand, she stroked the scar on his cheek, wondering for the hundredth time how he had come by it, then murmured, "It's going to be exciting being married to you. Any other man would have lots of memories about other women—but you'll only know me! I'm so selfish, aren't I?"

"Yes—just the way I like you," he responded. "You're what you are, and I take all of you—the bitter with the sweet. If it hadn't been for you, God knows what I'd have become. I'm so grateful to you!"

She stirred uncomfortably, saying sharply, "I don't want your gratitude—I want love! Sometimes I think you don't really love me at all—that I'm just a stranger who helped you out of trouble—that you're marrying me just to show your gratitude."

"Nonsense!"

"Is it?" she whispered, clutching him closer. "Kiss me!" she demanded. "Show me how much you love me!"

She had done this before, and as his lips fell on hers, he sensed again the possessive streak in her nature. Little as he knew about women, he realized that she was no humble girl submitting meekly to a caress. She met him with passion and a hunger that was greedy, pulling at him until he finally drew back, saying, "You have all of me there is, Blanche."

He shook his head and the moonlight made silver highlights on his dark face, throwing his eyes into ebony shadows. "That may sound like a good thing to a woman—but you have to remember there's not much to me. I can only bring you those things I've learned in the past few years. You're marrying a cripple, Blanche, and I've told you before, you should consider that. It's not fair to you—and it might not be enough."

"You're what I want—what I need!" Her voice was intense, and she clung to him in the warm darkness. Looking out past her head as she stood there in his arms, Hawke heard the sound of Morgan's fiddle and gazed at the bright stars. She was headstrong, this woman, and he knew that it was the novelty of his condition that had drawn her. It was not that he did not feel strongly for her; that was inevitable in view of the circumstances. But he had strong doubts about the love between them, for with only his limited knowledge, he realized with a keen insight that she would be a difficult woman to live with—demanding, possessive, and headstrong. She was, to offset that, beautiful, wealthy, and witty. Whether it would be enough—that he could not fathom.

He drew back and smiled at her. "Your father said once, 'Blanche likes to make things—dolls when she was young, and *people* now. Don't let her make you into something you don't want to be, Hawke!' I think he was right."

"I love you and you love me! That's all that counts!" she argued adamantly, and pulled his head down once more.

Well, it won't be a boring marriage—not with this one! he thought as they kissed again.

CHAPTER SIXTEEN

CAPTURED!

★ ★ ★ ★

"Deck! Deck! Sail—three points off the stern!"

Captain Rommey had been shaving, but the urgency of the lookout's call caused him to drop his razor; he charged out of his cabin, raced up the ladder, and emerged on deck heedless of the flecks of lather clinging to his face. The bright morning sun blinded him, and he moved close to Langley, who was staring over the stern toward the north. "What is it, Langley?"

"Can't say, sir—the convoy has drifted so far. But I thought I heard something just before the lookout sighted sail."

"Heard what?"

"Well, it was faint—but it could have been gunfire."

"Gunfire! And you didn't call me?" Rommey's face was red with anger and his blue eyes flashed. "You should have known better!"

"W-well, sir, it could have been thunder . . ."

A distant sound suddenly came to their ears. Rommey lifted his head and a blistering curse fell from his lips. "Well, *that's* not thunder! That's ship's cannon! Put the ship about at once!"

"Yes, sir—but there's so little wind we'll have to tack—"

"I don't give a farthing *how* you do it, Lieutenant—just *do* it!"

The deck was soon swarming with seamen, but the vessel itself could not be hurried. Slowly as the faint breeze caught the sail, she began to swing about, and Angus said to Hawke as the two of them stood in the bow, "Makes a man want to get out and push, don't it now?"

Hawke was staring intently across the sea, narrowing his eyes against the brilliant rays of the sun. "The convoy must be spread out over twenty miles! I'll bet my life there's a Yankee privateer nibbling away at the stragglers!"

"Probably that's it," Angus agreed. "Captain warned 'em to stay close, but they're a heedless lot. Looks like some of 'em will pay for it."

"Well, that fellow can't do much without a wind."

"More than *we* can. These privateers are the fastest things in the water. And with enough sail for a ship of the line! We're weighted doon with a crew of five hundred men, cannon, shot, supplies. She'll make twice our speed."

"Yes—but if we could get in range, we could blow her out of the water."

"Not much chance o' that unless the captain's a fool—and most of them aren't. They're a crafty lot. As soon as they spot us, they'll turn tail and run for cover."

★　★　★　★

The captain of the privateer was getting that exact advice. *The Gallant Lady* had encountered the convoy at dawn, and Daniel had shouted immediately, "Man the guns! They're out there like sitting ducks!"

At once the ship became a beehive of activity, but as the guns were run out and the ship was manned for action, Laurence Conrad hurried to where Dan stood beside Captain Alden to protest. "This is foolishness! We'll risk this ship for nothing!"

"There's no danger, Laurence," Dan replied easily. "Look— those merchant ships are loaded, and they're not armed. We can make a run right through the middle of them and punch the bottoms out of a lot of them with the long guns."

"And what about that frigate?" Conrad demanded.

"Why, in this calm she can't even move much faster than those fat merchant ships! We can walk away from her!"

"I don't like it," Conrad muttered gloomily. Then he shrugged his thin shoulders. "Well, there's one good thing, if you get us all killed in this crazy mess, we won't have to worry about getting caught by the British and sent to Dartmoor!"

"That's the cheerful way to look at it, Laurence," Dan laughed. "But there's no risk."

And for the rest of the morning his words were so accurate that the crew was convinced, and even Conrad, though he continued to prophesy awful messages of doom, seemed assured. The *Lady* moved steadily under the slight breeze, and by ten o'clock they were within range of a three-masted brig. "Look at them scurry around!" Rufus Middles cried gleefully. "They know what's coming!"

Charity had come to stand beside Dan, and she asked worriedly as he ordered the guns loaded, "Are we going to give them a chance to surrender?"

"What would we do with them?" Dan shrugged. "We don't have room for any prisoners, much less cargo. "

"But won't they drown?"

"No, they'll have plenty of time to get their boats off, and the other ships will pick them up." Then he gave the order, "Fire as you bear, Smith!"

Lige Smith grinned toothlessly and stated, "Like shootin' fish in a barrel, it is!"

It seemed like a merciless thing, and Charity couldn't bear watching the onslaught. Smith could not miss, and he put six shots just below the waterline of the ship that bore the name of *Portsmouth Belle* on her bow. She was already beginning to settle low in the water as Dan ordered, "That'll do her, Lige. Let me take that schooner."

Dan moved to his favorite long eighteen, and as they skimmed slowly and relentlessly across the smooth water, he hulled a schooner that was so loaded she could only waddle along in the light breeze. One of the shots went high and blasted the gun crew to bits. Charity could see the broken parts of flesh flying through the air, and the sight of a man's leg striking the mast made her turn away sick.

They had sunk four ships and were moving on when the lookout hailed, "Deck, there's a frigate bearing down, two points off starboard bow!"

"Time to get away," Captain Alden advised, and began to consider the direction.

"Wait a minute, Captain," Dan urged. He had seen an opening in the convoy and pointed to it. "If we go through that gap, we can get a couple more ships on our way."

"But that course will bring us almost within range of the frigate!" Charity protested. "Let's just put about and get out of here!"

"Wind's in the south, Charity," he reminded her. "We'll have to tack anyway. If we cut through like I say, we'll come a mite close, but she can't catch us. We'll get a couple more ships, and then we'll show them our stern."

Captain Alden opened his mouth to object, but Dan added, "It'll be striking a blow for Curtis." He saw that the words had power with Alden, so he exhorted, "Your boy died for this cause, Captain. Let's do it for him."

"That's not fair, Dan!" Charity cried, but her father's eyes had grown stern, and he nodded.

"We'll do it for Curtis," he agreed, and gave the order to turn.

As the *Lady* heeled and headed into the gap, every eye was fixed on the frigate—still far off in the distance but headed straight for them. A silence fell over the deck as the crew realized that they would pass close to the guns of the warship, and Laurence gave a melancholy sigh. "Well, I've often wondered what it would be like to look down the cannon of one of the King's ships—now God has blessed me with the opportunity. Let us be duly grateful for the bounties of the Almighty!"

★   ★   ★   ★

Rommey had watched helplessly as the privateer had destroyed the merchant ships, and his failure to drive his ship to the rescue enraged him. He had gone to stand beside the three lieutenants who were staring with loathing at the scene.

"Shall I have the guns run out, sir?" Langley asked.

"What for? We'll never get close enough to get a shot. They wouldn't be such fools."

At that instant, Hawke saw a movement that the others missed, and he yelled, "Look, she's putting about, sir!"

"What?"

Hawke's sharp eyes had taken in the maneuver of the privateer, and he reported hurriedly, "Sir, she's not going to run south—there's no breeze at all that way. She's going to cut through the convoy—see there? She's heeling around." Then his eyes blazed, and he cried out in excitement, "Sir, we'll have one chance—she'll *have* to pass fairly close to us on that course. Let me make a try for her with the bow chaser."

"That would be too long a shot," Langley argued. He had seen that the third lieutenant had done what *he* should have done, and it enraged him. "It would take a miracle!"

Captain Rommey snorted, "Well, we'll have a miracle then!" A glitter of excitement rose in his eyes, and he smiled. "You man the bow chaser, Mr. Hawke—and take Mr. Burns along to pray. That ought to cover God and man!"

The remark was taken seriously only by Burns, who said, "It'll do nae harm to invoke the favor of Jehovah. David prayed that God would help him destroy his enemies."

The others stared at him, Hawke in particular, fascinated by the religion of the dour Scotsman, but he grinned and agreed. "You pray and I'll shoot, then, Angus!"

It was a full two hours before Angus called excitedly, "There! I can read her name—*The Gallant Lady.*" He was watching the trim privateer as she glided between the merchant ships, and he added thoughtfully, "Beautiful craft. Be a shame to sink her."

"I don't have your mercy, I'm afraid," Hawke remarked. He was bending over his bow chaser, lining the gun up with the enemy ship. "I'll sink her with every man if I can."

"Weel, now, that's a man o' war speakin'—but I doot ye'll get the chance. Look, she's tackin' now. Ye'll not get more than five or six shots at her, I'm thinkin'."

"One is all it takes. I've put a double charge in the gun, and a single shot. Ought to be in range in a few minutes."

"One hole in her wouldn't do it, though," Angus surmised, shaking his head. "Even if ye hit her with two or three o' them six-pound shot, they could plug the holes and pump the hull dry before we could catch up with 'em."

"That's right enough," Hawke agreed. "But you just ask that God of yours to let me place one shot where I want it—and then we'll see."

Every member of the *Neptune's* crew was on deck, the gun crews gathered about their weapons, all watching the progress of the enemy ship.

"Do ye think the wind's going to hold?" asked Angus. "Looks like the sun's swallowing it."

"Can't say, but if we can get in a good shot, we'll have a chance of coming up to her. Ready to fire," he ordered, and there was a long moment as he waited for the slow roll of the ship. At the extreme point when the bow was lifted free from the white foam, he yelled, "Fire!"

The gun exploded almost before his words died, and the gun was driven backward, coming to an abrupt halt as she hit the end of her harness. All eyes tried to trace the flight of the ball, but under the force of the double charge, no one could spot it.

"Didn't see the ball hit," Angus said, but Hawke was yelling at the crew, who were toiling like demons.

"Load your powder!"

The cartridge slid down the barrel.

"Rammers—first wads!"

The wad was rammed down on top of the cartridge.

"Load roundshot!"

The ball rang and rumbled its way down the barrel.

"Second wads!"

The rammer damped the wad hard onto the ball.

"Run out the gun!"

The men clapped on to the side tackles and ran the gun down the slight slope of the deck, hauling it hard up against the ship's side, the black-painted muzzle jutting out over the green water.

"Handspikemen—train hard forward!"

The crowbar dug in and levered, inching the gun rapidly around until the muzzle was pointing as far forward as possible.

"Adjust your quoins—minimum depression!"

The gun muzzle rose as the wedge slipped into place. The gun captain, in this case the burly Dion Sullivan, crouched over his flintlock, waiting for the final order.

"Fire!"

The lanyard jerked, the spark flew, the muzzle belched flame and smoke and thunder, and the gun hurled backward, brought up sharply by the breechings.

This time Angus thought he caught a glimpse of a thin black line against the sky, and then he shouted, "Close miss! Too long by half a cable."

Hawke cried out the commands and the next shot was seen by all, falling too far by a cable.

"Ye're overshooting!" Angus yelled. "Lower the gun."

"Mind your praying! I'll take care of this gun!" There was a flaming light of battle in Hawke's eyes, and he once again cried out "Fire!" The thunder of the gun had not died away before a cry went up from the crew.

"You got her main mast!" Angus screamed and did a war dance on the deck. "Hit her again!"

Sure enough, the mainsail of *The Gallant Lady* was snapped off as if sheared by an invisible axe halfway up. The mainsail and the royals fell directly against the foremast, tearing down the top gallants and bringing a mass of wreckage down onto the deck.

"We've got a chance now!" Captain Rommey had come to stand close to the stern gun, and his eyes were alight with pleasure. "Good work, Mr. Hawke. I'll mention this in my dispatches."

"Thank you, Captain. Keep up firing, of course?"

"Of course. If you can keep up the pressure, we'll be close enough to swing about and give her a broadside—that'll take care of her!"

But that was not accomplished so easily. The crew of the privateer cleared the deck quickly; and even stripped of part of her sails, she was able to keep her distance from the *Neptune*.

Slowly the two ships moved through the water, and the first success of the warship was not repeated. The *Lady* presented a small target, and even though the six-pound shot came close, no more hits were repeated.

Angus was watching the fleeing ship through the brass telescope, and he cried out, "She's got stern chasers—look like eighteen-pounders to me! I think we're in for it!"

He had no sooner spoken than clouds of smoke rose from the stern of the *Lady*, and then they heard the roar of the stern chasers. Instantly there was a terrific crash midship, and Hawke looked around to see a section of the ship disappear. Bodies and parts of them splintered through the air. Lattimore received the full impact and lay still on the deck.

Confusion reigned, but Langley ran to the scene, and soon had the wounded carried below. Almost at once, another large shell struck the superstructure of the small cabin containing storage just below the poop deck. No one was hurt, but Angus yelled, "We can't stand up to that kind of pounding! She's got good gunners, sir! She can pound us to pieces with those long eighteens!"

"I thought we had her—but you may be right, Burns."

"We'll take that ship! As long as we can fire this gun, I won't quit!" Captain Rommey was startled, for Hawke's face was blazing with anger.

"We can't risk our ship, Hawke!"

"Hell loves a quitter, sir!" Hawke shot back, a fierce light in his eyes. "We came to destroy this ship, sir! Isn't that what the admiral said? I say we do it! Let's show those Yankees what Englishmen can stand!"

Rommey stared at him, then smiled and nodded, "I stand rebuked. Continue firing, Mr. Hawke."

For two hours the duel continued, the breeze tantalizing the British. It rose and fell, and the shots from the *Lady* fell, too, sending shrapnel whirring through the air. Bresington, a huge Swede, was crossing the deck of the *Neptune* when one of the shots exploded on the side of the ship, driving a splinter the size of his arm through his back, knocking him forward and killing him instantly.

There were other casualties, and the crew stayed away from the deck unless compelled by orders. By some miracle, none of the shots hit the bow chaser, and all the crew were awed by the way Hawke stood there giving commands as calmly as if he were in a living room at home. More than once he heard the *whizz* of a shot close to his ear, and he was amazed to see the crew fall flat. "What are you doing?" he demanded. "Get back to your guns. I'm ashamed of you!"

"The man has no more nerves than a brass statue," Rommey muttered to Burns. "I think he lost his fear the same way he lost his memory."

Ten minutes later a shell did strike one of the crew, a tall Cornishman named Wells. He was bringing up a round shot when a missile from the *Lady* hit him with such force that he fell to his death without a sound.

The crew flinched, and Hawke saw them ready to bolt. He knew at once that if they left, he'd never get a crew to stand exposed to the stern chaser. He spotted Captain Baxter immaculately dressed in his red uniform, and cried out, "Captain Baxter! Take the name of the next man who dies without permission!"

The crew stared at him unbelievingly, and then Sullivan laughed wryly. "Sink me! That's a good one!" Then the rest of the crew joined him, and they got off another shot as the body of Wells was carried away and the deck was covered with sand to soak up the blood.

"That's the way the good ones are," Rommey commented as he watched. "They can rise to any crisis and the men know they're not afraid. All the great fighters have been like that. I think you've seen the birth of a legend, Mr. Burns—Look! Got his rudder!"

Burns looked and saw the rudder of the *Lady* dangling by a cable, and the ship veered helplessly to one side. "We've got her, sir! She can't get away now."

Hawke came charging down the deck, pulled up before the captain and demanded, "Permission to fire broadside, sir!"

"Permission granted," Rommey answered. "I'll have the ship put about, and if she doesn't lower her colors, sweep her decks with the carronades. We can take her as a prize, I think. Have the guns loaded with chain."

"Aye, sir!"

Angus looked at the reeling ship, and said, "She'd better surrender. I hate to think of what a broadside with chain will do to those on that deck."

"It's their option, Mr. Burns. If I had God's ear as you do, I think I'd ask Him to give that captain enough sense to surrender!"

★   ★   ★   ★

Ever since the main mast had fallen, the crew of the *Lady* had been hard put to avoid panic. Captain Alden had shown no fear, and it helped the crew to see the old man standing straight and tall on the deck as unconcerned as if he were in his own garden at home. Dan Greene looked up from where he labored over his guns long enough to say with a grin, "Well, Captain, we're in a fight!"

"Blast the suckers out of the water, Daniel!" Alden cried. He shook his fist at the *Neptune* and shouted, "Come on, you blasted cowards."

Dan shook his head later and remarked, "Captain, I wouldn't say they're cowards exactly. They're standing up to our fire better than most. But unless they get more of our sail, we'll make it. Once it's dark, we can shake them off. Maybe we can get a little more sail on, do you reckon? Every yard helps."

Alden went off to see about jury-rigging a jib, and Charity came to stand beside Dan. Surprised, he shouted, "Charity, get below!"

"No! I'll stay here with you and Father." She ignored him as he begged her to leave, and after he got off the next shot, she asked, "Are they going to get us, Dan?"

"I pray not." He stared out across the water, then shook his head. "This is my fault. But I pray God will deliver us."

"And there are men on that ship praying that God will put us in their hands." She stared at him bitterly, bright anger in her eyes as she stormed, "I don't understand your God, Dan. I never will!"

He stared at her unhappily, and she turned and stalked off. He wanted to run after her, to explain. For now that would have to wait. She was angry with him for getting them into the danger, and rightly so, but he had no thought of being taken.

It was only when the shot from the warship knocked the rudder off that he knew they were lost. He felt the shot hit; then when the ship heeled to starboard, he knew it was over.

He walked slowly toward where Alden was standing beside Hobbes, the ancient helmsman. "We've got to surrender, Captain Alden."

"Surrender the *Lady*? Never!"

"No choice. Look, she's swinging around to give us a broadside."

Alden looked, but had no idea of what that meant. "Get to your guns, Daniel."

Greene stared at him, amazement in his face. "Sir, we can't stand a broadside from a frigate! Why, a ship of the line couldn't stand that!"

Alden seemed dazed. He shook his head stubbornly. "We'll fight her! Get to your guns!"

Dan saw that the old man had cracked. He turned and stated numbly, "I'll lower our colors, Captain."

He left the cabin and heard Alden shouting, but could not make out the words. Suddenly just as he approached the mast and was prepared to haul the colors down to indicate surrender, he was seized and thrown to the deck. He fought, but Olsen and three other husky members of the crew held him down. Olsen had never forgotten the whipping he'd taken, and now he laughed in delight as he pinioned Greene to the deck.

"Let me up, you fools!" Dan shouted. "They'll blow us out of the water!"

But Olsen only laughed. "Let's see how strong you are now, Mr. Greene!" he taunted.

Fear rose in Dan's heart, for he knew that as soon as the frigate made her turn, she would throw enough metal at them to blow the *Lady* to bits.

But he could not free himself. He thought mostly of Charity, and struggled frantically to break the hold. Others were giving the orders to man the guns, and he caught a glimpse of the port deck, lined with gunners. It seemed that every hand was on deck, not knowing they were about to be hit with a hail of iron.

Some of the guns fired, but then he heard Laurence Conrad cry clearly, "Look out! She's coming to bear!" He paused and then added, "For what we are about to receive—"

He never finished, for there was a terrific thunder of guns, and the *Lady* reeled under the blow. The air was full of sounds, and

Greene knew as he lay powerless on the deck that the *whirring* noise was six-foot lengths of chain that swept the deck of the ship like a scythe. The men who held him down were knocked off him as if with a giant fist, and as Dan sprang to his feet, he saw that Olsen had been cut almost in half.

A deadly silence followed, strange and eerie after the crash of the guns—and then the cries of the wounded and dying began. It tore against Dan's nerves, but he hurdled the bodies that lay squirming on deck and ran for the cabin. The sides of it, he saw, had been blasted away, and he flung himself through the door in an agony of fear. He saw the mangled body of Hobbes huddled against the bulkhead, and in the middle of the deck William Alden lay holding on to his stomach. He had taken the wound that spilled his life, and he was staring at the wound with eyes that were already beginning to cloud.

"Father! Father!" Charity came flying through the door, falling beside the dying man, weeping and pulling at him. "Don't die! Please don't die!"

He lifted one hand, and the blood ran like a stream to the deck. Touching her hair, he waited until she lifted her head. When he spoke his voice was weak. "Daughter, you have been my joy—but now it's time for me to leave. God will keep you—for I go to Him— I go to my Beloved!"

She shook in every joint, and her hands plucked at him. "Don't leave me!" she cried.

His face was pale as death, but he took his other arm and threw it around her. Then the strength drained out of him, and he managed to say only, "I—will wait for you—your mother and I—we'll be—"

Then he fell back, and she flung herself across him in a paroxysm of grief.

Dan Greene stood there silently. He had killed her father as surely as if he had put a gun to his head, and his heart was dark with hopeless grief.

He heard the sounds of the warship's boats arriving a little later, but when a British lieutenant entered and commanded, "Take him away, and see that this lady has proper treatment," he did not say a word, but turned and left the cabin without a backward look. His eyes were blurred, but he did not know if it was for the crew, for William Alden, for Charity, or for himself that he wept.

CHAPTER SEVENTEEN

AN OLD ACQUAINTANCE

★ ★ ★ ★

Captain Rommey waited until Langley came through the door of the great cabin and took his place beside Burns and Hawke. The captain had given them a day to repair the damage to the *Neptune* and to care for the wounded of both ships; now he rose from his chair and went to stand in front of them.

"I'll have full reports on the damage to the ship later, but first I want to know what disposition you've made of the prisoners."

"Captain," Langley spoke up, "the privateer had over fifty prisoners on board, taken from prizes. I had them shifted to the *Mary Ann*. She's got a cargo of lumber and iron products, but she can carry that many people without any problem."

"Very good. We don't need the added burden of nursing civilians on this ship. What about the crew of the—what's the name? Oh, *The Gallant Lady*."

Langley shifted uncomfortably, and there was a cloud on his face as he answered, "Well, sir, most of them were on deck when the broadside hit. Those who weren't killed outright were pretty badly hurt. I had Dr. Mann set up emergency surgery. Not many of them will make it."

"The captain was killed, I understand?"

"Yes, sir. His daughter was on board. She's taking it badly."

"I see." Rommey turned and began to walk back and forth, his hands clasped behind him and staring at the floor. It was a characteristic behavior, they knew, when he was wrestling with a decision; so they waited until he slapped his hand against his thigh and came to stand before them.

"I'll have a prize crew put aboard the *Lady*," he stated. "She's not badly damaged, I understand. She'll bring a good price, and I don't suppose you gentlemen have any scruples against taking prize money?" He smiled at them, then frowned and added, "There are problems, of course."

"We're undermanned as it is, Captain," Langley protested quickly. "Can't spare many men."

"It's always that way, Mr. Langley, but we can manage something. The problem, of course, is navigation. I want this ship taken to New York, and that's no easy job. With a skeleton crew it will be a difficult job at best, for I expect the convoy will pull away before the *Lady* is repaired." He glanced at Burns and said, "I'd let you go, Mr. Burns, but—"

"No, sir," Burns interrupted. "I'm still shaky on my navigation."

"Yes, I thought so," Rommey scowled. "It can't be you, Mr. Langley, of course—so, Mr. Hawke, I'll have you go as prizemaster."

"Yes, sir."

"You can fight it out with Mr. Langley about which of the crew you can take with you—and if there's any difficulty, Mr. Burns will make the decisions. I suggest you act quickly, for I hear that there's a wind rising. Be good to get out of this blasted calm!"

"How long do I have, Captain?"

"Take today. Get supplies and anything you need from our stores to repair the ship. I want to move at dawn. You should be in New York some few days after we arrive—now, I believe that's all."

"Sir," Burns spoke up, "there's one matter ye must decide—aboot Miss Alden."

"Who? Oh, is she the daughter of the captain?"

"Aye, sir. Well, is she a prisoner, or not, Captain?"

Rommey's square face grew sober, and he rubbed his thick chin with a forefinger. "According to the law, she's technically a member of the crew of an enemy vessel—but that won't answer here, will it, Burns?"

"I don't believe so, Captain." Burns had been busy sorting out the prisoners and had spent considerable time with the daughter of the late captain, and his heart had gone out to her. He put an energetic note in his voice as he made his plea: "She's lost her father—and, of course, the ship was all the family had for a liveli-hood. And her people are strong on family plots, Captain. She's been beggin' me to see that her father's body gets back to America."

"That's impossible!" Rommey snorted.

"Not really, sir," Burns responded quickly. "There's plenty o' alcohol on board. I could have the body sealed in a barrel full of spirits, and it would be preserved."

Rommey stared at the Scot in a mood close to anger, pausing to consider his absurd suggestion. "This must be a very pretty young lady, Mr. Burns," he allowed with a slight smile. "You wouldn't do as much for a homely woman."

"Perhaps, not, sir," Burns nodded, "but it would nae be to my credit to behave in such a fashion. The young woman is vurry attractive—but I trust my motive is somewhat more humane than that."

Rommey stared at him, shrugged, and continued. "Very well, Mr. Burns. If you will take care of the details, I will arrange to insure that Miss Alden is listed as a passenger, not as a crew member."

"Thank ye, sir. 'The quality o' mercy is not strained,' as the bard says."

Rommey snorted. "I'm not interested in your blasted poetry, Mr. Burns, and I want every man of that crew who's able to walk sent as a prisoner to Dartmoor—no exceptions, you hear me?" Rommey appeared to be apprehensive that someone would inter-pret his act of mercy to Charity Alden as a weakness, so he scowled at them sternly, adding, "Put them in that hellhole, Mr. Burns, every man jack of them!"

"Yes, sir. They're under lock and key—but there's not more than fifteen of them."

"You are dismissed!"

The three officers filed out, and it took the combined efforts of all of them to get the job done by dark. It was no minor matter to get the material for repairs shifted from the *Neptune* to the *Lady*, but the business of the prize crew brought Langley and Hawke into a bitter altercation, as the captain had known it would. Langley contested every choice that the other made, and Hawke deliberately set his sights too high, knowing he'd have to settle for less.

In the end, they were forced to hand Burns their lists, and he agreed to pick the prize crew. "On the condition," he demanded, staring at them sternly, "that my decision is final. No hard feelings toward me if ye don't agree. Both of ye are my friends, and no matter *what* I put on the list, neither of ye will like it!"

He was correct, but Hawke was secretly pleased when he heard the names—especially with Rhys Morgan, the best foretopman on the ship. He was not so pleased when Burns named Oscar Grimes—but he saw a twinkle in the Scotsman's gray eyes and knew he had done it to placate Langley. He was not sorry to hear the name of Dion Sullivan, for despite his differences with the man, he needed strong hands and good seamen. He received only fifteen men, but one of them was Robert Graves—a fine carpenter who could oversee the repair of the *Lady*. Once again, this was balanced by the addition of Spinner—but Hawke knew that the gunner was in such fear of him he'd cause no trouble.

The crew worked furiously all day, and it was not until after dark that Hawke came to the captain's cabin, having been summoned by the steward. He knocked, and when the captain called out "Come in!" he entered to find a table set and Blanche and her father sitting in the golden light of the lanterns.

"Come in, Mr. Hawke!" Rommey indicated a chair with a place set on the white tablecloth, and as Hawke took his seat, he said, "Better enjoy this meal, my boy. I've approved the list for your prize crew—and there's not a cook on it. You'll be eating poorly until you arrive at port."

"You're probably right, sir," Hawke smiled. "I don't suppose you could part with Hans for the rest of the voyage?"

"On no account! I'll part with any other man before I give up my cook!" Rommey responded. "Well, pitch in, Hawke, and you too, Blanche!"

It was the most ornate meal Hawke could remember, consisting of a large fish, beef-and-kidneys, a magnificent kidney pie, even some fresh vegetables. In addition there was a ragout of pork and a dish of brawn with dark specks, which the captain identified as truffles. For dessert, they were served a pudding rich with raisins and currants, jellies of two colors—all washed down by an ocean of fine wines.

Finally, Rommey pushed his chair back and stared at Hawke with an odd smile on his blunt face. "Now that you are hopelessly full and unable to argue, I must tell you, Lieutenant Hawke, that I have brought you here under false pretenses."

"Sir?"

"You don't see Mr. Langley or Mr. Burns here eating like a

king, do you? No. That's because I want you to do something for me."

"Why, sir, you are my captain."

"I'm also your future father-in-law, and as such I think it wise that you get a good look at the woman you are marrying."

Hawke glanced across the table at Blanche, who was looking smug as a cat who'd just eaten the canary. "She looks very beautiful, sir."

"That's on the *outside*, Hawke—but you are now to learn what a devious piece of baggage my daughter is." The captain leaned back and passed a hand over his forehead, made a slight groan, then slapped the table with his hand. "Sink me! A man must partly give up being a man to live with women!" Shaking his head, he went on, "Well, let's have it out, my boy. When Blanche heard that you were taking the *Lady* into port as a prize crew, she came to inform me that she was going along as a passenger instead of aboard the *Neptune*."

"Now, Father, I simply came to ask if I might have your permission," Blanche remonstrated demurely, but the dancing light in her eyes confessed that her father had pretty well stated the truth.

"There it is!" Rommey spread his hands. "Had her mother not taken passage to New York on a faster vessel, she would no doubt refuse Blanche's request. But what chance does a mere man have against this one? And you'll fare no better, I warn you, Hawke!"

Hawke smiled at the captain, reached his hand across to Blanche, and replied, "I am warned, sir—and I'll take the risk."

"Done you in!" Rommey grinned. "Well, I must tell you, my boy, that your engagement was somewhat of a concern to me. However, I must also say that it's brought a father and daughter closer together than they ever were!"

"I'm glad of that—but what about—" Hawke hesitated. How could he say it delicately? "Well, there might be talk—gossip, you know? I mean your daughter and I alone . . . ?"

"Oh, she's been quite able to take care of *that*, Hawke!"

"It's simple, sweet—I will share the cabin with the captain's daughter. I mean, after all, the poor girl needs a woman at this time!"

"I'm sure your concern does you credit, Daughter," Rommey acknowledged dryly. "But you'll have it your own way. I don't know how I'll explain all this to your mother—with any sort of luck, the *Lady* won't be too far behind the convoy. Now, you'd better get aboard the *Lady*—both of you. I'd planned to get under way at dawn, so I'll say goodbye now."

"Have a safe voyage, Father!" Blanche rose and went to put her arms around his neck, an act which pleased him greatly. He stood there with one arm around her, and put his hand out to the young lieutenant. He made a massive shape in the lamplight, and the years of rough living had toughened his features, but there was real affection in his face as he said, "I am entrusting you with a prize ship—but here is the real prize, my boy." He patted Blanche's arm and gave it to Hawke.

"I'll take great care—and thank you, sir—for everything!"

"All right—off with you!"

He did not follow them, but in thirty minutes, they were in the captain's gig on their way to the *Lady*. "Are you happy with your passenger?" she asked as they moved across the velvety waters.

"It's the best surprise you could have given me," he returned, and the answer contented her. She loved adventure, and this was, to her, an opportunity for an idyllic voyage with her sweetheart. *I hope it takes a month to repair the ship!* she thought as she snuggled close beside him in the darkness.

★　★　★　★

Charity rose from her bed stiffly. Her face felt drawn and tight, for she had wept until she had finally drifted off into sleep. But it had been a troubled sleep, filled with phantoms, and more than once she had almost awakened with her body twitching in terror. She seemed to hear over and over the sound of the thunderous broadside that had killed the crew, and she looked wildly around, not knowing where she was.

Startled by a knock, she stared at the door in terror. Lieutenant Burns had been gentle, but he had been forced to tell her that she might be treated as a prisoner of war; and fear of what could happen grabbed at her as she stood there helplessly.

"Miss Alden! We must come in!"

It was a woman's voice, and that confused Charity, but she wiped her tear-stained face as the door opened. It was a young woman dressed in a stylish gray dress, flanked by a muscular seaman with a large trunk on his shoulder. She came straight up to the startled girl and put her hand out, a smile on her lovely face, "Miss Alden, my name is Blanche Rommey." She turned and spoke to the seaman. "Put the trunk there." When he had put it down with a grunt, she gave him a coin, saying, "That's all."

"Thankee, miss!" He knuckled his forehead, grinned shyly, and left the room, closing the door behind him.

Blanche removed her cloak, tossed it onto one of the two beds, then came to stand before the girl, whose face was pale and tear-streaked. "This is very painful for you, Miss Alden," Blanche said quietly. She had not expected such a young woman, nor one who was obviously very pretty in spite of her swollen features. But there was a vulnerable air about the girl that made her reach her hand out impulsively and say, "I'm so very sorry about your father."

She had not intended to say that—in fact, she had not given a moment's thought to the woman on the privateer. She was not given to such compassion, but now that she saw the squared shoulders and the quivering underlip of the girl, she was moved. Blanche Rommey was a selfish creature, but she had sympathy for anyone in such a predicament—though it would have to be added that she would have been just as moved at the sight of a wounded puppy!

"What—what are you doing here?" Charity asked.

"I'm afraid you'll have to put up with me for the rest of the voyage—but I have good news. Lieutenant Burns told you that there was a possibility you might go to prison, I believe?"

"Yes . . . ?"

"Well, my father is Captain Rommey of the *Neptune*. And I'm very glad to tell you that he has made arrangements for you to be treated as a passenger."

"That's very kind of him . . . and my father?"

"He'll be buried in your cemetery—Lieutenant Burns is making all the arrangements. Does that make you feel any better?"

"Oh, yes! I'm—I'm very thankful, Miss Rommey."

"You had quite a champion in Lieutenant Burns. He was very determined. Not many lieutenants can move my father in that way."

"He was very kind."

Blanche nodded, adding, "I must tell you, I come with a double purpose." She hesitated, looked at the other girl, and smiled slightly. "My fiance has been appointed prizemaster of this ship. I asked my father to let me come with him—and he only agreed because there was another woman on board."

"Where will we go?"

"To New York. I am sorry about the loss of your ship. But I

suppose privateers look on that sort of thing as an occupational hazard."

"Yes, of course."

There was such sadness in Charity's face that Blanche went on quickly. "It will be a short voyage—and I'll see to it that you have no problems. There'll be no lock on the door or anything like that. And you'll take your meals at the captain's table—that's my future husband, Lieutenant Hawke." She hesitated. The girl looked so vulnerable. "Is there any way I can make this easier for you—may I call you Charity?—anything at all?"

Charity bit her lip. "What about the crew? I—I know that most of them were killed."

"I'm afraid so. The severely wounded are on board the *Neptune*. Those that were not are in the hold under guard. I'll get the names of the survivors for you."

"What will happen to them?"

"They'll be sent to a prison until the rebellion is over—Dartmoor, I believe." She gave Charity a close look, asking intuitively, "Is there one of them you'd like to see? Perhaps a relative? I'm sure I can arrange a visit."

Charity licked her lips and murmured quietly, "I was engaged to one of them—Daniel Greene. But he was the cause of all this—my father's death!" Her youthful face grew tense and she shook her head. "I hope I never see him again as long as I live!"

Blanche felt a sudden surge of inner pity for the girl. She herself had led a sheltered life, lacking nothing, never a tragedy. Now she looked into the eyes of the girl before her and felt a shame at her lack of compassion. *I must do what I can,* she thought. Going to her, she put her arm around Charity and said, "We'll talk about it later. There's going to be lots of time for that. But now, do you mind too much having to share your quarters with me?"

"No, of course not, Miss Rommey."

"Well, maybe you'll help me unpack. Perhaps tomorrow morning you can show me the galley and cook a breakfast. I understand there's no cook, so I hope you've more experience along those lines than I!"

It was a strange night for Charity; she was very conscious of the British woman in the bed so close to her, but she managed to get through the ordeal with some sleep. They rose late, not wanting to interfere with the crew's meal, and dressed. Charity led her to the galley where she cooked a fine breakfast of battered eggs and toast. The two of them sat down, and finally Charity ate a little. Afterward they went up on deck where the repairs on the ship were already under way, a mass of tangled cordage, ripped sails, and splintered timbers being removed by the crew.

"That's my fiance," Blanche told her, pointing to the bow where Hawke, surrounded by workmen, was supervising the repair of the outer jib. "But," she went on, "I can see we're going to be in the way up here." She glanced up nervously as Sullivan cut away a top yard, letting it fall to the deck with a crash, and said quickly, "We'd better get below. You can meet Captain Hawke at dinner tonight."

They went below, but Charity had a thought, and asked as they went down the ladder, "Some of the crew are still aboard—those who weren't badly hurt?"

"I heard so."

"We were a close ship, Miss Rommey. I know all these men—they're old friends, most of them. I wonder, could I go see if they need any help? Bandages or medicine?" Charity said, knowing that Dan might be among them, but refusing to let her anger stop her from helping the others.

"Why, of course, Charity." Blanche felt that it would be much better if the American girl had something to do other than dwell on her misfortune, so she added, "I'll go with you. Maybe I can help get what they need."

"I suppose they're in the hold?" Charity inquired. "It's this way." The young women descended to the lowest deck, finding there two of Captain Baxter's marines guarding the door.

"We'd like to see the prisoners," Blanche stated.

"Why, I'm sorry, Miss Rommey, but we can't let you do that—not without permission from the captain."

"Oh, very well. I'll go get an order. You may as well wait here, Charity." She made her way to the deck and threaded the cluttered passageway to where Hawke was working. "Oh, Captain! I need you," she called.

He raised his head, came to where she stood, and grinned down at her. "I'm not a captain, Blanche. Just a lowly lieutenant."

"Well, give me a note and sign it 'Captain Hawke.' "

"A note?"

"Charity Alden, the captain's daughter—she wants to visit the prisoners."

"I'm not sure about that!"

"Oh, it's all right," Blanche promised and reached up to straighten his collar. "She's a poor creature, and it'll give her something to do." She smiled at him coyly. "*Please*—and I'll give you a reward when we're alone!"

He flushed, and gave in. "Oh, all right. You write it and I'll sign it—or you might as well sign it yourself, I suppose."

"Oh, that wouldn't be right!" she giggled as she went off to find paper and ink. After getting his signature, she returned to the hold and handed the paper to the marine, who looked at it carefully, then unlocked the door. "You want us to go in with you, Miss Rommey?"

"I don't think we're in any danger," Blanche shrugged. "Go in, Charity."

The room they entered was a low-ceilinged affair, lit by several lanterns. It had been filled with supplies, but most of them had been removed to make quarters for the prisoners. The lanterns swung with the motion of the ship, casting a series of yellow waves of light over the makeshift bunks on which the men were lying. It was close, and there was the smell of waste and sweat, strong and harsh in the nostrils of the two women.

"Charity—!" Dan had risen from one of the bunks and stood before her, his eyes filled with pain. "I—I'm glad thee has come—"

"I came to see if I could help with the wounded." Even to Blanche's ears the words sounded flat, even angry, and they struck against Dan Greene like lethal blows.

He stared at her silently, his wide shoulders sagging in despair, and he responded simply, "That is kind." He stood back, and a voice suddenly rose from the side.

"Charity! Charity!"

She turned and strained her eyes in the dim light, then moved to stand beside a bunk. "Thad!" She knelt quickly and took the hands of young Alden. "Are you badly hurt, Thad?"

"Ah, not so bad," he answered, but his voice was reedy and thin. She looked closer and could see the pallor on his face even in the dim light.

"What is it?"

Rufus Middles appeared, and his round face gleamed with sweat in the yellow lamplight. "Got a splinter in his side, Miss Charity. He ought to have gone to the *Neptune* with the others that was bad wounded—but he begged so hard to stay, the Scotsman let him do it."

"Can't you take it out, Rufus—the splinter, I mean?"

He rubbed his cheeks, thought on it, then said slowly, "I tell you the truth, Miss Alden, just like I done told the boy here, it's a bad 'un. Got to do a heap o' cuttin'—and I warn you, he might bleed to death."

"But—it's got to come out!" Charity took Middles' beefy arm and insisted. "I'll help you, Rufus!"

He hesitated, saying, "Well, it's up to Thad. It's his life."

"Do it!" Thad gasped. "If you'll help, Charity, it'll be all right."

Charity turned to Blanche. "Can you get us a place where we can treat this boy?"

Blanche was overcome by the stench of the hold, and she croaked, "Yes! I'll see to it—I'll get everything ready—instruments as well." She turned and almost ran out of the room. Charity knelt beside Thad again, taking her handkerchief and wiping his brow. "It'll be all right, Thad—you'll see!"

"God sent you, Charity!" he cried, and he held on to her hand, his eyes bright with fever. She felt the feeble grasp, and tried to pray, but could not. Then she looked up and saw Dan sitting on his bunk with his back against the wall, his head bowed, the picture of grief—but she felt nothing. *He killed my father!* was her only thought, and though the rest of the crew spoke gladly to her, Dan did not lift his head, not even when a seaman came and carried Thad to the makeshift surgery. Even afterward, when Charity came back, drained and sick from the bloody operation, Greene was still sitting in the same position, with head bowed.

Blanche was shocked at the pallor of Charity's face when she saw her later during the day, and she was relieved that the girl seemed to crave solitude. "I feel so sorry for her," she said as she sat with Hawke under the shade of the afterdeck. "She's lost everything—even the man she loves. She blames him, somehow, for her father's death."

"Too bad!" he murmured. "War is like that."

"I want you to be nice to her," Blanche requested. Then she smiled archly and added, "Not *too* nice—because she's a very pretty girl! But I've asked her to eat with us. You clean up and I'll manage to get something fit to eat."

He agreed, and she spent most of the afternoon locating a sailor named Harrison who admitted having had some experience as a cook's helper, so the two of them worked the rest of the day preparing the evening meal. For Harrison it was an easier job than moving heavy timbers, and for Blanche it was fun—something different.

It was growing dark when she went to her cabin and found

Charity sitting in a chair, staring at the wall. "Come now, Charity!" Blanche cried out gaily. "We're having dinner with the best-looking man in the King's service. We must look our grandest!"

"I—I'd rather not, Miss Rommey."

Blanche went over and pulled her up. "I know you've had a hard time—but it will be good for you. Come now, I insist!"

Under Blanche's prodding, Charity put on a dress, a green one with white trim, and let Blanche fuss with her hair. "My, what fine hair! Beautiful!" She stood back and looked at Charity, then smiled gaily, "It's a good thing I'm not a jealous woman—or you'd do without supper tonight! Come now, we'll be late."

Reluctantly Charity allowed herself to be pulled out the door and up to the captain's cabin. It had occurred to Blanche that Charity might be saddened at seeing her father's room, but there was no choice. "She's got to start facing reality," she had said to Hawke.

When the two entered, there was no one inside but Harrison, who was wearing a white coat, acting as steward. "Captain will be here soon," he informed them. "Said for you two to wait."

"Well, I'll teach him better manners than this—after we're married," Blanche laughed. "You sit there, Charity, and I'll take this seat."

As they waited for Hawke, Blanche did most of the talking, telling her about her fiance, and Charity responded with a smile at her enthusiasm.

The door swung open and Hawke entered. He was wearing a blue uniform with white facings. His brass buttons glittered like gold in the bright lamplight, and his hair was neatly drawn back, tied with a blue ribbon. *Heavens!* Blanche thought with a burst of pride, *he is a handsome man!*

Hawke stepped to the table and smiled, his teeth chalk white against his dark tan. The scar on his lower jaw stood out like a white line, and his eyes were kind as he bowed and apologized, "I'm sorry to be late. This is Miss Alden, I believe?"

He paused, waiting for a reply, but Charity was staring at him, her eyes full of fear. Hawke was taken aback. He glanced at Blanche, who was openly puzzled.

"Charity—are you all right?" Blanche asked, concern etching her face.

Instead of answering, Charity abruptly rose to her feet, her face pale. She was trembling, they both saw. She quickly put her hands together, trying hard to control the shaking.

She sees me as the man who killed her father! Hawke thought, and a glance at Blanche confirmed his thought. He started to speak, saying, "I must apologize, Miss Alden. This is too much—"

"Winslow!" The name leaped to Charity's lips, and she threw her hands out in a helpless motion, her throat constricted. The dreams she had of this man—the dreadful nightmares that had come a hundred times to fill her with terror—came rushing back and she raised her voice and cried out, "Paul Winslow! What are you doing here! You're *dead!*"

The last word was a scream, and she fell back in her chair and put her face in her hands, weeping hysterically.

Hawke paled, and he and Blanche stared at each other, speechless. Then slowly, Blanche went over to the weeping girl. She was afraid, but she knew the time had come for something that could be a tragedy for her. She slowly pulled the girl's hands from her face, saying, "Do you know this man?"

Charity stared at him, shivered and whispered, "Know him? Of course I know him!"

"You—you may be mistaking him for another man," Blanche whispered, almost in a plea. "You can't be *sure!*"

Charity pushed Blanche away, stood straight and pointed at the man whose face had gone pale beneath his tan.

"There's no mistake!" Charity seemed to weave and she began to back toward the door, fearfully, as if afraid they would attack her. She reached the door, then turned. They were both staring at her, and there was an expression in the dark eyes of the man who stood before her that would have brought pity to her heart if it had been any other man.

"Not know him? *I put that scar on his face!*"

She turned and with a sob left the room. They heard her feet as she fled down the corridor, and then they stood silently.

Finally he spoke, his voice heavy with foreboding. "Well, my dear, we don't have to wonder about me anymore, do we?" He dropped his head, standing there like a statue. After a while he lifted his eyes, and a bitter smile touched his mobile lips.

"Paul Winslow—I wonder what sort of fellow I'll turn out to be? It seems we'll know pretty soon, doesn't it?"

They stood there like strangers, and she felt an ominous fear that he had gone far, far away—and that the man she knew as Hawke would never come to her again!

CHAPTER EIGHTEEN

HERO—OR VILLAIN?

★ ★ ★ ★

When Blanche left her cabin just after dawn, she nearly stumbled as the ship took a slow roll that threw her off balance. Twice as she made her way to the deck, she saved herself from being thrown against the bulkhead by sheer effort alone. Stepping out on deck, she saw at once that the sky was no longer blue, but was like a lead-colored bowl pressed over the sea, colorless and somehow ominous. The sea itself was different, for though there were no whitecaps, the surface was flowing with long undulations that slowly picked the ship up, then dropped it into the troughs.

The repair work was still going on, and Blanche sensed an urgency in the men as they drove themselves at a frantic pace. Hawke was standing beside the rail on the quarterdeck taking a sight with a sexton, and she hurried to his side. He turned quickly at the sound of her footsteps, his questioning eyes searching hers. Without waiting for him to speak, she began. "You look like you didn't sleep a wink," noting the dark circles.

"I got a few winks," he shrugged. "But you look worn out. I guess you didn't rest much, either." He turned his eyes skyward, then back at her. "I almost came to your cabin to question the girl— but she was in a bad state. I thought maybe she'd talk to you."

"Not a word!" Blanche drew her mouth together in anger. "I told her how you'd lost your memory—but she didn't believe it! Then I tried to get something out of her, and she just turned her face to the wall."

"She said nothing at all?"

"Well—she did tell me—"

"What?" He saw that she was uneasy, and understood the reason. "She obviously hates me. What did she say?"

"Oh, only that I'd be sorry if I married you. I thought all night about it, and I think the girl has lost her mind." There was a defiant stubbornness in Blanche's chin and she added, "The strain of losing her father has driven her too far."

Hawke smiled and shook his head. "I'm afraid that's wishful thinking. We can't ignore this, Blanche." He looked up quickly, lifting his eyes to the mainsail. It was furled, but a sharp gust of wind caught the loose ropes, causing them to whip around the mast sharply.

Seeing the uneasiness in his face, she asked, "What's the matter?"

"I think we're in for a blow—maybe a bad one. And if it hits before we get the rigging repaired, it could wipe us out." He stared at the sky steadily, shaking his head. "I can't leave the deck for long, but I'll get the working crews going. After that we'd better have a talk with the girl."

She stayed where she was, watching as he moved along the deck, giving orders calmly, answering questions and pointing from time to time at the rigging as he explained. There was an air of quiet command about him, and she'd been around the navy long enough to see that he was a natural leader. Finally he returned and took her arm, "Let's go below."

They made their way to the cabin, and Blanche opened the door and entered, followed by Hawke. Charity was standing with her back against the wall, her eyes hard and defiant. Hawke immediately began to speak, his voice quiet and even. "Miss Alden, I'm sorry to intrude on you, but I don't have much choice. . . ."

As he stood there explaining how he'd come aboard the *Neptune*, battered and without a trace of memory, Charity searched his face. He *was* different, tanned and lean, though his face was the same, and the white scar that traced its way along his cheek was like a flag. *He's better looking than ever*, she thought briefly, but she was caught in a rush of memories, not only of the terrible scene when she'd slashed his cheek, but of the countless nightmares that had haunted her ever since. Furthermore, there was the knowledge that he was the enemy who had killed her father and stolen her ship—this burned in her as well, and she remained silent, challenging him with cold eyes, her face pale as old ivory.

Finally he finished. "So you see, Miss Alden, it's been a difficult time." He bit his lip and the firm gaze wavered slightly. "It's been an ordeal that you probably can't understand: not knowing what you are is terrible."

Charity almost weakened, but once again the hatred that had taken possession of her raged within and she shook her head stubbornly.

"I think she made the whole thing up!" Blanche glared at Charity, adding venomously, "You probably heard of Lieutenant Hawke's problem and decided to get revenge for the death of your father. I think you're lying!"

"Do you?" Charity's eyes flashed in anger, and she lifted her head high. "I can prove what I say easily enough. All you have to do is send for Daniel Greene. I haven't said a word to him—but he'll know you as soon as he lays eyes on you!"

Hawke stared at her, then nodded, "Very well, we'll see." He stepped to the door and called loudly, "Sergeant! Sergeant!" He waited until a red-coated marine appeared and stood to attention. "Go to the hold and bring the prisoner Daniel Greene to this cabin—immediately!"

"Aye, sir!"

An oppressive silence pervaded the room as Hawke shut the door, and the three stood there stoically. Charity remained against the wall, waiting silently. Blanche bit her lip nervously as she looked at Hawke's expressionless face. It was a painful time; the only sound that broke the silence was the creaking of timbers as the ship rolled slowly with the swells. Finally they heard footsteps, and soon a knock on the door.

"Bring the prisoner in, Sergeant," Hawke called out. He walked toward the far bulkhead, pausing deliberately, keeping his back toward the door as it swung open. "Remain outside, Sergeant," he ordered. He waited until the door closed, then wheeled to face the prisoner.

Dan had been in the darkness of the hold so long that the light of day was painful, and he was forced to squint. As his eyes adjusted, he surveyed the scene quickly: Charity against the wall, the woman across from her who'd come with her to the hold, and an officer in a blue uniform, who now spoke. "Do you know me, Greene?" Captain Hawke asked sharply.

Greene batted his eyes, focused on the man's face, and as the truth dawned, his eyes widened with shock. "Winslow! Paul Winslow!"

"Does that satisfy you?" Charity snapped. She saw the befuddled look on Dan's face, and explained hurriedly, "He claims to have lost his memory."

Greene looked back into the dark eyes that were regarding him intently, and inquired soberly, "Is that true?"

"Yes. I can remember nothing that happened before I was brought aboard the frigate *Neptune* about two years ago. I was carried there by a press gang," he added, "and I had an injury to my head. Evidently it did more damage inside than out, because until Miss Alden called my name, I had no idea who I was."

Dan waited, listening carefully to the words. He glanced at Charity, shifted his gaze back to Winslow, and finally said, "Well, I can tell you that your name is Paul Winslow." He hesitated slightly before asking, "Don't you remember me at all?"

"No."

The monosyllable fell flat, and Dan shrugged. "Well, we were not friends, Winslow. As a matter of fact, we were enemies. I might as well tell you that we were scheduled to meet in an affair of honor."

"An affair of honor? What was the quarrel?"

Dan shook his head, but Charity spoke up. "*I* was the cause! You had dishonored me, Winslow."

He stared at her, his eyes expressionless. She was waiting for him to apologize, but he said nothing for what seemed like an eternity. When he did speak, it was not of her.

"Who am I, Greene? Will you tell me about my family?"

Dan was taken aback. He had never heard of such a thing, and his first thought was that Charity was right: the man was playing a role. He studied the face of the officer, and finally asked quietly, "Are you telling me the truth? You don't know who you are?"

"I do not."

Dan Greene was a perceptive man, and he could see nothing in the steady gaze that suggested Winslow was lying—and he had been doing some rapid calculations with dates. "I believe you—"

"Well, *I* don't!" Charity broke out.

"But, Charity," Dan protested, "remember how he disappeared? It was in March when we went to the Winslows'. That was two years ago—and they told us Paul had disappeared."

"But they said he'd been murdered and his body thrown into

the sea! Mr. Winslow said he *couldn't* have been pressed—he said he'd had it checked!"

"Obviously, whoever checked was not successful," Dan shrugged. "Was it in March when you were brought on board?" he questioned, turning to Winslow.

"It was the third day of March," Blanche declared. "That was the day my mother and I boarded ship to go to the West Indies— and I was there when Hawke—" She broke off abruptly, an odd look in her eyes. "Or should I say *Paul*? Anyway, I was there when he came out of his coma. He couldn't remember a thing about his past. I've been with him for these two years—and he's not lying."

For a moment the cabin was still, then Dan said in a subdued voice, "Well, I think it's obvious that you were injured and lost your memory. I'm sorry for it. Would you like to ask questions?"

Paul Winslow's eyes grew warm at Greene's willing spirit and he replied hastily, "Well, of course, I still want to know about myself. I mean, am I a criminal?"

"You're the son of Charles and Dorcas Winslow. They are a well-to-do American couple living in Boston. You have one sister, a girl of sixteen named Anne. Your people are Loyalists, but your father's brother is an officer in the Continental Army—Major Adam Winslow."

"A tangled web," Paul murmured. "And what about me, Mr. Greene? What was I?"

"A drunk, a brawler, and a lecher!" All three turned toward Charity, who, though she had not raised her voice, spoke with such anger that Dan shook his head in silent protest. She went on, "Your uncle Adam and your cousin Nathan, his son, are the finest men in America. But your father allowed his brother to save him from what the rest of the Tories got, and your parents have no more gratitude than a pair of vipers!"

"That's not quite true, Charity," Dan argued. "And you are being unfair to Paul as well."

"You defend him?" Charity scoffed.

"We're all weak, frail vessels, Charity," Greene remonstrated. "Thee has lost that quality that makes people love thee. Charity is your name, but thee has lost that quality," Dan finished softly, lapsing into the Quaker use of "you."

"How can you babble about love, Dan? Have you forgotten what he did to me? He didn't care if his own family died in that frozen waste of Valley Forge while he tried to ruin me when I sought his help. And now he's joined our enemies—and he was one of those who killed my crew—and my father!"

Blanche ignored the tears that gathered in Charity's eyes and declared hotly, "He is an officer in the King's service! It's his duty to fight the enemies of his country!" Then she said in a different tone, a guarded voice that was devoid of emotion but which all knew held the question most real to her, "What about—Paul Winslow? What did he—do to you? Were you lovers?"

"Lovers? Not likely!" Charity brushed the tears from her eyes and told the story that had led to the scene in the inn, and ended by saying, "I slashed at him with that candle snuffer, and it cut his face! There's the scar! And I wish it had cut his heart in two instead of his face!"

Dan interrupted her outrage, saying, "I think perhaps it might be better if you didn't press Charity too hard. She's not herself. I'll answer any questions I can, Winslow."

"I agree—and I'm in your debt, Mr. Greene." There was an enigmatic look in his eyes, and he added, "As long as we're on this ship, I will be Lieutenant Hawke. You can understand that."

"Yes, of course," Dan nodded.

"We're in for some bad weather, Greene. If we don't get this ship rigged and refitted, she may turn belly up. I don't know that there's a precedent, but I have an offer for you. If you will give me your parole, I'll set you and the others free to work the ship—with the understanding that you will still have the status of prisoners. Will you do it?"

"Yes! I'll do anything to get out into the air—and I think you are right. We're going to need every hand on board to weather this one. I feel it in my bones!"

"Talk to your men. I'll take your parole and theirs as well."

"Aye—Lieutenant Hawke!"

Hawke left the room with Greene, and the two women studied each other. Finally Blanche's shoulders sagged and she went to sit on her bed. "I know you hate all of us—but what you've heard is the truth. I love him, and I know he's not like you say."

Charity did not answer for a moment, but when she did, there was an unhappiness in her and she murmured softly, "I'm sorry about all of this, Miss Rommey. It was—it was such a shock—seeing him! I've—I've never gotten over that scene! The horrible dreams I've had—over and over!"

Blanche Rommey looked up in surprise, and her features softened. She had not thought for one second that the girl was truthful in her concept of Hawke, but now she intuitively knew that there was no reason why the man she had come to know would have been incapable of such things. She nodded slowly, "I suppose I let myself in for this when I fell in love with him. We always knew his memory might come back, or that we might run into someone who knew him. My worst fear was that he'd have a wife!"

Charity looked at the other perplexed. "Are you still going to marry him? Now that you know who he is?"

"He's still Hawke, Charity. You can *tell* him that he's Paul Winslow—but the man that fell in love with me is another man. Don't you see that?"

Charity replied wearily, "I don't know. I don't know—or even care—about anything anymore!"

But neither Charity nor anyone else aboard the *Lady* had any time or emotion to spend over personal grief, for by nightfall the ship was rolling like a chip in a white-water mountain stream. If the prisoners had not been released and allowed to work, the ship would have rolled over during the night. As it was, they managed to get enough sail on her to make a run before the wind, and that was what finally saved them.

All night they fought the raging seas that rose and fell like white-crested mountains, the force of the waves repeatedly striking the battered ship with terrific blows. "It's like gettin' hit with the fist of a giant!" Dan exclaimed, wiping the water from his face as he struggled to get a little more sail on the yards.

"Sure if that giant don't get tired pretty soon," little Rhys Morgan sputtered as a wave took him square in the face, "we'll be kindlin' wood by mornin'!"

While the crew worked around the clock, Charity nursed the wounded men. Thad was recovering, but the rolling of the ship made him sick, and she had to stay by him for long hours, holding him in the bed and trying to ladle broth down his throat.

When she wasn't tending the wounded, she was in the galley. Cooking was not a simple thing, for the galley was a constantly tilting platform, so that just to keep a fire going was a feat that called for all her ingenuity! Harrison helped some, but his skill was needed topside to work the ship, so Charity worked long hours to keep hot food and coffee for the crew.

Dan came from time to time to grab a quick bite, but there was a strange wall between them. He said nothing, but thanked her for the food; and on the second day when it seemed that nothing could save them, she was momentarily filled with shame at the way she had treated him. He had eaten a chunk of bread, washed it down with scalding black coffee, and murmured quietly, "That was good, Charity. Thanks."

That was all, but his steady gaze was a rebuke to her. She tried to shake it off, but the memories came quickly, and she thought of his kindness, and what a true gentleman he had always been. With shame she remembered how he had loved her father. Again she tried to shake off the thoughts, but the shame grew greater. Finally, she grabbed a covered pan, put some hot beef in it and headed for the deck, intending to take it to him. But she never made it.

When she stepped out on deck, the howling wind smote her with a terrific force, filling her with fear. But she saw Dan crouched over, working one of the jibs in the bow, and started toward him. She was halfway there when the ship suddenly nosed down and she lost her balance. A huge wave broke amidships, and she felt herself lifted high and thrown toward the open sea.

She opened her mouth to scream, but the water rushed in, and she knew she was lost. Just as she was even with the rail, staring down into the trough of raging water, a hand caught her wrist, and her entire body seemed to snap as her progress was checked. She grabbed wildly at the arm that held her, and clung like death to the man who had caught her. He had anchored himself to one of the davits, but the water was sucking with such force that his grip was loosening. She stared at his hand, watching the knuckles grow white—then she saw his fingers straightening out as he was inexorably pulled by the force of the waves.

"You can't hold me! Let me go—save yourself!" she screamed, but the hand tightened on the wood, splaying out the fingers with effort.

Charity saw another wave sweeping down the deck, headed for them, and knew that he could not hold on. She bent her head back to shout for him to let her go—and found herself looking into the eyes of Paul Winslow! The shock was so great that she was speechless, but he forced his head forward and shouted above the roar of the wind and water: "Hang on, Charity! Don't give up!"

"No—let me go!"

He shook his head stubbornly, and then in the midst of the storm, with death pulling them into its watery maw, he suddenly grinned. He put his lips against her ear and shouted, "Well, maybe

I'm not the fellow you talked about—he sure wouldn't have done this! Look out—here it comes!"

The world was water, and Charity gagged as the brine went down her throat. She clung to the hand that held her, thinking, *This is death*—but it was not, for the crashing of the water abated, and she heard the moan of the wind again.

"Better get below." She looked into a pair of somber eyes, and then she felt him lift her onto the deck. She staggered at first, and then he was gone before she could say a word.

Dan had seen the incident, and he came running along the deck. "Is thee all right, Charity?" He grabbed her in a hug and said in a joyful voice, "The good Lord was with thee!"

She waited until he released her; then a tremulous smile touched her lips. "I guess so, Dan—but it looked like Paul Winslow to me."

She left the deck, and he stood there staring after her. Throwing a glance at the form of the lieutenant, he muttered, "Well, you can't be *both*; which are you—Paul Winslow, the villain, or Lieutenant Hawke, the hero?" He grinned ruefully, saying softly, "I guess you are like all the rest of us—a little of both!"

★　★　★　★

"I don't think that's the same sea, sweet! It's so calm."

Hawke and Blanche were standing at the stern rail, looking back over the glistening wake of the *Lady*. Diamond-like flakes of foam were spread out in a large V, catching the light of a moon round and bright as a silver sovereign.

"It's the same sea—just in a different mood," he murmured. They both thought of the rolling seas that had nearly sent the ship to the bottom ten days earlier, and the placid, mirror-like surface of the water beneath them was so peaceful it did seem impossible that such waves could have driven them miles off course.

"Listen—that's Morgan's fiddle!" she exclaimed, and the plaintive sounds of the music came drifting to them on the slight breeze. The crew were all gathered around the mainmast enjoying the steady progress of the ship and content with the delicious supper they had just indulged in.

"The crew did very well," Hawke remarked. "Greene and his men saved us, of course."

Blanche responded instantly, "You would have managed."

"No. They knew the ship, what she could do. We'd all be

feeding the sharks if it weren't for them. It was a close call. I hope your father's all right—but then the *Neptune*'s weathered worse storms."

Blanche stroked his arm, thinking of the events of the past few days. "You've spent a lot of time with Greene and Charity since the storm," she commented, an edge to her voice.

He looked at her in surprise, discerning a sharpness that he could not explain. "Why, of course. I want to know all I can about my people."

"They didn't know them that well."

"Not my parents—but did you know that Dan and my cousin Nathan were in love with the same woman? She turned Dan down, but he and Nathan are great friends."

"And now he's lost another woman," Blanche laughed. "He's not lucky in love."

"Oh, I think Charity will come around. She thought at first that Dan had refused to surrender, but one of her crew—a fellow named Conrad—saw the whole thing. It was actually her own father who gave the order. Conrad told her, and it's made a difference."

Blanche was unhappy, but could not explain it to herself or to him. Ever since the name *Paul Winslow* had jumped out at them, she had felt a vague uneasiness that continued to grow. It had bothered her to see the three of them talking so often—probably because she felt left out and wasn't sure how he would handle the new identity. Now she broached the question. "What will you do? About your family, I mean? Will you go see them?"

"Not likely," he admitted. "I'm a sailor of the King, and if I left my ship and went to Boston, I could be arrested for treason. That's if I went in disguise and got caught. If I didn't conceal who I was, I'd be arrested by the Yankees and thrown in a prison as an enemy of the Colonies."

She shrugged, saying, "This stupid rebellion will be over soon. My father says it can't last much longer."

"Dan thinks it will. He says that if Washington ever cuts the British Army off from the support of the navy, it'll be over."

"But that's exactly what *won't* happen!" she argued. "You're an Englishman, Hawke. You can't even remember America—and your family is loyal to the King."

"That's true."

His admission did nothing to change her feelings of unrest,

and she announced petulantly, "I'm going to bed. It's getting late."

"Good night." He made no attempt to kiss her, so she turned and left, her back rigid with disappointment.

For twenty minutes he remained there, enjoying the music that floated up to him. He was about to retire for the night when he saw Charity leave the small group gathered around Morgan and move toward the stern. She did not see him, and would have gone down the ladder had he not spoken. "Beautiful music, isn't it?"

She glanced up, hesitated, then came to stand beside him at the rail. There was an uncertainty in her attitude, but her voice was decisive. "We've had several chances to talk—but never alone. I— I want to tell you that I'll never forget what you did during the storm."

"Anyone would have done the same."

"No, that's not right. I wouldn't have, I don't think." Her face was turned to him, and he was struck with the pale beauty of her features. Her eyes were light in the moonlight, and the curves of her cheeks were smooth and chaste. She had, he noted, a chin that was a trifle pronounced, a reflection of her character! But she was a beautiful young woman. She went on quietly. "You almost went over with me, trying to save me. Most men would have let go— but you didn't, Paul, and I'll never forget it."

He stared at her, then said pensively, "*Paul*—it's odd, but when you say that name it—I don't know. It tugs at me somehow in a way I can't understand. It seems—*right* somehow."

"You remember it!"

"Oh, nothing like that. It's just a vague thing—like some odor you know you've encountered—but when you smell it, you can't remember just where." After a pause he laughed, saying, "I'd ask you to tell me more about myself—but it's all bad."

She moved along the deck, and the two of them stared out over the wake. She was bothered by the man, and had been since he had saved her life. Before that night it was easy to hate him. But the following days found her being fretful, uncertain. Now standing by the rail, she spoke what was in her heart.

"I don't know you, Paul. The man I hated and had nightmares over is dead. You're not the same at all."

For a long time they stood there, talking quietly, and finally he blurted out in a voice of bitter resignation, "I'm the nobody man, Charity. I can't be Hawke—and I can't be Winslow. I'm a dead man who won't stay buried!"

Instantly she was filled with a great pity for him. Never before had she known what it was like to be locked in time with no past, and it made her want to reach out to comfort this man she'd hurt so deeply. Without thinking, she put her hand on his arm, and when he turned in surprise to face her, she whispered, "Paul— don't be bitter! Please don't!"

Her face was only inches away from his, and he could see that she was weeping. Tears glittered like diamonds on her lashes, and the sudden rush of sympathy shook him as never before. He had no notion of doing such a thing, but impulsively he leaned forward and kissed her. She moved against him, and the salt of her tears was on his lips.

Charity was swept with emotion, and his lips on hers made her shake like the wind that had battered the *Lady*! She seemed to lose all her strength, and she clung to him as she had the night when only his arm kept her from being pulled to a watery grave.

They were both shocked when a voice spoke mockingly, "Well, I see that you two are having another 'talk'!"

Charity pulled back, confused, and saw Blanche, who had come out of the hatchway and was regarding them with a twisted smile on her lips. She did not say another word, but turned and dashed down the ladder into the darkness.

And before she could answer, he whirled and left her alone on the deck, confused and swept with a painful feeling that she'd not be able to forget the moment—not ever!

CHAPTER NINETEEN

TELL HIM WE LOVE HIM!

★ ★ ★ ★

The blazing sun of August faded into a pale specter as September brought winds with a taste of fall and a hint of winter. *The Gallant Lady* forged steadily through the gray sea, making for New York with all speed.

Since the night that Paul Winslow had kissed her, Charity had found herself living in a state of restless confusion. Although she had tried her best to apologize to Blanche the following day, there was a strain between the two women. She wanted to talk to Dan— but even after she had asked his forgiveness for unjustly blaming him for her father's death, she could sense a definite wall when she saw him. She felt isolated, cut off, and the future looked empty, dull, without any hope of pleasure or satisfaction. The *Lady* had been her life, and now that both her father and the ship were gone, her heart was heavy when she tried to plan the next steps in her life.

Thad was the beneficiary of this time of her confusion, for she spent much time nursing him back to health. She tried as best she could to lay to rest his youthful love for her, but she had only partial success.

While she was changing Thad's bandages one afternoon, she had her first encounter with Paul Winslow since that fateful night. Charity had just pulled the old bandages free and was carefully sponging the wound when a shadow fell over Thad, and she looked up with a start to see Paul looking down at her.

"How's the patient doing?" he asked.

"Oh—he's doing well—no sign of gangrene."

"From all reports, you've done a fine job with these men," he remarked. When she didn't comment, he continued. "I'd like to have a word with you when you're finished here."

She glanced at him sharply, wanting to refuse, but heard herself saying, "I'll be finished soon."

"Captain?" Thad spoke urgently as the officer turned. "What's going to happen to us—the crew, I mean?"

Winslow looked down at the boy, regret in his eyes. "I'm afraid you'll be sent to Dartmoor. It's a naval prison for captured enemies of England."

"We been hearin' it's nothin' but a grave, Captain. Word we've had is that nine men out of ten just die there."

Winslow shook his head. "I wish I could tell you more—but I know little about the place. It *does* have a bad reputation—but I guess all prisons do."

The boy's eyes gleamed with anger, and he spat out fiercely, "Well, they ain't goin' to do me in, I tell you flat! I'm bustin' out of there!"

"Don't do that, boy!" Winslow shook his head sternly. "It's a bad place with lots of sickness, and men die—but from what I've heard the escape rate is nonexistent. Every man who's tried to escape has been caught—and most of them killed by the guards. Try to be patient. This war can't last long."

"Easy for you to say!"

"I'll see you on deck," Winslow nodded at Charity, and left the cabin.

After she finished the bandaging, Charity promised, "I'll bring you something to eat later, Thad. Try to sleep."

She left the hold and went up on deck, where she saw Winslow standing on the poop deck looking out over the bow. When she climbed the steps he turned, saying, "I'm sorry about your crew. It's one of the most terrible aspects of war—prisons. There are no good ones, I believe."

"What did you want to see me about?"

He seemed uncertain, and took off his bicorn, twisting the hat around nervously, staring at the object as if it held a particular interest. The brisk wind ruffled his crisp black hair, causing a rebellious lock to fall across his forehead. Finally he lifted his gaze and said quietly, "I want to apologize for my behavior. It was unpardonable."

His frank approach and the directness of his gaze pleased her, but at the thought of his kiss, she felt her cheeks flush. Quickly she ducked her head and turned to look out across the sea to compose herself. "It was not altogether your fault, Paul," she murmured.

"I must risk contradicting a lady—for I know that in this case you are mistaken. Am I forgiven?"

"Well . . ." She shifted her eyes to meet his, and the beginning of a smile touched her full lips. "You are forgiven as far as *I* am concerned, but—"

He grinned ruefully, and came to lean on the rail beside her. "Blanche? You needn't mention *that*! I've already discovered that a woman scorned is a fearful sight!"

"She'll forgive you. She loves you very much."

He didn't answer directly, but traced an intricate design in the encrusted salt coating the rail. When he looked up, he asked hesitantly, "Would you do something for me?"

"Why—I'm not sure," she answered.

"Let me ask—afterward you can feel free to refuse—and no hard feelings." He brushed the salt off his hands, and as he began to speak, she saw that he was tense. "I'm in a difficult position, you see. I'm an officer in His Majesty's Navy—and if I am apprehended by the authorities—the American authorities, that is—I'll be arrested. But I would like very much to contact my family."

"How can I help, Paul?"

"You could go see them, Charity," he responded instantly. "Tell them about me. They think I'm dead, so it'll be a shock. However, the truth may be even a worse shock, don't you see?"

"I don't understand."

"Well, I've thought about it a lot, and it seems to me that when my family hears I'm alive, they'll all rejoice—at least I would *hope* so! But they need to be told that they're not getting their son back again—because I'm not the same man. It's going to be terrible for them, Charity!"

She stared at him, nodding her head slowly. "I hadn't thought of that."

"You agree—to go, I mean?" He spoke faster, seeing that she was not convinced. "I know you have to bury your father, of course, but after that, if you could go to Boston and speak with them, I would be so grateful! You know what I'm like—as contrasted with what I evidently was before, and they need to be aware that the Paul Winslow they knew really is dead."

A small column of smoke was rising from the galley, and she smelled the acrid scent of coal burning. It got in her eyes and she blinked to clear them before she answered. "I'll go to Boston, Paul."

"You will?" He involuntarily took her hands, then dropped them instantly, saying, "I suppose *that* won't do! But it's like you, Charity. You seem born to take care of helpless creatures like Thad and me."

"It's no trouble," she assured him, and bit her lip. A sadness touched her green eyes, and she stated evenly, "I don't have anything else to do."

"That's my fault, too, isn't it?"

"No. We knew there was a risk of losing the ship," she answered. "Don't blame yourself. Now, what do you want me to say to your family?"

"Tell them what I am," he began slowly, his brow furrowed in thought. "And tell them that I think it best that we don't meet at all. I have another life now, and it will never be possible for me to be what I was."

"I'll try."

He nodded, a look of relief etching his face. "I'll do the best I can for the crew—but it's out of my hands. There may be a way to help make life there easier. I'll see what I can do."

"Dartmoor is a hell, they say." Charity's lips trembled, a sadness touching her eyes at the fate of her crew. "Most of them will die there." She turned hastily, and left him standing on the deck.

For the next two days she kept to herself, but she noticed that Blanche was almost always at Paul's side. *She'll fight for him!* she thought; and try as she could, she could see no happiness for the family of Charles Winslow.

★   ★   ★   ★

Twelve days after *The Gallant Lady* dropped anchor in New York harbor, Charity found herself for the fourth time in her life standing at the door of Charles Winslow's house feeling totally unsure of herself. The first time, she'd come seeking help for Nathan and his wife; the second time she'd come with Dan to apologize; the third time she'd been with Dan and the Winslows; but this time she was even more apprehensive.

She knocked on the door, and while she waited, she thought

of the events of the days since the docking of the ship. She had left the *Lady* with tears, for she'd said her goodbyes to the crew. Dan and the rest would be placed on an English warship and taken to Dartmoor the following day, and they all knew it was the last time they'd ever meet—at least for most of them.

She'd fallen into Dan's arms, grief and shame engulfing her. She knew she did not love him—at least not in the way a woman must love the man she marries—but he looked so alone standing there! "Dan—I'm so sorry!"

"Thee mustn't weep," he had encouraged steadily. "Let me see a smile. It'll have to do me for a time—that's better! Now, I'm believing the good Lord that somehow I'll see this country again—and thee must pray with me."

"My prayers aren't worth a farthing!" she had sobbed. "I don't know God! I'm not even sure I believe in Him!"

"Well, He believes in *thee*—and that's enough." Then it was time to leave, and he had smiled, saying, "Thee has my love, Charity."

The parting had been hard, and just as difficult had been her coming home to Boston to an empty house. She had not realized how much her father had filled the home, had made it happy and full of life. But now it was a burden on her to stay there, and she knew she could not live in the place alone for long.

She thought of the funeral, when the members of the church had gathered around the stark grave, and Pastor Johnson had spoken the old words about resurrection. She had stood there, her mind locked, frozen; when the black casket was lowered into the red clay, she had fainted for the first time in her life.

That had been two days ago, and during all that time she had tried to steel herself to keep her promise to Paul. As the door began to swing open, she had the absurd inclination to whirl and flee—but it was too late. Cory, the same house slave that had told her where to find Paul the first time she'd come, asked, "Yas'um? What can I do fo' you?" And when she recognized Charity, her obsidianal eyes filled with hatred.

"I would like to see Mr. Winslow."

"Mistuh Winslow—he not well."

"Mrs. Winslow? I *must* see one of them!"

"I go see—you wants to come in?"

Charity entered and stood there waiting. The morning sun fell in gold bars through the heavy glass in the door, but it was unable to dispel the depressing silence in the house. Cory came back after what seemed like a long time and said, "You kin come dis way."

Charity followed the servant down the wide hall, glancing in at the dining room where she'd been entertained on her last visit, but Cory led her past that, around a corner, and finally indicated a door.

"You kin go in, dey say."

Charity pushed the door open and found herself in a study that had been converted, it seemed, into a bedroom. Charles Winslow was seated in a leather chair with his right foot on a low stool. His wife was standing across the room, her eyes fixed on the visitor, a hostile expression on her face.

"You must forgive me, Miss Alden," Charles apologized. "This gout has laid me low. I'm bound to this chair, you see."

"I'm sorry to hear of it, sir," Charity responded. She hesitated, not knowing how to begin and it showed on her face.

"Is there something wrong, Miss Alden?" Charles asked. "You seem disturbed."

"Well, I have news for you—but I'm not sure how to go about it. Is the rest of your family here? It's something that concerns all of you."

"Why, yes, they're here. I can't imagine what—"

Charity burst out, "Perhaps it's better if I tell you—and you can break the news to them."

"Break the news?" Dorcas frowned, coming forward. "That sounds ominous. What news could you possibly have that would be of interest to us?" A thought struck her, and she asked quickly, "Does it have to do with my husband's family?"

"Oh, Lord!" Charles moaned. "It's Adam—he's been killed!"

"No! No! It's not about Major Winslow at all!" Charity wet her lips and tried again. "Perhaps I'd better tell you where I've been for the past few months."

"I understand from my brother you've been at sea—in your ship."

"Yes, that's true. And we had bad fortune. . . ."

She began slowly, telling how they'd encountered the convoy, and finally how they'd been captured. Then she said, "The captain of the *Neptune* put a prize crew aboard, and the prizemaster was a young lieutenant named Hawke."

Winslow noted that Charity was gripping her hands so tightly they were white. "Well, my dear, I don't believe I recognize that name."

Charity swallowed, and went on. "You don't know that name, Mr. Winslow, but you know the man. He is your son—Paul Winslow!"

A cry broke from the lips of Dorcas Winslow, and her face drained of color. "No! It can't be so!"

Winslow's countenance was white, but he admonished, "Sit down, Dorcas, before you fall." He waited until she sank into a chair, her eyes fixed on Charity, before he spoke. "I don't understand you, Miss Alden. Our son an English naval officer? You must be mistaken."

Charity protested strongly, "No, sir, I'm not mistaken. He . . . still has the scar from the blow I gave him." She flushed at that, but forced herself to be calm. "It was a shock for me to see him— so I can't begin to understand what it must be for you."

"But—how did it happen? Why hasn't he come back to us?"

Charity looked at Paul's mother. She had never seen the woman behave with anything less than iron control—but that was gone now. Her face was twitching, tears running unheeded down her cheeks.

"I must tell you something," Charity hurriedly went on. "Paul is alive. He was brought on board the *Neptune* by a press gang; he'd been badly injured—and not just in body. . . ."

The couple hung on her words as she related how Paul had completely lost his memory. Then under their questions, she told the rest of it—how he'd become an officer and was engaged to the daughter of a British captain.

"But, why didn't he come here?" Charles asked when she was finished. "You told him about us, so he *knows* we're his family."

"Yes, but he's a British officer. If he were caught here, he'd be arrested."

"Of course," Winslow nodded. He put his head in his hands, his voice breaking as he cried, "And I *can't* go to him—not with this foot!"

"Miss Alden, you must go back and persuade him to come!" Dorcas Winslow had risen and come to stand beside Charity. She held out trembling hands. "I must see him! Oh, God! I must have my son!"

Charles, too, voiced his opinion, but was more reasonable. "I realize it would be dangerous, but a thought has come to me. If

Paul comes here and sees all of us—might it not jar his memory? I mean, he's not seen anything familiar. But if he were here with us . . . ?"

"I don't know about that, Mr. Winslow."

"Will you try? He can wear his old clothes—and he'll have his papers! We can send it all. He'll just be Paul Winslow on a journey home from New York."

"Please do this for us!" Dorcas sobbed. "I know he'll remember us when we get him here!"

Charity was not certain he would, but she only said, "I'll do what I can. But he'll have to make the decision."

"I'll get his things!" Dorcas dashed out the door eagerly, her face alive with hope.

"Tell me more about Paul, please, Miss Alden," Charles begged quietly, and he sat there intently as she told him how he behaved, including how he had saved her life. He listened avidly, and his sharp eye did not miss the warmth that came into the girl's face as she spoke of his son.

Finally when she halted, he responded, his penetrating eyes fixed on hers, "I believe you are telling me that my son is a better man now than he was before." He ignored her protest, and continued thoughtfully. "Paul was a spoiled child. He had too much, and that was my fault. It would be good to believe that we could have the best of all possible worlds."

She grasped at his meaning. "You mean, have his memory return, but not lose this—this better spirit?"

"You are quick, Charity." He put his hand on hers. "Tell him we love him. Tell him we want him home! This is his place. He is a part of the House of Winslow!"

"I'll—I'll tell him, Mr. Winslow, but it may not work out. Things don't, for the most part."

She had told him of the death of her father and the loss of their ship, and now the doubt and fear showed in her smooth face.

Winslow felt her grief, and he spoke earnestly. "You know my brother and his family. They are all devout believers. Not like me. I'm a nominal church member." His lips twisted sadly, and he shook his head in disgust. "I heard a preacher once say, 'God deliver us from half-baked Christians!' Well, that's what I am—but I have always known that God is much larger than my thought of Him, for I've seen it in Adam and Molly. Nathan and his wife are probably the same."

"They are! When my brother died at Valley Forge, I'd have died with grief if they hadn't helped me with their faith!"

"Yes, I know. They have *something*, don't they? Well, I'm an impious man—but I am convinced that God didn't save my son, then put you in his way, then get him back to this country *by accident*! No, Charity, God is in this! Now, you go tell my son to come, and we'll see God do the rest of it—give him his memory back and restore him to his family and his place!"

CHAPTER TWENTY

THE TRAP

★ ★ ★ ★

Charity made the trip to New York quickly, but filled with apprehension. She had no desire to get involved with the family of Charles Winslow, yet there seemed to be no way out of taking the message. *I'll tell him what they said—and after that I'll pull out of the whole thing,* she promised herself as she got off the coach and made her way to the dock.

The sight of *The Gallant Lady* in the repair yard saddened her, and she forced herself not to think of how much the ship had meant to her. Paul had been aboard waiting when she had left for Boston, but the dockmaster told her that he had gone back on board the *Neptune,* anchored a half mile away. She made her way to that section of the harbor and waited until the captain's gig came ashore, and she saw Lieutenant Burns stepping out onto the dock.

She approached him as he walked away from the gig. "Lieutenant Burns?"

He turned at once and touched his hat. "Yes, miss?—why, it's you—Miss Alden!" His homely face lit up with a smile and he strode to her at once, adding, "I'm glad to see ye, miss."

"Thank you, Lieutenant." She offered her hand, saying, "I never had an opportunity to thank you for your thoughtfulness—and I do so now. You were so kind when I lost my father!"

"Nothin' at all, Miss Alden," he protested. "I only wish I could have done more."

"Would you be able to do me a small service?"

"Anything, Miss Alden!"

"I need to have a word with Lieutenant Hawke. Would there be any way you could get a message to him?"

"Certainly there is!" he nodded vigorously. "I'll be goin' right back to the ship as soon as I make one call in town. Just tell me where you'll be, and I'll tell Mr. Hawke."

"I'll be at the Eagle Inn—right over there."

"Shouldna be over a couple o' hours, miss. Captain Rommey's been generous with us aboot shore leave. We'll be shippin' out in a week, so he thought we might like to see a little o' America. Weel, I'll hurry on now—the Eagle, is it?"

"Yes, and thank you so very much!"

The officer scurried off, and for the next hour Charity walked along the beach, noting that the harbor was a forest of masts—most of them English warships. The fleet of England was the mightiest in the world, and she wondered how the tiny nation seeking a birth could ever survive matched against such a force.

She was several hundred yards down the beach when she saw Burns return, get in the gig, and set out for the warship. Less than an hour later, the gig pulled away from the *Neptune* and she saw Winslow in the prow looking landward. She hurried toward the dock and waited with mixed emotions as she saw him step out on the dock. There were eight men pulling the oars, and after catching her eye, Winslow turned to his men, ordering, "Those of you with overnight leave better not get so drunk you can't get back to the ship tomorrow—or you'll find yourself carrying my bag up the mast." He waited for the "aye" that came rather reluctantly from the men, then turned and walked toward her.

"Lookee, there, Sullivan! Blimey! If 'e ain't gone and got hisself another dolly!" Oscar Grimes kept his beady black eyes fixed on the couple as he got out of the gig. His stiff black hair was pasted down with grease, and he was dressed in his "town" clothing.

"He's a ladies man, right enough," the hulking Irishman agreed, staring avidly at the figure of the woman. "But I ain't got no doubts about findin' meself one that good, Grimes. Let's get to the liquor and the gals!"

Ordinarily Grimes would have joined Sullivan at the fleshpots, but he was a man capable of storing up hatred like a miser stores his gold. He had never forgotten how Hawke had treated him and his friend Sullivan; in fact, the memory had grown over the months until now there was a hatred like a fiery coal in the brutal mind of the seaman. Very rarely can a common seaman find any way to revenge himself on an officer, but an idea had leaped into his mind.

"You go on, Sullivan," he suggested, a crafty smile twisting his lips. "I got me another sort of pleasure in mind."

Sullivan stared at him, shifted his gaze to the officer and the girl, who were headed toward one of the inns, and grinned. "Oscar," he told him, "you ain't hard to figure out. You're gonna get some goodies on Hawke—then see that the captain's daughter gets wind of it, right?"

"I dunno—but I'll find some way to get some of me own back on him, blast 'is eyes!"

Sullivan shrugged his heavy shoulders. "You can get burned playin' with fire—but I know it won't do no good to talk to you when you see a chance to do him dirty. I'm out of it!"

Grimes scowled at him, turned abruptly, and followed Hawke and the woman. He kept well back out of sight, and when they entered an inn with a picture of an eagle on the sign, he found a spot down the street where he could remain invisible, yet see the door. "Guess they'll be goin' upstairs for their fun," he muttered. "But I'll get the goods on 'em!"

He was surprised when, twenty minutes later, Hawke came out alone and headed for the dock. "Wot's this?" he scowled. He watched to see if the woman came out, but she did not. Baffled, he kept Hawke in sight and saw him walk rapidly to the wharf and leap into the gig. He grew angry with frustration, for the situation seemed to offer no possibilities for revenge. He skulked about the street, still waiting for the woman to come out. He got a drink from a bar and took it outside to continue his watch, but finally gave it up and started to find Sullivan.

At that moment he looked across the harbor and saw the *Neptune*'s gig making for shore again with Hawke in the bow. He hid himself as he watched the officer come in sight—and saw that he was carrying a bag. He entered the inn and did not come out again.

"I'll bet the blighter went and got leave!" Grimes mused out loud. Slowly a grin split his face. "He's movin' ashore, sure as Sunday, to be with that gal. Now I'll git 'im for sure!" He was prepared for a long wait, but it was a pleasure for him to think about the damage he could do the officer. He was so caught up with his plans to ruin Hawke that when a man came out of the Eagle an hour later, he almost missed it. Only when the woman came out did he cast a startled glance at the man—and his mind reeled when he saw that the well-dressed civilian was Hawke.

"Wot's this?" he gasped. "Wot's 'e up to out of 'is uniform?"

He followed the couple as they made their way out of the harbor to a red barn-like building located on what seemed to be a main road. Grimes couldn't read, but he asked a man who was passing by, "Wot place is that, do yer say?"

"That's the coach station" was the answer. "Coaches out of New York all leave from here. You pay for your seat in there."

Grimes stared at the building uncertainly, noting that the pair had entered. But they were out almost at once and went to a small inn facing the red building. "Well, wot they up to? Leavin' town?" A light burned in his beady eyes, and he snapped his fingers. "Blimey! He's gonna take that little wench away from here—get away from where he's known!"

He was certain this was the way of it, but he was stymied as to what to do next. Finally he moved carefully down the street and entered the coach station. An elderly man with silver hair looked up from the desk. "You need a seat?"

"Why, no—not fer meself—see, wot I need is to find out if a man has already been here—and bought a seat."

"What's his name?"

"Why—that's the trouble!" Grimes was thinking fast, and he was a quick-witted fellow. "Me captain told me to check the station and see if one of our officers had already left—but I forgot 'is bleedin' name!"

The old man shook his head. "No naval officers have bought seats today."

"Well—maybe 'e wouldn't be wearing 'is uniform, seeing as 'e was on leave."

The clerk thought, then shook his head. "There are only five people on the coach that leaves for Boston—and there's no other coach until tomorrow. There's a woman with two small children and one couple—a man and a woman."

"Was the man a dandy sort of fellow—sort of dark and well set up?"

"Why, yes, he was. Said his name was Paul Winslow. You could find him down the street, I think. The coach will leave in an hour."

Grimes nodded and headed out the door, muttering, "Now— I dunno wot to do with this. Why would 'e change 'is name? Just to cover up 'is tracks, I reckon—but how the devil can I get the proof on 'im? They won't never take my word against 'is—not likely!"

His mind raced, and he stood there baffled. Just as he was ready to give it up, he remembered something he had heard one of the officers say: *If there's trouble with the men on shore, it'll be handled by the commandant's office—a Major Locke. He's Army—but he takes care of discipline problems—sort of a policeman.*

Grimes scurried off quickly, and by the simple expedient of asking an army officer, discovered the location of Major Locke's office. He went in with his hat in his hand, more than a little frightened at what he was about to do, but the hatred he had for Hawke kept him going.

He told a sergeant in an outer office that he had secret information for the major, which was evidently a common thing. He was taken to a larger office, and soon the English officer—a smallish man with a thin moustache and penetrating gray eyes—had pumped him dry.

"So this Lieutenant Hawke is now going by the name of Paul Winslow?"

"Aye, sir, and I gotter say 'e ain't never been no *regular* officer, if you know wot I mean!"

Locke listened, and although Grimes had no way of knowing, the principal job of the officer was not the discipline of unruly troops so much as secret service operations. The English were in the midst of an enemy people, and the Americans had developed an effective method of obtaining and passing along military information. It was, Locke had learned, not so much a formal organization as a loosely joined group who were as hard to pin down as running water.

He listened as Grimes spoke of how Hawke had come aboard, and thought with a shock, *What a clever way to get one of their men inside our service!* He rejected the idea at once as being too complicated and totally unrealistic, but he was determined to run the matter down.

"I'll see about this, Grimes. I can find you on the *Neptune?* Well, you keep what you've told me quiet—and that's an order."

"Right, sir. I was just doin' me duty!"

Locke waved the man out impatiently, and as soon as he was gone, called out, "Sergeant, get Mackley in here at once." He leaned back in his chair, staring at the wall until a nondescript man in civilian clothes came and stood before him. "I have something for you, John. Probably not worth much, but I don't think we can ignore it." He gave the details as he had gotten them from Grimes, and ordered, "Get going. The Boston coach leaves in less than an hour. Find out about this fellow."

"Take him in, sir? Might be a bit touchy, you know. I mean Boston is packed with rebels."

Locke frowned. "You're right, of course—but take McCoy with you, out of uniform, of course. The two of you should be able to get the fellow out of Boston. Use your judgment, John. These blasted Americans know every move we make before *we* do. If the man's a spy, he's in a position to do us tremendous damage—an officer on board one of His Majesty's ships! Think of it!"

"I'll be on the coach." Mackley turned and hurried out of the room. The major went to the window and saw him moving rapidly along the streets. "He'll be a clever fellow if he gets by Mackley!" he muttered with satisfaction.

★ ★ ★ ★

Hawke had been expecting a message from Charity, but when he got inside the Eagle Inn, he was taken aback by her proposal. He listened carefully while she told in detail of her meeting with his family, but shook his head at once when she told of their plea for him to come to Boston.

"That would be too dangerous," he replied immediately.

"But not if you went as Paul Winslow," she urged. "I've brought your clothes and plenty of papers. After all, you *are* Paul Winslow, so if we're stopped, what can they say?"

He hesitated, shaking his head doubtfully, "The ship will be leaving soon. I might not be able to get back—besides, I'm not sure it's the best thing—I mean, for my family."

"They love you—that's what your father told me to tell you." She studied his face, not missing the longing in his dark eyes, and she put her hand on his arm. "Do this one thing for them, Paul. You'll never be at peace until you do!"

He smiled at her, saying quickly, "You know me too well, Charity. For that is what's been on my mind." He thought rapidly, then replied, "I'll have to go back to the ship and get leave. You wait here, and I'll see if it's possible."

He had gone back and, as he expected, he found Captain Rommey willing to grant his request—but somewhat surprised. Blanche was not there, having gone to the country house to be with her mother, where they stayed when the ship was anchored in America. "You'll go by and check with her, of course?"

"I have a short trip to make, sir, but as soon as I return, I'll make my apologies."

"Well, take ten days," Rommey suggested. "You deserve it, Hawke. I feel we'll be having some hard service when we ship out again—perhaps we won't touch shore until this mess is over in America."

"Goodbye, sir, and thank you."

He had hurried back to the inn, changed clothes, and a few hours later, Winslow and Charity were on the Boston coach. It was a fast journey, and the coach was crowded. A burly man propped himself upright and went to sleep at once. A young woman with two children who were difficult to handle furnished some diversion. Charity, seeing her dilemma, took over as playmate for the two girls, allowing the exhausted mother to rest.

A small man, who gave his name as Samuel Wilkins, said little at first, but as the trip went on, he and Paul talked from time to time. At one of the stops for the night, they were forced to share a bed in a very dirty inn, and Wilkins remarked with a smile, "Not much your habit, Mr. Winslow. I can see you're used to better accommodations."

Before he thought, Paul answered, "On the contrary, this is not bad at all. It's about ten times as large as my cabin aboard ship."

He bit his tongue, but Wilkins did not react; and when Winslow added, "Oh, well, when we travel on a ship, we all have to take small space," he breathed a sigh of relief. He determined to say nothing more to the man, and managed to keep to his vow.

They got to Boston in the late afternoon and Winslow stepped down, giving a hand to the young mother and to Charity. Wilkins left immediately, and Charity and Paul rented a buggy from the stable that served as coach station. As he drove the team along the road that led out of town, she observed, "You drive well; you've done it before."

He looked at her and shrugged. "Yes, it's familiar—but I guess most men can drive a team."

They didn't speak again, except when Charity gave him directions. He was in a concentrated study, thinking of the strangeness of his position and wondering what the next hour would bring.

Finally they drew up in front of the big house, and he looked carefully at it, noting the huge pillars and the ornate structure. He said nothing, but got down and helped Charity out of the buggy. He tied the reins to a post, turned and took her arm, and they walked to the door. But before he knocked, he faced her and said, "Charity, no matter what turn my life takes, I want you to know how much you've meant to me."

She stared at him, her heart beating faster as he reached out and took her hands in his. "Oh, Paul—I've done nothing!"

"Not true," he murmured. He shook his head and gave her a fond look, and there was a quality in his voice—gentle and longing—that he'd never used with her. "You can't know what it's been like—being what I am. No past at all. No friend to think of from the old days. But you've helped to fill that gap. We *are* friends—aren't we, Charity?"

"Oh yes, Paul!" she responded quickly and squeezed his hands. She felt such compassion for him at that moment, yet she realized it was not altogether pity, for her heart would not race so madly if that were all. She tried to speak, but could not. Instead, she reached up, pulled his head down and kissed him. Then she gave a short laugh and dashed the tears from her eyes. "Now, don't you dare say *that* kiss was your fault, Paul Winslow! And you just remember, no matter what happens, we'll not lose each other!"

His eyes were moist as he lifted the knocker on the door. When it opened, he was confronted with a small, thin black woman who stared at him with eyes that widened like moons in her dark face. Her jaw dropped and she cried out, "Lord God! It's Mistuh Paul!"

She swayed for a moment, then whirled and ran down the hall, crying out, "Mistuh Charles! Mistuh Charles! It's you boy! He's done come back from the grave!"

Paul was unnerved by the scene, and he gave Charity a nervous smile. "I guess this *is* the right place!"

Soon the woman came back, saying breathlessly, "Go on to the study, Mistuh Paul—you folks is dere!"

Charity felt her arm gripped so tightly that it was painful, and looking up she saw Paul's ashen face. The strain made him compress his lips until they were a thin line, with beads of perspiration across his brow.

"Do you remember the way to the study, Paul?" she asked.

"No! I can't even *think*, Charity!"

"It's this way." She led him down the hall and Cory reached out and touched his arm as they passed, whispering, "Thank you, Jesus! Thank you, Jesus!"

The door was open, and Charity heard Paul take a deep breath as they went through it. She got a quick glimpse of the family—all looking as if they were posing for a portrait. Charles sat in his chair with his foot raised, his eyes wide; Dorcas stood by his side with her mouth twitching; Martha sat on the edge of a hard-backed chair, her dim eyes peering at the man who stood before them. And Anne, grown into a young woman with the Winslow look, stared at her brother silently.

"My boy!" Charles cried brokenly, "you're alive!"

He held out his hands and Paul moved across the room to take them. He may have intended to shake hands, but Charles gave a sob and reached up and pulled him down into an embrace. Charity saw that the cold formalism was broken; Charles Winslow was a man who prided himself on never showing emotion, but now his face was twisted as if in pain, though she knew it was joy. Tears ran down his cheeks and his eyes were tightly shut. He kept saying, "Thank God! Thank God! You're alive!"

Then he released his grip, and Paul straightened up in time to catch his mother, who fell against him, weeping, and she was soon joined by Anne and Martha. Paul stood like a statue, not knowing what to do with his hands. But Charles, wiping his eyes, saw his embarrassment.

"Dorcas, let the boy alone—and you, too, Anne and Mother!" He spoke roughly to cover the emotion that had welled up in him. Gazing up at Paul, he tried to smile as he said, "Well, sir, Charity has told us of your affliction. You must forgive us—because though you don't remember us, we remember you."

"I understand," Paul replied. He looked into the face of his father, then to his mother, his sister, and grandmother. "Somehow I feel as if I'm being very unfair—not knowing you."

"No, you mustn't think that!" Charles protested. "It's been horrible for you, Paul, but certainly not your fault." Turning to his wife, he sputtered, "Well, don't just stand there! Give the boy a chair, Dorcas—and one for Charity."

There was a bustle as the chairs were brought and everyone was seated. An awkward silence fell on the room as they stared speechless at Paul. He laughed lightly, attempting to break the stilted atmosphere. "I feel like a prize exhibit at the county fair, sir!"

"I don't wonder!" Charles exclaimed. "But let me look at you. You're so brown. And I've never seen you looking fitter!"

"You look so handsome, Paul!" Anne burst out in wonder. "I

wish I could see you in your uniform!"

"That will have to come later, Annie," Charles stated gently. Then he turned back to his son, feasting his eyes on him hungrily— as if he could never get enough of the sight of him. "Now, tell us everything! You can't think how we've grieved over you—and now you're here! I don't ever intend to doubt the mercies of the Almighty again!"

With a certain trepidation, Paul spoke, telling them of his recovery. They all listened avidly—drinking in the details, exclaiming over some of his trials and smiling in appreciation over the tale of his rise from seaman to lieutenant.

Finally he stopped and uttered, with a short laugh, "I can't tell you how strange I feel."

"Do you recognize anything at all, son?" Dorcas asked quietly. "Any of us? Anything at all?"

He looked at her, saying carefully, "It's so hard to tell. I—I seem to feel *different*. But this is so strange and bizarre—it could be that."

He seemed despondent, and Charles broke in hastily, "You're tired. Why don't you rest, and we'll have a good dinner—and you must stay, too, Charity!"

She protested, but he overrode her and held his hand out. When she rose to take it, he pulled her down and kissed her, saying with a twinkle in his eye, "I'm getting to be as emotional as a Methodist! But I just don't feel responsible—everything is so bright!"

At that moment there was a knock on the door and Cory stepped in with an angry expression on her face. She was stuttering with rage, trying to say something, but was roughly pushed aside by a short man, who was followed by a burly man in a black coat.

"Who the devil are you?" Charles demanded. "What are you doing in my house?"

"Mr. Charles Winslow?"

"That is my name!"

"My name is John Mackley. I am an officer of His Majesty's forces. My superior is Major Charles Locke."

The room had grown ominously quiet, and suddenly Paul cried, "Why, I know this man—his name is Wilkins!"

"That is not my real name—just as your real name is not Hawke." He stared at Paul coldly. "You needn't deny it—for we have proof that you are indeed Paul Winslow. He is your son, is he not, Mr. Winslow?"

"I won't answer any of your questions! Get out of this house!"

"I am leaving—but I am taking him with me." He turned to Paul and announced, "In the name of our Royal Sovereign, I arrest you, Paul Winslow."

"On what charges?" Charles broke in.

"On the charge of high treason."

A deadly silence fell, and then Mackley declared, "I'll have to ask you to come, Winslow."

"You can't take him!" Charles protested loudly. "This is Boston, not New York. You have no authority here!"

"This is my authority, Mr. Winslow." Mackley drew a pistol from beneath his coat, and the other man did as well. "We have a carriage outside, and if you try to stop us—or have us stopped— the first bullet will go into this young man's brain." He glanced at the large man, and added quietly, "See to that, will you, McCoy?"

"I'll shoot him at the first sign of trouble, sir."

Charles started to protest, his face pale, but Paul stepped forward, "No use, sir. I'll have to go."

"Well, try not to worry," Charles said quickly. "It's all a mistake. We'll get lawyers—"

"It will be a military court, sir," Mackley interrupted. "No civilians will be admitted to the court martial. Put the irons on him, McCoy."

He spoke sharply and McCoy drew a set of heavy manacles from his coat and fastened them on Paul's wrists. Paul looked at the others, saying sadly, "I'm sorry I've caused you such trouble— twice now."

As they left, led by Mackley, Dorcas collapsed on the chair, trembling in every limb—and weeping helplessly. "It's my fault! I never should have asked him to come! Charles, we must *do* something!"

Her husband replied quietly, "We must try—but I know these courts, and the way things are now in this country, he doesn't have a chance."

"Will they . . . hang him, Father?" Anne asked weakly.

He did not answer, his body slumped in the chair, his face a picture of abject fear and hopelessness—his son alive, and now facing certain death! Charity looked at him with compassion and murmured gently, "I'll go now. Call on me if I can help."

Charles stared at her blindly, and whispered hoarsely, "Only God can help, Charity! Only God!"

The next day, Charles had himself carried to a large coach that had been fitted with a bed. He had asked Charity alone to go with him, insisting that his family stay at home. His lips were white with pain as the carriage bumped over the road, but he uttered no word of complaint.

A week later he returned, weak and grim, and was helped back into the house by two servants. They put him in the study, and as soon as they were gone, Dorcas asked, "What happened?"

Anne was there, and Martha, the old woman looking as grieved as the rest of them. Paul had been her prize, and now he was gone. She sat rigid, her eyes fixed on her son.

"It's not death," Charles explained, but when they all gave a glad cry, he held up his hand. "No, listen to me—it's not death. Captain Rommey saved him—so they say. I wasn't there, but we heard that it was the captain's plea that kept the court from handing down the death penalty."

Burns had sat in on the court, and he had sought Charity and Charles out to give them the verdict. "He's nae goin' to die—but it's prison for life."

"Dartmoor?" Charity whispered.

"Yes, I'm afraid so." Burns bit his lip, and there was real grief in his eyes. "They're wrong! Wrong! There's nae treason in him! But he is an American who put on a British uniform—and that's all the court could see."

"Can we go to him?" Charles asked.

"No, sir—they say not. Some of the members of the court are still screaming. Your son will get to Dartmoor with a bad recommendation, I fear." Then he added, "But God is still merciful. I am goin' to pray that somehow this will nae be the end o'it."

Now sitting before his family, it was all Charles could do to hold back the tears, but he was a Winslow. He said adamantly, "We will not give up. We'll spend every penny, pull every string! I will have my son back again!"

Dorcas stared at her husband, for she had never seen him so determined. Neither had his mother. Martha Winslow had always known that Charles was not a man of character—that was why she had hated her stepson Adam. Now she said quietly, "God keep you strong, son!"

Dorcas stared at her husband incredulously, and then Charles drew himself up and repeated quietly but with an intensity that had never manifested itself in his life: "I will have my son back again!"

CHAPTER TWENTY-ONE

THE GATHERING OF THE CLAN

★ ★ ★ ★

"Get up! Get up!" The guard's voice echoed in the filthy hold of the frigate *Mantigo*. Paul gathered his belongings and joined the line of prisoners that waited for the door to open. The voyage from New York to Plymouth had been slow, for the ship was old. He had not complained, but others who had found the moldy ship's biscuit and rotten beef uneatable were chastised.

A short, muscular seaman with tattoos everywhere but his face laughed gruffly at them. "Yer don't like this grub? Wait till yer gets to Dartmoor! This'll look like a piece of cake! Why, a fine, prime rat goes for ten shillin's, and no lack of bidders!"

They were taken to the berth deck, then put ashore in a drizzle of cold October rain that seemed to freeze the marrow of Paul's bones. In spite of the early hour as they passed through the town, they found themselves surrounded by drunken sailors out of grog shops, old women carrying jugs of ale and baskets full of cakes, fried eels and boiled sheep's heads. Devon farmers in corduroy breeches and red vests that dropped halfway down their fat thighs stared at the ragged prisoners, colorless from the lack of sun.

The escort was a troop of Devonshire militiamen. As they left the city the wind roared down the abrupt roadways, and rain began to soak their tattered garments. It beat the road into a brown river of mud that sucked at their feet; and when one of the prisoners fell, he was prodded to his feet, shivering in every joint.

All morning they plodded, laboring up range after range of the rolling hills until finally, just when Paul was about ready to drop, they came to a long hill. Its top was lost in fog and rain, and there were massive granite-like knobs jutting out, as if God had stuck it together as an afterthought.

He caught the word "Dartmoor," and asked one of the round-faced militiamen, "Is this Dartmoor?"

"Aye, Dartmoor" was the answer. They crawled like blind insects upward until finally late in the afternoon they came to a halt; there below was a circular mass of granite, a sort of giant millstone. Paul stared down at it, then lurched drunkenly down the slope, a mud-caked scarecrow, not caring much whether he lived or died.

Prodded by the militiamen, the bedraggled group entered the huge gate and was immediately surrounded by guards with muskets. Soon the troop escort from Devon was on its way back to the coast, and a florid-faced, hook-nosed man with tiny eyes and a cruel mouth came to look at the prisoners. After a quick glance he snorted, "What's Snyder thinkin' of to send me a hundred prisoners—and me with nine thousand crammed in like sardines? Well, give them hammocks, blankets and mattresses. Oh, mess equipment, too, and spun yarn for slingin' their hammocks."

After receiving their gear, they stumbled forward, pushed by the sharp bayonets of the guards. Paul expected Dartmoor to be a warren of small cells, but suddenly he was pushed into an enormous room, with colonnades of slender posts extending from floor to ceiling along the length of it. Everywhere men were squatting around kettles in groups of six—eating, drinking, laughing, and shouting. Among them were flickering candles whose beams seemed to make their garments and faces appear yellow.

The newcomers were pushed into the room, most of them falling instantly to the floor, exhausted. Even as they fell, Paul saw the old prisoners begin to creep toward them, and a skeleton of a man began to go through the pockets of one of the new arrivals. *Got to stay on my feet!* he thought. *If I go down, they'll take all I have.* He had a knapsack stuffed with food and trading items, given to him by Burns the last time they'd met.

"Hang on to this, Hawke," Burns warned, calling him by his old name. "Ye'll need it in Dartmoor—and do nae give up on God!"

The words echoed in Paul's mind, but as he staggered around the hellish room, he almost thought that God had given up on *him*. But just when he was about to collapse, he felt a hand on his arm. He whirled around to fight off an attack—and found himself looking into the face of Daniel Greene!

"I've been looking for thee, Friend Paul," he greeted with a smile that gleamed in the semidarkness. "We got word of the trial—and I figured they'd send thee here."

"Dan? You're here?" Paul's mind was blurred, and the words came from his lips in a slur.

"Here, come with me—thee is about past going."

He took Paul's arm with a powerful hand and steered him to a stone stairway, then into a room filled with faces. He recognized some of the men—Thad Alden and Laurence Conrad among them. Weeding their way through the mass of humanity, Dan finally pushed Paul into a corner where he fell onto a straw-stuffed mattress and passed into unconsciousness.

It was no lighter when he awoke. He rubbed his eyes, trying to get his bearings. Fear gripped his confused mind as he began to remember. He sat up quickly and heard a voice. "Well, sir, you've finally come out of it. I thought you were waiting for the general resurrection of the dead!"

Paul squinted in the dimness and found the long face of Laurence Conrad peering at him. The tall man was even more cadaverous than Winslow remembered. "Have some grub," he offered, and then with his usual mixture of pessimism and cheer, remarked, "If it don't kill you, boy, it'll keep you alive for a time."

Paul found he was ravenous, and gobbled down the food without inquiring into the contents. He drank tepid water from a stone jug, taking huge gulps before setting it down. Ashamed at his crude manners, he said, "Well, thanks for the food, Laurence. I guess I was pretty hungry."

"Might as well get used to that," Laurence stated. "You'll spend most of your time trying to find grub." He nodded at the knapsack. "I kept an eye on your kit—and you'd better do the same."

Paul looked around and asked, "All of you in here—you're from *The Gallant Lady*?"

"Most of us—the rest are from our part of America. We don't trust each other much—but we don't trust anybody else at all."

"Well, if you hadn't helped me, that food would have been gone—so it belongs to the crew—all of you. And I'd like to be a part of it—if the men will have me."

Conrad stared at him with a peculiar intensity. Then he shook his head and remarked dryly, "Just when I convince myself that mankind is no blasted good—totally depraved—somebody like you has to come along and ruin my theology."

Dan Greene came over to the corner and sat down beside Conrad. "Well, thee is among the living again," he nodded to Paul.

"Maybe, but he's not in his right mind," Laurence answered with a shrug. "He just donated all his goods to our little group."

Greene gave Paul a thoughtful look. "Well, two is better than one—and a threefold cord is not easily broken." He slapped Paul on the shoulder, saying, "I'm sorry thee is here—but in this place no man can live without friends."

Paul was embarrassed, and replied nonchalantly, "Why, it's nothing. I'm grateful to you." He picked up the bag and hefted it. "There's gold in here—courtesy of Angus Burns."

"Gold! Good Lord!" Laurence exclaimed in a low voice. "Don't say a word to anybody, man!"

Paul looked at him strangely and asked, "Gold is rare here?"

"It'll get you anything you want," Conrad divulged. "Even a woman, so they say."

"Not anything, Laurence," Greene broke in. "It won't get you freedom."

Paul gave him a searching look. "I—I'd hoped it would help make an escape possible."

Conrad and Greene exchanged quick glances and Greene commented, "We wondered how long it'd take before thee got to that."

"We all get to that point, Winslow," Conrad explained. "But it won't pay to dwell on the subject. Nobody gets out of here alive."

"Nobody? Not even one or two?"

Greene stared at Paul and shook his head. "Well, there were a couple of cases—or so I'm told. But they all had one thing in common."

Paul waited for him to finish, and when he hesitated, Winslow inquired, "What did they have in common, Dan?"

Greene bit his lip and shrugged his shoulders. "They all had plenty of help from the outside—wealthy friends who were willing to pay any price to get them sprung. Which leaves all of us out, Paul."

"You have any relatives with a fortune they'd like to throw away on your worthless carcass, Winslow?" Conrad regarded the younger man with interest. "Your newfound father—he's got money, hasn't he?"

Paul thought of Charles Winslow, but he shook his head. "No."

He knew that as a Tory, the Americans would have frozen Winslow's assets, if not actually seizing them. "No, there's nobody out there who'd be able to redeem me."

Greene and Conrad heard the sadness beneath his steady tone, and Conrad said softly, dropping a friendly hand on Paul's shoulder, "Well, the good part of it is, my boy, if we die in this place, we won't have to go out and fight another war with the lousy British for our freedom, will we now?"

Greene was more sober, and urged, "It's no good thinking about freedom, Paul. I've found that out in the short time I've been here. The old-timers have lots of stories about men that go crazy thinking all the time about getting out. The way to beat this thing is just to ride with it. This war will end, and then they'll let us go."

"Not me," Paul informed them. "My sentence is for life—the penalty for treason." He stood up and looked around at the mass of men in the cell and remarked, "The rest of you have a chance of getting out of here. I have none. So I won't be able to stop thinking about escape."

"God help you, my boy," Conrad nodded sadly. "For nobody else will."

Winslow stood up and surveyed the cell, then walked to the end and gazed out on the massive room that held the rest of the prisoners, noting the thin, mean, pock-marked faces. There were ugly features, gray-looking even in the yellow light of the candles, and gaunt. All wore yellow rags and some nothing but a piece of cloth twisted around their loins.

He came back to stand before his two friends, and stated quietly, "I may go to hell when I die—but I'll die before I spend the rest of my life in this hell on earth." His lean face grew utterly serious and he added, "There's nobody out there who can help me—so I'll have to do it myself."

★　★　★　★

Paul had no way of determining that a small group across the sea had already come together, bent on getting him out of Dartmoor. Originally they had not met with the purpose of getting him free, but rather to ease another Winslow out of the world.

Charity had been drawn into the world of Charles Winslow's family almost against her will. She discovered that her own life was empty, and after several days of cleaning the old house on the sea, she welcomed a message from Charles: "My mother is ill. Could you help Anne and Dorcas with her?"

She had gone at once, and found her services almost hysterically welcomed. It was obvious that Martha Winslow was dying, and neither of the women knew what to do—in fact, they were both stricken with fear at the coming event. They had almost grabbed at Charity when she arrived, and from that time both of them depended on her desperately.

After two days, Charles came into his mother's room where Charity was sitting beside her, reading the Bible aloud. He sat down, his foot much better but still tender; and when she paused, he waved her on. She was reading in the Gospels, and his gaze never left her face. When she finally put the Bible on the table, he remarked, "You've been a blessing, Charity. I was afraid for Dorcas and Anne. They have no experience in this sort of thing. You're so calm. How did you learn to handle sickness and death?"

She bit her lip and answered quietly, "At Valley Forge. I don't like to think about that time. Every day—almost every *hour*—men died, most of them just boys. I never got used to it, but I learned to last through it."

Charles put his hand on his mother's and murmured, "She's going to die, isn't she?"

"I think so, Charles." The elderly woman had been ill for a long time, but a week earlier she'd been found unconscious on her bedroom floor, struck down by a stroke, they assumed.

"I've sent for Adam. He should be here any time." He looked at the Bible and asked, "Do you read the Bible to her often? She doesn't hear you, does she?"

"I don't really know, but when my brother Curtis was dying at Valley Forge, Julie would read to him for hours as he lay in a coma. When he woke up, I think it had somehow been . . . heard. It sounds odd, but Julie said there's a verse that reads: 'The *entrance* of thy word giveth light.' She told me that just *hearing* the Bible is a good thing. I hope so."

"All my brother's family are godly people—as you are, Charity." A painful light touched his eyes and he whispered, "I wish now I'd been more attentive to such things."

"It's not too late," Charity encouraged, adding hastily, "No, I'm not a Christian, Charles. When my father died, I cursed God. I'm not like Julie. But like you, I wish I were."

They sat silently for a long time, listening to the faint, labored breathing of Martha, punctuated by the sound of the ticking of a clock on the mantel. Finally Charles rose. "She keeps asking for Adam, have you noticed? Every time she regains consciousness, she asks for him."

"Yes. I hope he comes soon, Charles. I don't think she can last long."

Adam did come, early the next morning. His wife Molly was with him, and so were Nathan and Julie. There was a quiet meeting in the parlor, and all of them embraced Charity exactly as they did Anne. It did funny things to her heart and made her eyes sting with tears. She had no family, but somehow they had made her a part of theirs. Julie saw her tears and plopped Christmas down in Charity's lap. "There! You take care of this fat wad! He's almost worn me down." Julie was expecting again, and for the next two days Charity became a key member of the Winslow family. She helped Cory with the food and beds, she tended to Christmas, who was into everything that wasn't tied down, and she cared for Martha.

She found herself talking to Julie a great deal, for she still remembered the strength of the young woman when Curtis had died. She told her about Dan, and as she did so, a queer look came into Julie's eyes. Finally she said, "Charity, you're filled with guilt because you can't marry Dan. Well, so was I!" She touched her cheek and her eyes were cloudy for the first time since Charity had known her. "I loved Dan—but he would never have had all of me. Nathan had that—and if you can't give a man all of yourself, you're cheating on him even before you marry."

"But it's my fault he's in prison. If he hadn't met me, he'd never have been on that ship!"

"No, he'd probably be in a shallow grave at Princeton or Cowpens or any one of a dozen spots where our men have died. Charity, you can't blame yourself, for you can't know what God had in mind. Maybe He had Daniel on the *Lady* to keep him from getting blinded or torn apart in some battle. You don't know. All you can know is, God is good."

"I wish I believed that!"

"You will believe it someday. God has told me."

The calm statement hit her like a blow, and she got up and left the room. It angered her, somehow, when people talked in such terms, and she avoided Julie for the rest of the day.

It was almost midnight when Martha woke up for the last time. Charity was asleep in her chair, and she heard a voice calling, "Adam! Oh, Adam!" Charity sat up with a start to see the elderly woman staring open-eyed at the ceiling, her hands grasping at the counterpane.

She leaped to her feet and ran down the hall. Adam and Charles were talking quietly in front of the fire when she burst into the room, crying, "She's awake—she's calling for you, Major!"

"Go get the others, Charity," Adam urged. "Get them all."

The men walked rapidly down the hall, while Charity summoned Dorcas, Julie, Molly, and Anne from their beds. They threw on robes and hurried to the big bedchamber where Martha lay.

She was resting in Charles's arms. Adam was kneeling beside the bed, his face close to hers. Charity saw her lips move, and she heard Martha saying, ". . . was never fair to you, Adam—never!" Her voice was weak and thready, but her eyes were brighter than Charity had ever seen them.

"Don't fret, Martha," Adam assured quietly. He took her hand in both of his, and she grasped with the other until he caught that one as well.

"No, I hated you. I was jealous—wanted Charles to be first with Miles. And I made him hurt you—you know I did."

Adam pulled one hand free and removed a white handkerchief. He gently wiped the tears from her withered cheeks, remarking, "It came out all right, Martha. You must remember. Father and I became very close."

She sobbed, "Yes—and I hated that, too—I was so hateful!" She continued to weep softly. As Charity watched the scene before her, her throat ached under the strain. She wanted to run, for the old grandmother's guilt was terrible.

Finally Adam said, "Martha, you must listen to me—just lie there, and let me talk to you. . . ."

He began to speak of his own youth, and how unhappy he'd been. He told her how he'd felt left out, and then how he'd found God.

"I didn't see how God could forgive me, Martha. But Molly will tell you—she was there. I heard about Jesus and how He loved me in spite of my ways. And I called on Him—and Martha, He heard me! He forgave me! That was such a wonderful time—I can't explain how it was—but mostly it was like Bunyan's Pilgrim. I had a load of guilt that was wearing me out, but when I called on the Lord, it rolled away—and it's been gone ever since!"

She was watching him quietly, and there was a strange look in her old eyes. "Martha," he went on, "how could I not forgive *you*—

when God forgave *me*? I forgive you, dear Martha—but I want you to know more than that. Wouldn't you like to know God's forgiveness—wouldn't you like to meet Him with not a single sin or flaw in your heart?"

"Adam—I can't!"

"Yes, you must! Now, I'm going to pray, Martha, and you must pray, too, but only one prayer. Just tell God you're guilty. He knows you are. Tell Him you're not able to help yourself. He knows that, too. Then ask Him to forgive you—and ask it in the name of Jesus— He always hears that prayer. . . ."

Adam began to pray, and as he prayed Charity began to sob. She tried to stop, forcing her fist against her lips, but she could not hold it back. Through her sobs, she heard Martha Winslow calling on God in a feeble voice; then it became stronger. She heard Adam and Molly praising God. Soon she felt an arm around her, and she turned to see through her tears that Julie was there. She began to shake so violently that she could not stand, but slipped to the floor. She did not even wonder what the others might think, for something was moving inside her—a power she had never known before.

She was weeping and moaning, striking her hands against the floor. Julie touched her gently, saying, "It's your time, Charity. Remember what Curtis said? *I'll be waiting on you!* God is calling you right now. Martha has heard and answered. Now it's your turn."

Charity was filled with fear, but there was a longing such as she had never known, and she cried out, "Oh, my God, my God! Forgive me! In the name of Jesus! Help me!"

She continued to sob, but there was a difference. The fear left, and she was filled with a peace that seemed to flow over her. She felt light and free, and she knew that never again would she have the terrible emptiness and fear that had preyed on her.

As Charity rose to her feet, Nathan and Julie embraced her, both of them weeping. She saw Charles and Adam as they looked down at Martha—who had slipped away.

Charles stammered, "I—I'm glad you were here, Adam. She needed you."

"She went to meet God, Charles. I know it!"

"Yes, I know it, too." Charles brushed away the tears streaming down his face. "She was at peace—for the first time, I think. See how rested she looks—she's looked so tired for a long time."

They all left the room subdued, their hearts filled with the wonder of God's working in their lives. But the affairs surrounding death had to be carried out, so in a short while Charity prepared the body, while the rest went about the other duties.

The funeral was held the next day, with the pastor preaching a sermon. Afterward the family returned to the house that now somehow seemed so empty.

After the funeral, they were all seated around the living room and Charles announced, "I have something to say to all of you." Immediately there was a hush, and he looked around with determination in his thin face. "Mother is gone, but my son is in a prison. I want to tell all of you that until he's free, nothing else matters to me."

"Why, Charles, there's nothing to be done, is there?" Dorcas asked.

"Yes, there is and I'm going to do it. Maybe it might surprise you, Adam, but I've been reading the Scriptures myself a little bit." He smiled at his brother as he continued. "I even know a verse you may have missed."

"That's possible, Charles," Adam replied. "What's the verse?"

"It's in Ecclesiastes, chapter 10, verse 19, I believe. It says, 'Money answereth all things.' "

Adam looked curiously at him, as they all did, then asked, "I don't recall it. Does it say something to you?"

"It says that Dartmoor is like any other prison on this planet. It's run by men, and men can be bought. It's simple. I'm going to get Paul out of Dartmoor if it costs every cent I've got. If I need more, I'll steal it."

Adam shook his head. "Don't do that—steal, I mean. Your assets are frozen by the Congress until you lose your Tory ways—"

"I just lost them!" Charles interrupted. "I don't blame England for all our problems, but for whatever reason, I'm an American. I know people won't believe me, but it's the truth."

Adam stared at him, nodding slowly. "Well, I believe you, Charles—and I can drop a word here and there. I think we can get your property released."

This meant he himself would speak to Washington, and that was all it would take. Charles bit his lip, but said only, "I thank you, Adam."

"Nonsense!" Adam cried cheerily. "The boy's a Winslow, isn't he? Of course, we'll have him out of that place. But you can't go to

England. In the first place, you're not able—and in the second place you'd be under suspicion from the minute you set foot within a hundred miles of Dartmoor. And I can't go—nor Nathan. This war seems to be winding up to a climax, and we have to be here."

Charles looked at him, a haggard expression on his face. "I know—but *somebody* has to go!"

The room was quiet, and then without the slightest intention of doing so, Charity stated flatly, "I'm going!"

They all stared at her, and she reddened, but held her head high. "I was going anyway—to try to get Dan out of that place. I might as well get two as one."

"But, Charity, you're only a woman," Anne protested.

"I was only a woman when I was captain of a privateer, Anne, and I did that job all right. I'm going to sell my house and use the money to get Dan and Paul out."

Adam started to argue, but Julie interrupted him. "She will do it, Adam. The Lord said to me last night, 'I will deliver these men from prison—but not by the hand of man.' I didn't understand it at the time, but now I do. It'll be by the hand of a woman!"

Charles argued, "Charity! What could you do?"

"I don't know, but I'm going."

"And you're going as a Christian, aren't you, Charity?" Julie asked.

"Yes. I have given my life to God," Charity declared. Lifting her head high, she went on. "I'm only a weak woman, but God will go with me."

Charles snapped his fingers and leaped to his feet. "Of course! Adam—William! She can stay with William!"

Adam looked startled; then a smile broke across his wide lips. "That's right! His church is very close to Dartmoor!"

"Who is William?" Charity inquired, confused by this sudden burst of enthusiasm.

"William is Adam's older brother," Julie explained. "He is a Methodist minister in England, and very fond of Adam."

"He'll be risking everything, Charles," Dorcas warned.

"He'll do it! I know he will!" Charles assured, his face was alight with excitement. "Adam, how soon can you get something done about the property? I want Charity to start right away."

"I'll get on it—and I think with a little 'encouragement' in the right place, things will go pretty fast."

"I'm leaving this week," Charity added. "I can sell my house tomorrow, I know for a fact. I've already had offers."

"I can't let you do that," Charles protested.

"You can't stop me, Charles Winslow!" Charity was startled at her own boldness, but laughed, "Now you know the worst about me—I'm a stubborn female, bound to have her own way!"

"I think, Charity," Adam told her, "your way is God's way. And I want us all to pray right now for God's angels to go before you, and that our men will be delivered by the same hand that delivered two other men long ago from a jail in Asia—Paul and Silas."

"But that was in the old days!" Anne protested.

"He's the same God—yesterday, today, and forever! Now, let's pray to that God!"

As they all joined hands, Charity felt a moment of fear. But as Major Winslow bombarded heaven, the fear fled like a beaten dog, and she was convinced that God was going to England with her!

CHAPTER TWENTY-TWO

ESCAPE

★　★　★　★

Paul adjusted to the rigors of Dartmoor quickly, primarily as a result of those in his mess. There were six men, including Dan, Laurence Conrad, Thad Alden, Rufus Middles, and Miles Johnson, the white-haired ex-master of the *Lady*. The sixth man was introduced to the group by Paul himself, about whom he wrote in the journal he began keeping from the first day.

Dec. 25, 1780

Christmas Day—and my third month in Dartmoor. My beard is long and full of lice, I'm down to no more than a hundred and thirty pounds, and the Christmas dinner was a chunk of cold beef, stringy and well on its way to being spoiled, washed down by a cup of flat ale—but that's nothing!

Dan and the others have been my salvation—for since I've come here, more than one of the prisoners who came with me have given up and died. They were sick when they came and never had a chance. Our mess is a little band of brothers—reminds me of the words of Henry V in Shakespeare's play: "We few, we happy few, we band of brothers!" If it hadn't been for these men, I would have been swallowed up by now, for the survivors here become beasts of prey, vultures that swarm over the weak and destroy them.

So, I'm thankful for our mess—and it grieved me when Lige Smith died last week. He was wounded when we took the *Lady*, and despite all Lester could do, the wounds worsened and he died. All the men in the mess except Laurence Conrad and I are Christians, and they took it better than us—the unbelievers. Before we took Lige's body to the guards, there was a "funeral" service, and it was like nothing I'd ever seen. Dan did the talking, and he was smiling through his tears—they all were!—and it was like saying, "We'll see you soon, Lige!"

Well, it almost sank me. I was so depressed that I could hardly eat—but yesterday, a miracle happened. (I'll have to learn to believe in miracles if I stay with this group of Christians long!) I was amazed to see Enoch Whitefield brought in with a new group of prisoners. He was just the same as ever, calm as you please. He'd left the *Neptune* and gone to be with his cousin, the famous preacher, George Whitefield. Then he'd signed on an American ship, which had been captured by the British—so here he was. I was so glad to see the poor fellow, and so sad that he was in this place, but he said, "Why, it's God's will, sir!" I proposed him as a candidate for the vacancy, and all the men were glad. Conrad had to be opposed, just to keep his status as resident cynic. "He'll want to have all of us falling to the ground like those Methodist enthusiasts. Oh, for a group of sound atheists for me to have fellowship with!"

But Conrad's a fraud. He's fascinated by these men who can have joy in their God, even in this hellish place—just as I am!

I have tried all I know to find a way out of this place. My only ray of hope was one of the guards. When he saw my gold, he made me all kinds of promises and took the money—but I never saw him again. Conrad says I was a fool, and he's right. Now I have nothing—no money at all. It's hard not to give in. All I want to do is die—better that than this place for the rest of my life!

Paul wrote the last words, closed the small notebook, then leaned forward and put his head on his knees. He was sitting alone in a corner of the large room, in the cobwebby hours of the morning. The din of a thousand voices had not yet begun—only the groans and cries from dreams came to him as he sat there. He tried to pray—something he'd been doing for weeks, without much result—and he had no sense of God. He had observed that when Dan or Enoch prayed, a smile would come to their faces, and it was like they were lifted out of the dark and squalor of Dartmoor, lifted to a place of light and music and pleasure. They could pray like that for hours, and he longed to know what it was that could make the horrors of Dartmoor grow dim.

Now as he tried to pray, he did not have a similar experience, but something came to his mind—something so different that it frightened him.

It was the face of a woman, a beautiful face. He was half asleep but totally conscious of himself. He could smell the stench of the prison, feel the dank cold air, hear the bedlam of voices that was beginning to sound—but for a few seconds in his mind a scene unrolled.

He was at a ball, and the woman in his dream was there. She was outside on a terrace kissing a man, a very tall man with blonde hair and eyes bluer than any he'd ever seen. He felt a rage in him in the dream, and he saw himself going out on the terrace, seething with anger. The woman had fair skin, rich brown hair, and her clear hazel eyes were unafraid as he rushed out to meet the two. The blue eyes of the tall man were angry, and suddenly there was a violence of some sort—and then the memory faded.

By the good Lord! Paul cried out, coming back to the present with a jerk. *I remember! I remember it!* He sat there with his heart beating, his eyes hazy with tears, for it was beyond all doubt a scene from the shadows of his past. He did not know who the man and woman were, but it was *something!*

He was still sitting in the same position when Dan came in, and he immediately told him about the experience. "I don't know who they were," he ended, "But, Dan, I *remember!*"

Dan smiled at him and said gently, "I know who they are, Paul. The man is your cousin, Nathan Winslow—and the woman is Abigail Howland. You two both courted her. Nathan himself told me about that scene. He'd had too much wine, and the two of you nearly had a brawl over the Howland girl."

"It was so *real*, Dan!"

"Praise the Lord, I believe it's a beginning, Paul. I've been praying about your loss of memory, and God's going to give you back your mind and your memory."

★   ★   ★   ★

His words had been prophetic, for in the next three weeks, all through January, flashes of scenes, bits of memory, a parade of faces came to him. He'd be almost asleep, or eating or listening to the talk of his messmates, and some face would leap into his mind clear as a painting. He told no one except Dan, but the hope of regaining his memory revived his anticipation of escape.

He threw himself into the work of making soup bones into small pieces that would serve as planks for the fashioning of ship models to be sold. After whittling at this project for a while, he realized it would take six months, and at that rate he knew he'd never make enough money to bribe anyone; so he tried plaiting straw into baskets and boxes, but despaired. One day when Enoch stopped to talk to him, Paul grumbled, "We'll never buy our way out of this place! It'll have to be something else. Maybe we can get together and break out by force."

"It's been tried—and every man was killed," Enoch informed him. "Just pray, my boy. God has you here for a purpose."

"He has me here to be eaten alive by these pesky lice?" Paul had a bitter smile on his face as he spoke, but then added, "You're beginning to sound like Angus Burns with his confounded Calvinism!"

"Well," Enoch leaned forward to stir the soup he was brewing, "the lieutenant is a pretty fair Bible scholar. I remember once in Savannah a couple of years back, my cousin George was preachin' to 'bout twenty thousand people out in the open. He read a scripture from Romans—let's see, it goes like this: *And we know that all things work together for good to them that love God, to them who are the called according to His purpose.* 'Course, I can't say it like George, but I believe it like he does."

"Why, Enoch, that doesn't make sense!" Paul cried in exasperation. "How could a good God let us wallow in this place?"

"He let Joseph stay in a jail that was probably 'bout as bad as this one! Did that prove he didn't love Joseph? No, sir! It proved He *did* love him. 'Cause later on, Joseph faced his brothers—who'd done him 'bout as wrong as they could—and he said, 'You thought evil against me, but God meant it unto good.' Why, if it was the goodness of God that put Joseph in that prison, and if he hadn't gone through all that, he would never have been able to save 'is people from the famine."

Paul stared at him, and replied quietly, "I'd like to believe that, Enoch. It'd be a little easier to be in this place if I thought there was a purpose in it."

From that time on, Paul listened more and more to the words of the Bible, for each day Dan or Enoch would read aloud to the group. He borrowed the worn black Bible and pored over it, trying to find the secret, but day passed into day with nothing changed.

Winter wore on, and his hopes at times grew as cold and barren as the prison he was in. Only the flashes of memory that kept recurring and the encouragement of his friends kept him alive.

And then, one day late in the afternoon—though afternoon meant nothing inside the dark prison—he was walking aimlessly through the babbling crowd, looking at the wares brought in by the vendors that were permitted in from time to time. He had no

money, but it was something to do, and he found himself confronted by a short, fat man with a handful of chestnuts. "Hey, buy
some fresh chestnuts! Cheap!"

"No money," Paul shrugged, and would have turned away,
but his arm was caught in a steely grasp, and he stared at the vendor
who closed one eye in a wink. He held up a small sack and there
was, Paul saw, a slip of paper protruding out of it.

Paul's heart lurched, and he stared at the man, who grinned
and murmured under his breath, "Pretend to give me some
money."

With his hands trembling, Paul reached into his ragged coat
and pretended to bring out some coins and give them to the man.
The vendor handed him the bag and whirled away without a word.

Paul left the crowded area at once, and getting to his own
smaller area, opened the note and read:

Be selling something in the market one week from today—Jan. 22.

He stared at the words, then with his heart racing, he folded
the note carefully and put it in his pocket. He leaned his head
against the wall and cried out to himself, *Dear God! Somebody cares!*

For a week he waited impatiently, saying nothing to anyone,
but on the twenty-second he was in the market with a few baskets
he'd woven out of straw. They were poorly done, and none of the
buyers that came in from the villages for the sale looked more than
once, but he kept moving, his eyes searching for the fat man who'd
given him the note. When, after hours, he did not see him, his
heart sank.

He was about to leave the market area when he heard a voice
at his elbow: "Let me see your baskets."

He turned quickly—and found Charity Alden looking at him,
her greenish eyes gleaming in the flickering candlelight.

"Charity!" he breathed. "Good Lord, what—!"

"No time, Paul," she answered softly. "Show me the baskets
while we talk." She spoke quietly, and there was an assurance in
her manner that brooked no argument. "You'll walk out of here in
three days—you and crew of the *Lady*."

His head was spinning, and he responded, "How can we do
that? It's impossible!"

She gave him a smile, confident and fearless. "With God all
things are possible. Just be ready. Have the crew come to the east
gate. They'll be taken out as a work party. When you get outside

the prison, watch for a wagon with a canvas top. The guards have been bribed. They'll put you in the wagons; then they'll disappear."

He stared at her, and would have asked more, but she said hurriedly, "I can't stay—someone might suspect. Remember— three days!"

She took one of the baskets, gave him a coin, and left, threading her way through the milling crowd.

Paul walked back to the inner cell, his mind humming. He wanted to shout, but keeping a tight grip on himself, he said nothing until late that night. The prison went to sleep, and for a long time he listened as Dan read the Scripture. Finally, when the Bible was tucked away and the men were turning to their hammocks, he whispered, "Come close. I have news."

They stopped, moved in close, and he began, his voice barely audible. "We're getting out of this place in three days." Seeing the unbelief in their eyes, he pulled the note out of his pocket and showed it to them.

"That's Charity's writing!" Dan uttered excitedly, keeping his voice low.

"Yes—and somehow she's paid the guards off. We've got to be ready. The agreement is for six of us. Members of the crew of *The Gallant Lady* are paid for."

"Why, that's not me," Enoch returned quietly.

"Yes, you're one of us," Paul reassured. "You'll be going along in Lige's place." He stared at Enoch, saying, "I guess God took Lige home so you could make the escape with us. All things work together for good. That's what the Book says, didn't you tell me?"

There was a sudden burst of smiles on the men's faces, and Paul cautioned them, "Don't act any differently. Only the guards on the outer gate who take the work patrols out are bought. If one soul in this place gets wind of what's going on, it'll be over. Everybody in Dartmoor will be lined up to make the break."

"Paul's right! We've got to act as though we were in here for the rest of our lives."

"I promise to be as miserable as ever," Laurence Conrad predicted, but his eyes were gleaming. "If this comes off, Winslow, I fail to see how I can remain an atheist—because only the hand of God can open the locks of Dartmoor!"

★　★　★　★

The air was cold as the tall man and the girl left the house and got into a wagon pulled by a sturdy pair of roan horses. A large brown canvas covered the top, raised by steel hoops. It looked no different from many such vehicles used by merchants to haul their wares from the country to the port of Plymouth. The man helped the girl onto the high seat, climbed aboard, and gave the horses a slap with the reins. They broke into a brisk walk.

Charity said nothing for a time, but she was so nervous her hands twisted in her lap, and finally the man noticed it. "You don't have to worry, Charity. It'll be all right."

She looked at him, and the sight of his smile reassured her. She had instantly seen the Winslow look in William the first time she stepped inside the little house where he lived with his wife and five children. He was taller and more fair than Adam, but the family resemblance was there. He favored Nathan more, but when he'd read the long letter she had brought from Adam, he had smiled and set her fears at rest by saying, "We believe God for the deliverance of our men."

She had spent the next weeks with his family, posing as a distant relative from America. She'd been amazed to find that the congregation of the Methodist church where William was pastor was passionately opposed to the American war. It was not a popular war anywhere in the country, she was to discover, and William had encouraged her. "If Washington can hold out, America will win. The people here are angry at the whole thing. They'll quit if they can find a way."

Working out a plan to free the crew had been a matter of many meetings with many people. Charity had sold her house, and Charles had sent her what seemed to be an enormous amount of money—but getting it into the right hands was the problem.

William had proposed, "We'll ask God for wisdom—and I think I know a thing or two that might help." Charity never was sure how he did it, but she found herself at a luncheon in an inn in Plymouth with a man named Thomas White. He was some sort of official at Dartmoor—she never learned his exact position—and after the meal the conversation drifted to Dartmoor. William finally mentioned casually, "I understand there's no way for the prisoners to escape, Thomas."

"Quite impossible!" White shrugged. "And if they did, where would they go? There's no place to hide; we'd have them back in a few hours—or dead, more than likely. The guards are really callous. Just as soon kill a man as look at him."

They talked about that for a time, and then William commented, "Miss Alden here is quite saddened. Some of her people are in your charge at Dartmoor."

"Oh?" White suddenly stared at her with fresh interest. At William's direction, she had purchased expensive clothing just for the meeting and she felt the man's eyes on the diamond necklace that had been bought for an enormous price in London. "How is that, may I ask, Miss Alden?"

She told him of the *Lady*, and he listened carefully as she ended by saying, "I intend to buy a new ship, and I'll miss my crew." She looked carefully at the massive ruby ring that glowed on her finger and gave a little laugh. "It'll cost a fortune to train a new crew—and I was so fond of them. As a matter of fact, Mr. White, one of the men is my fiance. I am sick over it." Then she sighed and said in the saddest tone she could muster, "If it were only a matter of *money*, there would be no problem!"

White did not take his gaze from her, and replied, "How sad! We'll all be glad when this war is over. I as much as anyone." Then he sipped his coffee and remarked without emphasis, "I would be glad to do anything I can for you, Miss Alden. Let me know if I can be of any service."

After Charity and William had bidden their farewells and were on their way home, William chuckled and repeated White's statement, "I would be glad to do anything I can for you." He laughed aloud and put his arm around Charity, saying, "In translation, that means *I am for sale! How much will you give me to let them go?*"

And that had been the key. There had been many meetings, much bargaining, for White had to buy off others and at the same time protect himself. It would have taken the assets of Lloyds to give him what he demanded, but Charity, for all her tender appearance, proved to be a hard bargainer.

Finally the deal had been made. Half the price was in White's hand, the rest with William, to be paid when he received a letter from Charity saying they were safe in America.

Now as they headed for the prison, Charity wished it were over. "There are so many things that could go wrong!" she worried to William.

"O ye of little faith," he chided her. Then he asked, "You are engaged to this man Greene?"

"Well—we had an understanding once . . ."

He turned to stare at her, for they had grown close. She had told him much of her life, and he struggled to put into words what he wanted to say to her. They would not meet again after the escape, and he wished to make something clear. "Charity, you have said more than you meant about Paul Winslow."

"Paul?"

"Yes, my nephew." William thought hard, then spoke frankly. "I think you've grown attached to him without being aware of it—and I want to warn you about him."

"What about Paul?"

"The Winslows are a good family—but there are some bad seeds—and I fear that Paul is one of them." He talked about how the young man had been nothing but grief to his parents; and he ended by saying, "I am happy that you have found the Lord, Charity—but don't make the mistake of getting involved with a man like Paul. He would ruin your life."

Then he changed the subject, but his warning had not left Charity, and for days she thought about it, never easy in her mind, for she trusted the judgment of William greatly.

They reached a side road not far from Dartmoor about noon, and waited anxiously until late afternoon. Both of them were nervous, but at three o'clock William exclaimed suddenly, "There they come!"

A line of prisoners dressed in faded yellow uniforms appeared, and she counted six of them, with only two guards. William advised her urgently, "Be ready to leave."

The guards were on horseback, and as the line came forward, the two men watched the wagon intently. Not a word was uttered until they got even with where Charity and William were waiting, and then one of them ordered the men, "Here they are! Get in there!" As the six men scrambled inside with wild haste, the guards whirled their horses and dashed down the road at full speed.

"Let's go!" William yelled, whipping the horses and driving like fury. As soon as the wagon began moving, Charity pulled back the canvas and jumped into the back with cries of joy. "We made it! Oh, I was so worried something would go wrong!" The crew members of *The Gallant Lady* closest to Charity threw aside all restraint toward their captain and embraced her, joining their tears with hers.

The happy reunion was an emotional time for all of them. Even Laurence Conrad made no attempt to staunch the tears, and there was none of his usual cynicism as he embraced Charity and murmured with fervor, "God bless you, girl!"

Only Paul and Dan held back, and she had to turn to them, holding out her hands. They each took one, and stood there staring, unable to express what was in their hearts. Finally she said, "Let's go home!" and then whirled and left, saying, "Get out of those clothes! You'll find new ones in the chest."

As the men changed into new clothes, Dan remarked, "I was worried a bit about getting back across the ocean, Paul—but with a woman like that—what's a little thing like the Atlantic?"

And Paul Winslow responded with utter and complete sincerity: "Amen."

★ ★ ★ ★

Two months passed before they could leave England, for the men had to be hidden until the uproar over their escape died down. Then they had to obtain passage to America, and that was not a simple matter.

But on the third of March, Paul Winslow walked up the steps to his home, entered and announced to Charles Winslow, who stood there staring at him: "Father—I'm home! You brought me out of it as no one else could have." He turned and took his mother in his arms, and then the three of them wept.

CHAPTER TWENTY-THREE

CHARITY HAS A PLAN

★　★　★　★

Spring had come early to Boston, the freezing winds of January turning almost warm by the first of April. The fruit trees were deceived by the bright sun and the life-giving breezes, and all around the country the brown hills were spotted with white and pink blossoms of wild plum and pear.

Since his return to his father's house, Paul had done little but stay indoors. It was a strain on him, for he still had only flashes of memory, but he was conscious that he was needed there. His mother clung to him, and he had grown very close to his father. The two spent long evenings together in front of a fire. Charles did most of the talking, and to Paul it was fascinating, for the Winslow name went back to the *Mayflower* and even further. One evening Charles had handed him a book richly bound in red leather, saying, "This is my favorite book—your great-great grandfather's journal." He held the book, running his hands over the smooth cover, and looked up with a warm light in his blue eyes. "Gilbert Winslow was his name. I never knew him, of course, but his granddaughter Rachel stayed at our house a great deal while I was growing up. Adam was her favorite, which didn't always make me happy. But I never forgot her stories of how her great-grandpa had left England to come to this land on the *Mayflower*."

Charles stopped and looked intently at his son, then smiled and remarked, "You have something of him in you, Paul."

"I do?"

"Yes. Gilbert Winslow was the best swordsman in England in his day, or close to it. I believe you got that gift from him. Adam has his sword, and you'll want to see it. It's a fine piece of craftsmanship, and you'd appreciate it. Ought to be in a museum, but then perhaps not. Maybe Gilbert would like it better if one of his seed carried it."

"I—I'd like to see it."

"I'll tell Adam to bring it next time he comes." Charles hesitated, then said, "Take the book, Paul. Read it, for it's got the heart of this new country in it. He lived for a long time, and he saw something here that's haunted me. Adam sees it better than I— he's broken with England and is an American."

"I've wondered what to do—but I have no decision to make, really," Paul stated slowly. He took the book, opened it and read a few lines. "I'm a traitor to the English. I've got no choice now but to be an American."

Charles nodded. "You are right, and you know, Paul . . . I'm glad of it!" He slapped the desk, saying, "By the Lord, I'm going to do the same! Here's one Tory who'll never be an Englishman again!"

"Major Winslow will be happy."

"Yes, he will. I'm not so sure about Dorcas—but from the latest signs in Anne, she's not going to be far behind me."

Paul looked at him, and a smile touched his lips. "You mean that crush she's developed on Dan Greene. . . ?"

"Just that." Charles shook his head. "Of all the men in the world she'd be attracted to, that Quaker is the one I'd put last."

"He's a fine looking fellow, Father. Strong as a bull—and he's not only smart, he's as good a man as you'd want for a son-in-law—if it comes to that."

They thought about it—how Greene had come to stay with them when the crew had gotten back from England. He had spent much time with all of them, but Anne at the age of seventeen was captivated by him. Greene never noticed, for to him Anne was a child.

He found out different quickly enough when they were taken to a ball one evening. Charles had asked him to watch out for Anne, and he'd agreed. But when she'd come down the hall wearing a pale green dress that set off her red hair and molded itself to her fully developed young body, he had gazed at her speechless. She had left her arms and shoulders bare, and as she stood looking up at him, smiling and taking his arm, he had almost stuttered when he said, "Thee—thee does look beautiful, Anne. I never knew—" He broke off quickly, but she finished it for him with a teasing tone.

"Thee did not know I was a woman, did thee, Friend Greene?" Anne was a natural mimic, and he had to smile at how she used the Quaker words. They sounded strange dropping from her full rounded lips, and he had been very conscious of her womanhood from that day.

Anne had approached Charity with all the blunt manner of youth. "Are you in love with Dan, Charity?"

Charity had stared at her, a slow smile forming on her lips. "No. He thought he was in love with me—but he wasn't really." A touch of humor surfaced in her eyes, and she asked innocently, "Why are you asking, Anne?"

"Oh! I—I just wondered." Anne's face turned pink. "You're too quick for me, Charity," she laughed. "But isn't he *something*?"

"He's not very showy, Anne," Charity had warned her. "He's a Quaker, and his religion is very important to him."

"I know. We've been talking about that." The girl had paused and a look of wonder came into her eyes. "I didn't know people could *enjoy* being Christians—the way he does."

Charles and Paul had watched this relationship grow, and now Charles remarked with a smile, "Looks like this house is going to be turned upside down, Paul. From Tory to Patriot, and from Anglican to Quaker—or maybe even worse. Adam will make shouting Methodists out of us if he has his way!"

★   ★   ★   ★

Paul had read Gilbert Winslow's journal, then read it again, and one warm afternoon, he spoke of it to Charity. She had come to spend time with Anne, and he had encountered her as she was walking across the yard from the barn with a basket of eggs in her hand.

"Breakfast, Charity?" He took the basket, saying, "Look up there—the first of the purple martins. They're early."

As she lifted her head she saw a pair of bluish birds circling the house. "Purple martins. I've seen them but didn't know their names."

"I built that house up there—see, on that pole?"

She studied him for a moment. "You're remembering a lot, aren't you, Paul?"

"Well, more all the time. I met a fellow in town last week whose face was familiar, and I remembered that when I was just a boy he came to our house and plowed our garden. His name was Tom Tillis and he loved to sing folk songs. I remembered that—but other things just aren't there."

"It'll come, don't worry."

He sat down and pointed to the seat, "Rest for a minute, Charity. You work all the time." He looked at her as she sat close to him on the small bench, then said, "I've been reading my ancestor's book. He came over on the *Mayflower*."

"Yes. I've read it. It's a wonderful book."

" 'He was a man, all for all. I shall not look upon his like again.' " He flushed and wrinkled his brow. "I can remember lines from Shakespeare, but can't tell you what my first teacher's name was! Anyway, they don't make men like that anymore."

"Oh yes, I think so."

"Name *one!*"

"All right," she responded with a saucy light in her green eyes. "Adam Winslow."

He thought about Adam, smiled, and nodded. "You have me there. He's some man! My father thinks there's nobody like him."

She traced the design in the pattern of her dress for a moment, then looked up at him and said with a rush, "You could be like him, Paul—if you wanted to."

"Me?" He stared at her incredulously, threw back his head, and laughed. "I thought you were a bright girl, Charity—but that's crazy!"

"No, it's not." She had bathed that morning, and he caught faint whiffs of lavender as she moved; her skin was almost translucent in the sun. He had never seen such lashes, long and thick, shading eyes that were sometimes blue-green like the sea. She put her hand on his arm, and if she did not notice it, *he* did, and his arm tingled under her touch.

"You could be anything you wanted to, Paul. Look what you did on the *Neptune*. You rose from a battered pressed man to become an officer in the Royal Navy. Why, some men try for years and never manage that!"

He looked at her unbelievingly, still conscious of her touch, and stated flatly, "I didn't have any choice."

"Well, you have a choice now, Paul Winslow!" She snatched her hand away, adding, "You could do as much for America as you did for England—but you won't!"

"I won't *what?*" he asked, taken aback by her flash of anger. He didn't understand her reaction, but he saw that her face was pink with indignation.

"You won't be an American—because of Blanche Rommey!" She was sorry the moment the words slipped out, and a wave of scarlet touched her neck and crept into her cheeks. "Oh, Paul! I had no right to say that!"

He grinned at her, saying ruefully, "You do have a temper, Charity! But you're wrong."

"You don't love her?" The question leaped to her lips, and she waited for his reply, a shade of doubt in her eyes.

"Why, it's not that easy, Charity," Paul returned. He stripped a splinter from the wooden bench, bent it into a U, then dropped it. "It's not like I am only one man, is it? Blanche fell in love with Lieutenant Hawke—and now I'm just half of that man. I'm half Paul Winslow. Why, I'm a traitor to her country, Charity! How do you think she'll feel about that?"

"If she loves you, it won't matter," she answered warmly. "A woman doesn't fall in love with a man's politics!"

He smiled. "It would be a little awkward, wouldn't it, for the daughter of a British captain to be in love with a traitor? Play havoc with the social life, I'd venture."

"Oh, hang the social life—and you take care of your own love affairs!" Charity snapped. "Anyway, I really have wanted to ask you something."

"Ask away."

"What are you going to do, Paul? I mean, are you going to work or what?"

"Don't know. I could work with father—or I could join the Army. I'm no soldier, but I could learn."

"Why, you'd be wasted as a soldier!" Charity protested. "You're a sailor, and that's what you should be doing."

"Not much in that line available, Charity. No warships looking for lieutenants as far as I know."

Charity bit her lower lip and leaned closer to him. He breathed the lavender again and gazed at her curiously. She was being very secretive, and he was sure there was no one within a mile to listen.

"Would you go to sea again—if you could get on an American privateer?"

Startled, his eyes searched hers, for it had occurred to him.

"I'd go like a shot—but do you know of a ship?"

She moved closer, the pressure of her firm body pressing against him. He almost asked why she was getting so close, but decided against it. He liked lavender.

"I know of one. It would be a little trouble to get her, but she's the best there is."

"I thought you always said *The Gallant Lady* was the best."

"Yes—that's what I'm talking about!" she explained excitedly, her hand gripping his arm.

"But—Charity!" he protested, "she's in the hands of the British!"

"She's in the harbor in New York right now, Paul." She spoke softly as if there were spies hanging from the boughs of the huge cherry tree ten feet away: "Paul—we can take that ship!"

He was not sure he'd heard her. "Take her how, Charity?"

"We can get a crew, sneak on board some night, and sail her out of the harbor."

The humor of it struck him, and he laughed out loud. "Why, sure we can! There are only about ten ships of the line, no telling how many frigates under the British flag there to stop us—not to mention most of Howe's army running all over the streets of New York. Charity, it's the wildest thing I ever heard of."

"That's why it can be done, Paul." Her eyes were wider than he'd ever seen them, and they seemed to set off sparks. "Do you think they *expect* someone to steal a whole ship? They're watching everything else in the Colonies—*but they're not watching that ship!*"

He stared at her, not knowing whether to laugh or just walk off and leave her. He opened his mouth to tell her how ridiculous the idea was, but instead, the thought of the *Lady* flashed into his mind. With a frown he reached up and stroked his chin, and after a long silence he voiced his thoughts. "I remember how it was when we tied up there. The harbor is busy enough by day—but at night it's a ghost place."

"It could be done, Paul. I know it could!"

Her excitement was contagious, and he began to think out loud: "We'd need to get a good crew—some hearty fellows who aren't afraid to take a chance. We could filter into the city a few at a time. Then we could go out in small boats after dark and take the ship."

"We can get plenty of men—all we need," she added. "And when we get clear of the harbor—"

"Wait a minute!" he interrupted. "You're not going—and that's final!"

Anger lit her eyes, and she jumped to her feet and challenged him with clenched teeth. "I'd like to see you try and stop me!"

He was on his feet, and before he thought he grabbed her shoulders and cried, "You may think you're a man, Charity Alden, but this time you're going to act like a lady. You'll stay ashore—ow!"

She had lifted her hand and given him a crack on the cheek; without meaning to, purely as a reflex action, he slapped her full in the face. The blow was far from his full strength, but it drove her head back and she stumbled, falling to the ground with her cheek glowing red from the force of the blow.

"Oh, Lord!" he cried out, and in horror he stooped and put his arms around her. She was sitting there with a blank expression, not hurt so much as shocked, but when she saw his agony and grief, she knew the day was hers. Ordinarily she would have given him another slap across the face, but a streak of feminine wisdom ran deep in Charity despite her mannish ways. She let her body relax, and with no trouble at all began to sob softly, and as he frantically muttered his apologies, she allowed herself to fall on his shoulders, holding tightly to him.

Paul was dumbfounded. He had hit plenty of hard-headed sailors, but the sight of Charity's head being driven back under his blow was frightening, and he continued to pat her shoulder as she lay in his arms sobbing as though her heart would break.

Carefully, as if she were made of fine crystal, he pulled her to her feet and whispered, "Oh, Charity—I'm so sorry . . . !"

She made the most of it, clinging to him with both arms and pressing her face against his shoulder. He began to be uncomfortably aware that he was holding a beautiful woman in his arms, and soon he could do nothing but stand there thinking of her soft beauty.

"Charity—please don't cry!"

She looked up and the soft, damp eyes smote him like a blow. "Paul," she begged, "don't be mean to me—please don't!"

Her lips were inches from his, and he lost all consciousness of the world. Only she was real, this desirable young woman who was melting in his arms. He said huskily, "Charity, I—I . . ." Then one of them moved; he never knew which, and it didn't seem to matter. Her lips were soft as down, and he felt her hands on his neck pulling him closer. Time seemed to stop, and all he knew was the fragrance of her and the soft vulnerable figure pressed against him.

"Paul! Oh, Paul!" she whispered as they parted.

His eyes searched hers. "Are you all right?"

"Yes." She dropped her head, and then asked quietly, "You won't leave me behind, will you, Paul? When you go for the ship?"

"No," he assured. "We'll go together." They turned and walked down the path talking of the ship, but her heart was crying, *He can't love Blanche! Not if he kisses me like that!*

He was thinking of how he was going to explain taking her along on a dangerous exploit, and not once did he stop to realize that he had never consciously made the decision even to try the thing. It was fortunate for Charity that he had no memory of affairs with women, for the old Paul Winslow would have laughed at those tears, seeing them at once as a weapon a woman uses to get her way.

But he was not sorry, and as they walked along the fresh blooming boughs of the apple orchard, he was more aware of her soft hand in his than of the plans they made to capture *The Gallant Lady*.

★   ★   ★   ★

It took three days to convince Charles that the plan to take the *Lady* was worth the risk. It took another week to collect the men for the venture, but Dan Greene and the old crew knew every seafaring man in Boston—and more important, they knew which of them could be trusted. Dan was in and out of the house constantly, with Anne like a shadow, staying as close as possible.

Charity and Paul were inseparable, Charles noted, and mentioned it to Dan one day. "That is a remarkable young woman," he commented. "She's been good for Paul. Look at them!"

Dan glanced to where the pair were sitting at a table. Charity was arguing, her arms flailing, and Paul was watching her quietly, with his head moving from side to side. "They fight all the time, Charles. I hate to think what would happen if he married her!"

"They're both strong people—and if they don't kill each other, I think it might work out. But of course, he has a fiancee, I understand."

Plans for taking the ship continued. Then one day Charles disappeared, telling no one where he was going. He came back in a few days with a strange smile on his face. He called for a meeting, and the leaders of the venture gathered in his living room.

"How would you like to be farmers?" he asked with a droll smile.

"Farmers?" Laurence Conrad frowned. "They grub around in the dirt and grow things, don't they? Not for me!"

"What's in that devious mind of yours?" Paul inquired.

"I thought it over, and I decided that to take the ship by force in the harbor was too great a risk. So I came up with a different plan."

"What does thee propose?" Dan asked.

"I propose that the entire crew go as passengers on the *Jupiter*—that's the *Lady*'s new name."

"Passengers!" Paul was staring at his father with bewilderment. "Passengers to *where*—and for *what?*"

Charles Winslow's face had a light of excitement clearly evident to everyone, and he looked much younger than he had the first time Charity had seen him. The lines had faded and his voice was clear as he continued. "I've been to New York and done a little ground work. The *Jupiter* was sold to a man named Whitaker. He's taking a load of cannon and powder to Admiral Hood's squadron in the West Indies."

"What's Hood doing there?" Dan inquired.

"I talked to Adam, and he told me that the French Admiral de Grass is out there with a large force—nearly thirty ships of the line. Washington has asked him to come and pin the British down at Yorktown. If the French Navy can hold the sea, Washington can take Yorktown and force Cornwallis to surrender—and it'll be the end of the war!"

"Glory to God!" Enoch exclaimed. "But it'll be hard for de Grass to get through Hood. That man is a hawk!"

"So Adam said. Well, the *Jupiter* leaves in a week for the Indies. Adam talked to General Washington, and His Excellency said— and I quote: 'If those men could take the ship and make it to the Indies, they could be the eyes of de Grass. Poor fellow has no fast ships like an American schooner!' "

"Washington said that?" Paul's voice was filled with wonder. Then he looked around and declared fiercely, "By heaven, we'll take that ship or die!"

"But not in New York Harbor," Charles stated. "Here's what must be done—I met the master of the *Jupiter* and I told him that I was starting a farming venture in sugar in the Indies. I asked him if he could take my crew of planters when he went. He said no at first, that it was against the custom for naval ships to haul passengers. But he somehow discovered that it was a custom which had lost its importance—when I waved more money at him than he'd ever seen!"

"Mr. Winslow—you can't afford that!" Charity protested.

"Well, no—but then I don't expect the good captain will keep it long," Charles smiled. "Because when we seize the ship—just before we get to the Indies—I'll get a refund from him."

"By Harry—it'll work!" Conrad exclaimed, and the room buzzed with excited talk.

"I never thought of you as a schemer, Mr. Winslow," Charity told him. "But you've come up with a real plan."

Charles Winslow ducked his head, and then raised it slowly. Both Paul and Charity could see by the stiffness in his patrician features how he was struggling with his emotions.

"All the Winslows have fought for this land. I've been the only one who hasn't—but if I could do this one thing, I could think of myself as a *real* Winslow—and an American!"

"I'm very proud of my father, sir!"

Charles took the hand that Paul held out, and his eyes were suddenly blinded. He whispered, "I have something for you."

Paul and Charity followed him to his study, and he picked up a sword that was on his desk. He handed it carefully to Paul.

"It's the sword of Gilbert Winslow, Paul. Adam said that you're the Winslow who can use it best."

Paul took the shining blade, lifted it, and made a pass. "Beautiful!" he breathed.

"It's been red with the blood of our enemies, Paul."

A firmness tightened Paul's jaw, and his eyes were bright as he declared, "I may die with this sword, sir, but I'll never dishonor it!"

Charles's eyes misted as he murmured wistfully, "I wish your grandfather were here—my father, Miles. He would think better of me—but that's the past. Now, let's make ready for this thing as best we can!"

CHAPTER TWENTY-FOUR

CAPTAIN WINSLOW

★ ★ ★ ★

Over a hundred men dressed as farmers were standing on the dock on the morning of March 15. Captain Whitaker came ashore and looked at them with distaste. They all wore rough clothing, and had bags and chests piled high beside them. Whitaker spotted Charles Winslow standing at the back of the crowd and made his way through the milling crowd, a frown on his face.

"Ah, Captain Whitaker, here you are!"

"Look here, Winslow, you've got more men here than we agreed on."

"Why, there may be a few more, but all the more profit for you, eh, Captain?"

Whitaker opened his mouth to argue, but when Winslow tossed him a soft, heavy leather bag, he clamped his teeth immediately. "Well, all right—but no more!" he warned. Then he turned and yelled, "Stevens! Get the passengers stowed away—on the double!"

"What time do you sail, Captain?" Winslow asked.

"Dawn tomorrow—and if any of your blasted peasants ain't on board, they get left!"

Winslow replied cheerfully, "Oh, you needn't bother about that. My men are all anxious to get to their work—isn't that right, men?"

A chorus of assent rose from the pseudo-farmers crowded around, and Whitaker grunted and moved away.

"I wish I were going with you, Paul, but your mother wouldn't hear of it," Charles said wistfully. Then he nodded toward Charity, who was moving among the crew, laughing at something Conrad had said. "I still think it's a mistake to let Charity go—but she's hard to deny."

"She's that, all right. I'm too big a coward, but I've told Miles Lester that when the action starts, his one job is to get her below and sit on her if he has to!" An odd look leaped into Paul's face, and he added, "There's something I have to do before we leave, Father. I'll be back in plenty of time."

Charles stared at his son knowingly before he replied, "If you must do it—whatever it is, Paul—that's all there is to it. I'll be here when you return."

Paul nodded, and turning quickly, moved across the dock and disappeared into the teeming crowd that swarmed the harbor. Charity saw Paul leave and came up to Charles, inquiring, "Where's Paul going?"

"Oh, he had something in town to take care of."

Charity fixed her eyes on him, a strange look in her eyes. She said nothing, but there was a stiffness in her shoulders as she whirled around and went back to the crew.

It took many trips for the small boat to get all the men on board, but finally as dark was falling over the gray sea, Dan reported to Winslow, "Well, Charles—they're all on board."

"I hope none of them drops his bag. If one of those sailors gets a look at the weapons and the uniforms those men have stored, it'd be all we need." The men's bags and chests did not contain farming tools as Winslow had told Captain Whitaker. They were stuffed with pistols, cutlasses, muskets, bayonets, dirks and a variety of other weapons. And Paul had insisted on the uniforms. "We're not pirates but seamen of the Continental Navy, and when we take the ship, it'll be in that uniform." Adam had obtained the commission for the men, naming Paul as captain and Dan Greene as lieutenant.

"No fear," Dan shrugged. He looked around quizzically. "I haven't seen Paul all afternoon. Did you send him on some duty?"

"No—he had some personal business."

Dan looked at him searchingly, but said only, "I'd better get aboard." He put his thick hand out and smiled. "Thee is as good a man as Adam Winslow, Charles!"

Charles waved his hand in denial. "Oh, that's not so, Daniel!" He smiled and added, "If I didn't know you for a man without guile, I'd think you were trying to butter me up. I expected to have to listen to you asking for Anne's hand in marriage. What's holding you up?"

Dan's broad face burned, and he answered quickly, "Oh, she's too young for me, as I've told her, Charles."

"You're twenty-seven and she's seventeen."

"Well, it's not that, really. I'm not a rich man, and she's used to fine things."

"That's not it, either, is it now?" Charles took Greene's arm firmly. "I used to dream of a rich man marrying Anne, but I've had some sense beaten into me lately, thank God. Now I want more than anything else for Anne to have a man who's honest and good. And you're the finest example I've found."

Greene regarded Charles Winslow for a moment, then said huskily, "Thee is kind to say that—"

"It's the girl's religion, isn't it, Dan?"

"Well, sir, it is." Dan's lips turned up in a rueful smile. "I've courted two women, and both of them have turned me down. I'll be pretty slow to declare myself to any woman. Anne is a beautiful woman, and any man likes that—but the woman I marry will have to love God."

"I honor you for that, my boy," Charles replied seriously. "And it's true that Anne has little religion. But that's my fault. She has a warm and loving heart, and if I'd been wiser in my own ways before God, she'd be different." He paused momentarily. "I think she's in love with you—and it's my notion that with a little help from you and other real Christians, Anne will find your God."

Dan smiled at him, and remarked, "I think thee is hard on the track of God, Charles."

"It's the other way around, I think. I feel like God is on *my* trail—and I have the joyful sense that He's about got me cornered!"

The night passed slowly, but Dan did not go to his bunk. There was too much to think about. He leaned on the rail of the ship and looked at the thin clouds sliding across the sky, masking the yellow moon. *I wonder what will come of this desperate venture*, he mused.

"Dan—" Charity interrupted his thoughts as she joined him on the deck. For a long time they stood there watching the stars and talking about unimportant matters. She was, he discerned, tense and restless. She was always an active girl, but the nervous movements of her hands and the abrupt starts and stops of her speech told him she was not herself.

About an hour after she joined him, they heard a hail from the port side, and Dan looked down to see a small boat making for the *Jupiter*. "It's Paul," he told her, turning back.

They waited until the boat was alongside and saw Paul leap over the rail. "Paul," Dan called. "Over here."

There was a hesitation in Paul that neither one missed. For a moment Charity thought he would turn away, but instead he came toward them. His eyes were shaded by the cap he wore, hiding any information they might glean. "You two still up?" was all he offered.

"Couldn't sleep," Dan stated.

"Everything go all right?"

"Fine." Dan hesitated, then said, "I was worried about thee. If thee hadn't made it back, the whole affair would probably fail."

Both Dan and Charity were waiting for him to explain his errand, but he only replied, "Oh, there was no danger of that," and turned to go. "I guess I'll turn in. Whom am I bunking with, Dan?"

"With me and Enoch. I'll show you."

"All right." His eyes fell on Charity. "It's late. You must be tired."

"I am, a little. Good night."

She left without another word, and Dan led the way to the small section of the crew's quarters where he and Paul strung their hammocks. Some of the *Jupiter*'s crew were already occupying the quarters, so there was no possibility for talk. Dan fell asleep thinking, *He is surely behaving in a strange way!*

Paul lay awake for a long time, immobile in his hammock, thoughts running through his mind that left no mark on his face. He stared blindly at the deck overhead, oblivious to the watch sounding the calls that night.

In the morning the crew ate in shifts. There was no room for all the sailors to eat at once, not to mention the passengers, so in the days that followed, life consisted of shifting from one section of the ship to the other, eating and moving out of the small cabin so that others could come in and have their turn.

Usually some of the ship's crew were close, so meetings between Dan and Paul and the other passengers had to be rare. Charity seemed to keep to herself, and Paul found himself missing her, but there was little opportunity for a meeting.

Day followed day, and everyone became more edgy with the strain of the situation. Finally Conrad growled, "If I have to talk about potatoes or beans one more time to fool these dolts, I'll die."

"Don't you like vegetables, Conrad?" Paul asked with a twinkle in his eye.

Conrad drew himself up to his full height and answered solemnly, "I ate a pea once!" As everyone burst into laughter, he stalked off, offended at their rudeness.

The one completely happy person aboard was Thad Alden. He found Charity willing to talk to him more than she ever had. They spent time together in the bow of the ship, talking about the days back in Boston before the war. Charity should have known better, but she didn't notice how her attention brought the lad into a state of blissful joy.

She was scarcely listening to him one day when he inquired, "You figure a man like me could ever get married and have a family, Miss Charity?"

She was half asleep from the warmth of the tropic sun, and answered, "You, Thad? Why, a girl would be lucky to have a fine man like you for a husband." She almost named Lucy Gambell, knowing that the girl, daughter of a local butcher, was wildly in love with Thad. But she didn't, and she failed to see the flush that came to his face.

"Thank you, Charity."

★   ★   ★   ★

On Sunday the thirty-first, the group met for church on deck, the only place large enough. Dan preached, and the rest congregated around him. Charity felt someone squeeze in between her and Laurence. She looked up to see that it was Paul. He smiled at her, and asked, "Room for one more sinner?"

"Why, I think so."

She sat there so disturbed that she was unable to concentrate on the sermon, but when she glanced at Paul, he was listening intently. After the service was over and they got to their feet, he said, "Come to the stern. I want to talk to you."

She followed him, and by some miracle there was no one at the rail. He was silent at first, just gazing across the shattered water that the ship sent boiling in its wake. Finally he asked quietly, "Charity, are you angry with me?"

"Why—no."

"You've not said ten words to me on this voyage."

She bit her lip, shrugged, and replied evasively, "I . . . I suppose I'm a little bit afraid."

He searched her face, trying to read beneath that facade. "You've been so distant. I . . . I've missed you."

She looked at him, startled, and fingered her bodice nervously. "I didn't think you would."

He saw that she was unhappy, so he hurried on. "Charity, we take the ship day after tomorrow."

"Paul!"

"And I want you to promise me something."

She smiled, the sadness leaving her. "I know. You want me to hide until it's over."

"That's it. You see, I'm very fond of you, Charity. If anything happened to you, I'd—"

She waited for his next words, and prompted him. "You'd what, Paul?"

He searched for an answer, then turned his dark eyes on her. "I don't know what it would be like—not having you." He reached out and stroked the rail nervously. Suddenly he blurted out, "I don't have much to think about, Charity. My memory's coming back—but it's very limited. I have a few items stored there—a few people. But if you were to be taken away, it would be like having the sun disappear!"

She dropped her head, feeling a mixture of joy and hope at his words. She heard the hissing of the water and the flapping of sails, but there was an ease in her heart, a diminishing of the weight she had felt since they had left New York.

"I'll stay out of danger, Paul, if that's what you want."

"I thought I'd have to beat you again." She looked through the darkness to see him smiling in the old way.

"I'll be glad when it's over. Keep yourself safe."

"I will," he promised as he turned and disappeared down the deck.

★ ★ ★ ★

It had been decided to seize the ship just before dawn. That was when the majority of the crew were asleep. Paul met with Enoch, Dan, and Conrad at dusk. "We've been over this a dozen times, but remember, if we can get the marines disarmed, that'll be the best we can hope for. I'll take that detail—oh, and be certain the men wear their uniforms. Enoch, you take care of the watch, and Dan, you take the captain and the officers. All right?"

"It'll be a piece of cake," Conrad yawned.

Dan stared at him, shrugged, and said, "It ought to be."

The night slipped by, and finally Paul whispered quietly, "All right—it's time."

He had tried to time the attack so that no one element of the crew would be able to unify against them. His was the hardest job, for the marines were tough, and he gripped his sword tightly in one hand and saw that the others had only cutlasses. Those taking the crew would have muskets, but the marines would have to be hit hard and swiftly.

He stopped the group of ten men that he had chosen, and murmured softly, "All right. They're not expecting us. They'll be asleep, so when—"

He gave a start, for a musket had gone off midships, and the explosion rocked the night air. Cursing the fool that had thrown them all in danger, he yelled, "Come on—they'll be armed in a minute."

It was too late, he saw, for the door of the marines' cabin burst open, and the deck was filled with the figures of marines half dressed but carrying muskets and sabers. "Cut them down!" Paul screamed. A musket exploded almost in his face, and he heard a scream and a body hit the deck. He cut the marine down with one stroke of his blade, but was nearly skewered on a bayonet that he avoided only by twisting his body to the side in a violent movement. He was too close to use his sword, so he pulled the pistol from his belt and fired it straight into the staring face of the startled marine. The man fell at Paul's feet.

As he cut down another marine who came at him with a wild swing of his saber, he heard the sounds of gunfire and yelling from forward and from below. The crew of the *Jupiter* came swarming up the ladders, and soon the deck was a bloody tangle of men, screaming and slashing at one other. The rising sun cast reddish beams on the deck, and Paul saw Dan and a small group besieged and fighting like madmen at the foot of the mizzenmast.

He lost track of time, and once he was knocked to the deck by a blow of a musket barrel, and came to his feet blinded by the blood that ran into his eyes. He wiped his eyes free with his sleeve and yelled, "Come on—we've got them now!"

He had no idea if the men would follow, but as he went charging across the deck, he heard the pounding of feet behind him, and his group struck the knot of men that was about to annihilate Dan's small team. It was knife, club, bayonet, and saber now—all the muskets and pistols had been fired.

The clash of steel was a ringing chorus that sounded over the screams of battle. Paul was all over the deck, lifting Conrad up where he'd fallen beneath the attack of a burly sailor, directing a counterattack at the stern where Middles and Lester were cutting their way through a wall of flesh. He saw Middles lift his sword, but a seaman with only a dirk leaped under it and cut Middles' throat. For one terrible moment the man stood there, trying to yell, then fell to the deck grabbing his throat and died as Paul watched, helpless to aid the man.

Others went down, and as Paul raced across the deck, he saw Captain Whitaker with his first lieutenant driving his remaining men toward the center of the fray. *If I don't break up that charge—we're whipped!* Paul thought. He yelled at Dan, "Look! We've got to get those officers—then the crew will quit!"

The two of them hurdled side by side over the bodies of the dead and dying, and Whitaker looked up to meet them, his face livid with rage. He lifted his pistol and fired—and Dan went down on the deck. Paul lunged at the captain, who was trying to draw his sword—but it would not come free. The lieutenant leaped forward and caught Paul's blade on his own sword, giving the captain time to draw. The two officers lunged at Paul, and he parried both flickering blades and took one step backward.

"Get him, Stevens! He's the leader!"

They pressed him, and he kept his feet by a miracle, for the deck was slippery with blood. Both of the men were good swordsmen, and they divided so that he could not keep his eye on them at the same time.

He knew it was a matter of time until he was caught, for they were playing him just right. One would lunge while the other waited; then when Paul's blade was engaged, the other would strike. Three times they maneuvered him into position, and only by fighting like a madman did he escape.

Finally their lethal thrusts came as he knew they would. The lieutenant pulled his blade to the right, and he saw the captain to his left driving forward at his unprotected side! He expected to feel the steel driving through his body—but instead he heard a cry and someone fell against him.

He looked down to see Thad Alden, who had come to his aid,

the blade of Captain Whitaker buried in his stomach almost to the hilt. Thad looked up at Paul with unbelieving eyes and whispered hoarsely, "Please!"

The eyes of the lieutenant were fixed on the boy, gaping at the captain's blade trapped in Alden's body. Quicker than a striking cobra, Paul ran the lieutenant through the throat and even as he fell to the deck kicking and gagging, Paul whirled to face the captain.

Whitaker saw Paul's red blade, and his eyes bulged as he saw the merciless face of Winslow, but he could not move fast enough, and instantly the blade that had killed his lieutenant was buried in his chest. He touched it almost delicately with one hand; then a dullness came to his eyes and he fell backward, dead before he hit the deck.

There was a shout, and Paul heard men crying for quarter. Looking around he saw that it was over. He dropped his sword and knelt to lift Alden's head. The boy opened his mouth to speak and was gagged by a rush of crimson blood. Paul wiped the blood from the boy's lips and Thad moaned, "Now I never—won't never be able to—marry Miss Charity—take care of—" Unable to finish, he died in Paul's arms.

Winslow rose to his feet sick at heart, but then he saw Dan getting up, holding his head where the ball had creased it. The big man was smiling, and he came and threw his arms around Paul, saying, "God has been good to us, Paul."

Paul looked around at the dead men and those that would soon die but who now were crying out with pain. He bowed his head, filled with sadness. Then he looked at Dan and cried, "Why do men treat each other worse than beasts?"

Dan shook his head, compassion filling in his eyes. "Why, God's not finished with us yet, Paul. One day we'll study war no more."

"I wish I never had to lift my hand against another human being!"

"Why, thee *should* feel like that. Don't thee suppose that Gilbert Winslow and all thy people felt the same? We're weak vessels, Winslow, but God will see us through."

Winslow nodded, and began tending the wounded and the dying. Charity came running up and stopped short as she saw his bloodstained garments and bloody head.

"I feel like something out of the sewer, Charity," he groaned, and a wave of fatigue and horror gripped him. "Thad is dead. He died with your name on his lips." She gave a cry and fell down to touch the forehead of the boy, and when she looked up Paul had moved away and was speaking to the crew.

All morning the cries of the wounded sounded as the surgeon tried to sew them together, and by noon the warship *Jupiter* of the Royal Navy was *The Gallant Lady* once again, under the command of Paul Winslow, Captain.

CHAPTER TWENTY-FIVE

ADMIRAL DE GRASS

★ ★ ★ ★

Lieutenant General de Armees Navales, Le Comte de Grass, Commander in Chief of His Most Christian Majesty's naval forces in the West Indies, paced the high poop of his flagship, swinging at anchor in Port Royal bay. Fore and aft, he paced, taffrail to quarterdeck.

He had fought in thirty campaigns, this man, and for more than forty-five years he had served French kings. In the American war for independence he had already taken part in eight engagements. His thoughts turned longingly toward home—the Chateau de Tilly, near Versailles. He yearned to feel the rich earth of France underfoot, treading his family estate instead of hard oak decks. His love for home and France was written in his will; no matter in what part of the world or on what sea he might expire, his heart was to be sent to repose eternally in the chapel of his chateau.

But short of death, the count knew that months must pass, perhaps years, before he would see home and family again. There was much to be done for his king on this side of the Atlantic, and he had done little. Rodney and Hood, the English admirals, had checkmated every attempt he had made to bottle up the American coast.

His second in command called from the wheel, "Ship is arriving, monsieur."

The count moved to starboard and saw a fleet three-masted ship that could only be American-built skimming over the water.

As he admired the way she seemed to glide in the peculiar fashion of her type, he mentally added up his triumphs since arriving in the West Indies with his fleet two months before. He had attacked St. Lucia, where the English fleet was a constant threat to French ships, and had driven Hood farther north. He had captured the island of Tobago, but had been repulsed at Barbados, one of England's richest and largest naval supply bases.

All in all, it had been a stalemate—a duel of the minds, a threat of fleets. Thrust and parry and thrust again. He had not succeeded, but M. de Grass well knew the final test was still to come. The war for American independence would be decided not by armies but by ships. The sea lanes along the American coast would be decisive. If he could gain control of those water routes, the war would soon be won. Yet he dared not leave the West Indies until Rodney's fleet had been drawn away.

He said, "I will speak with the captain of that American schooner." Going below, de Grass spent the next two hours poring over maps, as he did every day. So engrossed was he that he did not hear the steward enter, and he looked up with a start when he heard the man say, "Sir, the American captain—he is here."

"Bring him in, Pierre."

He straightened up stiffly, and moved in front of the map table to meet the three Americans who came through the door. He greeted them politely, surprised to see that one of them was an attractive young woman dressed in a man's trousers. *Ah, who can tell with these wild Americans?* the count thought, but he said only, "Welcome to my ship. I am Count de Grass." His English was flawless, and the richness of his French accent gave a fluid motion to the language that invested it with life and interest.

"I am Captain Paul Winslow, Continental Navy, and this is my first lieutenant, Mr. Daniel Greene." The trim young captain introduced the third member. "And may I present Miss Charity Alden."

"We have so few ladies out here, it is indeed a pleasure to have you, Mademoiselle Alden." He moved forward and took the hand she extended, then bent to kiss it.

The gesture brought a blush to Charity's face, and she said in a flustered tone, "Oh, thank you, sir!" The count was a handsome man, over six feet tall, powerfully built, yet moving with agility and grace. His advanced years were evident only in his graying hair, drawn back from wide temples and gathered by a ribbon at the back of his neck. His eyes beneath heavy brows seemed aware of everything; a patrician nose marked his noble lineage.

"Are you attached to any commander, Captain?" de Grass asked, motioning them to take their places around the large oak table.

"Well, sir, we are in a rather peculiar position." Paul spoke quickly of the way they had recaptured *The Gallant Lady*, and the count was properly impressed.

"Indeed, you have done well!" he exclaimed. "I have never heard of such a thing in all my years in the navy." He gave Charity a warm smile and said, "I take it that the ship will be in your name as the original owner?"

"I . . . I'm not certain, Your Excellency," she answered. "Captain Winslow's uncle, a major with General Washington, persuaded the general to give us a commission. If we could recapture *The Gallant Lady*, she was to be under the authority of the naval forces of the United States until the end of the war. He also gave Paul Winslow a commission as captain."

"Ah, and what were his intentions—General Washington?" the count asked, his face intent. "I have had a recent communication from His Excellency—and he is very insistent on our plans."

"General Washington sent us word through Major Adam Winslow that we were to come to you as soon as possible, to be of any aid we could," Paul spoke up.

"Good! I have no ship as fast as yours. You will be my eyes, Captain! If we are to be of service to your country, we must somehow slip through the fingers of the English admiral and strike the British fleet off your coast. That is what General Washington urges. He thinks the time is ripe—but it will not be easy."

"You will take your fleet to America, sir?" Charity asked.

"My fleet needs to be in three places at once," the count replied. "To escort the trade home, to go to the American coast to aid Rochambeau, and to protect our West Indies while the British fleet remains."

"My uncle thinks that Rodney will take his fleet from here to reinforce the British blockade. And he says if that happens, there's not much hope of winning the war."

"Yes, that is what General Washington warns me of in his dispatch." A frustrated look came to the count's eyes. "I must decide," he stated slowly, "for this is one of those times when history hangs in the balance. Most of the time, history is slow, seeming not to move at all, or if things do happen, they have little impact.

But every now and then, there comes a moment of destiny, and the decision rocks empires. I think we are now at such a time—and what happens now will change the nature of America—and of the world."

"I agree, sir," Greene replied. "If this war is lost, England will rule North America. That would be the end of France as a world power, as you well know—and it would mean that America would remain forever a minor colony instead of becoming a powerful nation."

Count de Grass smiled at him. "Lieutenant, you have said it well. So, I would have you be at my call at all times. I must find a time when Rodney is looking the other way—and when that moment comes, we will drive across the sea at full speed. I will need your ship desperately."

"It will be our pleasure to serve you, sir."

The count rose and the others followed. He went with them onto the deck, saying as he walked, "I will give orders for your ship to be supplied, and if you need men, I will have them transferred to your ship. I want you to be battle ready as soon as possible."

They left the ship and returned to the *Lady*, where they brought the crew up-to-date on their new assignment. There was a meeting with the nucleus of the original crew—Miles Lester, Laurence Conrad, who would be the second lieutenant, and Benjamin Smith, the new master gunner. They met in the captain's cabin, and as Paul outlined the plan, speaking swiftly and moving with authority, Dan leaned forward and whispered to Charity, "He's a born leader!"

They all received their assignments, and Paul continued. "We'll take on all the powder and shot we can carry. Smith, you'll get some new hands, experienced men, and I'm expecting you to hit with those guns like they were Kentucky long rifles!"

Ben Smith, a wiry brown man of few words, spit on the floor before he thought, wiped his mouth with embarrassment, then said, "I'll shoot the eyes out of them Britishers, Cap'n!"

"We'll go out every day for firing practice, and I want you to get the crew so sharp they can spin the *Lady* around like a shake of a duck's tail! We'll likely run up against ships with more fire power, but if we're ready, they'll never be able to get a shot at us. Anything else?"

"I think we ought to investigate Port Royal's social life, Captain," Conrad spoke up. "I mean, if we're going up against the whole British fleet, why, we ought to have a fling first, don't you agree?"

Winslow's white teeth gleamed as he smiled at the lean form of Conrad, and he nodded. "Shore leave for everyone—but in shifts. I want the ship manned and ready for action twenty-four hours a day. One third of the crew can ruin themselves at a time."

Conrad let out a long sigh. "Well, then, here I go to the flesh-pots to get drunk again." He shook his head mournfully, and added, "And do I dread it!"

★ ★ ★ ★

There are few spots on planet earth more beautiful than the West Indies in spring, and for the next two weeks the crew of the *Lady* had the most pleasant time of their lives. The fitting of the ship was not difficult, but the training was hard, though brief. Captain Winslow was a hard-eyed slave-driver during morning drills, pushing the men with a single-minded determination; but when the ship returned to her slip in the afternoon, a third of the crew piled off and eagerly headed for downtown Port Royal.

Dan and Charity found time to explore the town, though Paul refused to leave the ship until everything was to his liking. It was a time of relaxing pleasure to stroll along the narrow streets, which appeared to have had no preconceived plan as they wound through the ancient city. The two also spent time shopping and watching the pageant.

One afternoon when they had stopped for a fruit drink, Dan asked suddenly, "Does thee think Paul has changed?"

She sipped the sweet drink, shrugged, and thought for a moment. Her skin was already a golden color from the southern sun's rays, and very becoming to her. "Oh, I suppose—but it's just the responsibility."

He studied her profile a while and smiled. He was such a big man that the cup of juice looked fragile in his large hands. He rolled the drink around, took a sip, then commented solemnly, "We have changed, too. How long is it since we were engaged? Now look at us."

"Poor Dan!" she comforted teasingly, and her teeth gleamed against the tan as she added, "Be glad you didn't get me, Dan. I'll be a frightful wife. Bossy and mean!"

"Not true!" he protested.

"Anne will be perfect for you—if you can convert her."

He blinked at her in surprise, and she laughed at him and shook his shoulder. "You think I'm blind as well as stubborn? She's so much in love with you she can't see straight!"

"I—I don't want to rush into a marriage, Charity. Once bit, twice shy, as they say."

"Oh, you're still sensitive over getting passed over by Julie— and by me," she shrugged. "Does a man no harm to get rejected a few times, Dan. Makes him humble."

"It's not much pleasure. Makes me feel like a fool."

She got up and pulled at him until he arose. "Come on, let's walk. Maybe I'll make you buy me a parrot."

As they left the crowded street and walked along the white beach, she had a thought, and asked him, "Did you ever hear the old tale about how lovers find each other?"

"Not in the Bible, is it?" he grinned. "Then I don't know it."

"Well, it seems that when God created the world, He made a creature, a beautiful creature and it was both male and female. But this creature did something very wrong, so God tore it into two parts and threw it into the world. Now there were many of these creatures, but all of them had been torn in half, just like you tear a sheet of paper in half, you see?"

"Not really."

"Why, when you tear a paper in half, only the other half of that paper will really fit, you simpleton! So the male half and the female half of this creature spent their lives searching through the whole world to find each other."

"So they could fit properly together again?"

"Of course! So in this world every man has to search for the one woman that's a perfect fit for him—and the woman does the same. And I think that Anne Winslow is the one you're looking for, Dan. Neither Julie nor I would really 'fit' you."

"And who is the other half of *thee*, Charity?" Dan asked quietly, pulling her to a stop and looking at her intently.

She was taken off guard, and to her extreme disgust, tears gathered in her eyes. He put his arm around her, murmuring softly, "I think that thee does know the answer to that."

She sobbed against his shoulder, her words muffled as she uttered, "I do love him so, Dan!"

He held her until she finally pulled herself away, then handed her a large white handkerchief. "It's clean," he remarked.

"What are we going to do, Dan?" she moaned. "We've both

given our lives to God—though I'm just a baby at such things—
and we can't marry anyone who's not going after the Lord."

"Why, we must ask God to change them," he replied. "He is
able to do exceeding abundantly above all we ask or think."

"Well, I can *think* a lot," she spouted, a tremulous smile touching her lips. "But it's a big order—even for God."

They got back to the ship to find Paul bright-eyed with excitement. "Where've you been? Never mind—I've got a word from de
Grass!"

"We're pulling out?" Dan asked, his eyes shining.

"Not right now, not today—but soon. Here's what he told me
this afternoon. He's let word get to Rodney that he's sick, that he's
going to take the fleet back to France. And he's even giving a farewell ball to make them swallow the bait."

"Then what?"

"After the ball when Rodney is lulled to sleep, de Grass will
slip away, but not to France. Our fleets will go to drive the British
fleet away from the coast, and then Washington can move on Yorktown to whip Cornwallis."

"It will work!" Dan agreed instantly. "Always before, when we
whipped the British, they'd back up to that fleet, and we couldn't
do a thing. With the French there, Cornwallis won't have anyplace
to hide."

"Get your best dress ready, Charity," Paul laughed happily.
"I'm taking you to a ball, and we have to make the English spies
think it's the real thing!"

"I don't have a dress!"

"Well, *get* one!" he commanded. "I'm not taking you to a fancy
ball in those breeches, and that's final!"

"Aye, Captain Winslow!" She snapped to attention and gave
him a mock salute. "I'll be in uniform when you come to take me
to the ball."

The secret was guarded so carefully that even the men in the
fleet were persuaded that the armada would sail for France. The
ball was the talk of the whole island, and everybody with any pre-
tension to social standing wrangled an invitation.

On the evening of the ball, Paul put on his uniform: snowy
white breeches and a blue coat with one epaulette on his right
shoulder. He wore Gilbert Winslow's sword at his side, and his
long black hair was tied back with a white ribbon.

He went on deck, and saw that the gig was ready. Just as he

was about to ask where Charity was, she came up the ladder. He stared at her as if she were an alien creature from another planet.

She had managed to have a dress made by a woman on the island who sewed, and it had not turned out quite as she expected. The woman had spoken little English; she had done a beautiful job, but she was accustomed to making dresses for her own people— who wore their dresses cut much lower than was usual in Boston.

Charity had picked up the dress the day of the ball, and had not tried it on until she got back to her cabin. She slipped it on, then stood aghast, staring into the mirror. It was a beautiful dress, made of some frothy material she did not know, with ribbons of green interwoven through the hems of the white cloth. It fit perfectly—but she gave a gasp when she saw how low the seamstress had cut the neckline. She quickly gave a tug to lift it higher, but it was useless, for the dress fit like a glove.

"I can't go like this!' she wailed, and stood there staring at herself. "He'll think I'm a—a *hussy!*"

But it was only an hour before the gig left—so finally she set her jaw and declared through clenched teeth, "I'm going to that ball if I have to go stark naked!"

And when Paul Winslow looked at her as she came up to him on the deck, he batted his eyes, for he had never seen anything more beautiful!

She stood there challenging him defiantly with her large green eyes and said, "Well—are we going, or are you just going to stand there staring at me?" Despite her words, her face was red, and she pulled a thin shawl around her shoulders.

"You look ravishing, Charity," he replied, taking her hand and leading her to the gig. The boat was full, and Dan took one look at her, then smiled broadly, though he said only, "Well, thee is all dressed up for the party, I see."

The ball was held at the great ballroom of Government House. It was a grand affair, with light from a thousand candles flashing on gold sword hilts, setting aglow the decorations of noble and distinguished officers. The Count de Grass, with the wife of the governor on his arm, led the grand march, the blue, white and gold of uniforms making a splash of color.

"I've never seen such a beautiful sight!" Charity murmured, clutching Paul's arm tightly. She looked carefully at the beautifully gowned ladies, their white shoulders and bosoms bathed in soft loveliness from the golden light of the candles, and felt less conspicuous in her own dress.

The evening sped by, and she found herself in Paul's arms, gliding across the floor. He held her loosely, but she was conscious of his strong arms around her. She danced with other officers, and when he came to her and suggested, "Let's get a breath of air," she was ready.

They stepped outside, moving away from the palace until they came to an open garden. The music and the sound of voices were muted as she stood beside a fountain with him.

He said nothing for such a long time that she began to get nervous. But then he looked at her and said, "I remember a time like this, Charity. It was the first thing from my past that came to me—and now it's all as clear as if it happened yesterday! I can remember all of it!" His voice rose with excitement, and he took her hands unconsciously as he cried, "All of it! Not just bits and pieces!"

"Tell me, Paul!" she begged.

"Why, I was in love with Abigail and so was Nathan—but both of us were fools, though we didn't know it. And it was at a ball like this that Nathan took her out to a garden and I followed them. I was ready to kill both of them." He shook his head in wonder as he continued. "I betrayed Nathan to the British, and he was almost executed. What a fool I was!"

She asked quietly, "Do you remember—about us, Paul?"

He stared at her, then nodded grimly. "Some of it I do. I remember you coming into the inn looking for help for Julie—and I remember getting drunk and taking you upstairs."

She reached up slowly and touched the scar on his face. "Do—do you remember when I gave you this?"

He put his hand on hers and shook his head. "No, thank God. I was too drunk, I suppose—and that's *one* memory I never want to come back. What a swine I am!"

She left her hand on his face and shook her head swiftly. "No! You've changed, Paul. Your father spoke to me about it. He said you *did* die in some ways—that the man you were doesn't exist. And he's so proud of you—and so am I!"

"Are you, Charity?" he whispered, his face pale in the silver moonlight. "Are you fond of me?"

"Yes!" she whispered, letting him take her in his arms and press his lips to hers. It was not a demanding kiss, but gentle and sweet.

When he lifted his head he said evenly, "I want to marry you."

She stared at him and stammered, "But—what about Blanche?"

"What about her?"

"Why, you're going to marry her."

"No. I went to her before we left New York. You do remember I left to go into the city?"

"I—I believe I do remember something about it."

He laughed and squeezed her in a delightful fashion. "Oh, Charity, you didn't speak to me for days! You were jealous, weren't you?"

"Of course I was!" Her eyes flashed and she pulled back from him. "And what did you two have to say? Was it a loving reunion?"

"Not exactly," he said dryly. "I managed to sneak out to their summer place and send a message inside. She sent a note back. Would you like to see it?" He pulled a slip of paper from his pocket.

She took it from him and held it to the yellow light shining from the windows of the house.

You are a traitor to your country! it stated in large letters. *If you don't leave at once, I'll notify my father and you will be shot as you deserve!*

"So much for my hopes," he sighed. He took the paper, tore it to shreds and tossed it into the air, saying, "Now that is settled—will you marry me?"

She longed to throw herself into his arms, but she shook her head. "I want to, Paul. I love you so much! But something has happened to me."

"Can you tell me about it?"

"It was when your grandmother died. I called on God—and He came into my life." She peered up at him, her eyes filled with tears, and said, "I belong to God, Paul—and the man I marry will have to belong to Him, too."

He stood there, his face lean and his eyes fixed on her. Finally he said, "I seem to be running into God at every turn. All I can say is, I can't go to God just to please you. That would be wrong—but I tell you this, Charity, everything I've seen that's good in this world has been in the form of one of God's people. I want that goodness in my own soul."

She touched his cheek gently, and then whispered, "You will find God, Paul! You will find Him!" And her eyes were filled with faith as they turned to go inside.

CHAPTER TWENTY-SIX

THE DUEL

★ ★ ★ ★

The plan of de Grass to pull Hood's eyes away from the French fleet was a success—or so it seemed from the reports of the informants who brought news to the count. He waited for two weeks, and was gratified to learn that Hood's squadron had moved away from their position toward the north. De Grass acted immediately, issuing orders that the entire fleet move out. The fleet set sail two days later, and according to the count's orders, took a course that would lead to France rather than America.

"He's a wily old fox," Dan remarked to Charity as they stood with Paul on the *Lady's* deck admiring the fleet. They had taken station off the flagship, and had a clear view of the white sails of the warships as they followed in order. "I think we've fooled Hood—which is a pretty hard trick to bring off!"

"What happens now, Paul?" Charity asked.

"Oh, we'll fake him out on this course for a day or two, then turn and make a drive for the coast. There are just a few British warships there now, and this fleet will drive them off, bottle up the army—then Washington will move in and have Cornwallis in the palm of his hand. And that'll be the end of the war. But," he went on thoughtfully, "if we run into trouble, remember your promise to stay below. I'll need every man I've got."

Two days later, de Grass ordered a change of course exactly as Paul had predicted, and for the next four days every square yard of canvas was put on the yards, for surprise was the essence of the scheme. If word of the attack got out, Hood or Rodney would race to meet the French fleet and parry the blow.

On a bright Sunday morning Dan hurried into Paul's cabin with a message. "Signal from flagship, Captain. You're to report to the admiral aboard his flagship at once. I've had the gig put out for you."

Paul wiped the lather from his face, threw on his clothes, and was soon in the gig headed for the flagship. He climbed on deck, and was escorted at once to de Grass' cabin.

"Captain Winslow reporting, sir."

"Winslow—you made good time." The count's face was tense and he told Paul hurriedly, "We're in trouble, I fear. Our lookout spotted a ship up ahead just at dusk. He got only a glimpse, but she was there this morning—a frigate, he thinks."

Winslow saw the danger at once. "You think she's a British ship?" That was what they had feared most—the fleet being spotted and a report made, alerting the English forces.

"It has to be," the count concluded gloomily. He struck his hands together and cried in anger, "It will destroy our plan!"

"We'll have to capture or sink that ship, sir!"

De Grass stared at Winslow with a set jaw. "It's our only hope—but she's a frigate. We have only ships of the line. None of my ships could catch her—" He paused and seemed to be weighing the quality of the young captain as in a balance. He studied the dark eyes, the firm mouth, the air of determination, then added, "No ship—except yours, Captain Winslow."

A fire leaped into the eyes of Paul Winslow, and he said instantly, "We'll do it, Admiral!"

"Think of it, Winslow!" The count came close and looked down into the face of his officer. "She carries three times your guns, as you well know. Her crew will be well trained, and I don't know of an instance of a sloop defeating a frigate in a close action duel."

"We've got to try, sir," Winslow urged. "If that ship gets away, I think it will mean America loses the war."

De Grass nodded slowly, his eyes moody. "I believe you may be right. Washington can't hold the army together much longer. We're his last hope. You know the odds, my boy. Are you certain you want to attempt it?"

"We must do it, Admiral—there's no other choice!"

"Then go, Captain!" De Grass' French blood got the better of him, and he impulsively threw his arms around Winslow, giving him a mighty hug, and then to the younger man's shock and amazement, kissed him soundly on the cheek! The admiral stood back, smiled and apologized, "Forgive me, Captain. We French are so emotional!"

"Oh—that's all right, sir," Paul answered as he turned to leave. "I'd better get back—and, sir, it's an honor to serve with you!"

"Captain Winslow, the honor is mine! Now, God go with you!"

Paul drove the oarsmen of the gig as if they were galley slaves, and as they sent the craft skimming back toward the *Lady*, he kept his eyes fixed on the horizon where the English ship was lurking. He knew that as soon as the English captain was convinced a French fleet was making for America, he'd drive his ship toward the coast to give the warning.

He hit the deck running and shouting commands. "Lieutenant Greene! I want every inch of canvas at once! Change course three degrees south. All officers in my cabin immediately!"

He hurried to the cabin, followed by the officers as they rushed to his command. He gave them the news, then the ultimatum. "We've got to stop that ship! I don't have to tell you what that means—and I don't know how we're going to do it. But it means the war, I think."

"She's a frigate, Captain," Laurence Conrad stated grimly. "One broadside and she'll blow us out of the water."

"Then we'll have to be certain she doesn't get a good shot at us, Lieutenant! The only plan I've got is to use the qualities built into this ship. We can sail rings around that frigate—and thank God for the long eighteens! We can keep up a running fire and maybe knock her sticks off—dismantle her. If we can slow her down, it'll give de Grass time."

There was an air of uncertainty in the faces of most of the men, a fact Paul knew he could not change. *If I could only speak better— somehow convince them that we have a chance!* he thought, but nothing came and he stood there watching their doubt grow.

"I'm not afraid." Charity suddenly spoke up, and every eye turned to her. She was attired in old blue breeches and the red-and-white checked shirt she wore as her uniform aboard ship. Her heavy mane of auburn hair was bound with a white silk scarf, framing her tanned face and enormous eyes. Her countenance was set, confident, even content.

"My brother died at Valley Forge. My father died on the deck of this ship, and some of your comrades with him. We've all shed our tears for the fallen—but that's not enough!" Her voice rose and she searched them with her gaze. "It's not enough! If our country goes down and becomes a rag for England to wipe her feet on, my father and my brother and your family and friends will all have died—for *nothing*! I say we may go down, but I'd rather go down fighting than run like a whipped dog and let the British put a chain around my neck."

"I says the same, miss!" Ben Smith, the master gunner, had been brought to the meeting by Dan, and he nodded his head with grim determination. "I was born in Devon, and I done my share below decks in England's ships—but I ain't no Englishman. I'm an American. Let's send that there ship to the bottom!"

The air of the cabin was altered immediately, and Paul, seeing their sudden shift, asked, "We're all agreed, then? Good! Now, to your stations—but first, Dan, it might be well for you to offer a prayer."

Dan looked with surprise into the face of the captain, but saw there only an honest light in the dark eyes. He bowed his head and prayed, "Thou art our God—and we are thy people. I know, Lord God, thou hast some of thy children on the ship we'll soon do battle with. We are but weak, foolish men. We have no way to know the mind of our God—but we fight to make a land where the songs of Zion will be sung, where the Gospel of Jesus will be preached, where we can raise our children in the fear of a holy God. We remember the words of thy servant David: 'He teacheth my hands to war, so that a bow of steel is broken by mine arms.' Lord of Hosts, teach all of us to war—and break the bow of steel. Set thy people free—in the name of Jesus Christ."

"Amen," Paul Winslow murmured, and his eyes were fixed on Dan as if the words had somehow gone deep into his spirit. He did not move, and they all saw that he was stirred by the prayer. Then he shook his shoulders, saying quietly, "Take your stations. Tell the crew the situation. They need to know how important this mission is. God be with us!"

The Gallant Lady, carrying full sail, seemed to shoot out of her station, and as she passed the flagship, the signalman, Simmes, called, "Signal from flag, sir." He stared at the pennants and read them to Winslow with a smile. "Little David—slay your Goliath!" He shrugged when Captain Winslow gave him an unbelieving look. "That's what the flags say, sir!"

"Signal *Thank you—and Amen*."

The *Lady* ran before a breeze all morning, and at noon, when all that could be seen of de Grass' squadron were the top gallants of the ships, Dan Greene spotted the frigate. "Sail! Two points off port bow!"

"Where does she bear, Lieutenant?" Winslow shouted from the deck.

Dan peered through the glass, then answered, "She's turning, sir—I think she's spotted us!"

"Stay where you are, Lieutenant. Keep me posted."

In two hours of hard sailing, with the masts bending under the weight of full sail, Paul could see the enemy ship for himself. He was standing beside Blake, the helmsman, when Greene came to his side. There was, Paul saw, an odd look on his face. "What's wrong, Mr. Greene?"

"Well, sir, that ship there—"

When he hesitated, Paul asked impatiently, "Spit it out, man!"

"Well, sir—she's the *Neptune!*"

His words caught Paul off guard, and he could not say a word. The *Neptune!* His mind raced as he thought of what that meant. He had been prepared to do battle—but he had never once thought that he might be directing the deadly fire of his guns against men he knew well! He thought of Captain Rommey, blunt and hard, but who had been almost a father to him—and Burns, that dour Scot who had been his friend—and even Langley, who had been jealous of him, but fair. To fire on them? And the crew! He knew most of them, and soon he would be sending the shot that would mangle them, leave them dead and crippled.

It's not fair, God! he cried out in his mind, and he tried desperately to find a loophole. *I'll let Daniel command,* he thought, but one look at the honest face of the big man told him that was hopeless. He was the only man capable of fighting the ship. *Go back and let de Grass appoint another captain!* But it was far too late for that, he realized in despair.

He turned and walked to the rail, motioning Dan to follow. When they were out of Simmes's hearing, Paul asked, "You know what's eating at me, Dan?"

"Those men are your friends," he nodded. "You are facing the choice of killing men who aren't faceless anymore."

"What can I do?"

Dan stared at the tortured face of the man he'd learned to love. He wanted to put his arm around Paul Winslow, but discipline had to be observed. He answered quietly, "Some things a man must face alone, Paul. This is your Gethsemane—and you only can make the decision."

"I can't do it, Dan! I can't!"

Dan Greene forgot the eyes of the crew. He put his big hand on Paul Winslow's shoulder, and with tremendous compassion in his warm brown eyes, said, "One thing is good—the old Paul Winslow is gone—for he would never have hesitated to do this. I think God has you about whipped, Paul. His grace will see you through and bring you in. Into His house."

Paul slowly nodded, saying in a heavy tone, "Thanks, Dan." He looked up and his eyes were bright with pain as he spoke. "We'll be engaging in an hour. Get the gun crews ready."

"Aye, sir."

A sudden thought struck him, and he lifted his head to glance at the *Neptune*. "Dan—for all Rommey knows, this is still a British ship!"

"Why—I suppose so."

"Quick—run up the British flag! This may be our chance."

Dan saw it at once. "Get in close and blast them? It may work—if they don't blow us up first!"

"I'm hoping that Rommey won't think of that. Get those colors up! Have the gunners rake the decks with the carronades and hit their gun ports with the eighteens!"

"Aye, sir! And I guess you might say that the Good Lord is answering my prayer—teaching our hands to war!"

★   ★   ★   ★

Lieutenant Burns turned to Captain Rommey, who had come on deck to take command. "Sir, that ship that's been shadowin' us, weel, I don't know what it means—but she's the *Jupiter*!"

Rommey's eyes grew large and he took the glass from Burns with an impatient air. "Impossible!" he snorted. The captain froze for a moment, then lowered the glass, his eyes puzzled as he muttered, "It *is* the *Jupiter*! Now what the devil . . . ?"

The two of them watched as the ship grew larger, coming closer by the second. "I can't fathom it, Burns! What is she doing out here? I heard she was being used to take supplies to Admiral Hood." He stared at the English flag on the *Jupiter* and pondered. "Perhaps she's got dispatches for us."

"Perhaps, sir." Burns's voice was doubtful, and then as the

ship drew closer and tacked to come broadside to the *Neptune*, he yelled, "Sir! Her guns are run out! Look! She's pullin' doon the British flag and flyin' the Yankee flag!"

Instantly Rommey bellowed, "Change course! Full about! Beat to quarters!"

The two officers remained in position, stoically willing the frigate to wheel out of range of the guns that threatened them from the sloop, but it was hopeless. "She's goin' to give us a broadside, sir! I'll get to my guns."

"Do the best you can, Lieutenant." Burns disappeared and Rommey stood there listening to the sound of men scrambling and guns being run out, but his attention was on *The Gallant Lady*. He saw that she bore that name on her bow, and she was close enough now to see the officers at their deck stations.

He had never felt so helpless! Ordinarily, he would have laughed at the idea of fighting a single-ship action with a sloop of war. But this was different! Two things ate at him. He remembered the guns aboard the ship, and what Burns had said in his report. "Sir, she's nae such a big ship—but Lord, the guns on her deck! Why, I don't doot she could sink a ship of the line if she got in the first broadside!"

He remembered saying to the Scot with a smile of disbelief. "And do you think a ship of the line would let her get close enough for that? Why, any captain would have her blown out of the water before she could get off a shot!"

But I let her come alongside without a thought! Rommey beat his fist against the rail, and then gripped it with all his might as he heard the lower ports open and some of the guns put in position. *Too late! It's going to be too late!* The deck of the enemy ship was visible now, and it seemed to bristle with guns. His practiced eye could see no flaw in the arrangement, and he thought, *Those big eighteens are aimed low to knock out our guns and hole us below our water line—and those carronades—Lord, how many are there?—will kill every man on deck! They can't miss!*

Then the two ships were even, and the air was filled with the mighty roar of cannon. The *Neptune* reeled beneath the shock, and Rommey fell to the deck. The fall probably saved his life, for the helmsman, who was directly behind him, was transformed into a mass of raw flesh by the whirring chains that ripped up the wheel even as it killed the man.

The air was full of death, as canisters of grape—small musket balls in cans that exploded—sent a deadly hail of fire over the deck, cutting the crew down as with a scythe!

Rommey struggled to his feet and looked around in despair. Most of the men were either lying still in death, or were twisting on the deck in their own blood, and the ship was helpless. One of the eighteens had struck the foremast dead center, and it had fallen back into the mainmast, killing several men as the heavy yards crashed to the deck. The ship was reeling like a drunken man, for the wheel was gone and the rudder flapped and thrashed in the water.

Rommey began to cry out orders, rallying the crew. "Baxter, get the marines to the tops! Have them pick off the gunners of that ship! Lieutenant Rogers, rig a line to the rudder—get us some control. She's turning to give us another broadside!"

He would not have believed a ship could turn so quickly, but he saw that the American captain was doing just what he himself would have done—seeing the terrible damage the first broadside had caused, he was driving the sloop around and in a few minutes would be in position to deliver another!

Down in the lower gun deck, Burns was misled. He heard someone cry, "Here she comes again!" and he thought the enemy would come to his starboard. There were too few gunners left alive to man both batteries, so he commanded at once, "All gunners, man starboard guns!" The men obeyed, but then as the guns were run out, Dion Sullivan, captain of number-three gun, rose up with wild eyes. "Mr. Burns! She's comin' on the port!"

Burns stood there, his mind reeling. He dropped to stare out one of the ports—and there she was, *The Gallant Lady*! She was beginning her run, and before he could even reverse his orders, the bow guns fired and he saw the first two gun crews blown to bits by the explosions! He began to weep as once again the *Neptune* shook beneath the hail of heavy metal. "God! Our enemies have triumphed!" he whispered, and tears ran down his cheeks. After the broadside had shattered the lower deck, there was a babble of cries, and then he heard a command: "All hands on deck to repel boarders!"

When he got to the deck, fighting his way through the press, he reached the forecastle deck, and saw the captain staring at the enemy ship that had completed her turn and was gliding in, her decks lined with boarders.

"We must not lose the ship, Mr. Burns," Captain Rommey told

him quietly. His face was pale, but calm. And he added, "We've been outdone—but we have more men than that sloop. We must win the battle on this deck!"

"I doot, sir," Burns replied, "that we have more men." He stared about the deck and thought of the carnage below. "But we'll nae give up, sir!"

"Look at the enemy. That's their captain getting ready to lead the boarding party. Do you recognize him, Mr. Burns?"

Burns followed the direction of Rommey's hand and breathed a name. "*Hawke! It's Hawke!*"

"Yes!" the captain hissed. He looked at Burns and asked, "Do you still believe in predestination, Angus? Did God put that man on this ship so we could save him and train him—in order that he would one day be the instrument of our destruction?"

Burns did not answer, for his mind was blank. "Shall I command the deck defense, sir?"

"Yes. We must not lose! If that fleet gets to the coast, we will have lost America—so have no mercy, Mr. Burns! Save that for later!"

★ ★ ★ ★

As the two ships converged, Paul stood beside the rail, his sword drawn. The crew had gone wild as the *Lady* had shot the larger ship to pieces without taking a single blow. Several men had gone down, the victims of the marines firing from the tops of the *Neptune*, but a murderous blast with the carronades had ripped through the tops, shredding men and sails alike.

"Ready!" Winslow yelled, and there was an answering cry as the men waved their swords in the air. He looked at the deck of the *Neptune*, and it gave him a queer feeling, for he knew every inch of it. Now it seemed to be carpeted with dead men—dead and wounded. He looked midships where Angus Burns and Captain Rommey were ready to direct the battle on the deck, and almost parallel with him, he saw Langley. Suddenly their eyes met, and Langley's jaw dropped, for he had not known until that second who was in command. Then his mild eyes blazed with fury and he screamed, "Ready, men! Kill them all!"

Paul saw two of the marines in the tops drop like red fruit from the foretop, their screams lost in the battle cry that came from both crews. Beside him, a young seaman named Trent took the full impact of a musket ball. The sound, like someone thumping a ripe fruit, went through Paul like fire. Then they were on top of the enemy.

"Ready, lads!"

He watched the sea rising and breaking against the *Lady*, the pressure mounting against her yards.

"Now!"

He gripped the rail as the helm went over and the bows started to pull toward the enemy. Sunlight flashed on the sloop's quarter-deck, and then her side exploded in a crash of musket fire, blowing great gaps in the crew of the *Lady*.

Winslow almost fell as the man next to him crashed against him, killed by a musket ball. He dragged himself up, and threw himself over the side. Paul waved his sword above his head and ran toward the deck where Rommey and Burns were waiting. *If we can take them prisoner, it'll be over,* he thought.

"This way!" he screamed, and then he was in the thick of battle. The steel of the English was ready, and Winslow crossed swords with a petty officer and then slipped on the deck, the breath driven from his body as he pitched headlong across the other man. He felt the man jerk and kick, and saw the awful agony in his eyes as Whitefield pulled him away. "Be watchful, sir!' he cried out. "We can't lose you!"

The deck was so packed with fighting men that it was almost impossible to move; but somehow he made his way to the ladder that was already crowded with men—some of them English, some American. He glanced up and met the eyes of Captain Rommey—but at the same moment he was struck by a blow in the back and turned to put his blade through the chest of a wild-eyed seaman.

The fight raged from stern to bow, and there was no quarter asked and none given. He saw Dan Greene duck under a blow of Langley's sword, and then leap onto the man like a tiger, the two of them rolling on the blood-spattered deck. Benjamin Smith was killed, fighting beside Winslow. He was run through by a bayonet, and the marine who killed him died instantly, shot in the right eye by Conrad, who was fighting like a madman.

It could not go on long with such intensity, Winslow knew, and the issue was in doubt. *Got to get the captain!* he thought des-perately. With a gargantuan effort he scrambled up the ladder and found himself in a fight with the small group that had ringed Rom-mey.

Angus Burns saw him instantly, and came at him with his saber lifted high. The Scotsman knew he had no chance—not against Hawke's sword! He had seen the dark American play with the best swordsmen on the *Neptune* as if they were children. Nevertheless he threw himself between the two captains in a wild attempt to save Rommey!

Paul could have killed him with a single thrust—but he could not do it. He avoided the wild slash of Burns; then pulling his heavy pistol from his belt, he struck the man on the head. Burns went down like a dead man, and someone yelled, "Sir! Behind you!"

He whirled to see that a lieutenant with battle-crazed eyes was lifting a pistol, and there was no time to duck. He was frozen to the deck, expecting at any moment to feel the pain of death—and then a form was in front of him, and he recognized Enoch White-field's face. There was an explosion and he felt the man's body jolt, then go limp.

"Enoch!" he screamed, and struggling to his feet, saw that Conrad had cut the officer down. Dan Greene was there, blood all over his chest. He had a sword, and seeing his captain down, he had leaped forward and Captain Rommey had parried his thrust. Their blades rang like bells, but even as Winslow got to his feet, he saw Dan's strong blow drive Rommey's sword upward. Then with another slash, he drove the blade out of Rommey's hand.

The rage of battle was on Dan's face, the tears streaming down his cheeks. His mild expression was gone, and there was madness in his eyes.

Rommey stood there helpless but with no sign of fear in his eyes as the American drew back his blade, and he knew he was a dead man.

Then, as Greene's blade leaped forward, it was deflected, for Paul Winslow had made a lightning-like move with his sword; and Greene's blow went to Rommey's left, doing no harm.

There was a single instant when the eyes of Rommey and Winslow met. The older man was bitter, and in the agony of defeat, for one moment he wished more than anything else to destroy this man who had been like his son. Then he nodded and the light in his eyes dimmed.

"The ship is yours, Captain," he said quietly. Rommey shouted to his crew, "All hands, *Neptune*, surrender!" He stooped, retrieved his sword, and tendered it to Winslow.

"Keep your sword, sir." Winslow shook his head, saying, "I didn't think it would come to this, sir." Then he turned and knelt down on the deck over Whitefield.

"Enoch!" His voice cracked and he shook his head helplessly.

"Sir?" Whitefield was breathing, but his lips were flecked with blood and his eyes were glazed with death. "I—I'm proud you're safe—sir!"

"Whitefield! You shouldn't have done it! You're dying for me!"

The eyes of the sailor opened, and he smiled. His voice was so faint that Winslow had to lean forward to hear it.

"Sir—I'm not—the only one—who died for you! Jesus did!"

Winslow felt his eyes fill up, and he nodded, unable to speak.

"Sir—would you—like to take Him? He's come for me—but it'd please Him—and me, too, if'd you'd ask Him to be—your savior. Would you—do it, sir?"

Winslow's heart suddenly broke and he whispered, "Oh, God! I ask you to forgive me! Jesus, save me!"

At the words Whitefield gave a glad cry, and he reached up to touch the face of his captain. "Sir—it's happy—I am—"

And then he slipped away, slumping in Winslow's arms. Paul Winslow knelt on the bloody deck, holding the body of his friend. And looking up to heaven, he said, "I'll serve you all my life, Jesus!"

CHAPTER TWENTY-SEVEN

IT'S GOD'S WILL

★ ★ ★ ★

The damage done to both ships had been considerable, though the *Neptune* had suffered the most. More than a dozen balls had punched holes below the water line, so for several days it took every effort to keep her pumped out. Finally the damage to the hull was repaired, but there was not an available spar to replace the foremast, so Winslow commanded Greene to go aboard as prize captain.

"You'll just have to keep her afloat the best you can," he said as the two of them met on the deck of the *Lady*. The battle and the loss of many men had etched lines in both their faces. But for Winslow it was worse, for he had stood at the rail to bury his own dead, and then beside Captain Rommey as the still forms of the *Neptune*'s crew slid into the deep.

"Aye, sir." Dan paused for a moment before asking hesitatingly, "What will happen to the prisoners?"

"Prison for most—but I expect Captain Rommey will be exchanged."

"His career is over. He'll never live it down, a frigate being defeated by a sloop!" Greene's eyes were bright with admiration, and he added, "It was tremendous, sir! Nothing like it ever!"

Winslow allowed himself to smile, saying, "It was—but the credit goes to the crew—and to you." His face darkened, and he groaned, "Poor Langley! He was a good officer." Langley had gone down under Greene's sword, and though he had not been a close friend, he was part of Winslow's life, and the loss saddened him.

"Aye, sir. But think of it as a thing that had to be done."

"It's still hard." He forced himself to smile, then said, "Well, off with you, Lieutenant! Make the best speed you can and we'll lag along behind."

"Aye, sir."

"And tell Captain Rommey I'm expecting him and his officers to dinner tonight."

Actually, Paul had been wondering if he should issue such an invitation. He had slept badly, riddled with guilt as he thought of the captain. The officer had done him nothing but good, and it cut him sharply to know that he had engineered Rommey's downfall.

All day he walked the deck silently, speaking only to issue necessary orders, apprehensive over the meeting with Rommey and Burns. He made a trip to the hospital area, thankful that it was not in the same condition he'd found it after the battle—*that* had been a scene from hell itself!

Lanterns had revealed a seaman named Cates strapped and writhing like a sacrifice on an altar, his leg already half amputated by Rafe Morgan, the ship's surgeon. The latter's face was devoid of expression as his fingers worked busily with the glittering saw. His assistants were using all their strength to restrain the struggling victim and pin his spread-eagled body on top of the platform of sea chests, which sufficed as an operating table. The man had rolled his eyes with each nerve-searing thrust of the saw, and had bitten into the leather strap between his teeth until he passed out from the excruciating pain.

It had taken more out of Winslow to stand there and share that agony than it had to tackle the *Neptune*, but he knew such was part of his duty.

He had been sickened by the sight all around him, as the other wounded had awaited their turn, some propped on their elbows as if unable to tear their eyes from the gruesome spectacle. Others lay moaning and sobbing in the shadows, their lives ebbing away, and thereby spared the agony of knife and saw. The air had been thick with the stench of blood and rum, the latter being the only way of numbing the victim's senses before his turn came.

He had gone around to each man, speaking a word of encouragement, and was surprised to find Charity in a corner of the room putting a bandage on the stump of a young man's leg. The heat was terrible; he saw that she did not have on a dry thread, and her face was worn with strain.

"Don't do this, Charity," he said thickly. "It's not a job for a woman."

"It's a job for who will do it," she retorted, her pugnacious air forcing him to nod and smile grimly.

"If you won't obey the captain's orders, then the captain will have to join you." He had stripped off his coat and all day they had borne the burden of the pain and death that lay heavy in the small room.

They had been drawn closer than they'd ever been, and now as he entered the surgery, he was pleased to see that it was different. Charity had put the surgeon to rout, demanding fresh air for all the men, so that a place had been made for them on deck where they could soak up the life-giving sunshine. She had commandeered the galley, seeing that the wounded men got the best of the food, and even now as Paul entered, she was bathing the chest of a boy not over sixteen who had lost his left arm.

The boy's name, Winslow knew, was Tommy Hooks, one of the lads from Boston. He'd been a powder monkey and one of the most cheerful members of the *Lady*'s crew, scampering up the rigging very much like a real monkey. Now he lay with his face turned to the wall.

" . . . won't have to worry, Tommy," Charity was saying. "You'll be able to get a place on a ship. There are lots of jobs for a bright young fellow like you."

"With only one hand?" he retorted bitterly, and turned his head to look at her. "Wot could I do, Miss Charity?"

"You can serve on the next ship I get, that's what!" she promised. "I'll need a quartermaster, and you're quick with figures and write a good hand."

"Would—would you really take me, miss?"

She laughed at him, and slapped his chest sharply. "You know what I think? I don't think you're worried about a job. You're worried about what the girls will think!"

His face grew red, and he mumbled, "Aw—who cares what they think?" He swallowed hard and asked timidly, "Do you think they'll mind much?"

She picked up the towel she'd been using, put it in the basin, then bent over and whispered so that Winslow barely caught it.

"Tommy, I'm a woman, and I'm in love!"

"Are you, miss?"

"Yes! And my sweetheart's got a wound, too. Not his hand—

but he's got one. And I'll tell you a secret—I don't mind a bit. As a matter of fact, I'm so crazy in love with him, I wouldn't care if he had both his arms cut off! And neither will the girls. When that arm heals, you'll get a shiny steel hook, and when you go to church with your new white uniform on, and the girls see that hook, they'll start whispering, like girls do! And one of them will say, 'That's Tommy Hooks, the one who fought on *The Gallant Lady!* He lost his hand—see that hook! He's a hero!' And then they'll fairly jostle each other to get to sit next to you! Oh, won't you be something, though!"

Winslow saw the boy swallow; then with his face working to keep back the tears, he had suddenly seized Charity's hand and kissed it.

"Oh, getting a little practice, are you, Tommy?" She had laughed, and as she turned Winslow saw the worship in the boy's eyes.

"Why, Captain!" she exclaimed, "how are you today?"

"First rate," he smiled. "Are you about ready to leave?" he asked Charity.

"In a few minutes."

After they left the cabin, they walked to the rail and stood looking down at the waves lapping against the ship.

"I heard what you said to Tommy," Paul began, breaking the silence.

"About the girls? Well, he needs some encouragement."

"Not about that—though that was wonderful—but the way you handled it. You always know just what to say to the men to make them forget their loss. But that wasn't what I meant."

"Why, what did you hear?"

"I heard you tell him about your sweetheart—the one with the scar that you—how did you put it. Let me see . . ." He put his finger on the scar on his cheek and said, as if he was having trouble remembering, "I think it's something like: *I'm so crazy in love with him, I wouldn't care if he had both his arms cut off!*"

Charity stared at him and her face flushed a fiery red. "You—you had no business eavesdropping!"

"That's one of my minor sins," he replied, taking her hand in his. Then he sobered. "Charity, do you love me?"

She looked at him quietly, finally whispering, "You know I do, Paul!"

"I love you, too. And I'll say as much for you as you said for me—nothing can change what I feel for you. If you lost your beauty, I'd still love that girl that's inside."

They stood there looking into each other's eyes, searching, probing the depths. After a while, he dropped her hand and leaned on the rail. "I want to tell you something. It's about Enoch."

He told her how the man had died, and how it had made him call out to God. "It's been different since then, Charity," he concluded. His eyes were happy and he added, "I'm not what I ought to be—and I'm not what I'm going to be; but I'm not the man I used to be—that Paul Winslow has died somewhere."

"Paul! I'm so happy!" She forgot all about protocol, and there in the bright sunlight, threw her arms around him and kissed him soundly. Then she drew back, her face rosy. "There! That's the kind of woman I am—no propriety at all! Will I make a captain's wife?"

"I hope you never change!" he smiled. "And you have to marry me, because I've got to go home and tell my family I've become a shouting Methodist! It will shame Mother frightfully."

She laughed at his rueful face. "Oh, Paul, it won't be hard. She's been worried about Anne marrying Dan and dressing up in gray and becoming a quiet Quaker woman. Now she'll be so busy trying to keep you from acting like an enthusiast, she'll have no time to worry about Anne!"

"I hope so. Father—I think he'll come around. He's been hit on all sides with the Gospel."

"So the House of Winslow is coming to the Lord!"

"Yes."

They stood silently for a moment, each lost in thought. Paul was the first to speak as he remembered his invitation for the evening meal. "Rommey and Burns are coming to supper tonight. I want you to be there to help me. I feel terrible about them. I owe both a great debt, but look what I've done to them."

She agreed, and that night she took all the strain out of the meeting.

When they were all seated, she looked across the table at Angus and said, "I have a treat for you, Lieutenant Burns. We have a cook who comes from your country—and he's made a special dish for you."

"For me? What is it?"

"You'll have to wait and see," Charity replied. Then she turned to Rommey. "Captain Rommey, I'll be blunt with you."

"Oh?" Her manner amused him, and despite the gloom that

shadowed his eyes, he smiled. "What form is this bluntness to take?"

"A personal remark." Charity told him frankly, mystifying him further. "I have stolen the heart of your prospective son-in- law," she stated calmly.

Paul, who had taken a sip of wine, suddenly choked on it, shocked at her words. "Charity!" he exclaimed, "for heaven's sake!"

She gave him an impatient look, saying, "Oh, Paul, did you think we'd manage to get married without his finding out about it? Be sensible."

"I don't know what to say to you," Rommey returned, wonder in his eyes.

"Well, I know what to say to you. You're a man of sense, Captain, and I tell you to your face that Blanche and Paul would have been perfectly miserable if they had married—and I suspect that you've been aware of that."

Rommey nodded. "I have thought it would be difficult. She's a willful girl—and Mr. Winslow has proven to be quite a rugged type. It would have been like fire and gunpowder."

"Of course it would!" Charity declared emphatically.

Rommey smiled at her and remarked, "I must say, however, that the same problem seems to be in your future, Miss Alden; for you are a very *forceful* young lady yourself."

"Yes, but Paul loves me—and when two people love each other as we do, they'll make a marriage work."

At that moment the door opened and a small, sandy-haired man brought a dish in and with a single glance went straight to where Lieutenant Burns sat. He put the bowl down and said, "Sir, I trust you'll find this a bit of home."

"Haggis!" Burns nearly shouted when he lifted the lid. He looked up with his eyes gleaming and a huge smile. "Oh, man, how did you do it?"

"It's a bit of what we brought from the Indies, sir."

"What is it?" Winslow asked.

"It's a dish made from a sheep's head, Captain," Angus explained happily. "Would ye care for a leetle bite?"

"No!" Paul responded quickly, restraining a shudder. "I wouldn't want to deprive you, Mr. Burns!"

The cook brought food for the rest and the supper went well, and just before Charity left, she reached out and shook hands with

Captain Rommey. An impish light touched her green eyes, and she said, "I couldn't give you a sheep's head to make peace with you, Captain; but I think I deserve your thanks for taking Paul off your hands."

"Well . . . thank you, Miss Alden," he answered. "Perhaps you're right— and I can tell you that Blanche is such a nationalist, she'd never marry an American. But it will be a comfort to me in prison to know that I won't have to adjust myself to a Yankee son-in-law."

She stared at him, saying soberly, "I do have one gift for you, sir—but you can't have it until we land. Then I think you'll feel better."

"No man feels better about prison—but I am grateful for your kindness, Miss Alden. Captain Paul Winslow is a lucky man!"

"What gift are you going to give the captain?" Paul asked as soon as they were alone.

"I'll let you know when we're almost home," she promised. Then she put her arms around him and kissed him thoroughly. "And I know what I want for a wedding present."

"Something expensive?" he smiled. "I'm a poor officer."

"You'll find out when we get home."

He teased her for several days, but she would never tell him. Finally they were on deck one evening and he said, "We'll be home tomorrow or the day after. Tell me what you want for a wedding present."

So she told him.

Two days later the ships reached the coast, and to Dan Greene's surprise, he received a written order from his captain.

Lieutenant Greene:
> See to the docking of the *Neptune*—I will take *The Gallant Lady* for a short cruise to the north. Have Captain Rommey and Lieutenant Burns sent to *The Gallant Lady*.

Greene obeyed, but as the *Lady* sailed away, he scratched his head, wondering, "What's that woman doing to Paul now?"

Rommey and Burns were soon standing on the deck of the *Lady*. They looked up to see Charity and Paul coming across the deck.

"Captain, it's time for you to have your present."

"Indeed?" Rommey asked politely. The dark future of a prison had dimmed his eyes, and he could not say more.

"I hope you appreciate your gift, Captain," Paul said with a smile. "It's what Charity asked for her wedding present."

"Her wedding present? How could that—?"

Charity looked earnestly at Rommey, stating quietly, "I want a *whole* husband, Captain. Paul was so consumed with guilt over you and Mr. Burns that I don't think I could have stood living with it—nor could he."

"He did nothing wrong, Miss Alden."

"Perhaps not—but he has grieved over what he feels was a wrong. So I asked him for something for a very selfish reason. I want a whole man, not one who's eating himself alive over guilt."

Rommey looked puzzled. He shook his head, saying, "I don't understand."

"Why, I asked him for your freedom, Captain—and he agreed."

Both men stared at her. "But he can't do that!" Rommey exclaimed. "He has no authority!"

"But he's not English! He's an American!"

"What difference does that make?"

"You English have traditions that are hundreds of years old," she answered simply. "There's a rule for everything. But in America, why, we're *making* our traditions right now. So, Paul has said that both of you can go free."

"Well, not *quite* free," Paul broke in quickly. "I want your paroles—that you'll not serve against America again."

Burns replied instantly, "That's very generous, Captain." He gave a half-sour look at his superior and remarked, "Now that the French have broken the blockade, there won't *be* any action against America in a short time."

Rommey nodded slowly. He walked to the rail, stared out at the coast line, saying nothing for a long time. A gull was crying in the wind, and the sails flapped in the brisk breeze.

Finally he turned and there was relief on his stern face. "Mr. Burns is right. You have won." Then he went to Charity and reached for her hands. "You are a lovely woman—and Mr. Paul Winslow will have his hands full with you. But I am in your debt." He looked up at the sails, then shook his head with a light of gratitude in his eyes. "Miss Alden—this is a very fine ship. But to me *you* will always be the gallant lady!"

He stepped back, and Angus took her hands. "It's a bonny girl ye are! And that man is nae deservin' o' ye." The haggis seemed to have thickened the burr of his speech, and there was a fond light in his eyes as he took Paul's hand. "I'm not going to over-thank you, Paul."

"I hope not. It was Charity's gift."

"I beg to differ." Angus Burns lifted his head and said, "It was God's will! As ye should nae be forgettin', Mr. Paul Winslow!"

"I'll remember, Angus."

Burns shook his head and looked at them, a canny light in his eyes. "The trouble the guid Lord went to—just to make America free! Every man carryin' a musket, and here He has to knock you on the head and have the British make a fine officer out o' ye—so that ye can save the day for Washington!" He lifted his hands and exclaimed, "Marvelous are His ways—but the guid Lord has found a strong man of war in ye, Paul Winslow. God bless ye both!"

They got into a small boat that Winslow had made available to put them on board a British ship anchored off shore, and Angus shouted as the boat moved away from *The Gallant Lady*: "It was God's will! Remember!"

The two of them watched until the small craft was out of sight, and then Charity questioned him anxiously, "Paul, will you be in trouble? for letting prisoners go, I mean?"

"A fine time you picked to think of that!"

"You won't be. Adam will tell His Excellency, and that will fix it."

He stared at her and shook his head. "It's a good thing you're such a beauty! At least I'll have something to look at when I get home after all the trouble you're going to get me into."

She smiled and asked demurely, "Am I beautiful? You must tell me more often—every day!"

"I'll be too busy winning the war!"

"Will it last long?" she wondered.

"There's no way for England to win now." He put his arm around her and they looked at the shore. "It took a French Navy to pull the English out—but our country is going to be all right. And we won't be just a loose collection of colonies. One nation will arise, Charity. And our children will be *Americans*—not Englishmen!"

She lifted her face to gaze at him, her eyes shining. "And we'll be a part of it? Together?"

"Together, Charity—on the Lord's side," he murmured, kissing her softly. Then they turned and looked again at the land—at America that was to come.

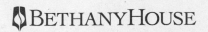